EARLY PRAISE FOR ALTERATIONS

Kate Maruyama invents a magical refracted Hollywood history and a lusty, coded story of forbidden love in Lotusland.

—Matt Tyrnauer, director of *Victoria's Secret: Angels & Demons* and *Scotty and the Secret History of Hollywood*

In this stunning literary novel, *Alterations*, Kate Maruyama has stitched together a multi-generational tapestry of women with entwined journeys of big love, profound loss, and the wonder and allure of cinema. As this superbly-designed story unfolds through time, locations, and from regrets to hope, it wraps around the reader's heart. This is a deeply moving, dazzling, and delightful read.

—Toni Ann Johnson, author of *Light Skin Gone to Waste*, winner of the Flannery O'Connor award, *Remedy for a Broken Angel*, and two time NAACP Image Award nominee

A gorgeous, exquisitely plotted, humane, warm, real, and unpredictable book.

—J Ryan Stradal, author of *Kitchens of the Great Midwest*, *The Lager Queen of Minnesota*

T0283758

Alterations is flat-out wonderful. A warm, sensitive and beautifully-written novel about complicated families, thwarted love, and the heartbreaking difference between old movies and real life.

—Peter Blauner, NY Times bestselling author of *The Intruder* and *Picture In The Sand*

ALTERATIONS

KATE MARUYAMA

RUNNING WILD

ALTERATIONS
Text copyright © 2025 Kate Maruyama
Edited by Aimee Hardy

All rights reserved.
Published in North America and Europe by Running Wild Press. Visit Running
Wild Press at www.runningwildpress.com. Educators, librarians, book clubs
(as well as the eternally curious), go to www.runningwildpress.com.

ISBN (pbk) 978-1-960018-75-5
ISBN (ebook) 978-1-960018-74-8

for Toni Ann Johnson

PROLOGUE

Hollywood, California, 1941

Adriana tucked her sore feet up under herself on one of the streamlined, red velvet chairs in the Paramount screening room and settled in for another long night of dailies and notes for *Ball of Fire.* Her boss, Edith Head, sat to her right, and Barbara Stanwyck sat behind them. When the film started rolling, Adriana was only half-focused on the screen, half on the notebook in which she was doodling. She was waiting for her dress to appear – Sugarpuss O'Shea's sequined barnstormer that she had spent hundreds of hours and thousands of sequins putting together.

Onscreen:
   Black and white.
   The joint is jumping. It's one of those impossible nightclubs with a black, reflectively shiny stage floor and a big band surrounded by tables, each with its individual lamp.

1

A close shot of a curtain. A woman's hand emerges, beating out a rhythm; it's all you see of her, that red nail-polished hand, those long fingers.

Adriana had worked with Stanwyck for a few years now, but she had never truly seen her before this moment:

Barbara Stanwyck walks onto the stage, not with the slinkiness of your regular movie nightclub singer, but with a confident skip. She's here to have the best time, and she's gonna let you join in. The band starts the song by hollering, "Boogie!" and Stanwyck sings, swaying subtly, just enough to keep the beat, moving her shoulders, keeping rhythm with her feet, and snapping her fingers.

That dress, that ridiculous dress Adriana worked so hard on.

Stanwyck makes it sizzle.

Edith always knew what worked for a girl. Stanwyck's body was unusually long. For her role in this film as a nightclub performer, Edith broke up that long torso with a bare midriff. Adriana sewed sequined strips onto the delicate webbing of the sheer top four times before she got it right. Edith insisted on Adriana's assistance, especially for her tiny stitches—none of the girls in the shop had stitches as delicate as hers.

Stanwyck was overall a good egg. She had a genuine immediacy for a star and insisted everyone call her "Missy." Adriana always felt like she couldn't cross that line, but something was happening to her perception of Stanwyck as she watched ...

... the "skirt" works. Shiny jazz pants dangle long strips of sequins from her waist to the floor. The garment moves with every dance step, revealing Stanwyck's long, shapely legs.

Stanwyck's singing ends, and Gene Krupa goes into a collar-popping, wild-haired shoulder-wagging drum solo. "1... 2... 3..." Stanwyck counts out the solo which seems to end the song. She leaves the stage, and the number could have ended there. But at the demand for "more," Stanwyck takes charge of the audience, asking them to clear a table and gather 'round this tiny impromptu stage where they recreate the song, using the audience's vocals with Krupa playing drums on a matchbox. Yep, a tiny matchbox, two wooden matches his drumsticks. At least thirty people circle the small table, and Stanwyck keeps the crowd at her intimate command. With the enthusiasm and control of a big sister sharing a rare treat, she guides Krupa and the crowd through the number. They whisper, "Boogie!" and she sings so softly with them, "Ya, da, da, da, da, da, da!" Krupa scratches out his full concert rhythm. When he finishes, he lights the matches, which he and Missy blow out.

When the Stanwyck on screen was singing softly to Gene Krupa's matchbox drum section, Adriana was acutely aware of the star sitting behind her in the screening room. Despite having spent two years in dailies just like these, prickles ran up and down her arms, up her neck, and into her hair. When the number came to a close, *Missy* leaned her head between Edith and Adriana, and her warm hands grasped their shoulders. She smelled of freshly washed hair and cold cream, mingling with a trace of cigarettes.

She said, "That dress is genius, ladies. Thanks." Adriana was thrilled with that Stanwyck-brand husky voice, that strong, supple New York accent. The same soft resonance that had just held a crowd captive around a matchbox whispered warmth onto her neck. And Adriana knew that she had fallen for Missy. Hard.

CHAPTER ONE

LIZZIE

My nonna always said that life isn't a tapestry so much as a patchwork. You sew and you sew and stitch the pieces together as best you can. The stitches don't always look perfect, the joins don't always look great, and the colors sometimes look like they don't match, but when you stand back and make some alterations here and there, and get it just so, that patchwork is something to behold. It took work to think this way, to make sense of life and our cobbled-together family, but Nonna wasn't wrong.

My part of the story started on the day I lost everything.

Pelham, New York, 1998

I didn't know what she was saying at first. I woke up to someone shaking my shoulder, and I was trying to understand what Mrs. Dunford was doing in my room hovering over me. From that angle, it looked like Billie Joe Armstrong from my

Green Day poster on the wall was jumping over her head. I would have laughed if it wasn't so scary and weird.

I was thirteen. People weren't supposed to be in my room without my say-so. Especially not goofy old Mrs. Dunford who was all jeans and weavy banana-yellow sweater that went with her banana Oil of Olay smell and no sense of humor. And why was she waking me up? And why didn't my alarm go off?

Mrs. Dunford was warbling something at me. "I'm so sorry, your *mwah mwah mwah mwah mwah...*"

I sat up fast, realizing I was wearing my hot-pink tank top – *embarrassing*. I hate it, but it's super comfortable, so I wore it to sleep in. I pulled the covers up around me like a cape and noticed that the light in the room was weird. It was waaaaay early. In the morning. Why was Mrs. Dunford in my room in the *morning*? Where were Mom and Dad?

And her words were starting to take shape. "Lizzie? Honey? Did you hear me? Terrible news. I'm so very very sorry."

She handed me a glass of milk. I took it from her, not sure what to do with it. It was cold and wet on the outside. I started noticing everything like you do first thing in the morning after you've slept really hard. My pajama bottoms were screwed around sideways, and I had a slight wedgy, but with the milk in my hand and the woman hovering over me, I couldn't fix it. There was cold air seeping through the window at my back, and my foot kicked the giant sketchpad I'd been drawing in when I fell asleep the night before. I was very, very warm, like bed warm, but my shoulders were cold, and the glass of milk was freezing. Mrs. Dunford was standing too close to my tower of manga. I started collecting two years ago, and I'd gotten twenty of the squat Japanese comics to balance like a side table. But they weren't that sturdy. I saw them sway when her rear end knocked them. Why was this woman in my room in the *morning*?

Mom and I fought last night about how I was plenty old enough to take care of myself for one little evening out. Mrs. Dunford was the result.

And Mrs. Dunford – this lady with the pants that made a *zhoozh* noise when she walked – she was the one who told me that my parents were dead.

"A taxi accident. Last night. I wondered where they were, then I fell asleep. The phone woke me up. Becca and George, oh my God. So *young*. I can't... I'm so sorry, Lizzie."

Her face was curling up in pain and tears from something I couldn't get a handle on. Her words didn't make sense. "What?"

She started talking to me loud and clear like I was deaf. "Your parents were in an accident in the city last night. The taxicab. There were no survivors."

There was a riddle about a plane crash. You draw a little map and a line between two states or countries. You tell the person about the plane crash and then ask them, "Where were the survivors buried?" The trick, of course, is that no one buries survivors, but if you have the person focusing on the map and the border, they forget that and take a guess anyway. I suppose it's to make them look like an idiot. One of those kinds of riddles.

"What?" I was stuck on what. Other words were beyond me.

Mrs. Dunford was getting frustrated, and she said, slowly and clearly. "Lizzie, your mother and father are dead. In a taxi crash. In the city." She was stuck on the city.

It was like when the weird dream you're having becomes a nightmare and you realize there's no escape. Maybe if I went back to sleep, I could wake up again and start over.

KATE MARUYAMA

But that morning, a cold seeping into my pajama bottoms brought the painful realization that I had spilled the glass of milk I was holding, and things were going to start sucking. Big time.

LAURA

Sherman Oaks, California, 1998

In her dream, Laura's with Becca under a sheet with a flashlight. They're nine. But they are also grownups. Becca is reading very slowly from a spooky book. Laura can't figure out what it's about, but she knows that she's afraid. Her fear grows and Becca looks at her, also frightened, then sad, and says, "CRASH." Her kid face is now her grownup face, and her grownup face morphs into a crushed face and there is so much blood.

Laura startled awake, her heart pounding and her chest tight. It took her a moment to orient herself. The cold creak of the cantilevered windows and the hum of the extra refrigerator with which she had been sharing her sister's sleeping porch for three months closed in around her, along with the newfound reminder that her cousin Becca was dead.

Still dead.

And she was still at Janelle's. Still unemployed. Still twenty-nine, and – thanks to her cheating jerkoff boyfriend,

Dexter – still single. Alone. Despair almost had a chance to settle in when she remembered it was moving day.

She threw off her nephew's discarded Winnie-the-Pooh quilt and swung her bare feet around to hit the cold linoleum with purpose. Today was the end of an era of depression and the end of living off her sister's good will in the late 1970s makeshift porch off the kitchen. Today was the beginning of something new. She tried to go with the positive feeling and not think about the fact that she was leaving Los Angeles in defeat— that by leaving, she had proven she couldn't cut it in the film industry. That she couldn't run with the big boys. That she had failed in her one live-in and fabulously glamorous relationship. She got out of bed, pulled on her jeans and jacket, and started packing a bag with her remaining things. She had packed the car the night before and, while Baltimore might not have all the answers for her, it was somewhere new, and she could live rent-free in her grandmother's house. *Some* kind of change was needed. She had to get out.

She grabbed her nephew's *Aladdin* lunchbox from on top of the fridge and went into the powder room off the kitchen where she grabbed some necessities for the car – a bottle of lotion, a travel-sized mouthwash, a toothbrush, gum, and a hairbrush. A small container of baby wipes lay on the toilet tank. She grabbed those as well.

Before the sun came up, Laura crept out to her car; this sort of escape was best made under cover of darkness. The car was a two-tone beige 1986 Ford Escort with an orange pinstripe that she bought from a friend in Beachwood Canyon for nine hundred bucks. Her Mercedes, intended to keep her running with the movie executive crowd, was leased in Dexter's name and had to be returned when she left him.

Laura had already packed her two suitcases into the trunk, and a box of books and easy-grab necessities in the back seat.

She tossed the Aladdin lunchbox in with them and climbed into the car. It smelled of that burnt-by-the-sun-too-long-in-LA-melting plastic.

The engine rattled when she started it. She had it tuned up for her trip, and her mechanic, Tito, promised her the car would last, at least until Baltimore. She would take Route 40 across the country for a slightly less stressful route than the 10. She would then hop on the 95 and go North to Baltimore.

Janelle was the one who suggested going to see Nonna. Laura balked at first, but she couldn't live on her sister's sleeping porch forever. Janelle was starting to expect things from her in return – help with the housework and babysitting her twin nephews, Skyler and Tyler.

She hadn't seen her grandmother in several years but, right now, Baltimore was *elsewhere,* a destination. That was enough. And maybe going back to the house where Becca grew up, back to the place they had spent their childhood summers together, would help her make sense of things. Nonna was always a touchstone for them, the house on Exeter Street a place filled with food and laughter, where Becca wasn't her cousin, but her real, long-lost sister. Maybe Laura could get rid of the guilt she held for drifting away from Becca. The guilt for having missed so much of her cousin's grownup life. And the sadness that there was no making that up now that she was dead.

Laura couldn't go to Nonna's empty-handed. She would bring her a gift. Instead of getting right on the freeway, Laura turned left on Ventura Blvd and rattled toward the Hollywood Hills. She was going back to her failed life in the house on the hill one last time to get her china. Dexter at least owed her that.

LIZZIE

Everyone was nice to me, but it didn't help much. They kept bringing food and thank God Uncle Bart came to stay with me to "help me through it," and there was the funeral, which was beyond bizarre, and people kept coming up to me and crying. I stood on the front steps of the church with Uncle Bart and some of Dad's friends from work.

It was a cold day for May. The leaves had just finished growing to full size and everything was green and summer-colored, but today was cloudy and there was a chill in the air. The wind blew through the trees like bad news. No one else seemed to notice, but the world was colder because Mom and Dad were gone. I kept looking at different places because if I looked at one thing too long I was going to start crying again.

Everything was panels of Sad, like close-ups in a manga comic when something awful has happened. The wind blew the leaves of the big maple tree in front of the church backward and up like a skirt, and they showed their paler gray undersides. Freeze frame: Sad. Closeups of people's black shoes: Sad. The church was tall, brownstone, and nothing but Sad. Only rain would make that picture sadder. I looked out at the street where there were two sad, black cars.

Any decent artist who drew this day would add rain.

Everyone was strange. Nonna was a wreck – Nonna was Mom's grandmother, but she raised her, so she was more like her mother, I guess. She broke her hip two months earlier, and she looked two feet shorter with her walker – and worn out like crying had taken it all out of her. I never in my whole life saw Nonna cry, but she cried the whole day. Quietly, like her eyes were leaking. She hugged me and patted me, but she didn't say anything. Her *not* talking was a pretty big Sad indicator. If I drew her, she wouldn't have a thought bubble, she'd have a gray smudge over her head.

I kept waiting for people to say something of use. I don't know what I expected – maybe incredible bits of wisdom people could give me like they do in the movies. Things I could *use* to live by. Each grownup walked up to me, their eyes full of pity – in that droopy downward way you would draw, like a kidney bean at an angle – plus maybe a little "phew, not my problem," and as each of them got up his or her courage to talk to me, I kept hoping for some explanation of where my parents went or some life-affirming thing about the future. But what did they say?

"I'm so sorry for your loss."

"A terrible, terrible thing."

"Wow. Both of them. I am so, so, so, so *sorry*." That was some neighbor guy. Like he'd done it. But I don't think that neighbor guy gets into the city much, so it wasn't likely.

"Every cloud has a silver lining." I wanted to punch the old lady who said this to me.

The day was panel after panel of these one-liners and drooping eyes, and nobody talked to me about what was going to happen next. I hoped Uncle Bart would stick around. Maybe live in the house? Commute to Manhattan? A few days after the funeral, I asked him when he was leaving, and he said, "Soon." I asked what happened next, and he got a depressed, distant, kidney-beans look on his face. I saw that look on a lot of people at the funeral, and it scared me – like they knew I had this horrible future, but they couldn't tell me about it, like I'd been sold to an evil colony of witches or a sinister uncle or a workhouse, or they sold me as a familiar for a nest of vampires. Uncle Bart touched my cheek and went to the other room. Maybe to cry. I thought it was nice of him not to cry in front of me.

Dad was his brother, and they were close – best friends close. Dad used to tell stories about the two of them getting in trouble together, running out in the fields behind their house on their strawberry farm, and finding dead animals. Before my parents died, I saw Uncle Bart once a year at Easter. A couple of times in New York and before that at Nonna's house.

Nonna's house. But I'm getting ahead of myself.

Uncle Bart told me he was leaving in two days and told me to pack up everything that was special to me. I didn't know how to "pack" that desk. Or the dishes. Or that casserole dish. Mom was a genius of the casserole. I really wanted our desk in the living room where Dad worked on his computer at night. The desk was older, from a time before computers. It had pigeon-holes on the front of it where I would leave Dad notes or drawings, and he would do the same for me.

And what about my stuff? My bed? My manga tower? All my sketchbooks? My science experiments I kept out back? I didn't know if "pack" meant a suitcase or a moving van, but pack meant leaving this big-windowed sunny, cozy house, and I didn't want to leave. When I asked Uncle Bart where I was going, he squeezed my shoulders, got that look in his eyes, and left the room again.

When I woke up in the morning a week later, I forgot for a moment. Then I opened my eyes and saw that my posters had been taken down, and the cardboard boxes were on the floor. The aching started new and all over again.

I squeezed my eyes shut and buried my face in my pillow. It smelled like home, and I wished and wished so hard that it was the before home with them in it. The sunlight was shining onto my bed like it did every morning, making a warm spot on my foot. Mom would be downstairs in front of her computer with a cup of coffee. Dad would be showering. I would get dressed. If I came down to breakfast just at the right time, I'd catch Dad, leaning against the counter in his suit, fresh and clean, holding a cup of coffee. When I was little, I'd hug him tight and bury my face on his shoulder, and I'd feel safe. I could forget about who was being nasty at school, a homework assignment I'd missed; I could forget about how bad I felt after arguing with Mom the night before. Everything was a starched, blue shirt and clean with a touch of dryer sheet and soap. I'd give him a peck on the cheek and slip a drawing into his pocket. He always pretended not to notice so he could fake a fuss later.

I should have seen the signals then. Whenever there was a happy beginning like this in a manga, whenever everything was heartbreakingly normal – that's when the bad stuff happened. The both parents dying type stuff.

When Dad was gone, I'd have breakfast with Mom, pressed and ready for work, full makeup, cup of coffee, snappy come-back, and some interesting thing from the news she'd saved out for me – usually about science or animals. Sometimes a new planet the scientists had come across in the next solar system over. Sometimes some new discovery about an old species of lemur. Sometimes a new treatment for cancer. I was worried Mom would get cancer like my friend Lisa's mom and die. I was always happy to hear about a new treatment.

Too bad there wasn't a miraculous breakthrough treatment for high-velocity collisions or bad drivers.

Uncle Bart called my name from downstairs.

What if I'd forgotten something? Everything was packed up. Things were being sent away. Where, I wasn't certain. I opened the door to go downstairs when I remembered something with a suddenness that rushed blood to my ears. I closed the door, opened my closet, got down on my hands and knees, and crawled past my clothes, which were stuffed into garbage bags. In the far corner of the closet was a loose panel that led to the eaves. I jammed it with my fist three times, it squeaked sideways, and I reached into the hole. I almost forgot it. It was stupid really, but it was a thing. A piece of my mom.

In among what must have felt like treasure years before – five glass marbles I found in the backyard, a single pearl from a broken strand that I realized now was probably glass, my third-grade class photo with Celeste Ewing crossed out in black marker – was an antique tube (Mom told me it was a lipstick case) that hung from a silk cord. I think it was made of ivory or something. It was very old. It had a screw top and was lined with very old, yellowed paper that smelled of long-ago perfume. I wasn't sure *what* to do with it when Mom handed it to me after I'd asked about it (she said it had been in the family for generations, she wore it for good luck at her wedding), but I used it to hide spy messages for a while. It had its secret spot in the back of the closet, and that's where I'd stashed it and forgotten about it around eleven years old, at the age secrecy stopped seeming so important.

I looped it over my head, and it hung higher than it used to, round about my stomach. I headed downstairs.

In the strangely bright kitchen, Uncle Bart sat at the table, the crunch of his Honey Nut Cheerios echoing in the emptiness. The curtains were gone. Everything was packed. Uncle

Bart looked like Dad, and he didn't. Their heads were different shapes. Uncle Bart was short and wiry, and Dad was taller, broader. Dad's eyes were also brown, but they were lighter, kinder. Uncle Bart's eyes looked darker, antsy. I suppose I should mention that Uncle Bart and Dad are/were Japanese. Well, American, but with Japanese parents. Mom was white: Italian and something else.

Dad was only thirty-five when … well, even though he was young, he had an older gentleman look about him. Uncle Bart was only two years younger, but he looked like the hip, twenty-something city dude. Fancy clothes with labels, a close haircut, aftershave that smelled expensive. Dad's smile glowed, Uncle Bart's flashed.

But now, stooped over his cereal, he just looked tired and worn out, like someone had turned down the color on him. If you were drawing him, you'd have to bring all his features down at least one inch and put some charcoal smudges under his eyes. He had three days of stubble. Until that morning I didn't even know he could grow facial hair.

His eyes had shut off inside.

I didn't want to ask because I didn't want an answer, but I had to ask.

"Uncle Bart?" It echoed.

"Yeah?"

"When you go back to the city, where am I gonna live?"

His furrowed brow relaxed, and his whole face went back up two inches. He looked relieved I was asking the question.

He coughed. "Well, honey, the thing is. We did a lot of talking about this, me and your Gramma." He looked me straight in the eyes, steady, determined to tell all. I thought it would beat that distant look, but it was scary. Intense.

I said, "Nonna."

"Nonna."

"She's my great-grandmother."

"Of course. Your mom's Gramma."

"Nonna."

"Nonna. Your Aunt Sally's not. Um. Like together enough?" Aunt Sally, my mom's mother's sister, was making bead jewelry on a reservation in Oklahoma. There was no Native American in her, but she'd scored a Kickapoo name and a place to stay. I had some cousin-aunts, Sally's kid – Janelle and somebody – who knew my mom, but they weren't really an option.

Uncle Bart breathed in and went on. It was obvious this was taking all his strength, and that made me nervous. "And I'd love to take you." Even though his saying this meant that he wouldn't, my hopes rushed at hearing these words together: love-to-take-you. "... but I travel so much for work I couldn't offer you anything like a home."

We could make it work, Uncle Bart. I'm already thirteen. I could come to your black and chrome-furnitured high-rise apartment. I'd read books and draw or watch Food TV, I wouldn't take up much space. We could hang out. I could shop for manga comics after school on my way home. I hear there's this store on Bleecker ...

He must have seen what I was thinking because he said, "I really wish I could, Lizzie, but my life isn't any place for a teenager. You need a community, a school, a home to go to after school. Not an empty bachelor pad."

He stopped. He was the living version of a character delivering bad news, and they show, like, five panels of his face, all on one page, each one zooming closer, each one with the face a little more serious and intense. He spread his hands and put them on the table, leaned in, and put on a cheerful face as carefully as if he'd taken it out of his pocket and hitched it on behind his ears. "You're going to live with your grandma ... Nonny."

"Nonna."

Crap. I loved Nonna. I grew up having holidays in her house. I loved her cooking and the stories about Mom growing up there. But after Nonna broke her hip, the life sort of – went out of her. She was old. She couldn't even say anything to me at the funeral. She was going to be the number one grown-up in my life? How the hell did that happen?

CHAPTER TWO

ADRIANA

Hollywood, California, 1937

When Adriana stepped off the platform into that gorgeous, high-ceilinged train station in Los Angeles, she knew she had arrived. She thought about the one-bench bus stop she'd come from in Bethlehem, Connecticut and she knew she'd never have to go back there. The place where she was abandoned. The woods that killed her sister.

She took in the detailed ceramic tiled walls, the deep, streamlined wood-and-leather chairs, the stencil work on the lofty wooden ceiling, and heard the click of her heels on the cool terra cotta floor. The morning light streamed in the high windows through circles of dust like it was a cathedral. It was the beginning. Of something, if not good, then at least better. She could throw it all aside and, in the bright, open sunlight, look at things anew.

Out front of the train station, she hopped on a bus going to Hollywood. No more lichen and dark and green. No more running water and noisy bugs. No more endless icy winters stuck in a moldering house waiting for the worst to come. Gone was the dark of the woods and the closeness. Here was open air. A chill breeze, smelling mysteriously of ocean cooled her cheeks, but the sun warmed her shoulders. The sky was bright, the bus was shiny and clean. As the bus traveled down Sunset Boulevard, she saw the low-lying beige buildings, the brown-grass-covered hills with only a few trees, and she felt the warmth and smelled the dust, it was like she was going home again. Back to Sant'Agnello, Italy. Back to baked grass and sun and sage. This was a place where things could happen.

She got off at Schwab's Pharmacy, not because she thought she'd be discovered right away, but because that is what you did when you were a girl arriving in Hollywood from a small town in 1937. She took hold of the historic handle for a moment, smoothed her best-flowered dress, and straightened her carefully styled hair before she swallowed deeply and went inside.

The ceilings were high, and the walls lined with dark wood glass-covered cabinets, but the center of the store was dominated by a lunch counter, thronged by women interspersed with a few men in suits. The girls who lined the counter had clever seams, suits, cunning hats, and beautiful shoes. Those shoes – handcrafted to their feet. Their lipstick was carefully drawn, they wore face powder, and had no blemishes. Each woman looked sparkling and singular at the noisy ice cream fountain, and they had something that Adriana didn't have yet: confidence.

LAURA

Hollywood, California, 1996

When Laura was twelve, on Thanksgiving night in Anchorage, Alaska, she found *It's a Wonderful Life* on television and fell in love. She had ignored black and white movies before, but two years later, thanks to the film series at the local community college, they became her religion. It became the life that she chose – one different from the life various grownups and their choices had pushed her into. She found families where mothers didn't leave their daughters but stayed and worked through the hard times; she found romances with handsome, clever men and women who were smart and quick with a comeback – when being clever was seen as a positive thing.

She had discovered a world outside her small tidy ranch home – a world she would find and live in when she was old enough to leave town. The promise of these movies prompted her to work harder in school and get into USC, which brought her to Los Angeles and closer to the movies.

Before she met Dexter, Laura was quite content living on

her own. She had a second-story walk-up in the Hollywood Hills on Gower Street with wood floors and 1930s plaster details combined with the most beautiful, green, hand-glazed tile vintage bathroom she'd ever seen.

She woke up in her 1940s wood veneer bed, scored at the Rose Bowl Flea Market. The lead casement six-paned windows on her 1930s apartment probably hadn't changed in as many years. If she ignored the noise of the freeway and her upstairs neighbor relentlessly playing the same three chords on his electric bass; if she focused on the sound of the birds chirping and the bougainvillea growing outside her window, she could imagine that it was 1942, and she was going in to work as a script girl at Universal.

She did work at Universal, and while things had probably changed a great deal since the forties, it was still an intriguing mini-world with enormous sound stages where movies were actually made. She drove on Lankershim past the entrance to the amusement park and up to Gate Two where her dashboard marker gained her access with a smile of recognition from the guard in the booth.

The lot still had machine shops, costume departments, and anachronistic visions, such as gothic vampires and vintage 1960s hippies on cigarette breaks lurking outside soundstage doors. On one "road," she passed a horse and carriage and a futuristic hovercraft. She drove the winding asphalt path carefully, around golf carts and past the tourist tram. It tickled her to see the regular folks from all over the country peering out of the sides of the tram at her bungalow, where the magic happened. She swung into her hard-won assigned parking space on which was painted *Director of Development*, a promotion she had earned two weeks before. She didn't get an assistant, but she got her own office and a modest expense account.

Laura was in her element, on top of her game, a woman of means. She worked for Roadside Pictures, a small indie company that had scored its coveted bungalow for its sleeper hit the prior year. *Windblown*, starring Steve Buscemi and Greg Kinnear, was a hyper-violent drama about two gangster brothers on the lam from the FBI. Part buddy movie, part heavy drama, *Windblown* was made for ten million but had earned ten times that through word of mouth and a clever marketing campaign involving posters of its two stars with guns drawn against each other's faces against a brilliant red and yellow paint-splashed background. It was the hippest movie of 1997. Laura came into the company just as the movie hit theaters and got caught up in the company pride that followed. The day Roadside Pictures moved into their bungalow, champagne, and caviar flowed, ordered by the crusty old assistant who basically ran the place. Laura felt she was at the beginning of something big.

The company was small, and Laura's boss, VP of production, a clever but snappish Brit Kevin Trilling allowed Laura access to almost all his meetings, which meant she sat in with writers, actors, and most importantly, studio executives. She was learning the inner workings of the industry and was on a career path beyond what she had envisioned for herself when she graduated from USC's film program.

One more year at this place, and she would find herself a VP at a similar production company, or at least a Creative Executive at a studio on her way to becoming VP. She was "good in a room" and could handle even the most eccentric writers with an equal amount of flattery and criticism that would send them back to their drafts feeling cared for and ready to write.

She kept her small apartment in the Hollywood Hills, her rent-controlled refuge where she would return, exhausted after a 9 p.m. trip to Gelson's for a plastic clam-shelled salad, and collapsed in front of the television to watch Turner Classic Movies. If it was in black and white, it was home.

Who did Laura want to be? Barbara Stanwyck. A clever, witty, quick-talking, don't-mess-with-me, tough-as-nails gorgeous dame.

Who did Laura want to marry? Cary Grant. The banter would be unbelievable. He was so clever, so sure of himself. Even while playing the bumbling David in *Bringing Up Baby*, you could see the controlled comic timing at work. When Dexter came along, she fell fast and without much thought.

The night she met Dexter was unusually warm for September; the Santa Ana winds were blowing. Laura had to walk sloping backward in her heels down the steep road in front of the house where the party was to maintain her balance. She wore a simple black dress and black pumps, and she knew she looked pretty good, but when she got to the front door, she wanted to go home, turn on TCM, and sink into black and white. She double-checked the address against the one in her bag. There was a low throb of music, which was comforting, but no voices. She leaned her head against the door when it opened, startling her.

A very stoned young man wearing a black T-shirt, jeans, and no shoes smiled at her.

"Hey, man," said Stoner boy.

"Dude," Laura replied.

He said, "You here for the party?"

Laura's visions of martinis, swanky outfits, and clinking glasses abruptly switched to scenes from *Animal House*.

A rather tall, mercifully well-dressed, and sober fellow stepped up behind Stoner Dude, and her hopes were restored. He had broad shoulders and dark brown hair, a lock of which fell rakishly over his eyes, and he was solid in his weight. He wasn't classically handsome, but he wore his face well. His large, brown eyes and look of confidence made up for any short-comings in his chin or cheekbones. He settled against the wall next to the door right behind Stoner, arms crossed, ready to watch the proceedings. He raised an intelligent eyebrow, smiling at Laura in a way that made her want to shine.

She answered Stoner, "No. Actually, I'm a singing telegram."

Stoner stared at her long and hard, puzzled. She raised her eyebrows and put her arms out. "So, you going to let me get to work?"

Stoner's puzzlement turned into a grin, and he nodded, laughing. "Yeah, yeah. Shoot."He wasn't moving. She stood and folded her arms. Handsome was amused, waiting.

Stoner said, "You gonna sing?"

Laura smiled, "The telegram's not for you..."

Handsome filled in, "Sam."

Laura said, "Sam."

Sam said, "Riight ..." He opened the door and stood back, allowing her passage.

She stepped in, uncertain of what to do about Handsome. But he took care of that for her. He held out his hand. "I'm Dexter Bellows." She was surprised to find his hand cool and dry.

Comforting on such a hot night. *Dexter.*

"Laura Mullen."

He used the handshake to turn her around to face the party. He said, "Allow me to buy you a drink. Wet your whistle."

She said, "I do sing better after a martini."

He placed his hand, ever so gently, on the small of her back and guided her through the dimly lit living room, which was strangely unfurnished. That guiding hand made her feel safe and cared for. One table, lined with tea lights stood in the center of the room. The crowd stood around with drinks in their hands. She recognized some of the cast of characters from Universal and raised her chin in greeting. An overpaid woman Laura referred to as Bitch Girl from Sunrise Productions was there, laughing too loudly. She was drunk. A girl stood with her – also laughing too loudly – clearly her crony. Bitch Girl was known for her malevolent gossip and a tendency to knock fellow junior executives down to further her own gains. Laura loved working with writers and fixing stories and focusing on movies, but the socializing for her job was like going back to high school with its pecking order, cliques, and basic syco-phantery. On nights like this, Laura wondered if she wanted to be associated with these people.

Dexter put a martini in her hand and steered her past them and onto a balcony. The smell of California dirt, fennel baked by the sun, and eucalyptus combined with the retreating sounds of the party struck her with an exhilaration she hadn't felt since she was a teenager. Beneath them lay a view of Sunset Boulevard and the city below.

Dexter looked out at the view, so comfortable in his own skin that his silence became an awkward, stretching substance, a conveyor belt onto which Laura felt the need to put something.

She said, "Wow this place is incredible. Who owns it?"

Dexter said, "Sam. Long story. So, are you a D-girl?"

Laura hated the term for being in development. D-girl sounded demeaning.

She said, "I'm Director of Development at Roadside." She loved her new title; this was the first time she'd tried it on for size.

Dexter raised his eyebrow, impressed. He said, nodding, "*Windblown*. Well then," and laughed, but it didn't feel like he was laughing at her. Just with her. In an only slightly conde-scending way. Maybe because she was a girl? Maybe he was so damned cute? Either way, she didn't care.

She said, "And you?"

He squared his shoulders and puffed up a little. "Well, as of today, I'm a CE at Paramount."

She shoved him on the chest, "No *kidding!*" Creative Exec-utive slots at the studios were hard to get. They were a sure way to climb the executive ladder quickly and involved a grueling series of interviews. Becoming a CE at a studio was officially getting in the door.

"Congratulations!" She said a bit too enthusiastically, but Dexter blushed and smiled. "Are your friends, like, *stoked* for you or what?"

He shrugged. "They threw me this party."

"Wow." Did she say that out loud? "I didn't know. Suzanne from Amblin invited me."

He put his arm around her waist and pulled her to face him. The view, the heels, the martini, the firm grip on his arm, she was dizzy. He said, "I am very, very glad she did." And he kissed her. He smelled of clean soap and some sort of tropical shave cream and he smelled of *guy*.

And his name was Dexter. Like Cary Grant in *The Phil-adelphia Story*.

Swoon.

ADRIANA

Hollywood, California, 1937

Adriana checked into a woman's boarding house on Franklin, right off Vine on an unusually hot March day in 1937. She had saved some money from sewing for neighbors over the years and had enough for the train ticket and two weeks' stay in a room on the third floor right next to the communal bathroom. The building was nice enough, but the setup reminded her of the first place she had lived in New York when she was very little. Something about the smell of old paint and old carpet, the bathroom in the hall, and the sounds of the city outside took her back. When she woke up on her first morning in Hollywood, she thought her sister Maria was lying next to her. But a new smell let her know where she was; the odor of perfume mixed with jungle mixed with warmth drifted in from outside the window. Only later did someone explain to her that it was night-blooming jasmine, the all-consuming odor that filled Los Angeles for two months out of every year.

She went to the Paramount lot first because she could walk

there. They sent her to central casting where she sat for six hours in a room full of women who seemed like they'd been doing this for a while. Some of them brought thermoses of coffee, cosmetic cases, books, magazines. A lot of them knew each other. One redhead caught her attention right away. Her hair was bottled auburn, ratted up top and loose behind. She had a straight nose, gorgeous, enormous mascaraed blue eyes, and her lipstick was perfect. Women approached her and talked to her with a regularity that made her seem the presiding godmother of central casting. Adriana watched her for hours as she pulled whatever a girl needed out of her pocketbook: a bobby pin, lipstick, makeup sponges, bandages, or an extra pair of stockings. She never once got bored or tired-looking, and she talked to anyone who came to her.

Adriana managed to sit a little closer to her when one of the chairs near her cleared out. She pretended to look at her magazine, trying to seem like she wasn't watching Rose. Rose was the woman's name, Adriana learned this about two hours in when woman number five approached her. One by one, the girls were called into that coveted place behind the closed door, and Adriana, who hadn't brought a lunch, was getting hungry. About two o'clock, she felt faint. Then Rose spoke.

"You new?" At first, she didn't know Rose was talking to her. "Honey, you new?"

Adriana looked up and nodded before she remembered to smile.

"Come sit by Auntie Rose." Rose couldn't have been any older than Adriana, but she had a maternal air about her. She shooed the woman sitting next to her out of the way and patted the seat. Adriana picked up her magazine and purse and sat down.

Rose's voice was full, friendly, and warm, "You look starving, honey. Didn't know it would take all day, did you?"

Adriana shook her head.

Rose leaned across the aisle to a rather mousy-looking blonde who was smoking a cigarette. "Marjorie, you got an extra sandwich in there?"

Adriana said, "No, really, you don't have to."

Rose's accent spoke strongly of New York. Brooklyn, though. "Oh, forgedaboudit. Marjorie, give her a sandwich."

Marjorie reached into her pocketbook and pulled out two half-sandwiches wrapped in wax paper. "Salami or liverwurst?"

Rose asked Adriana as if she hadn't heard. "Salami or liverwurst?"

Adriana's voice quavered. "Oh, salami would be very nice, thank you."

Marjorie handed the sandwich to Rose who handed it to Adriana. She gave Marjorie a big smile and said, "Thank you," and carefully opened the wax paper. The smell of salami and good bread made her feel a bit like New York again. Before Bethlehem.

Rose leaned her arm over the back of Adriana's chair and started talking. Adriana liked the sound of everything Rose said: it was frank and real. She said, "It gets easier as time goes on. I remember that first day I was a total nervous Nellie. Didn't know if I was coming or going, which way was up, and I forgot about the food too. By the time they called me in, I was ready to eat my own arm. Funny, they hired me to be an extra at Robin Hood's feast. The joke? We didn't get to eat all day. We sat in front of some nasty, cold-looking meat and sipped water out of nasty-tasting metal goblets, careful not to spill or costume would get us fired. But I saw you there, and I knew that look. 'Rose,' I said, 'There's a girl who needs a sandwich and some advice.' Where you from?"

But Adriana's mouth was full.

"Oh, don't tell me, let me guess." She looked Adriana up and down, from her hair to her suit. Adriana had put on her best hand-tailored suit for casting. It had taken her two months to make. The way Rose's eyes lingered around her breasts made Adriana feel peculiar like she hadn't felt about a woman before, like she hadn't felt about *anyone* before. She knew Rose was looking at the cut of her suit. Rose surveyed her shoes and said, "New York. Lower East side."

Adriana coughed with surprise.

Rose smiled, "Your bag, honey. You bought it at Marty's. No one else does work like that. The shoes, also. But that suit? That suit I can't place. Nice craftsmanship and flair."

Adriana said, "I shopped in New York ... I used to live there. I come from Connecticut."

"So, you're a hick."

Adriana flushed. "I'm a city hick."

Rose's laugh was sudden and loud. She was so slim, but her laugh sounded like it came from a strapping young man. Adriana found it infectious and joined her. She was uneasy divulging private information to a stranger, but how was she supposed to make friends otherwise?

Rose said, "So, where does a city hick shop for a suit as gorgeous as that?"

Adriana blushed as she said, "I made it."

Rose's eyes changed from maternal to awestruck. Adriana thought that Rose could be a real movie star, able to change her expression like that on a dime.

"No!" Rose was incredulous.

Adriana nodded.

"Marjorie come over here! Tammy! Louise!"

Adriana was soon surrounded by women oohing and aahing over her needlework, her tailoring, her workmanship. It was overwhelming for a girl who had been listening to nothing but crickets and blowing leaves for the past ten years, but she smiled and thanked them and eventually, they dissipated.

Rose took her hand and looked fervently into her eyes. It was then that Adriana fell. She told herself it was just the excitement of the new place, that Rose was her first friend, but she knew she wanted to spend every moment that she could with this woman for as long as was humanly possible. Rose's eyes were anxious and sweet, her brow furrowed, and she said the most enchanting thing that Adriana had ever heard, "You are *talented*. We need to get you out of here."

With one borrowed Tin Lizzie and a giddying whirlwind of well wishes, Rose and Adriana were bumping over the potholes of Melrose, up, around the far side of the studio to another hidden gate. With a wink from Rose to the security guard, they wheeled around a corner and up to a small row of buildings.

Rose leaned over toward Adriana and before she could object or stop her, she kissed her on the lips. "For luck," she said.

Adriana opened her eyes and Rose was already out of the car, bounding into the building. Girls weren't supposed to kiss like that. But lots of things weren't supposed to happen. Mothers weren't supposed to leave. Nine-year-old girls weren't supposed to die of neglect. Adoptive parents weren't supposed to beat you. This was Hollywood, and anything was possible. It was the first really good feeling that Adriana had about kissing since her mother kissed her goodnight on that last night in New York. This was something to pursue.

Rose dragged her into a building, hollering, "Get me Edith! I've got a live one here!"

Within minutes, with no introductions, a short, dark-haired, prim-mouthed woman with severe bangs, a chignon, and darkened, horn-rimmed, circle-framed glasses was surveying Adriana's suit. Adriana's eyes adjusted to the light, and she looked around to see a room full of women working on dresses from every period imaginable: bodices from the French Revolution, tunics from Roman times, contemporary suits, and beaded gowns.

Realizing she was being closely examined, Adriana turned her attention to the intense woman whose hands were running over the lines of the seams of her jacket and pulling on its shoulders. The woman fingered the seams of the skirt and felt for the fitting where the jacket flared out at the bottom. Adriana had taken two weeks on a dress form in the barn with some pin-striped, gray wool she'd snuck in from Brooklyn one full year before. Her years of training in sewing for local families and making her own dresses had made her swift and accurate. Her seams were cut on the bias, sewn carefully and straight. The fabric on this suit was costly, and she didn't want to make any mistakes, so she took her time sewing it. Despite the close scrutiny, she stood firm, knowing her craftsmanship was good.

The woman came around the front of her and looked her in the eyes. Adriana flashed her a smile, not a pretty, winsome smile like she'd taught herself in the mirror when she imagined she'd be an actress. But a real one. The woman smiled back. "You're hired. Come in at seven tomorrow morning. Bring lunch. Don't be late. We work hard, but comfortably here. One week trial, if you stick, salary the second week." She held out her hand, and Adriana took it; it was rough with callouses. Her handshake was firm, real. "Edith Head, nice to meet you."

"Adriana Morello."

And with that, Adriana had a job, and Edith was back to work.

LAURA

Hollywood, California, 1997

Every Friday, Laura lunched with Dexter on his expense
account, which was slightly larger than hers; it was, in fact,
limitless. Fridays were notoriously light days in the industry, so
long lunches were expected. They ate at various tasty selec-
tions close to Universal. Ca del Sol, Sushi Nozawa. Sometimes,
somewhere unexpected. They played footsie under the table
and had quick, dry exchanges. Shot the shit about work. She
felt kinda cute in those days, hair cut to her shoulders, suits
bought from J. Crew tailored by a clever seamstress whose shop
was in a mini-mall. Being with Dexter made her feel cuter.
Roadside Productions was still flush with Hollywood's good
graces, and she had the feeling that she could do anything, She
imagined working her way up to producer and somewhere
down the line hanging out a shingle, getting a studio deal.

Sundays were just for them. Breakfast at his place, reading
scripts in bed until noon, a midday hike, luxuriating in each
other. Dexter worked Saturdays at the studio and sometimes

had dinners to which she wasn't invited. She understood. It was an executive thing. Laura Mullen and Dexter Bellows were becoming the couple to be seen with. They were invited to parties with fellow executives, to fundraising events, to premieres.

Soon, her nights in front of TCM were few and far between. A guilty pleasure. Life became a whirl of development parties that were filled with the same faces. The Bitch was named Meredith, and their small circle of friends was comprised of the junior executives, the script trackers, the movers, the shakers of a social scene which, to Laura, became more like high school every day. There was a great deal of puerile teasing, a lot of sleeping around, and a few liquor-induced blow-outs between friends who had circled the small watering hole together for too long. But Laura didn't mind. She was half of a power couple, and after a while, even Meredith started to look up to her.

One liquored-up night at the Roxy, screaming over an up-and-coming band, Meredith yelled into Laura's ear, "You hooked a good one there. He's going straight to the top!" Laura hadn't thought of Dexter as hooked, but she suddenly felt very, very lucky.

Dexter and Laura went to the Universal Christmas party together. It was enormous. They parked in Laura's coveted spot near the bungalow and caught the tram. The studio tour trams were retooled from the Universal Studio tours, decorated for Christmas and blasting Christmas carols. It was 75 degrees, but Laura wore a long-sleeved black shirt, jeans, boots, and a red scarf – a little Christmas flair. Dexter looked extremely handsome in his casual wear – a dark green golf shirt (that cost too much but allowed him to hang out with the senior executives), some khaki pants, and running shoes that cost half her weekly pay. As they waited in line for the tram, he put his arm around her, squeezed her, and kissed her hard on the temple. She was proud to be taking him to one of her parties for a change. She was proud that he was happy to be with her.

The tram took them on the long, winding ride down to the back lot where it stopped in the town square featured in so many movies. Laura still got a geeky surge of excitement as they dismounted by the actual clock tower from *Back to the Future* set right in the middle of a completely fake but real-looking downtown USA. The buildings were bedecked for Christmas like Bedford Falls, fake shopfronts adorned with fake snow and Christmas wreaths, real snow blown into piles for kids to play in, lampposts wound with garland, a band playing in the gazebo at the center of town. There were vast tables filled with food and drink everywhere they went, and each time they went to a new area, the menu changed. Downtown USA had burgers and hotdogs and cookies, Rome had pastas and antipasti, Europe had grapes, cheese, wine, and fruit, and the Old West had stations serving chili and cornbread. She and Dexter wandered until they found themselves in ancient Rome on the steps from *Spartacus*.

They knew a lot of people to say hello to. Laura was always friendly around the lot, and she got some happy waves and greetings as she walked around the party. One particularly slick-looking fellow gave her a high five and a Merry Christmas. Dexter looked at her, eyebrow raised; impressed. She shrugged bashfully, not having the guts to tell him that it was a guy who worked the food line in the commissary.

When they had parked themselves on a fencepost in the Old West village to eat chili and cornbread and watch cowboy actors demonstrating roping techniques, Dexter let out a sigh of contentment. And then he said it. "I love this crazy town."

Laura leaned against him and said, "Me, too."

He pushed her away from him so they could look each other in the eyes. He had a shadow of whiskers, which was the style for studio men on their off days. He looked so handsome. He said, "And I think I love you."

Laura's heart surged. It wasn't until later that she thought about the "I think" part. She chalked it up to the awkward Cary Grant he was playing.

"Oh, Dext." She purred, trying hard to sound like Katharine Hepburn.

A light came into his eyes like it did when he was excited about a script. Like it did when he had an idea for a movie. "We make a good team." It had only been a few months, was he going to propose? Here, now? *Don't be ridiculous.*

Dexter said, "Baby, will you shack up with me?"

Laura's mind went very fast. Dexter had a tiny apartment on the west side. But they could make it work. Cardboard boxes and one-pot dinners. They could watch classic movies together. And maybe it wasn't as intense as "hearthfires and holocausts" speech from *The Philadelphia Story*. But he said he loved her. Right?

Dexter said, "Baby?" He looked anxious and a little angry.

She smiled, threw her arms around him, and said, "Of course. Yes. Yes!"

On Monday morning, she picked up *Variety* to find a head-shot of Dexter on the bottom of the front page. He had been promoted to Vice President of Production for Paramount. When she asked him why he hadn't told her earlier, he shrugged and said it was business. This distinction puzzled her, but only later did she realize that it was everything.

CHAPTER THREE

LIZZIE

Sitting in the car, I tried going over what we packed. I looked back for Calzone, who had wedged his fat body in the back window of the rental like an invisible force was holding him there. I could tell by the way he hunched his shoulders and breathed quickly that he was cross. I tried grabbing at him, but he wasn't coming out for anything. He had been huffing for a while but now settled into a low-pitched growl. A small circle of steam had formed on the back window near his face. Cats hate to be moved.

Worrying about Calzone had gotten me off track about what I'd packed, and an icy grip of panic hit me that I'd forgotten something. I grabbed for my shirt; the secret message tube rested underneath my jacket. Why I'd chosen to hide it, I don't know. Its secrecy seemed somehow, once again important. Or maybe I was getting weird. Grief made you sad, but did it also make you weird?

"Uncle Bart?"

He said, "Yeah."

"What did you do with the rest of the stuff?"

"It's in storage. Some stuff went to Goodwill."

That was terrifying. I thought for a moment before I asked, "Mom and Dad's wedding album?"

"In your box."

Phew. I remembered the picture boxes, but not that. "Dad's desk?"

"Storage."

"Mom's favorite lamp?"

He sighed and said, "Which one?"

Oh, crap. "That glass one with the orange shade."

Uncle Bart breathed in through his teeth and didn't say anything for a minute like he was holding his breath. "Lizzie, that was broken. I tossed it."

Calzone's growl turned into a yowl.

"You what?" I didn't mean to sound so upset.

"I tossed it. We couldn't keep everything."

"She *loved* that lamp! She got it at a swap meet with my dad back when they were dating." I started crying. I was angry with myself for doing it, but I was more pissed that Uncle Bart threw out something precious to my mom without even asking me. What else was gone? I stopped trying to hide the fact that I was crying.

His voice cracked, angry, "What the fuck was I supposed to do? A whole house full of shit. No one else to help, I had to sort it out somehow."

"You could have asked me about it!"

He said, "I didn't want to put you through that. Lizzie, do you know what it's like, all those pieces of them? All of those things – to decide which is important and which is just junk?"

I was arranging a snappy comeback, but I heard a sob. Uncle Bart was crying. His tears dripped off his face into his lap, and he didn't make any noise, but his face went down and sideways like the tragedy mask in comedy and tragedy. His eyes were kidney beans but with another twist, turned up at the sides.

I said, "I'm sorry."

He wiped his face with his sleeve and cleared his throat. "No, Lizzie. I'm so. So. Sorry."

I looked out the window where the local mall was just passing out of view, the MACY's where mom, knowing I hated dresses, got me a very cool outfit with pants I could wear to a friend's birthday party, where she was going to drop me to hang with friends this summer. The mall I wasn't likely going to set foot in again. I said, "Everyone's been nothing but sorry."

We were quiet for a while. Calzone's growling subsided, and all I could hear was the noise of the engine and the cars whizzing by on the opposite side of the freeway.

Uncle Bart said, "It's all my fault, you know."

I said, "What?"

He paused for a moment and then said, "Never mind."

I didn't know if he meant that the lamp was his fault or the fact that I was going to live with my aging great-grandmother. I kept looking out the window so I wouldn't have to look at him. At least not until his face came back together.

LAURA

Somewhere off Route 40, 1998

When Laura pulled the car into the Motel 6 in Amarillo, smoke was pouring out from under the hood. Originally, she thought she'd take her time and see the sights on her way to Baltimore, but by the third Motel 6, she found that the road was a lonely and creepy place, and all inspiration for adventure had left her in the kitchen of the Hollyridge house in her final confrontation with Dexter.

As the fastest rising star at the studio, Dexter Bellows was given a company Beamer, a huge bump in pay, and was expected to turn around and buy a house. He was so busy with his new tasks at Paramount that Laura was left to do the house hunting. She found that if she cut her business lunches down to twice a week and left by seven-thirty each night, she could maintain her job but still look for a home for Dexter. And for herself of course. But Dexter's money was buying.

With some guilt and some exhilaration, Laura went house hunting. There was a huge learning curve of loan qualification, interest rates, neighborhoods. She was surprised by the enormous prices for the houses in the Hollywood Hills a few blocks above her $800-a-month apartment. They chose a 1930's Tudor house up Beachwood Canyon on Hollyridge. It had one story facing the road but went down the back of the hill two more stories into a garden. It had modest bedrooms, but the entertaining space was enormous. The house was imbalanced to Laura, something was missing, out of place, but once Dexter saw the grand living room with oversized Batchelder tiled fireplace and stained wood cathedral ceilings, he was sold.

The mood of the relationship changed abruptly the moment they moved in together. Laura tried to match Dexter's banter, his wit, but soon found that now that he'd won her, he didn't want to trade quips with her anymore. He just wanted a personal assistant, regular sex, and the appearance of a stable relationship. He sought his banter in the men's club of male movie executives and agents, in cigar rooms, at the Sky Bar, after hours in lounges where only men were allowed, where he could work toward his goal of world domination.

Turned out he didn't even like old movies.

Laura kept at it. Unfortunately, she had imagined her fantasy life with Dexter so firmly that she forgot about her own Hollywood dreams. Her shorter hours, taken initially for house hunting, were now taken up with the necessities for running a Hollywood household. Parties, catering, staff, appointments. She did more business with his slick male assistant Kirk than with her own business contacts. But she did it without question. They were becoming a power couple after all.

The dinners were gorgeous, catered from toney places like Bite. She had begun collecting Cottura, Italian plates imported from Italy. She was bringing her Italian heritage to the table.

Memories of lavish Italian holidays at her Nonna's house, spectacular cooking, great wine (when she was old enough) brought life to the parties for Hollywood's up-and-comers. Her work life kept her in the know and her training in black-and-white quips made Laura confident at her dinner table. She wanted Barbara Stanwyck's certainty, indomitable spirit, and steady delivery for these conversations. Stanwyck was a woman who knew who she was, whether the reporter, the moll, or the mistress. Laura didn't mind when Dexter didn't bring up her job in mixed company. These people worked for the bigwigs, and her small indie company, which hadn't produced anything since *Windblown,* was hardly worth noting.

Her bosses came into the office less and less. They had been unable to get a project greenlit or close to greenlit during their year in the bungalow. Laura knew it was time to start looking for a new job. She'd get to it next week after the cocktail party she and Dexter were throwing this weekend to celebrate director Andy Davis's birthday.

Laura let Dexter have his little put-downs at these parties. Sometimes he'd refer to her as "the little woman," or in a more sardonic mood, "my power-hungry common-law wife." She thought this was just boys' club talk and that he didn't mean it.

But in a matter of months, Dexter started talking over her when she'd have an opinion on a movie or a book. He contradicted any comment she made, no matter how minor. It was clear she was no longer allowed a voice. She sort of let it happen. She would have her day. As soon as she got the next job.

When Kevin Trilling called her into his corner office in the bungalow, he sounded elated. Laura hoped that her pet project, *Kindness* – to which she had managed to get an A-list star and a B-list director attached – had finally been greenlit.

Kevin said, "Good news. We're going home."

Laura wondered if she'd been fired. "Home?" she asked.

"We can't make movies here. The system's too big, the shit too thick. Anything we've brought into the studio has been smacked down, and they are always, always looking for someone to be attached. And then when that happens, they aren't content unless we bring in private backers. They're the *studio*, they're meant to be footing the bill. I've told Piers that the simple answer to the situation is to decamp. Go back to our roots. But he was insistent. If you want to know the truth, I think he likes the bungalow."

"Does ..." *does that mean I'm fired?*

He tilted back in his chair and steepled his fingers under his nose. This was a stance he always took when proposing a new idea to a writer, an employee, or a studio exec. Kevin said, "But look darling, I am *desperate* to take you with me. You are the only one who gets how I work. You're crackerjack with the writers, and in London, you wouldn't have to waste your time with all of this ..." he made air quotes, "*schmoozing* that seems to matter so much here. I mean you've *hardly* been in the office."

Guilt surged in Laura's stomach as she hadn't exactly been schmoozing for the company.

London.

It sounded so foreign, exotic, full of possibility. Trench coats, flats and taxi-cabs, and actual rain. One year ago, she would have jumped at the chance.

But Dexter. And her life here. She had a house. A home.

Kevin's eyes crackled with the confidence in the asking of a question already answered. "So? Will you move with us?"

Laura's face scrunched up, and her stomach sank, and she said, "No. I'm so sorry. No. I don't think I can."

Kevin stared at her sternly for a long moment. Then he looked disappointed. "It's a shame. A damn waste. I didn't figure you the kind of girl who would throw over an opportunity for a *man*." His poncey English accent that she had always loved, that had always made her feel important, became detestable and derisive. He picked up the handset on his phone, her signal to leave. He said, "I do hope he's worth it, dear."

It stung because on some level she knew he was right. Later, during long nights on her sister's un-insulated sleeping porch, she played this scene over and over, again and again, writing a different ending, imagining herself single in London, making movies, becoming something.

Laura went back to her office and sat in her comfortable chair at her swanky dark wood desk and stared at the poster for *Windblown*. Steve Buscemi's face was darkened with anger at the gun pressed to his cheek, his gun pressed to his brother's. The bright colors that swam behind them, that buoyed her during her workday said, *big movie*. But her cozy existence, Berber carpeted, and dark wood-blinded office, her parking spot, and expense account were finished.

It shouldn't be too hard to find a new job.

Whenever she tried to broach the subject of her job hunt with Dexter, he became tremendously unhelpful and feigned a phone call or a meeting, or an errand. She called a few of his friends, whom she thought of as her friends, asking them for help in finding a new gig, but they gave her the Hollywood brush-off. "Sure, honey, I'll keep my ear to the ground." And no call back. People never told you *no* directly in Hollywood. Their "no" was the mute hopelessness of the phone that wouldn't ring.

After a month of looking for work, Laura confronted Dexter. He was in the shower, the only place where she could corner him for conversation anymore. She leaned against the overpriced English shabby chic wood chest of drawers opposite the shower and forced herself to say in the general direction of the steam, "Why won't you help me find a job? Don't you give a shit?" Her voice came out shaky and wimpy, and she wished she could unsay it.

He pulled back the shower curtain, squinting from foam that was sliding down his forehead, and said with those once warm and witty brown eyes stone cold, "Oh, get real, Laura. Off Roadside? The one company with a golden three-picture deal who couldn't get a movie off the ground in an entire *year*? You'll be lucky to land a job as an assistant. You don't have enough hustle, honey. You weren't cut out for this business." The water coming off his mouth made it look like he was spitting his words. He shut the curtain on her.

That morning, when his BMW X5 burned out of their driveway, Laura realized she wasn't Barbara Stanwyck at all. She had become Joan Fontaine in *Jane Eyre* or her sister, Olivia de Havilland in *The Heiress*. She had become invisible.

Laura called Kevin that afternoon, but she didn't get the chance to ask if the position was still open. The first thing he said to her when he picked up the phone was, "Good news, Stephanie's coming with." Stephanie. The mousy girl who had only been promoted to assistant from script reader two months before. As a further dig, he said, "We'll miss you, Laura. It's a shame. A damned shame." He then begged off for reasons of London calling.

Her one real bridge burned, six months of increasing invisibility and total unemployment passed, and a picture of Dexter tonguing a mid-list actress showed up in the Hollywood Reporter. The photo was captioned "Moving Up" and coincided with Dexter's promotion to Executive VP of Production. They were caught in this makeout session on the red carpet for a movie premiere for which Laura had bought a new dress but to which Dexter had neglected to bring her. He said that he was stuck late at the office and forgot to call.

Three hours later found Laura on her sister's doorstep in Sherman Oaks with her car full of everything she owned.

Each day Laura drove along Route 40 until she thought she'd fall asleep or simply go crazy. She stopped, grabbed a bite to eat, jogged once around the parking lot, visited the bathrooms, and got back in the car. Then she drove until sunset when she found the next place to stay. She'd seen too many horror movies to have any notions about driving after dark in a car that might break down any minute.

She thought of this trip as a vision quest. She would wander the country, free at last, see the world, and get in touch with herself. That was what her mother had done when she left – gone in search of herself. It was her turn. And Laura didn't have any kids to abandon. She had fantasies about sitting on a perch overlooking the Grand Canyon and writing in her notebook. Playing pool with the locals in Albuquerque. But now, all she could think about now was that comfortable bedroom in Nonna's house where she spent summers sleeping over with Rebecca. That bedroom became her objective, her drive and her destination. Out here on Route 40, there was nothing left of her.

LIZZIE

Baltimore, Maryland, 1998

When we pulled up to Nonna's, it was getting late. The street looked dull and dark – undrawable. A swathe of black with two lit windows – Nonna's. We climbed the stairs to the porch, and I had Calzone wrapped in a sweater for his own safety. The street smelled like old city. Some cooking smells, old cars, a little bit of mold. The air was heavier than at home, and try as I might, I couldn't smell any green. Our neighborhood always smelled green and woody. Uncle Bart hadn't said a word since we reached Baltimore. I looked at him for guidance, and I knew that he knew that I was looking, but he kept his eyes on the door in front of him. He looked like he was screwing up his courage. You don't want the grownup in charge to look like he's screwing up his courage.

I loved going to Nonna's house when I was little. She was such a busy, bustling woman and ran around like a wind-up mouse. She knew all the neighbors and their business – not in a gossipy way, she just knew the comings and goings of their lives. She took me out to the bakery, the butcher, the greengrocer, the fish store and bragged about me to all the people who worked there. She seemed to have a lot of friends who worked in food. They rolled their eyes at Nonna's fussing, but they liked her – she was good people. She and I sang goofy songs I knew from school, and she always asked me to tell her a story while we walked. She wasn't like other grownups who try to correct your story or guide it. She let me make up the loopiest, most awful things full of demons and bunny rabbits and bubblegum – stories where everybody died at the end. She laughed at the funny parts, and I knew she enjoyed *me*. Enjoyed the company we kept.

She was a *crazy* good cook then. Italian Catholic – you couldn't go wrong. She made meat sauce, sausage, pasta, zabaglione, baked ziti, chicken parm, and knew the best bakery to get these amazing almond cookies in pastel colors. Nonna's house was a place to look forward to, especially at Easter. Roast lamb, rice cake, artichoke pie, and Nonna made that fancy Italian braided Easter bread that had to rise three times for the Holy Trinity, and she added three colored eggs in it for the Holy Trinity. Italy's all about the Holy Trinity. She'd bring it to the table, brown and citrus smelling and sweet and shellacked, the colored eggs gleaming in their braided nest, and everyone was amazed. Nonna was the coolest.

Nonna's brick townhouse was in Jonestown, right next to Little Italy. Before she broke her hip, Nonna would do the rounds of her old friends who were still around, checking in on them, bringing them groceries when they were driving them to doctor's appointments when they needed it.

When Nonna fell on her front steps and broke her hip last spring, I wondered if a part of her didn't fall out, also. Something small and shiny that they didn't catch slipped from her brain, popped out of her ear, and skittered across the sidewalk.

Maybe a passerby picked it up. The next time we went to see her, her glow had gone, like some evil villain had stolen her power – like Superman when a piece of Kryptonite was near. The house was dark and messy. It didn't smell homemade anymore; she ate only freezer food and TV dinners and had a walker. She couldn't get down the front steps, so she stopped seeing her neighbor friends. I tried to tell her a story, but it was like she'd forgotten how to listen. Her smiles were gone. Mom was really worried about her. She said, "You need to get out, Nonna. You can't just sit here forever. What about Gina? You could give Gina a call."

Nonna didn't want to trouble anybody. Her life had gone from bright color to a dingy gray. She kept the curtains closed, she stopped cleaning the floor and dusting, and soon she became one with her beige BarcaLounger, watching her gray and black movies. I never saw her so much as look at the television before her hip.

Mom was talking about putting her in a home before the accident. Like a *month* ago, it was all, "Nonna can't take care of herself anymore. She needs help." Now I was here with everything I owned, moving in with her.

Mom hadn't gotten around to changing the will and she probably put Nonna on the will when she was still *Nonna*. When she could put a meal together for fifteen friends and neighbors. When she was always laughing and walked around to all the shops so fast I couldn't keep up. Mom wouldn't *want* to wish this new Nonna on me.

Would she?

Uncle Bart rang the doorbell, but it didn't seem to make any noise. He rapped on the aluminum-framed storm door. It rattled. No answer.

I saw the curtains move. About two thousand years later, the front door opened, sucking the screen door in with a slam.

Nonna stood there, her eyes fishy behind her glasses. She was wearing a housecoat – a flowered type thing with pockets. She'd been wearing this since her accident. Before she fell, she was always so *put together*.

She leaned on her walker and yelled, "You gotta open the door! I can't reach it!"

Uncle Bart pushed in the square button on the handle of the storm door, which squeaked in a teeth-hurting way, and pulled the door open with a metallic *sprong*. A whoosh of yuck came out the front door. It was hot inside like she was running the heat even though it had to be seventy out. There was a green bean smell and some kind of nasty meat.

And no real greeting, just, "Come in, then. Don't let the cool out."

Uncle Bart got loud, like people do with old people, like Mrs. Dunford had that morning with me. He half-yelled, "How are you doing Mrs. Morello?" That tone gave me a sick, sinking feeling of dread.

"Fine, fine." Nonna turned her walker in and headed back to her beloved BarcaLounger, while Uncle Bart and I struggled with the front storm door, me trying to not let go of Calzone, him trying to get my suitcase through. There was a lot of clattering, and by the time we made it in, Nonna was already tilted back in her chair. She was watching one of her movies with no color. Some lady with too much hat was crying plastic-looking tears.

The TV was turned down, but from the glow on Nonna's glasses, I could see she was watching.

I sat down on the sofa opposite her and gently unwrapped Calzone while Uncle Bart got the rest of my stuff. Calzone scratched me in his scramble to get free and ran up the stairs, ears back, hind legs low, fur raised like a raccoon's.

I called after him even though I knew it wouldn't do any good. "Calzone!" Some sidekick.

Nonna thought I was talking to her. She said, "No. But I have some leftover hash if you're hungry."

Hash? Calzone was gone. I got up to go after him, but Uncle Bart was at the front door with my two boxes. I let him in. He put the boxes down and hollered, "Mrs. Morello, like I said on the phone, Lizzie's going to live with you for a while."

The only way I could tell that Nonna had heard was that her glasses no longer reflected the television. She said, "I know, Bart, I haven't lost my mind."

Uncle Bart was embarrassed, "Uh. I know. I just ..."

Nonna shushed him and pointed to the television. The weeping woman was shaking her head and talking, all worked up.

How could he just dump me off here? This wasn't living. I mean Mom and Dad were dead, and I *loved* Nonna, but this was like some sort of green bean and hash mortuary. It was no place for a kid – least of all a teenager. The windows were grimy, even the television had months' worth of dust on it. I looked up over Nonna's brick fireplace and saw an enormous cobweb the size of my head dangling with God-knows-what caught inside it. I grabbed Uncle Bart's hand and squeezed it hard. *Pleasepleasepleasedon't leave me here.* He patted that hand and then extricated his own.

He was going to leave me there.

He was still trying to communicate with Nonna, but she was somewhere back in another century in black and white. Bart said, "She can help out, cooking, cleaning, fetching groceries."

This is the part in a manga where the orphan is sold into servitude of some Samurai master. Only this was Baltimore, and Nonna didn't look qualified to train me in much of anything anymore.

She looked at me, her eyes all fish-big in her glasses. "That's nice. I could use some help. But I want you to have a good time, okay Lizzie? You've been through too much, and you're too young for this fucking old-age crap." I don't think I'd ever heard Nonna swear before. She continued like the swearing part was normal, "You'll get your shit together, go out, and make friends. Don't mind your old-lady grandma."

"Great-grandma." Bart corrected her. He was an expert all of a sudden.

Nonna turned her head back toward the TV and ignored him. It was disturbing that she referred to herself as an "old lady." Only three months ago, the term wouldn't have even come up.

We sat for a long while. The music on the movie was reaching a violin crescendo. Bart's leg jiggled; he was itching to get out of this situation – leave me in Hell and go back to his fabulous New York life.

The movie warbled on, turned down low. The air conditioning kicked in, blowing the stinky smells around in the closed air and making the giant cobweb dance menacingly. None of my dreams for becoming a teenager, growing up, like, maybe *dating* someday, having friends sleep over – none of that fit *here*. This couldn't be my life. This was somebody else's life.

Uncle Bart smacked me on the knee and squeezed it. He didn't look at me. He'd probably feel pretty awful if he did. He got up off the sofa. I grabbed his arm.

He said, "Well, I'm going to leave you two ladies to it. I have to work tomorrow, so I'd better hit the road. I have a long drive ahead of me."

Nonna didn't say anything. She just nodded at him.

And he left.

Just like that.

Just like my parents. Out the door. Never to be seen again.

I sat where I was and knew I was going to start crying if I didn't get out of there fast. I said, "Nonna, where am I going to sleep?"

"Upstairs. Left of the bathroom. Your mama's old room."

That was something. I got up and reflexively went over to kiss Nonna, but when I got near, I realized she smelled gross, so I backed off. I don't think she noticed, so I patted her on the shoulder. "See you tomorrow!"

And I lugged my suitcase up the carpeted stairs, *kathunk-slide-kathunk*-slide, and went to find Calzone.

CHAPTER FOUR

ADRIANA

Hollywood, California, 1937

Because of Rose, Adriana left central casting and went to work at Paramount as a seamstress for the only woman designer in the industry. Irene, famed fashion designer, would make gowns for a film, but Edith was the only female head of a studio costume department. She oversaw every gown, men's suit, and pair of shoes on the movies she designed.

When a room became available in her little house off Melrose Avenue, Rose called Adriana and moved her in by the weekend. Rose single-handedly changed Adriana's entire picture of what her life in Hollywood would be like. No casting calls, lipstick tricks, silk stockings. She often wore trousers. Aside from lipstick, she usually forgot about makeup. She wore her curly hair down to her shoulders. She rarely indulged in more than a few hairpins to keep it in place. She worked countless hours at the studio, fussing over velvet, putting boning into silk linings, fitting actresses. Her fingers traveled through miles of muslin, brocade, gingham, silk, through France, England, backcountry USA, to Manhattan, Boston, and Africa. Adriana possessed speed, accuracy, and a strong work ethic and rose through the ranks quickly. Soon, she was the first at Edith's side for fittings, ideas, or project changes.

Evenings and sometimes late at night, she rode her bicycle across the sun-baked pavement, not yet cooled by the evening ocean air, the few blocks home where she usually found Rose waiting with dinner, such as it was. Rose was no chef.

When she first moved in, Rose showed Adriana to her room, a small, sunny space at the back corner of the ten-year-old Spanish bungalow. It had a built-in vanity and dresser and a view of the back garden.

One night after a dinner of cold cuts and salad they sat on a wrought iron bench in their tiny patch of a garden. Not really a patio, just a square of concrete. Their wooden fence was crawling with jasmine which became more fragrant as the light faded and the air cooled. Adriana breathed in deeply, inhaling the scent of the fresh cut grass, the salt air of the marine layer rolling in, and Rose's face powder. She said, "Thank you."

"For what?"

Adriana raised her arms wide, gesturing to the yard, the rows of houses, the Santa Monica Mountains in the distance, and said, "All of it."

Rose leaned over and kissed Adriana, who was less surprised than she thought she would be. She had never been properly kissed before, except once by a boy of a man in New York who gave her such a distaste for kissing that she decided firmly against it.

But when Rose kissed her, softly, gently, and full, it tasted right, it felt right, and there were no questions. They remained on the sofa a long while, kissing, touching, taking in every inch of each other with a wonder Adriana had never known before. Rose was solid, strong, full-breasted with dancer's legs. Her strength made Adriana feel safer than she had in years. In that evening light, she became everything Adriana had never known that she wanted. They drifted into Rose's bedroom and out of their clothes, and Adriana knew that she would never leave this woman. She wanted this kind of night to be waiting for her at the end of every day that followed.

New York, 1931-2

In 1929, Mama brought them over from Sant'Agnello. Mama had had it with their papa, who beat them, so she secretly sent a letter to America to her aunt who lived there. She arranged boat passage to New York for all of them.

Things were okay at first. They lived in a one-bedroom apartment off Canal Street. Adriana was ten, and her oldest brother, Angelo, was twelve. Her next brother, Antonio was eleven, and her sister, Maria, was seven. Adriana got plenty of love from her Mama, who called her "il mio bambina," even though Adriana was big enough to dress and feed herself and take care of her baby sister. But Mama's money, taken from the jug in the kitchen in Sant'Agnello where she'd been saving it for years, ran out too quickly. A shifty-looking twenty-year-old named Guiseppe came by to change the lire into dollars for her twice. The second time, she gave him what was left – it seemed like a lot – and he gave her five crumpled dollar bills for it. He said the exchange rate wasn't so good.

Angelo and Antonio went to work in a meat factory. They came home stinking of something dead and rotting but with some bits of meat wrapped in paper for the family to eat and a few coins for Mama. Mama went to work as a seamstress, and

Maria and Adriana stayed home and took care of the apartment. Mostly, they cleaned and fought.

Adriana had to scrub and rinse her brothers' stinking clothes two times, just to fade that stink to bearable. Angelo and Antonio came home from work hunched over, ate wordlessly, stripped, and climbed into their cot, going to sleep before the girls had even finished with the dishes. Mama would come home late and give them each a kiss and mutter to herself in Italian. She said, "God" and "Jesus" a lot and wove in some words Adriana didn't know the meaning of, but she knew were naughty. But they were together, and she felt safe in a world where the foreign words were only just beginning to make sense.

Then Mama met Carlo. Carlo was handsome and kind to them. He always came with an apple in his pocket, a ready hand to tousle the boys' hair, ribbons and little gifts for the girls. Mama was happier and started dressing better. Adriana didn't know where she got the money. The color returned to her face, and she brought home fresh fruit and vegetables to cook with dinner.

After a few weeks, Mama told the boys they didn't have to go to work anymore. They stayed home with the girls, but Mama started staying out later and later and some nights wouldn't come home at all. The boys took the opportunity to run wild in the streets while Maria and Adriana stayed home.

One day, they were all sleeping in the pre-dawn hours, and the building hadn't yet started making its morning noises. The door swung open quickly and startled Adriana with its whiff of smoke, perfume, and alcohol. Mama and Carlo came in laughing and giggling. Mama was wearing a sparkly dress Adriana hadn't seen before and Carlo wore a suit. Mama turned to the room and said, "Children, children wake up. We're married!"

For a hazy moment, Adriana thought that they'd all gotten married together, and she was happy. But when she was fully awake, she saw something had changed in Carlo's eyes. He wouldn't look directly at them. And despite being flush with excitement, Mama moved nervously around the apartment and jumped at the slightest sound. Her smile didn't go all the way up to her eyes and she was worried about something.

Two days later, they were all on a bus to the country in Connecticut. They were moving to a farm. Adriana was excited, imagining the farms in Sant'Agnello, but what she saw out the bus window looked nothing like it. It was so much greener here that she didn't see how there could be farms. There were so many trees that she thought they were driving through a jungle. For a while the roads were wide, two lanes going each way, but then they rode up a narrow, winding dark road. Adriana leaned to look out the bus's front window and saw a truck coming directly for them. She gripped her seat and squeezed her eyes shut, but when she opened them, the truck had somehow passed. While she saw a narrow strip of sky out of the front of the bus, when she looked out the side window, it looked like they were going through a green, leafy tunnel. As far as she could see on either side were trees and low, stone walls which trailed off mysteriously into the woods. They had stone walls in Italy to divide farms, but what was being divided here? One plot of trees ran into another in the dark and dead-leafed jungle.

The bus finally came to a bus stop – just a roof and two walls with a bench underneath. Hanging from the roof was a wooden sign that read, *Bethlehem*. Adriana smiled. This looked nothing like where she imagined Jesus being born, but there was hope in the name and in the shingled bus stop. They got off the bus.

She had gotten used to the city and its noises and the pipes in the walls and screaming children and arguing parents. Before that, she was used to the quiet of Sant'Agnello, its rolling hills, few birds, and remote morning voices. But here, there was an oppressive, alien noise that she didn't recognize. A whirring and clicking vibrated deep in the forest and there were constant chirpings that didn't sound at all like birds. Something let out a desolate piercing noise bigger than Adriana had ever heard before and all around her, the leaves shifted and stirred like a large dark force was moving through them, coming toward the family that had seemed so big in that small apartment. A family that now was small and vulnerable.

Terrified, Adriana was not comforted by the looks on her brothers' faces. Antonio was resigned, but Angelo, the biggest – the one who laughed at the stormy days on the steamship which pitched and rolled when they were crossing the ocean – Angelo was obviously frightened.

Carlo lit a cigarette. Adriana was anxious that she should work harder, make him like her. She walked over toward him, her boots crunching on the gravel under her feet. Carlo looked up as she approached. He turned away, throwing aside his match. She moved up alongside him and slipped her hand into his. He'd held her hand before when he was courting her mother, but his hand wouldn't close on hers now. It hung limp, unengaged. Adriana got a lump in her throat and gave his hand a friendly squeeze. Carlo shook her off and walked away.

Adriana turned back toward Mama who sat on the two suitcases that held everything they owned. She had packed all the children's clothes into one suitcase. All of hers into another. The children's suitcase was bulging at the seams and hers still had a little room, but when Adriana suggested moving a few things, Mama said no.

The wind rustled the leaves again, and they stood for a while. Antonio was chucking gravel into the woods. Mama looked around her and pulled her shawl over her shoulders. Adriana put her arms around her, which would usually result in a pat on the arms, or a slight snuggle back. Mama stiffened. She carefully extracted Adriana's arms, one by one, as if they were unwanted appendages.

Adriana walked around the front of Mama and looked into her eyes, which were welling with tears and would not meet her own. Adriana leaned in, putting her face right in Mama's, but no matter where she moved, Mama averted her eyes, looking past her. Adriana grabbed her mother's face when the sound of a truck breaking through the woods' clamor caused them all to look to the road. An old farm truck emerged from the woods, its insect-eye headlamps glimmering dimly. It looked like it came from the time when cars were invented. Its motor rattled loudly. Its flatbed back, surrounded by a fence of wooden planks, was empty except for a few bales of hay.

Whoever was driving waved his arm out the window and tooted his horn, which made an *oweega* sound. Adriana looked to Mama inquiringly, but she said nothing. She thought she saw her wipe some tears away. When the man cut the engine, the wind kicked up and whatever was in the woods stirred again.

The man who got out of the car was Italian, Adriana knew immediately. He had a certain jaunt and machismo. There was some country about him, too. He wore dungaree overalls and a gray shirt. She couldn't tell if it was white gone dingy with lack of washing or simply gray, faded from frequent washing. He seemed friendly enough and smiled. She felt Mama's hand on her shoulder as she was herded over next to her brothers and sister. They lined up, and the man looked them over, up and down like he was buying horses or goats. He grabbed Angelo's arm and held it up, motioning for him to make a muscle. He did so, and the man squeezed and smiled. His face fell when he got to Adriana and Maria. He took a hold of Adriana's chin and held it, peering into her eyes. Never letting go of her chin, he stood back and looked her up and down in a way that should be left for grown ladies. Adriana jerked her chin away angrily, and he laughed.

The man handed Carlo a small wad of money and hoisted their suitcase onto the truck. Adriana noticed he didn't grab Mama's suitcase.

She turned to Mama and threw her arms around her waist, looking up into her eyes, but Mama wouldn't look at her. "Mama? Mama, where are we going?" Mama wouldn't look at her and stared across the road with tears running down her cheeks while Carlo pried Adriana's arms off and pulled her away. Adriana screamed and kicked, doing anything to dislodge herself, but Carlo wouldn't let go. Angelo ran to them and tried to slug Carlo, but he was three times his weight.

Angelo sized up the situation and calmed his face. He said, "Por favore. Signore, Por favore." He lay his hand on Carlo's arm, and Adriana stopped kicking for a minute. Carlo conceded, and Angelo put his arm around her shoulder and pulled her away gently.

Adriana wailed, "Mama! Mama!"

Angelo's voice was sharp, commanding, and comforting all at once, "Adriana."

She stopped and let him help her onto the back of the truck. He sat her down so that she could lean against the hay bale at her back. Maria came and sat next to her and took her hand. Maria may have hated her, but they were all they had.

Adriana didn't learn until later that Mama had sold them off as farm hands to Carlo's cousin Giovanni because Carlo wanted his new wife to start a family ... his family.

Mama never learned that she had sold her children into misery, her sons and daughters into slave labor. Mama caught

the next bus to her new life and left them to fend for
themselves.

In Bethlehem, the children worked for the diGiralomos who
ran a small farm. The boys worked in the fields, and Adriana
and her sister worked in the house. They were fed enough only
to keep them working and were relegated to the fringes of the
diGiralomos' lives. The boys slept in a small outbuilding, the
girls in an uninsulated attic room.

Maria took ill one winter when she was nine and Adriana
was twelve. It started as a cough, then a fever, and she kept up
her chores with extra help from Adriana. Then, Mama diGiralomo, afraid of contagion, confined her to her cold attic room.
Adriana slipped food, broth, and water to her when she had a
spare moment. The boys would sneak into their room in the
early morning to check on her. They pleaded with Mama diGiralomo to fetch a doctor, but she shrugged and said, "A doctor
will cost money and won't make a difference. Que sera, sera."

Two weeks passed. Adriana slipped into bed with her
Maria, who was hot to the touch. She mopped her brow until
she fell off into an uneven sleep. She roused to feel her sister
cooling, and she knew that her fever must have broken.
Relieved, Adriana fell into the deepest sleep she'd had since
Maria fell ill. The next morning, when she woke, Maria was
cold and still. There was a shrill screaming coming from somewhere. Only when Mama diGiralomo stormed into the room,
grabbed her arm, and slapped her across the face, did Adriana
realize the screaming was her own.

The following summer, Angelo ran away. He left a note for
his sister that read, "Forgive me. Come find me in New York
when you are of age." Antonio followed a year later with a
similar note. She didn't forgive them. They left her like Mama

had. They left her like Maria had. They left her with nothing to do but bide her time, endure more beatings, and plan her own escape.

Hollywood, California, 1937

Adriana and Rose fell in together easily, without question. Rules were so different in Los Angeles, but they made more sense than anything she had grown up with. Instead of being baffling, cruel, and sudden, everything was simple, straightforward, and right.

They fit. They shared Rose's bedroom and turned the second bedroom into a studio for Adriana, which she never really got time to work in, and an office for Rose, who was trying to write screenplays. They had a small group of friends who came over for Sunday breakfast every week to talk, smoke, drink coffee, and laugh. Adriana sewed for work and cooked to relax. She cooked also because a girl could only get so far on takeout deli foods and macaroni salad, which for Rose constituted her daily diet. On the weekend, Adriana cooked recipes from the old country, taught to her by her grandmother, which she had perfected in the diGiralomo's kitchen.

Slowly, Adriana's old wounds turned to tough scar tissue, and the specter of Bethlehem subsided. Mama diGiralomo's constant criticism of her cooking, her sewing, her cleaning, her breathing, and those beatings in the barn receded with Rose's constant encouragement and love.

What Rose had done through her admiration of the suit, she did with her admiration of Adriana's looks, humor, and especially her cooking. When Adriana created a simple pasta carbonara, Rose not only raved, but invited their friends over the following Saturday night to try it out, complete with flowers, several bottles of wine, and long toasts. On Rose's urging, they planted a vegetable garden. Adriana found that in Connecticut, she needed to substitute ingredients in so many of her recipes, but Los Angeles's Mediterranean climate grew everything from the old country. In their tiny backyard, Rose and Adriana grew feasts of tomatoes, zucchini, peppers, greens, small bunches of oregano, enormous bushes of rosemary, and a basil plant that had somehow grown into a small shrub. The orange tree and lemon tree that had been growing there for years made the dishes complete.

The earth seemed magical there, so dry and dead-looking when you tilled it, so rich in harvest. Adriana began to think that Rose had magical powers – with gardens and with people. On the Saturdays they were alone, Adriana took the entire day to cook something special for Rose: gnocchi, ravioli, squabs in lemon and garlic, panna cotta, vegetable tarts. Rose scolded her for letting her get fat. But the acting work was steady for Rose, who had that enviable figure that could eat its weight and not gain an ounce.

Adriana and Rose had created their own Eden, but Adriana worried about the world outside that wall. They sat over roast chicken one evening at a small table in their garden. Rose, flush from only one glass of wine raised her glass to Adriana and said, "To my very beating heart." Adriana flushed and made up her mind to enjoy it while it lasted, all the time, thanking God for her brief gift of heaven.

CHAPTER FIVE

LAURA

After that stop in Amarillo with an air filter change, a new fan belt, and a warning that her head gasket was about to blow, the car made it to Bumblefuck, Tennessee before it died. Laura had pushed on one hour past dark, thinking the next town would be nicer. A town name nowhere in sight, somewhere outside of Nashville in a pitch-black downpour, her car came to a dead stop near a deserted gas station.

She said a little prayer as she stepped up to the phone booth outside the station, which clearly had not been functional for several years. Ridiculously enough, there was a dial tone. She called AAA. They put her through to a tow company that sounded like it was out of *Deliverance* or maybe *The Texas Chainsaw Massacre*. For Chrissake, she was a woman alone in the middle of Tennessee at night. The second guy who got on the phone with her twanged, "And you're alone?" and started laughing uproariously before she hung up on him. She was *not* getting a tow from some psycho she didn't know. Horror movies started this way.

She had no choice but to call Nonna collect.

"Hi, Nonna? It's Laura. *Laura.*" She wondered whether Nonna had lost her hearing or her memory. "Look, I'm lost. Well, I'm not lost. I'm on Highway 40 in Tennessee somewhere, but I don't know where I am, and I ... well, I'm stuck." She didn't want to tell Nonna that her credit card was maxed out and aside from a trunk full of cottura, she hadn't a dime to her name. What could Nonna do? She was 82 and in Baltimore. "Do you know anybody in Tennessee?"

Nonna drew in her breath sharply, a sign of thinking or gearing up for a tirade. Laura hadn't heard any of her tirades since she was much younger, and they were usually in Italian, so she waited. But Nonna said, "You sit tight. I'll call you when he's close. And don't get out of your car."

Laura wondered how she would answer the phone if she couldn't get out of the car, but she figured Nonna must know someone local. She put the car in neutral and, thanks to a slight decline, glided it down close to the pay phone so she'd hear it, even with the rain. She pulled a blanket out of the back seat, tilted back the passenger seat as far as it would go, and fell asleep more easily than she would have imagined a week ago.

Five days earlier, Laura rolled down her windows as she drove up Beachwood Drive one last time. The smell of fennel warming in the sun and dirt and sage reminded her of her morning hikes, the only time she was ever really happy in this place; climbing up the dirt paths at the end of the road: past the horses, up the mountain, through the crunch of the gravel, the heat of the sun on the back of her neck, and the quiet. Here, she spun the image of herself that she wanted to project: she was one with nature, she was creative, she was woman, hear her roar. She was a *producer*. Or would be one soon. With these thoughts, she was usually trying very hard to whistle away Dexter's put-downs of the dinner party the night before.

Her shitty car labored up the hill to the right on Hollyridge Drive, and she pulled up to the 1930s Tudor-style house on the right. The million-plus dollar home with the recently redone granite and walnut kitchen. The master bath was so enormous it could house a living room set. As her car sputtered to a stop with the stink of exhaust, she realized she was leaving this. Leaving the foothold she thought she once had. The life that seemed so fabulous on paper.

Dexter's Beamer was parked in the driveway, a mockery of her rattling Escort. She thought about going back to the car and hitting the road. But it was her fucking china, and she had picked each plate so carefully, each platter, paid for with her own salary, and she was going to take it with her. She slipped her key into the front door. Surprisingly, it still fit. Dexter didn't think her enough of a threat to get the locks changed. For some odd reason, that diminished her further.

The place still smelled the same, a lemon oil wood cleaner, fresh paint, rosemary. She walked across the smooth wood entryway she had crossed so many times before and knew it didn't ever really belong to her.

She went directly to the kitchen and started removing the china from the cabinet over the side counter. It was painted in the Italian style, brightly colored. She'd been all over LA buying it from consignment shops; the cottura dealer had closed just after she started collecting. She had some platters with rooster patterns, a pitcher with sunflowers, dinnerware with a woven gold braid against a cobalt background, all bright and carefully chosen. When she was buying it, each time she found a new piece, she was making a home. A home for her and Dexter. And in her choice of cottura specifically, she was bringing a part of herself into the house. The Italian part. The

Easter bread and trips to church with Nonna part. It made her feel connected to a culture – that she came from somewhere – as she tried to reinvent herself daily in Dexter's life.

Nonna would love the china. Maybe it would get her cooking again.

As she got the second stack of dishes down, their weight seemed to open a black pit in her stomach. She had succeeded in nothing in this house. Her career failed here. Her relationship failed here. She had pedaled as fast as she could to keep up with the Joneses: the car, the suits, the mani-pedis, and the highlights. And here she was, back in her holey jeans and man's jacket, driving a piece of shit car, stealing into a house that wasn't hers to get some china bought in search of herself.

Tears dripped out of her eyes and one hit the counter audibly. She couldn't hear herself sobbing, just the too-loud clank of the china on the granite, and she reached for the pitcher covered with sunflowers.

Dexter said, "Laura?"

She startled and dropped the pitcher. It landed with an impotent clunk and a crack as the handle broke off. He stood there with a clueless, caught little-boy look on his face. In his overpriced Adidas jogging pants and matching slinky sleeveless shirt, covered in sweat from a run, he looked as if he had narrowly escaped the law only to be caught in his own home.

Had Laura thought it out beforehand, she'd be the one on the defensive, but all that filled her now was hate and immediate anger. She said, "Asshole."

His expression changed from bafflement to guilt. She had an edge.

She continued, "Cheating, lying, self-absorbed piece-of-shit asshole!" The words were the strongest she could think of, but they came out sounding weak, pathetic.

"Okaaay ..." Appeasement was clearly his method. Dexter

stood stock-still. He wasn't allowed to not react. She walked toward him, and her toe hit the fallen pitcher, which spun with a low rolling noise on the Spanish tiled floor. She put her hands out in front of her and shoved him on the chest.

"You made me feel like crap, you jerkoff. Every fucking day with your little put-downs, and me not being good enough, and your not *helping* ..." She shoved him again so hard that he slammed into the cabinet. "... or giving me *anything*. What were you accomplishing with all of that?" She wanted to say that he had ruined a perfectly good person. That she was amazing, and it was his loss. But something was hollow about it. She didn't feel very amazing. She felt like ... nothing. She had no claim to make. Just some overpriced Italian china, a shit car, and a key to his house.

The strength by which she came there was draining out of her, and nothing was left but paper and ash. She needed to get out before she blew away.

She looked at him leaning against the cabinets, gauging his next move. She couldn't stand the sight of his face. She stacked her twelve plates with the platter wobbling precariously on top and tried to lift it. It was too heavy. Fucking china.

He stepped forward and said, "Here, let me help."

She couldn't let him help. She had to take what was hers and get the hell away from there. But she couldn't carry it. She put the platter down gently, picked up about five of the plates and walked out the door without saying anything to him. Dexter stood back to let her go and went to get the rest of the dishes.

It took him three trips, but she sat in the car with the engine on, crying, pretending not to, trying to ignore him, while he loaded the dishes into boxes in the trunk. On his last trip, he brought the two pieces of the water jug and an electric teakettle. As he passed the driver-side window he said, "You always did like tea." He put it in the trunk and closed it. He walked over to her car window. He was working his way up to saying something. "The thing is ..."

She put the car in reverse and backed away from him with a skid of dirt from the side of the road. She threw the car in drive and squealed too loudly down the hill.

He wasn't allowed to have the last word.

LIZZIE

Breakfast at Nonna's was toast and microwave oatmeal. I don't usually like microwave oatmeal, but it was cinnamon raisin and made the house smell good. Nonna stank the night before, but this morning she was freshly washed and wore a clean house-coat. She was making an effort.

Nonna did a lot of gesturing when she wasn't talking. She motioned me over to the chrome and fake brown leather chair. I sat and scooted up to the table. The legs of the chair scraped on the linoleum floor since two of its rubber feet were missing. The table had pictures of flowers on it and a cigarette burn right in the middle. That cigarette burn had been there as long as I'd known Nonna.

This kitchen was all brown and beige and no angles – there was no drawing this room. Even Peter Parker's Aunt May's kitchen had more going on.

Nonna shuffled over to the counter with her walker and popped open the microwave, pulling out a bowl of oatmeal. She was so *old*. So *suddenly* old. The kryptonite-affected Nonna was bothering me. I so desperately wanted to find what was doing this to her and cast it out, blast it into space. Then the real Nonna would come back.

She was having trouble picking up the oatmeal bowl.

"Nonna, I can get it."

"Tch. Tch. I think I can take care of my great-granddaughter." Nonna had this Italian accent that came and went. Ever since she broke her hip, it stayed. Before she broke her hip, when she was whirring around the kitchen, laughing and chatting with her granddaughters, she sounded like a New Yorker, cracking jokes, mixing in perfect Italian where it seemed appropriate. Now she sounded like a stereotype of an old Italian lady from a bad movie.

She took the bowl of oatmeal in one hand and walked, pushed her walker with her belly and her free hand, and then walked some more. I was glad her kitchen was small. It was hard to watch. She put the bowl in front of me and gestured again, "Mangia."

I said, "Grazie." I didn't know why. Maybe because Mom always said *grazie*.

Nonna's face contorted like she was going to spit something nasty out, and she started laughing in a wheezy sort of way that sounded like it wasn't good for her. She thunked my head hard with one of her rings and tousled my hair. I smiled and watched her do the whole walker thing over to the counter again for her oatmeal.

"What a cut up!" Her city voice was back. It made me feel more comfortable. "Your mama was always so funny. So funny. She and Laura would have me in stitches. Janelle? No sense of humor, and Sally?" This whole stream of Italian came out about Sally, and I could tell it wasn't good. Sally was Mom's auntie, Nonna's younger daughter. My grandmother's sister. The Kickapoo-named lady.

By the time Nonna had gotten her oatmeal, stirred it,

maneuvered it over to the table, and sat down, I was done with mine. I sipped my orange juice slowly to compensate. It was weak, and I could see when I looked at the Tupperware pitcher on the counter that a chunk of the concentrate hadn't melted yet. *Get me out of this place.*

Nonna was out of breath by the time she sat down. She wasn't big, just round in the middle. Her face was narrow, and her hair was all straight and white and short now. She used to get it permed and dyed orange all the time before her hip. It made her look crusty. Now, with it clean and straight and pushed to the side, she looked totally different. If I squinted sideways, I might be able to catch a glimpse of her when she was young. But I'd have to squint pretty hard.

She spooned up some soupy oatmeal and blew on it. She had put her teeth in, which made her less scary.

"Elisabetta, I am sorry I didn't talk to you at the funeral."

"No, Nonna, it's okay." I didn't want to have a heavy conversation right then. I was just getting used to the place.

"I didn't think I had the words. The right words. And you're just a girl. You didn't need some old lady crying all over you." She made an awful face, sticking out her tongue. "Yitch."

It made me laugh. Nonna grunted two laughs and started slurping her oatmeal. I looked away as she some got on her chin.

ADRIANA

Hollywood, California, 1939

Adriana slept late that Saturday morning. She and Edith's crew had been up until three the night before working on a dozen silk Chinese suits for *The King of Chinatown*. It was an Anna Mae Wong picture, nothing destined for huge success, but Edith's work ethic demanded that each picture she designed be treated like an Oscar contender. They had scoured Chinatown for the right clothes, but Edith had her head set on a very specific fabric for Sidney Toler's suit and had decided that the others needed to match in cut and look. Adriana loved her job, but every once in a while, she wanted to point out that this movie wasn't *Gone with the Wind*. This would be a sore point with Edith. Even though she was quite happy at Paramount, she couldn't help coveting the lushest costume budget in town.

Adriana snuck home to find Rose already asleep. She slipped into bed next to her, exhausted. No matter the time she came home, Rose would usually wake up, rub her back, and talk over their day. But Rose, tired from an extra-long shoot the night before, put out a conciliatory hand and rubbed Adriana's back gently once with an unconscious, *phnpmth* before falling back asleep.

When Adriana woke the next morning, she smelled coffee and cigarettes and heard typing. She knew from the angle of the light on the wall that it was very late. Her hand reached for the clock on the bedside, and she brought it close. Eleven-thirty. Rose had probably been at work on her screenplay for several hours. She was determined to break into screenwriting, despite the fact that it was male-dominated field. She never let Adriana see her work, no matter how she pleaded. Rose said, "It's not ready for you yet."

It was already hot in the room. Adriana realized that, in mid-July, summer had finally come to Los Angeles. She had been working too hard to notice. She slipped out of bed, padded into the kitchen, and poured herself some coffee. It was lukewarm, but it seemed the right temperature for the day. She went to the icebox for some milk. Coffee cup in hand, she walked past the kitchen to the office where she saw Rose sitting precariously atop the back of her chair, feet under her, her knees crammed up against the desk. Rose's hair was tied up in a blue paisley silk kerchief, and she was wearing slacks and her slip shirt. There was a cigarette in her mouth and her fingers flew over the keys. Badabadabadabada*ting*, then the rip as she hit the typewriter return. Then a few more taps and a rip of the typewriter return.

Dialogue.

Adriana laughed. "Look at you!"

Without turning around, Rose took the cigarette from her mouth and halted with one hand in the air.

"Don't talk to me. I'm onto something!"

Adriana wanted to throw her arms around Rose and pull her out of the chair and just squeeze. She loved this woman. God had given her a woman to love, and she loved this woman.

Instead, she turned and went into the kitchen to examine the refrigerator. They had potatoes, eggs, and flour – that was enough to get started on some gnocchi. Adriana started a pot of water boiling and peeled the potatoes. She found the ricer, got out the eggs and the flour and the cutting board. This little kitchen had become so dear to her. Small, but sunny, it looked out onto their back yard. The tile was a cheery yellow, rimmed with black, and the cabinets were wood, plain white. The floor was yellow and maroon-checked linoleum and smooth and cool under her morning feet. There was a gas range, a small icebox, and a sink. They kept fruits and vegetables from the garden in a bowl on the counter. On the window ledge above the sink sat a collection of curiosities Rose pinched from movie sets after wrap. There was a blue and white Chinese dragon, salt and pepper shakers in the shape of cacti, and a little china dog. Adriana loved them for their randomness and a bit more for Rose's petty larceny.

The water at a boil, Adriana put the skinned, sliced potatoes in. She spooned a few cups of flour on the cutting board and made a well. When the potatoes were done, she drained them and put them aside. Into the well of the flour, she cracked an egg and scrambled it with a fork.

Then, very carefully with her hands, she began to bring the flour and the egg together. She paused periodically to push a potato through the ricer into the mixture. She loved these smells together, the egg, the potato, the flour. The feeling of the dough in her hands reminded her of being very small in her grandmother's kitchen in Sant'Agnello, before everything changed.

She remembered how her grandmother let her help with the gnocchi dough, telling her to knead it gently in circles. To keep the dough tender, it needed to be handled very lightly. She rolled the dough into a rope. She hadn't noticed that the typing had stopped.

Rose said, "What's for dinner?" It startled her.

"What're you doing, trying to kill me? Can't you see I'm cooking here?"

Rose threw her arms around Adriana's shoulders and kissed the back of her neck. "You always sound so Italian when you cook." She lowered something over her head and pulled her hair out of the way. It was a necklace.

She murmured, "I *am* Italian," as she reached an object hanging from the necklace and turned it in her hands. It was a small white cylinder made of something too white to be ivory. There was a deco pattern etched on the outside of it.

"What's this?"

Rose slid into the breakfast nook and looked at her coyly. "Open it."

Adriana puzzled on this for a moment, turning the tube. There was no hinge, no seams, except at the top. She unscrewed what could be a lid, cleverly fit into place and realized it was some sort of elaborate case for carrying lipstick.

"This is very fancy. Thank you, Rose." She could tell by Rose's expression she hadn't made enough of a fuss.

Rose said, "Look inside."

Adriana reached inside, which seemed to be lined with paper. She inserted her finger, twisted a bit and the paper slipped out. There was a simple line drawing of the shape of a heart on it, and it smelled a bit too strongly of Rose's perfume. She smiled, puzzled, and looked up at Rose.

Rose said, "Be careful, it's my heart."

Adriana flushed with love but couldn't think of anything appropriate to say. No one had taught her how to say the right thing in these situations. No one had given her a present since she was small. She kissed the paper, folded it carefully, and put it back into the tube, screwing it shut as she turned to kiss Rose.

She was home.

LAURA

Laura and Janelle grew up with their dad, the lanky, blue-eyed, handsome, but bewildered Bruce in a small town outside Anchorage, Alaska. He was a good man who fell hard for Sally one inexplicable summer on a salmon fishing boat. He later told Laura that he loved a woman who was secure enough to keep up with the men. Sally was a hard worker, both at fishing and at pleasing the people around her. Bruce confused Sally's need to be loved with actual love, and when he proposed to her after two months of wooing (one on sea, and one on land), Sally consented. She said that she had found herself a "sea dog."

Bruce and Sally married, not knowing that Laura was already on the way. They settled into a double-wide not too far down a winding road, and Bruce was delighted when his first daughter was born. Janelle came along two years later, around the end of Sally's rope. Laura's only early childhood memory of her mother was her writing madly in a notebook and waving Laura away while the baby Janelle cried. More solid memories came later, with infrequent visits and phone calls and the occasional postcard. Every visit and postcard contained a mix of promise, dread, and longing. Every time Sally left, the feelings of abandonment were fresh and new. By the time Janelle was two, Sally was gone. By the time Janelle was three, Judy had taken up residence.

Judy kept house and took care of them. Judy didn't ask questions. Bruce was a great, loving, one-note dad. He had plenty of hugs for the girls after work, and pithy advice that was just a little off what they needed. He was always there for them, but when Laura reached age twelve, she realized Bruce wasn't quite as deep as she hoped he would be. She loved him but went to her friends' parents for advice and to movies for clues about the world and how people behaved. Judy, she tolerated, and mostly avoided. Laura knew how to listen to her step-mother's speeches respectfully, to make them end more quickly, but Judy's lectures and ideas about "good girls," and "reputation," and "finding a good man" were wasted on Laura while Janelle subscribed to Judy's mothering hook, line, and dress code. It was around that time Laura turned to Rebecca for sisterhood. Their periodic letters turned into weekly correspondence, and her summers at Nonna's were *home* unlike this world posing as home in Anchorage.

The character Laura painted of her mother vacillated between the glamorous, world-traveling free spirit she yearned for with a deep, frightened longing – and the thoughtless, selfish mother who didn't have time for her and so clearly didn't love her. When the postcards came (Baton Rouge! Goa! San Francisco! Mexican Hat!) she hung them in her room, hoping that one day, her mother would swing back into town and whisk her away on her world travels, on her soul-seeking missions. Maybe Sally was just waiting for Laura to get old enough.

Somewhere around age fifteen, Laura realized her mother was never coming back. She was stuck doing time in Anchorage with an alien family from someone else's story. The empty black hole in her, dug by years of yearning, filled in with a depressing sludge. It sat next to her stomach, and she only felt it in extreme situations, like when Dexter belittled her or when he finally stepped out on her, or during quiet moments alone in Janelle's house with the humming refrigerator. It was when Becca died that the sludge seemed to metastasize. She was hoping that the move would dislodge it, let her breathe again.

As she grew up, Laura wrote her childhood as The Little Princess, the Misplaced Orphan, whatever worked. Now, tilting back her seat in her road-trip stinking car, rain battering the windshield into a blur, she imagined herself as the down-on-her-luck heroine, poised at the edge of some sort of montage leading to a fabulous life. Narratives fit so neatly into ninety minutes or between the covers of a book; there really couldn't be any alternative outcome.

The ringing phone startled Laura awake. It had stopped raining, but it was still foggy. It was daytime. She couldn't tell what time it was by the light in her car, but the pain in her back and her disorientation told her she had been asleep for a very long time. The clock in the car read nine-thirty. Impossible.

She stepped out into the chilly morning air, and her feet hurt on the cold, wet gravel as she scrambled to answer the payphone. Maybe it was 1970s movies that made a ringing payphone so ominous. She should have put her shoes on.

"Hello?" The phone was cold and slightly oily.

"Laura?" It was a man's voice.

"Yeah."

"I'm coming to get you." He sounded cross. For a moment she thought it was Dexter. He continued, "Where are you? I'm coming out of Nashville right now." Not Dexter. The voice was vaguely familiar in that she knew it wasn't anyone creepy. It was someone she knew, but she couldn't place it. It was a city voice. Hip, if a voice can be hip.

She asked, "Who is this?"

He said, "Where are you?"

She said, "Who *is* this?"

"*Bart.*" He sounded angry that she didn't know. "I'm driving west on the I-40 about a mile outside Nashville. Where do I look for you?"

Bart. Bart is Rebecca's ex-brother-in-law. Not ex. Brother-in-law until she died? Or still her brother-in-law, as she's the dead one. It didn't make any sense, Laura thought he lived in New York.

"Oh. Oh. Oh. I'm about an hour outside Memphis. I can't ..." she looked around her frantically. There was a sign she hadn't seen in the dark of the night before. "I'll be on your ... left side. It's a run-down gas station called 'GAS' near ..." she squinted into the woods where a street sign poked out from behind the trees. She laughed. "You're never going to believe this. I'm near Bucksnort Road."

He didn't laugh, which was disappointing. He said, "Uh. Um. Hold on. Okay. I gotcha. I'll be there. What kind of car?"

"A piece of shit 1986 Ford Escort. Beige."

He snorted before he hung up. She ran tiptoe back to the car and started to look for some socks.

She had met Bart only briefly on the receiving line at Rebecca's wedding. He was best man. He was flush with alcohol that day and seemed too slick. One look at his compact, slim body, his perfect hair and his sparkling brown eyes, and she knew he was a ladies' man. There was a slight electricity when she shook his hand and he smiled at her; like he knew who she was, the real Laura, the great things about her. She'd never had a stranger look at her that way before and planned to somehow get into a quick, clever romantic spar with him. But later that night, when she saw him nuzzling another bridesmaid on the dance floor, all desire left her. The fine line between ladies' man and smarmy womanizer had been crossed in her mind.

Laura knew that Rebecca got the catch of the two in George. He was the grounded, warm, dependable one. He was clever and funny, too, but there wasn't any mischief about him. When George and Rebecca said their vows, the entire congregation wept. They made those standard vows – so often repeated in movies and on television – sound like something new and real. They meant them – all of them.

Laura looked around in the car in a panic. It was a total mess, and she'd need Bart to help her move all this stuff. She hurriedly grabbed a plastic bag and started throwing the fast-food containers, cups, gum wrappers, and water bottles into it. He'd have to help her clear the trunk and the back seat. Where would she stash the garbage? She tried cramming it under the back seat, but once full, the bag was stretched almost to the size of the contents of a kitchen garbage can. She pulled it out of the car.

Cars and trucks whizzed by as morning commuters made their way on a two-sided freeway of what last night had seemed an abandoned road. She was a little embarrassed about not having gotten a tow. Things seemed much more frightening last night in the rain in the dark of the South. But if Bart lived in Nashville – what was he doing in *Nashville?* – it wasn't a huge hardship for him.

She panicked, realizing she probably looked a fright, and got back into the car. She flipped down the driver's side mirror … not as bad as she thought. Her brown hair was chronically curly, so it always looked a bit wild. Her freckles accentuated her pale skin in the early morning, but the rings of stress and exhaustion that had been under her eyes in Los Angeles had miraculously disappeared in the night. Or in the fog. A quick pit wipe with a wipee, some powder, and some lipstick and she wasn't gorgeous, but she wasn't embarrassing. She got out of the car again and faced the garbage bag that lay there, accusingly. She couldn't fling it. It would be just her luck to have a cop see her and pull over. She began kicking the bag underneath the car. She was going to abandon this car. She knew this now. She'd resuscitated it too many times. She'd call AAA and have them tow it to a junkyard. One of the larger water bottles lodged the whole bag and it wouldn't move. She pulled, but the bag started to rip. She tried kicking it, to wedge it under the car.

The bag burst, trash spewing out, quickly soaking up the rain collected in puddles on the side of the road. She squatted down and started picking up the individual pieces of garbage and shoved them further under the car. She heard some gravel move nearby and looked up to see a white Dodge Neon pull up. She stood quickly, a wadded wet napkin still in her hand.

She couldn't see into the car for the reflection on the windshield, but she knew it was Bart. The Neon was definitely a sub-par car for ... what did he do? Some kind of banker? She dropped the napkin and kicked it under, but it was hopeless, there was not much explanation to offer for garbage which looked ridiculous strewn all around her. She stepped forward as Bart got out, hoping to obstruct the mess with her body. She'd have him empty the trunk. How was all her stuff going to fit in that tiny fiberglass excuse for a car?

"Bart?" Of course, it was Bart. Idiot.

He didn't look as slick as he had at the wedding. What a tux will do for a man. Despite the rings under his eyes and his two days growth of beard, he was a good-looking guy, in a more human sort of way. He was on the shorter side, but still taller than Laura. His hair was somewhat awry, the top longer than its close-clipped sides. The growth of beard took away the slickness and, as Bart looked at her pile of garbage, in his leather jacket and decade-old T-shirt, and adorably worn pair of jeans, he rubbed his face in amazement. The fact that his skin moved like skin caught Laura unexpectedly.

She was being ridiculous. She had a sinking feeling as she put together what Bart was looking at and scrambled for five ways to explain it that were all terrible. She walked to the trunk, keeping her body between Bart and the embarrassment of garbage. She opened the trunk and did what she always did when she was nervous: she talked. "I hope your drive wasn't too hard. I have most of my stuff in the trunk and some stuff in the back seat. If you get the trunk, I'll get the back seat. Be careful, that's really fragile, at least the two big boxes. I'm not crazy for bringing dishes. These are special dishes from Italy. They're for Nonna. I have about five suitcases. I'm sorry, that last one's heavy. It's full of books and stuff. Watch it ..."

Bart winced as he lifted a too large, overpacked suitcase out of the trunk. He dumped it onto the ground with a grunt.

"I'm so sorry. It didn't seem like that much when I put it in, but then I added a few things after it was in the trunk, so that's what must have made it so heavy. Have you had breakfast? I'm starving. Maybe we can stop for breakfast in Nashville. Unless you have your place there. I mean we could. We don't have to. I guess I have to figure out what to do without a car. Maybe I can score a plane ticket. Or a train."

Shit. She really should be talking more like Barbara Stanwyck, clever banter, parry, thrust, turn, but she sounded like Katharine Hepburn in *Bringing Up Baby*, "David likes George, David loves George, David thinks he's such a nice dog."

She blamed Dexter for her inability to hold even simple conversations anymore. She stopped talking and got a box out of the back seat, and when she turned around, Bart was trying to smush the giant suitcase in the tiny trunk of the Neon. He wasn't so much listening to her anyway. And she was making an ass of herself. She needed to thank him, to talk to him, to get a real conversation going.

He came back to the trunk for another load, and she laid her hand on his arm. He looked at her. She said, "I'm so, so sorry about your brother. I'm sorry I didn't say that earlier. It's awkward. I was a total ... mess about Rebecca, of course, but a *brother*. I can't even imagine." She really meant it. She felt horrible, especially when she said it and realized, *brother*. But it came out sounding wrong, somehow.

Bart's eyes shifted suddenly downward, and he said, "Uh. Thanks." And grabbed a box, pulling it out of the trunk a little more violently and moving past her with almost a shove of his shoulder to get to the Neon.

Shit.

She got the cardboard box out of the back seat. Bart's head was in the trunk, and she said, "Rebecca and I were really close." This would be the time to shut up. If he was as close to George as his face had betrayed, he would *know* that she hadn't seen Rebecca in around ten years, and now, not only was she a flibbertygibbet, but she was a liar. But she couldn't stop. "I mean, our whole childhood. We fell out of touch when she got married. She got so ... busy. I only met Elizabeth once. How is she doing with all of this?"

At that moment, he slammed the trunk shut and walked around the side of the car. He said, "Is that everything?"

"Almost." She went back to the car and took her registration and her sunglasses out of the glove compartment, her purse and her blanket out of the passenger seat. She grabbed a tube of lipstick, one credit card, one packet of tissues out of the change well and threw the small things into the plastic lunch box. Finally, she took the keys out of the ignition. She held them for a moment. If she was going to leave the car here, she'd have to leave the keys. Maybe someone would steal it. She was light-headed with hunger.

The Neon still had new-car smell. It was only when Laura got buckled in and had settled her things that she noticed the rental car badge dangling from the keys. She said, "You rented a car to come get me? You didn't have to. Is public transportation that good in Nashville? You don't have to own a car?"

He looked at her incredulously and shook his head, starting the engine. They pulled off into traffic.

She asked, "When did you move from New York?"

He said, "Last night."

"What?"

Bart said, "Are you kidding me?" He was angry now, fuming and Laura was at fault, but a rush of frustration tight-ened her chest. She was the one who spent the night in her car, why was he all pissy?

She said, "What?"

"Mrs. Morello called me in New York last night, made me fly to Nashville and rent a car, and come get you."

Mrs. Morello. Nonna. It didn't make any sense. Why would Nonna do that? Why would he obey her and not tell her to fuck off? Why didn't she just trust the tow company? The shame of the last conversation, her guilt over not being there for Rebecca's funeral, her further shame about her predicament, her lack of a job, money, means, and the car she was aban-doning on the road all converged in pressure and noise and made her want to claw her way out of this tin covered roller skate. But there she was with an annoyed, petulant teenager of a grown man. Bart was once again extremely unattractive. She was angry with herself for even thinking he was cute for a minute there.

New York, though. Laura said, "I'm sorry." Why would he

tell Nonna yes? It was a ridiculous favor. Something's weird about that. "She's not even your grandmother."

"THANK you!" He sighed, exasperated. She got why he should be angry, but his edge made her feel defensive of Nonna.

She *did* apologize, and he was all overreaction and antagonistic energy. He was the opposite of Dexter, who was passive aggression and silence. That she knew how to deal with. This pissed her off. She snapped, "So why'd you come?" It came out brattier than she'd anticipated.

He huffed. Like a teenager. He started to say something, but his head just waggled around with his mouth open as he looked for words. Apoplectic was the only way Laura could think of describing it. He closed his mouth and slammed his hands on the steering wheel. He turned on the radio, which was playing a country song. He punched the "seek" button about six times, and it kept hitting country songs. He huffed again and turned it off.

She sat back in her seat, looked out the window, and tried not to cry. Her fatal flaw in any situation was that she cried when she was pissed off. Add exhaustion, and it was an inevitability. The tears started rolling. She wiped them away and refused to sniffle, but her nose was filling up.

Bart looked over at her. She turned her back to him so he couldn't see her face, but she knew she looked like a sulking child, facing the window entirely.

In a voice that could have been interpreted as apologetic, but it would have been a stretch, he said, "It's been a really, really long night."

Laura pulled the Aladdin lunchbox from the back seat and cracked it open, digging for those tissues. She said, "I'm sorry. I wouldn't ask you to come here from New York. No sane person would do that. Nonna was probably just confused about where you lived."

He said, "Oh, no, she knew where I was."

"No, I meant, like, that New York was far from Nashville."

He laughed drily.

Laura continued. "She wouldn't ever ask anyone to go out of their way..."

He said, "How long has it been since you've seen Mrs. Morello?"

"You can just call her Nonna."

He winced. "No, I can't. That would give her an edge."

Laura laughed. "I don't know. It's been a while. I mean, long before she broke her hip."

"Ah." He was quiet. Like he was judging her, her not being there for Nonna, her needing her now, her not going to Rebecca and George's funeral.

She started spewing excuses, "I've been very busy and tickets to Baltimore aren't cheap. I meant to go one Easter or another, but things kept happening. I moved. I lost my job. I ..." *moved in with my sister's linoleum sleeping porch and sulked for two months. Whatever.*

Bart said, "Relax. I don't think *anyone* should have to go to Baltimore who doesn't really want to go there. Mrs. Morello. Your Nonna. She's changed. A lot. And she may play the innocent granny, but she's always got something up her sleeve."

"You didn't have to come."

He said, "No, I didn't. But. I didn't. I. George's kid."

"Elizabeth?"

"Lizzie. I didn't take Lizzie."

She said, "Why would you take Lizzie?" She tried to say it like she always knew she was called that.

"THANK you." He meant it.

Laura tried to put it together, "So you came all the way to bumblefuck, Tennessee to give me a ride to Nashville ..."

"Baltimore."

Laura said, *"Baltimore?"*

"I'm driving you to Baltimore. Only thirteen hours, and I fly out from there.

"Wow."

"Thank you."

"You flew to Nashville to drive me to Baltimore and fly back to New York to assuage guilt you felt over not taking in an orphan girl of nine?"

He said, "Thirteen."

"Shit. Thirteen already?" When she saw Becca ten years ago she was taking a day in the city away from the baby. She must have been three then.

"Thirteen. A teenager. What was I going to do with a teenager?"

"Wow."

The mood quieted a bit. Bart said, "It wasn't about guilt." The defensive teenager was back.

Laura laughed. She said, "You're not a Catholic, are you?"

Bart snorted. "Do I look Catholic?"

She didn't know what that meant. She said, "It was about guilt." She smiled and teased, "Nonna got you."

"No, she didn't."

"When I first called her from the road, before she even picked up the phone to reach you, she said you were on the way. She got you."

He squinted at her, then at the road, then back at her. He smiled a little. "Well, shit."

He wasn't attractive anymore. But he was less *un*attractive.

For the first time in the ride, she settled back in the car seat and made herself comfortable. It was good not to be at the wheel ... for a little while at least.

CHAPTER SIX

LIZZIE

After I helped Nonna get the dishes in the dishwasher, I went upstairs to see if I could coax Calzone out with a can of tuna Nonna gave me. He wasn't having it. I could see his nose working to smell the tuna, but he backed up further under the bureau. The hair on his head was squashed backward. I called his name, and he started growling at me, so I stopped. I left the tuna next to the bureau.

I spent a good while arranging my room to look nicer. My manga tower didn't balance so well in this room – maybe the floor was crooked – or maybe it was just another example of nothing working right again. I put them on the bookshelf instead. There were a few books left from when my mom was little, but they were all duds. By the time I emptied my book box, the shelf was full. I tucked the extras in the little space between the bookshelf and the wall. I hung my old secret message case, the ivory thing, from the corner of the bookcase. Books, my quilt from home, and that talisman established my corner of her room. I'd need to find something for the walls.

I sat down at Mom's tiny wooden desk and flipped open my

sketchbook. I was going to free draw. That should break whatever dry spell I was having. I wouldn't think about it. I moved my black ballpoint back and forth in the corner with my wrist loose and let it take me where it took me.

It made a shadow, first. A squiggly wider at one end, growing smaller until it peaked out. But it looked more like a reflection. I drew a curved rectangle around it. It was definitely a windshield. I knew what this was – this was the rear windshield of the taxi before the crash.

I drew Mom and Dad inside. I outlined the backs of their heads in silhouette; Mom's hair with the flipped sharp edges at the bottom that whipped out, side to side. Dad's haircut as stiff as a brush. I probably needed to put her head on his shoulder, but I'd do that in the next frame. It would make it more intimate.

I filled in the back end of the taxi and put in some skyline and something seized hold of me in the shading and coloring. I got that fudgy overwhelming pulled feeling you have when you're drawing well, only, instead of comforting, it was a dark black opening up. My hand started shaking. I put the pen down and chucked the entire sketchpad under the bed. I should have closed it. I knew I couldn't rip it up. It would be like ripping them up.

I got out of there and went downstairs. The noisy clock on the mantle ticked. I looked at the time, feeling like I'd burned at least a few hours, given everything, but it was only nine-thirty. I'd killed exactly half an hour.

Nonna had settled into her chair and was reading a book. I hadn't picked up a book since – since that day. I tried when I was with Uncle Bart, but every time I tried to get back into *The Dark is Rising*, the book I was reading when it happened, the sentences sort of lay there, dead. Even *Akira*, the coolest manga of the past decade, held no appeal.

I stood up and walked around the living room to snoop. I ignored the cobwebs on the ceilings and the dust beasties in the corners and looked at the art on the walls. There was a plaster Madonna on the white-mantled brick fireplace alongside some saint dude. On the wall hung a framed color line drawing of Jesus, the one where his heart is sticking out of his chest and glowing. I hadn't thought of Jesus as a manga hero before, but he clearly had superpowers.

I kept going on the perimeter of the living room. The room was painted olive green, which I think might have been hip sometime a long time ago, but now it looked dark and depressing. On top of a built-in bookshelf, there was a framed black-and-white picture of two beautiful movie-type ladies with what must have been a movie star. The movie star looked familiar; she had brown hair to her shoulders and a broad smile. She was wearing long, slim pants, rebellious, the way women wore them when they weren't allowed to. She looked pretty but more like a real person than a glamour puss. The two women next to her were prettier, but they didn't have as much makeup on, so they didn't look as impressive. They also were wearing pants. I squinted close to see better. There was a dark-haired woman and a lighter haired woman, maybe red hair? Hard to tell in black and white.

I said, "Nonna, who's this?"

"Who?"

"In the picture, the three ladies."

She said, "You don't recognize Barbara Stanwyck?"

"Who?"

A stream of Italian came out of her, disappointed and shocked. Then she said, with no accent whatsoever, "That's me on the left, with the dark hair."

I looked closer and squinted. She looked a little like Mom, a little like someone from another time, but the gorgeous woman with the sparkling brown eyes couldn't possibly be Nonna. I said, "Wow."

She laughed a little. I kept snooping. Maybe if I looked more at where she came from, I'd find clues to where Nonna went.

After I had looked at absolutely everything that was in the living room from baby pictures of my mom and my aunt to a few more glamorous pictures of the ladies who weren't Barbara whatzerface and one tiny watercolor of a cityscape that hung in the corner, I ran out of things to look at. I figured at least an hour must have passed.

It was only Nine-fifty. Twenty more minutes had passed.

I didn't know how long I was supposed to be polite. "Nonna?"

"Yeah, honey."

"What happens now?"

She didn't look up from her book. "You can go outside and play."

I was thirteen. I didn't really *play* anymore. "No, I mean, I didn't mean *now*. I meant like, what about school?" *What is my life going to be like? Will you make dinner every night? How do your groceries get here?* I didn't even know if Nonna had any friends anymore or if the neighborhood was safe. Would I ever have any friends my own age? I wondered how different Baltimore was from New York or if there were any mixed people like me. I'd seen white people and Black people, but were there any in between? Did kids here love one sports team I'd never, never heard of? What do they do at recess? I didn't bring my bike. It wouldn't fit. How could I bike around? Was there a corner store? Could I get some gum? Was there a comic book-store? *Are you going to give me an allowance or do I have to like, get a job? Oh God what happens when I need a new toothbrush or underwear? Or tampons for God's sake?* I started thinking about dentist appointments and doctors and everything Mom took care of. And those things cost money. Did Nonna have money? Did she have income or did she keep it under the floorboard in coffee cans?

And you, Nonna? What about you? Are you coming back or is this just the way you are now? Is this it, family-wise? Long days in front of the television?

Then the tears came. I couldn't help it. I sobbed seriously embarrassingly loudly and started with the *wah-wah.* Not cool.

Nonna put down her book and looked at me long and hard. Her mouth was set, and her brows were knit. I felt bad for her all of a sudden. Here she was, cozy in her days – or non-days – and her oatmeal and her books and movies, and I came in with all these demands.

I tried to stop crying, I stopped sobbing at least, but the tears kept dripping, like an embarrassing runny nose. I wiped my eyes with my sleeves and tried to meet her look. But the worst thing about crying these days is it made me feel like a total idiot.

She said, "All right. It's gonna be all right, Elizabetta. We've got you enrolled at St. Casimir. But you don't have to worry about that until at least August."

Catholic School?

The truth is, I seriously could have used a hug, but it's like Nonna was watching me, like an experiment she couldn't tamper with, and I was supposed to show that I could do things on my own, but I had no idea what to do.

"Okay. Okay." She was making a decision about something. "Go into my purse on the table. Take out five dollars. Go outside, turn left at the sidewalk. Four blocks down across the street is a video store, called Video Planet. It's a lot smaller than its name. I want you to go inside and rent *Robin Hood.* Not the one with that bozo from the eighties, not the one that just came out, but *Robin Hood*, with Errol Flynn, Claude Rains, Olivia de Havilland. 1938."

I wiped my eyes, snurfled, and went into her purse, which was tidier than I expected, pulled five dollars out of her wallet, and headed for the door. It was something to do.

I had to get out of the house where time had slowed to cobwebs forming. A little walk around the neighborhood might prove to her whatever she was looking for in me. "I ..." My voice came out all phlegmy. What I hate most about crying is the stuff that hangs around after you're done. Evidence. "I'll see ya later." I opened the front door.

Nonna nodded and didn't say anything.

She was my only grownup. I'd have to figure out a way to make her better at it. At least like she used to be.

LAURA

Laura tried to strike up conversations with Bart here and there, but they all fell sort of flat. Bart didn't watch movies. Laura's three years of Hollywood training and the art of industry conversation were a dead loss with movies off the table.

She said, "Not even on television? I mean the old-timey movies?"

Bart said, "What, like black and *white?*" The disdain with which he said this coiled in Laura's gut, burning.

She said, "Some of the greatest movies of all time are in black and white."

He scoffed.

She said, "You don't have to be so judg*mental.* Have you even seen *The Philadelphia Story? Citizen Kane? Holiday Inn?*" She realized how ridiculous her choices sounded together. They weren't the ones you would name at a Hollywood party to make you sound well-educated in cinema. She got addled when she was angry.

Bart said, "Now who's being judgmental? Just because I

don't watch a certain form of media, I'm worthless or something?"

"No, I never said that. I ..." She trailed off.

Bart said, "I don't have time for movies. There's too much real stuff going on in the world. Music. Art."

She said, darkly, "Movies are only the reason for my whole existence or whatever." She knew how stupid she sounded.

He said, "Music is like a *living thing*. When you go to a concert, or even just a little club, the energy of the place, the dynamics of the arrangement just pop out of you, seize hold of you."

Bart got all excited listing several bands, but when she hadn't heard of the fourth band he listed, he gave up. He *was* totally addicted to reality television, which she couldn't stand. She did like that he approached it with a sense of humor, but she had no viewing experience with which to share in his glee, and it turned out that reality television was a *you-had-to-be-there* experience and dulled considerably in the retelling.

She searched for something to talk about. There was a sign on the side of the road that read PEECHES, *29 cent*. Laura laughed and said, "Wow. Spelling's not a huge priority in this part of the country, is it?"

Bart said, "What?"

"There's a sign, it reads *peaches* only it's spelled with lots of Es. And it says 29 cent."

He said, "So?"

She should have known to shut up, but she drew it out, "Peeeeeches, 29 cent." She put on a Southern drawl and said, "That's gonna be twenty-nine cent, lady."

Bart turned his head to her and snapped, "Really?"

"What? It was funny," Laura couldn't gauge whatever misstep she'd made, but she knew something got to him.

He said, "Wow, what a snob. Do you think that farmer has

time for spelling? Do you have any idea what it *takes* to run a farm?"

Oh, crap. She remembered that George and Bart had grown up on a strawberry farm somewhere in California.

He said, "The bugs, the frost, the planting season, the whimsy of the market. Your peaches, however they're spelled, took a lot of time and energy to grow, but depending on how crops did overall that year, selling them will either pay the mortgage for the next year or they won't clear enough for another year's farming. After fighting off blight or drought or being outside with smudge pots in the middle of the night during a frost, you may end up having to take on an extra job in the winter and have your teenage kids take over the farm work just so you can stay afloat. And maybe your sons missed school that year, or missed the class where spelling was taught."

Laura said, "You and George finished school just fine though, didn't you?"

He turned and glared at her.

That shut her down for about two hours.

She tried to sleep, but couldn't, so she pretended.

They drove on I-40 forever and flat roads gave way to gloomy pine-covered mountains. They pulled over to a small gas station for a bathroom break on Route 81 in West Virginia.

When Laura got out of the car, she felt she had stepped onto a different planet from that morning. The air was thick with pine, rotting leaves, and wet dirt. The sound had changed from open and tinny with the passing of cars on a wide highway to close and foreboding. The mountains rose up on both sides of them, blocking out any sunlight. Laura had to squint up through the topmost trees to see it was still sunny.

The gas station was something out of a fifties movie. Every-thing about it was rusty and old, only the pumps were modern. She crunched over the gravel and followed Bart into the small

old clapboard house that served as the pay station. It looked
more like a veterinarian's waiting room than a convenience
store. There was a high wooden counter at one end with an old
manual cash register. In front were racks with some snacks and
a refrigerated cooler whirred in the corner, water pooling
beneath it. Mismatched chairs were placed around, and two old
white men were sitting at a table playing cards and drinking
soda. They looked up at Bart, and once they recognized that he
was *different,* their eyes locked on him as if he was an alien in
their midst. Maybe they'd never seen an Asian guy before.

Bart went over to the cooler, got a soda out, and picked up
some chips, putting them on the counter. He must not have
noticed the tension in the room, because he smiled at the slack-
jawed middle-aged lady behind the counter drowning in her
oversized STP (the oil, not the band) T-shirt.

Bart said, "Good morning. Twenty dollar's worth of
unleaded please and," he turned to look at Laura, "You want
anything?"

She shook her head no. It was best to get out of here.
Quickly.

The woman closed her mouth and rang up the items with a
noisy clicking of keys and shuttling out of paper. "That'll be
$24.95."

Bart took twenty-five dollars out of his wallet and laid it on
the counter. Laura realized her window to pee was closing fast,
but she didn't want to leave Bart alone with these people.
They'd probably tie him to a tree and carve him up or
something.

Bart said, "Restroom?"

The woman looked at Laura as if she'd only just noticed
she was there. She looked at Bart and back at Laura. Her eyes
squinted up. "Round back. Don't need a key."

Bart said, perhaps too cheerfully, "Thank you, ma'am."

And walked past Laura out the door. The screen door closed behind him with a squeak and a slam.

One of the men at the table wolf-whistled and said, "Mmm-mmhmmm ... what a waste. Yep, a waste."

Laura burned under the collar and wanted to light into the guy, but she'd been playing out four horror movies in her head since they arrived at this place, and she was not willing to see any of them enacted. When she got outside, Bart was already in the car. She made an apologetic motion to the bathroom and went in quickly.

When she got back in the car, she hummed the banjo song from *Deliverance*, but Bart didn't get it. He did say, "Let's get out of here. That place gave me the creeps."

Laura wanted to bring up a conversation about racism, but she couldn't figure out how to word things without sounding like a dumb white chick. And she didn't want him to know that the guys inside thought she was wasting herself on him. It wasn't going to make his day better, so she kept silent.

Bart shifted in his seat and smelled funky after his travels, but Laura noticed that he smelled good. *That's trouble.* When a guy smelled bad, it was one thing. But when she *knew* he smelled bad, and he still smelled good, deep attraction was definitely at play.

Despite growing up in the woods of Alaska, these woods gave Laura unsettled Little Red Riding Hood feelings. These were woods on steroids, blotting out any sunshine or hope or goodness. Talking was the only way through.

She said, "Bart, what is it you do for a living, anyway?"

"I'm a financial consultant."

There were professions that gave way to further questions, but this was not one of them. If he'd said eye doctor, she'd have something to go with.

She tried, "What company?"

"Chase."

"Oh. I have a credit card from them."

Bart said, "That's actually why I'm here. Your credit card charges have gotten out of hand. Sixty pounds of Italian pottery? And the other stuff, don't get me started ..."

Laura said, "I can't help it, I have a thing for antique paper towel cozies. I'll bid on anything."

"Oh, the antique paper towel cozies aren't the problem, Miss. It's the floral chair covers that are driving you into the poorhouse."

They laughed. A shared joke. They fell quiet, but the tension had left the car. They were comfortable enough to settle into their separate thoughts.

The roads widened, and the mountains turned to rolling hills, and the landscape opened up. Laura really had no idea what she was going to do at Nonna's, but Baltimore would be a change of scene. Jobs would be different, and she could rethink. She was a failure in LA. But in Baltimore, she had yet to be defined. What does one do in Baltimore aside from eat crabs and visit old people? All she really wanted was a comfortable bed and no small children to babysit.

CHAPTER SEVEN

LIZZIE

When I closed Nonna's front door, I stood on the front porch for a moment and looked up and down the street. It was like that effect when you stand between two mirrors that are facing each other. You look one way and see twenty yous and look the other way and see twenty yous.

Only here, it was identical brick front porches with white trim like Nonna's. Tons of them. Both ways. I tried to figure out how you could draw that without it looking like a long hallway. I suppose two panels. One resembling a deck of cards fanned out one way. Smaller and smaller heads. Then another panel with its mirror reflection.

It was warm. The cool of the morning was gone, and I could tell it was going to be hot and muggy. The melt-your-popsicle-off-the-stick-in-chunks hot. I made sure to jump the last two steps of the porch because that really put you in a place. The smack through my sneakers felt good. I had landed.

I had five years before I could leave for college, and so far, not counting sleeping, I'd only gotten through two hours. If I figured out Nonna, it would go faster.

There was some grass growing between the cracks in the sidewalk, but this street didn't have any trees. They got the houses right but completely forgot to put in trees. There was no other wildlife. No ants, no nothing. I had to find a way to get Nonna out of the house. Out of the neighborhood. Maybe we could get to nature somewhere. Baltimore had to have parks, right? Didn't every city? Every time we came here, it was straight to Nonna's or walks to the markets, so I didn't know.

Step on a crack you'll break your mother's back. I tried avoiding cracks, but then I realized it didn't make any difference now, so I stomped on every crack I saw. It was awful and good. *Stomp.* Step. *Stomp.* Step. In about ten stomps, I'd stomped my way sick. I looked one way and then the other. More brick row houses. Nobody out. Just garbage. I crossed the street. There were a few stores. There was a corner store with bars on it that made it look like an evil lair or a bad part of town. There was a clapboard house and a little greengrocer, then a gas station. Across the street from the gas station was Video Planet.

Video Planet was cool, almost chilly. Empty, except for the girl behind the counter. She wore her black hair and giant hoop earrings like a high schooler, but she was definitely in her twenties. She looked totally bored, but I thought I'd be bored if I worked in a video store.

There were too many movies to look through. I walked up and down the aisles just to pass some time, sappy movies, action movies, comedies that I couldn't tell what they were about, and they were usually rated R. Alien movies, dark, strange grown-up movies, horror movies. I couldn't find anything like old movies.

I had to ask. I told myself it couldn't be any worse than that first day of school in the fall and I had to talk to somebody sometime.

I walked up to Ms. Totally Bored who was coloring her fingernails black with a Sharpie. I had to clear my throat so she'd look up.

She said, "Yeah?"

Corporate at Video Planet was obviously all about courtesy.

"Um. I need to get. For my grandmother. She wants *Robin Hood*, but not the new one? Not even the kind of old one? But the way back one with ... Earl. Flynn?"

"How way back?"

"I don't know. Like, great-grandmother way back."

She laughed; she wasn't a total waste. She came out from behind the counter and went to a wall in the corner. "You want classics. Classic is the other word for 'great-grandmother way back.'"

"Thanks. I can find it."

Maybe I was giving her something to do. I followed her as she walked alongside the shelves, turned her head sideways, and ran her fingers along some of the tapes like they were piano keys.

"Got it." She pulled out a box and handed it to me. The art on the cover looked *really* old. I mean, classic. It had this poncey guy in a hat laughing and this woman smiling in an all-white nun hat. Well, it was a movie. I wondered if Nonna wouldn't mind me bringing home something a little more modern. A comedy or something. But I could see Nonna trying to make sense of *Mrs. Doubtfire* and thought better of it.

I said, "How much is a rental?"

"$4.50"

With only five bucks, I knew I was stuck with *Robin Hood*. I should have brought my wallet. My last allowance was in it.

Was I going to get an allowance anymore? I'd work on that after getting Nonna out of the house.

When I stepped out of the rental store, it was obvious that the day had decided to be *hot*. I thought about checking out the school I was going to; it was supposed to be a few blocks away. I thought, right now, things aren't so bad. If the school was great, it could wait another day, but if it sucked, then why not just spend one more day of it could be great. Mom used to say something like that.

"You never know what's coming until you have to deal with it so what's the point in ..."

No. That's wrong. *What was it?* I was forgetting already. I had to write these things down before I lost them.

I started home. I was going to watch an old, crappy movie with my Nonna. Given the fact that half a block of walking had me dripping sweat, it didn't seem like a terrible prospect. I flipped the disk over and looked on the back, 102 minutes of viewing. 102 minutes of not having to think about anything too big. That was something.

ADRIANA

Unlike her male compatriots, Edith Head consulted with her actresses. She knew they were people and had needs. Adriana admired how Edith handled them; she wouldn't stand for their temper tantrums but never scolded. She'd laugh good-naturedly and accept whatever changes they needed. She knew that these women, objectified, who had fought for their roles, wanted their flattery delivered straight, no-nonsense. They trusted Edith implicitly, and Adriana helped her with the women's problem areas, filling out hips here with some folds or drapes, hiding expanding waistlines, boosting non-existent bust lines. Adriana watched and listened and never put a suggestion straight to the actress. She waited until Edith was in her office or working on a piece to give her suggestions, subtly, quietly, because Edith was the vision. Adriana saw herself as her seamstress. She never doubted she was working for the best.

The next movie Adriana worked on was to be called *The Lady Eve*, which starred Henry Fonda and Barbara Stanwyck. The ladies in the costume department cooed when they heard the second name.

Adriana asked her co-worker, Dorothy, what that meant, all the girls cooing. Dorothy was a petite powerhouse of a woman whose voice was deepened by chain-smoking and long hours. She wore circular wire frames and always had her hair up in silk kerchiefs, which changed colors with her wardrobe. Today, it was bottle blue.

They were working together on a particularly complicated French bodice with boning when Adriana asked, "Why all the fuss over Stanwyck? We worked with Katharine Hepburn last week, and no one said 'boo.'"

Dorothy smiled, causing the pins in her mouth to fan. She was pinning together two bodice pieces that weren't aligning smoothly. It was tricky with satin, any flaw caught the klieg lights and looked terrible. Edith was adamant that each dress for this French Revolution movie be given the care of Marie Antoinette's couturier.

Dorothy said, "Look, an actress is an actress is an actress, and a star is usually always a star. We do our job, they do theirs; we're not allowed to stare too long or get too intimate. But Missy's different. She's a *working* actress. She may do well at the box office, but she never became a star. When she's on the set, she learns everyone's name, keeps after them, sends gifts on their birthdays. She's ..." Dorothy paused to pull the five pins out of her mouth and whipped them into the seam. "She's real people, you know?"

Adriana didn't know. Aside from Rose, she hadn't been very impressed by the actors. It was glamorous and exciting the first time she saw Katharine Hepburn, but when she noticed that she only talked to her costars and the director, she started to understand how things worked. The lighting techs, set dressers, costumiers, even makeup folk who touched up the faces of the actors while they were working, were meant to be invisible. She didn't like the idea that a star deigning to speak to the crew was, by sheer virtue of not being a snob, elevated to a personage that could make a hard-working costume shop coo.

Adriana loved the sound stages. For two years she'd worked only in the costume shop, fallen in with her fellow sewers, patchers, patternmakers, dressmakers. It was a happy vault there. But now that Edith had taken a shine to her, she was brought along to set for adjustments, or sometimes just to look at her handiwork under the lights for signs of flaws.

The first day of *The Lady Eve* was shot on the backlot version of the deck of an ocean liner with two curving stair-cases, around which curled a solid wooden banister. Stanwyck came down those stairs wearing a simple white dress shirt and plaid skirt. She was petite and pretty enough, but she didn't have the star-like zing that Adriana had seen when the lights hit other actresses. She was no Susan Hayward or Claudette Colbert. There was no whiff of entitlement around her. When the director called cut, she resembled a kid. She plopped down on the stairs and talked to her costar or wandered the set, visiting people behind the scenes. Her demeanor was easygoing.

At one cut, she walked right up to where Adriana and Edith were standing. She threw her arms around Edith and hugged her. "Edie! I didn't see you standing there. How's things?" Edith murmured that they were fine, fine. Stanwyck continued, "How's Harold? Is his back still troubling him? Did that trick with the aspirin work?

Edith flushed. She never talked to her crew about her private life, and Adriana was clearly overstepping some boundary by hearing this conversation. Edith put her arm in Stanwyck's, and they strolled off together. Adriana knew better than to follow. She watched them, heads bent together, talking intently. This actress was obviously nice and involved, but Adriana didn't see what the cooing was about. She probably just wanted Edith to feel a part of things to make her feel good enough to make Stanwyck look good. Big deal.

Edith and Stanwyck circled back around to Adriana. Edith talked steadily, and Stanwyck looked Adriana up and down, like she was surveying a horse. When she got to her, she held out her hand, "Adriana, Edith has told me you're quite a craftsman. Pleasure to meet you. I'm Missy." Adriana took her cool hand and was surprised by the firm shake.

She said, "Nice to meet you, ma'am."

Stanwyck held her hand too long and looked in her eyes. She stopped a moment, and a vague smile played on her face. She finally broke, saying, "Well, I'd better get back to my place or Pres'll have a fit. Ladies, you do good work. Keep it up." Calling the formidable Preston Sturges "Pres." Goodness.

Without thinking, Adriana asked Edith, "What's her story?"

Edith looked at her for a long moment, and Adriana thought she'd overstepped. But Edith smiled, looking over to Stanwyck, and said, "She, honey, works for a living."

LIZZIE

I put the movie in and got Nonna set up with some water and her TV tray. I put a sketch pad – not the one under my bed – on the sofa just in case the movie was *really* boring. The phone rang, and Nonna's head turned sharply sideways.

I said, "Do you want me to get it?" *Ring.*

Nonna said, "No, it's a telemarketer." *Ring.*

It could be Uncle Bart or someone. Or maybe my best friend Emily. Not that she'd have my number. When my parents died, apparently I disappeared. Now add Baltimore, and I was gone altogether. But maybe it was *someone*. A friend. Someone Nonna should see. I said, "Are you sure?" *Ring.*

She looked straight at me and said, her voice scary serious, "Don't answer the phone." She must have seen the look on my face because she said, "The machine will get it."

If I couldn't get her to answer the telephone, how was I going to get her out of the house?

We watched the movie. The sound was different and tinny, and when the credits came up there was a lot of fanfare, which was pretty funny because they were just a bunch of words on old-fashioned parchment with pictures of Robin Hood painted on here and there. The art wasn't very good, and the credits didn't even MOVE. Then there were like five pages of history to read before we got started. The Prince John dude was short and wimpy. He didn't have enough oomph to be a villain.

Then the Flynn guy came onscreen, shoulders back, hands on hips, laughing like he could give a care. He had a spring in his step like a Christmas elf and I couldn't help it, but I snorted a laugh. It was louder than it was supposed to be.

Nonna looked over at me and put her bony finger to her lips, shushing me. Her face looked more *there*. It took a minute for me to realize that she'd put on makeup. She looked kind of good. Not quite the girl in the picture, but more like Nonna from last year ... before she broke her hip. Maybe I *could* work on her.

I leaned back into Nonna's sofa, pulled my feet up, and kinda relaxed into the movie. This was 102 minutes where I wouldn't have to think about how much everything sucked. I missed Mom. She'd know what made me laugh without my having to explain.

Everybody on the screen delivered their lines with a lot of vigor and a lot of music, but the story got better. More interesting. King John wasn't really the king, but a petty kind of weenie who ruled the kingdom with the help of this guy named Guy that Nonna kept calling "Basil."

Now *he* looked like a villain.

There was this one scene where Robin Hood came into a big banquet hall with a deer over his shoulders. Nonna paused the movie there. It was stopped on a row of ladies eating at a table, not much to look at. The lady in pink looked over her shoulders because Robin Hood had entered the room. It got quiet for a minute. Nonna had just *stopped*.

I said, "Nonna?"

She said, "Hon, could you get some more water?" Her voice sounded funny.

When I came back with the water she was leaning in toward the screen. It was that same shot of people eating, the ladies' heads turned. I thought I saw a tear trickling down Nonna's cheek. She took the water and smiled. I sat down, and she started the movie again.

NONNA

Rose.

LIZZIE

They talked too much in this movie, but it was all right and funny in parts, and by the end, I really wanted Robin and Marian to be together. The costumes were beautiful, and the color was totally saturated. The greens were so green, and the reds were so red, I didn't think my paint box could recreate them.

The closing credits came, and I didn't want it to end. And I wondered why my parents had held out on me all those years. There were probably other totally color saturated old movies out there that were great to watch, and we were stuck on the Discovery Channel.

Nonna pulled herself out of her chair and went over to the television to turn it off. I turned it off with the remote before she got there. She stopped for a minute, and I felt bad, like I had taken away something she needed to do. But she turned to me and smiled, saying, "Too quick for me, Lizzie."

The temperature was still almost comfortable inside, but the air was getting close, as the heat seeped in from outside the house. Nonna said, "Lizzie, figure out how that cooler thing on the window works, and I'll make us some lemonade. It's going to be a hot summer. I can tell that now."

I wanted to ask her why she was crying during the paused banquet, but I knew she might have been thinking about Mom, and I didn't want to have that conversation yet. What about *Robin Hood* made her think about Mom, I didn't know. She might have shown Mom her old movies, too. Maybe she was remembering when Mom was a girl, and they spent time together. Maybe Mom watched movies and had lemonade with her. Maybe nothing was wrong with Nonna. Maybe she was just sad like I was.

Maybe I could tell her a story to take her mind off things. But I didn't feel like I had any stories left in me.

LAURA

It was around 9 p.m. when they started seeing signs for Baltimore. Laura was disappointed. Now that she was there, what was she going to do? She tried to be Zen about it, or at least Tao, take what came, deal with it, but her sense of failure re-emerged to engulf her. She had no career and no prospects.

She glanced over at Bart, who looked completely exhausted. The drive was getting to him. She felt hugely guilty about his having come all this way. It was a bonehead move, but Nonna was good with the guilt. Not only was Laura going to live with an old lady, she was going to live with a teenager. She hated babysitting Janelle's kids and hadn't really put it together until now, that she'd gone from one babysitting post to another.

This was turning into some bizarre afternoon special. Aging grandmother, unemployed screw-up, orphaned second cousin, and Baltimore. One of them was going to have to develop a drinking problem for the plot to advance.

She tried to break the quiet in the car and stifle the noise in her head. She said, "So, um, when you flying back to New York?"

Bart said, "Tonight."

"Wow, drag. You can't stay over?"

He looked at her like she was crazy, and was about to say something to that effect, but his monotone answer showed he thought better of it. "Nope. Need to get home." She wondered if he had stopped a comment to spare her feelings. Something about Nonna's place. Or Baltimore. He said, "Have to go to work tomorrow, after all."

She said, "You must be exhausted."

"You could say that." As if looking for something to do to take the pressure off, he squinted up at an overhead freeway sign. "It's okay though. It hasn't been, like, torture or anything." He laughed nervously.

Laura laughed too. It was like they were coming to the end of an extremely awkward date. She got the distinct feeling he was trying to find a way of not asking her out again. Only this wasn't a date.

They pulled off the freeway and started going down narrow streets. The topography was so close and cluttered, compared to LA. It was flat, but Laura had that dizzying awareness of being somewhere totally *else*.

Bart said, "You gonna be okay here?" He sounded apprehensive.

"I'll be fine."

"I mean, Baltimore's a bit different from the big city."

No place to hike, that's for sure. But no Dexter, no constantly rejecting movie industry. It was different. That was good. And some part of Becca might still be there, some part of the *home* they'd had together. She said, "Yeah." She couldn't think of anything else to say.

They pulled up out front of Nonna's house, and when she got out of the car, Laura was surprised by how soggy and heavy the air was. It was too warm for evening and too damp to move. Twelve years in California, and she'd forgotten humid.

She fetched the heaviest suitcase out of the back of the car to spare Bart, and he got one box of cottura. It clanked when he lifted it, but Laura found that she cared less about the cottura than she had when they set out on this drive. It was a box of dishes again.

By the time she got to the top of Nonna's front stairs, she found it hard to breathe. It was all coming back, summers where a walk to the corner store seemed like a hike up a mountain with lead weights, the air so damp it was hard to draw oxygen.

It was late. The front porch light wasn't on, but the flicker of a television came from inside. Laura rang the doorbell. Bart put the box down on the porch and went back to the car for more stuff. Her heart jumped to her throat, and she half expected Becca to answer the door like when she and Janelle visited. They would scream and hug and run off to Becca's room. She was sad all over again.

A girl who looked about twelve came to the front door. She had long, straight, black hair in bangs, big brown eyes, freckles on a tan face, and a slightly glazed look about her. She was wearing shorts she was clearly growing out of and a T-shirt that somehow managed to be both tight and baggy. She saw Laura, and her eyes sharpened, her brows knitted, and she frowned. She looked behind her as if to ask for help, but it seemed that whoever could help wasn't there.

"Who are you?" She asked. Not rude, but a straightforward, honest sounding question. Laura liked the way she asked it, but then anger and uncertainty swelled. She was coming there to live, and no one had mentioned it to the girl.

Before she had time to answer, Bart was behind her saying, "Open the door, Lizzie, we've got a lot of shit to bring in."

Laura took umbrage at her life's possessions being classified as *shit* but Lizzie opened the door, and Laura heaved her suitcase in. The room was chilly. The warm damp outside gave way to cool damp, and the air smelled heavy with house – fresh air hadn't been in this place in a long time. The television was playing too loudly, something old, melodramatic, and full of music with tall chords. Laura could see Nonna in her chair, her slack jaw lit by the flickering light from the television. She wasn't sure she could see her breathing.

Laura looked back at Lizzie, who was staring at her. She shrugged her shoulders and sank to the sofa, saying, "She's not dead. I checked."

Laura laughed. "Good to know."

She turned to see Bart standing with the box of cottura. She took it from him and brought it into the kitchen, which looked reasonably tidy. Laura's apprehension gave way to a faint glimmer of hope that maybe things weren't as bleak as they had seemed. Somebody had done the dinner dishes and the counters were clean.

By the time she got back to the front door, Bart had brought everything in and left it in a heap on the patch of carpet at the foot of the stairs. He was standing there with his hands by his sides, eager to be dismissed.

He said, "Whatcha watching, Liz?"

Lizzie got up and went to stand by Bart, her hands shoved in her pockets, her head tilted sideways toward the floor, half shrug, half lean. Her entire body language was filled with a confused mix of forced casualness, teenage indignation, hope, and anxiety. Laura felt an irrational sorrow and worry for her.

Lizzie said, "Just an old movie. Ever see *Robin Hood?*"

Simultaneously, Laura said, "With Kevin Costner?" and Bart said, "Nope."

Lizzie looked at Laura, baffled again. Then at the stuff

piled by the stairs. She looked hopefully at Bart and said, "Are you moving in?"

The shame, fear, and betrayal that crossed Bart's face made Laura want to shield him somehow or buy him several beers and a long talk at a bar. Now his flying to Tennessee to pick her up came clear.

He said, "Oh, no, honey. Wish I could." He really didn't. It came out patronizing, and Laura could tell by Lizzie's expression that it smarted. Her chin set a little, her brows went down.

Bart said, "But Laura here's coming to stay for a while."

Lizzie flashed a suspicious look at her, like she was some sort of nanny for hire or social worker. Bart didn't volunteer any information.

Quickly, Laura said, "Lizzie. I haven't seen you since you were ..." Wait, did she see her or was she remembering someone else's kid? She really was a shitty cousin. "I'm your cousin Laura."

She held out her hand. Lizzie looked at her, and then, as if all her effort were put into it, she removed one hand from her pocket and shook it.

She withdrew it again. She squinted at Laura, putting it together, and said, "Laura and Janelle."

Laura nodded. The girl's face softened a little. Laura could see her reconfiguring her newfound orphanhood with a new character in it. Laura wasn't ready to be part of whatever picture Lizzie was dreaming up in her head. She had some work of her own to do.

She tried to fill her in, "I ..." she looked at Bart. She had an audience for summing up a part of her life she couldn't figure out herself. "I lived in LA. I'm starting over here. It's a place to stay, and Nonna could use the help." She kept it casual, with no onus on her or on the girl. There was no reason to figure it out all at once.

The pressure of caretaking lifted from both parties, Lizzie's shoulders relaxed, her hands came out. She swept her arm around the room and said, "Well, welcome to the manse."

Laura smiled and said, "Fabulous." She looked around the room. Despite the tidy kitchen, Nonna's place had darkened since she'd last been there. There was a lot of dust and a general pall had fallen over a place that was once full of promise and warmth – that was once home. Rebecca's absence became screamingly loud.

Lizzie's sarcasm was unaccustomed and therefore heavy-handed, "We do our best to ensure that everyone is welcomed in the greatest of comfort and ease."

They both laughed a little. Bart's entire *being* relaxed. He was less anxious than he'd been all day. He said, "Well, ladies, if you're all set, I've got a plane to catch..."

Laura felt like she'd been passed a very heavy object she wasn't allowed to put down. Weird that after their long journey together he should just, pouf, disappear. Laura said, "You don't need the bathroom? Or a cup of coffee or something?"

He said, "No, I'm good."

"Thanks for the ride."

Lizzie wheeled away from her and went back to Bart throwing her arms around him in a hug, which he hesitantly returned. "Bye, Uncle Bart. Come visit again, soon."

He said, "Uh, yeah."

Laura turned back to the kitchen so she didn't have to watch him go.

CHAPTER EIGHT

LIZZIE

Nonna never really talked about my grandmother, Anna Maria, the one who left my mom with her, but she would often rant in Italian about her youngest daughter, Sally. Sally had two girls, Laura and Janelle, and one of them was here. The possibility of *family* opened up a little hope in my belly.

Laura reminded me of those waif-like rock n' roll characters in the section of the comic store I wasn't allowed to buy from but could sneak a look at once in a while. All torn jeans, black eyeliner, messy gorgeous reddish-brown curly hair that looked completely unkempt but attractive. I'd never have hair like that in a million years. Big, wide crescent silver earrings, and she seemed a lot younger than Mom even though I knew they were around the same age. Mom told me about how they used to play together when she was little. The cousins who pretended they were sisters. But whenever I asked Mom what happened to Laura, she never really had an answer.

Laura got quiet the minute Bart slammed the front door, like he did it on purpose. She looked like she was somewhere else. I tried to keep the conversation going, but it was hard. I asked her about her drive here. What LA was like? She said, "Well, it's big and really hard to describe."

I couldn't talk about the one thing I *wanted* to talk about because it would make me cry. I think she had the same idea, so Mom didn't even come up.

We roused Nonna, who didn't say much. Just, "Glad you're here." It didn't sound like she meant it, but Laura didn't hang around. She dragged one suitcase up the stairs and disappeared.

Laura must have been the reason for Nonna's makeup and shower. I didn't know why she hadn't told me she was coming. It seemed like it would be important. But old people forgot stuff. Maybe they spent all day in their memories and forgot where they were or that they were in a housecoat and had huge cobwebs hanging from the corners of their rooms. Maybe they forgot who they were. Maybe Laura and I being there together would wake Nonna up again somehow. Makeup was a start.

I woke up early the next morning and listened to the house. I hoped I'd smell coffee or hear conversation or something to let me know there was life happening. Nonna's house, the prison, now had an echo of hope to it. It was too hot to sleep with more than a sheet that night, and when I stretched, I felt a hot patch of fur on my ankle.

Calzone!

He must have crept out from wherever he was hiding during the night. He looked a little manky, like he hadn't cleaned himself since he got here. But when I started petting him, he purred. I picked him up and opened the door. Someone was in the kitchen. I slipped Calzone into the laundry room where Nonna had told me to put the litter box and food.

I went through all my stuff and found my holey jeans. I got

out a T-shirt Dad had bought at a Rolling Stones concert, looked at my hair in the mirror, and tried to tousle it, but it was no go. Even in the total humidity of summer, it was straight and flat, and if it got tousled, it ended up with one bunch of hair forming a loop and just looked uncombed and stupid. Some jerk at school said that I had "Hair like an oriental." I thought he meant like a fringed carpet, but after a minute, I caught on. Yup, I had my dad's hair, black and forever straight. I unlooped it, and it fell flat, like it always did.

I went downstairs. Nonna was sitting at the kitchen table reading the newspaper. There was coffee in the coffee maker, probably for Laura. Nonna looked up in surprise. "You're up early!" She said this really loud, like for someone else's benefit. Was she trying to wake Laura up?

I said, "Uh. Not really."

Still projecting like she was onstage she said, "It's only six thirty!"

Oh. Wow. It must have been the light or something. No way was Laura going to be up, but I was and there wasn't any way to backtrack out of it. I was embarrassed that I'd been so excited, like a little kid.

Nonna put on her hearing aids with two loud whistles, and I got out the oatmeal.

LAURA

Laura woke up, and it was dark, and things smelled funny, old and heavy. She was in a room she'd woken up in on many a summer morning just like this one, only now she was tall enough to knock her feet against the foot of the single bed. She closed her eyes again. She knew that right across from her was an identical walnut-framed bed. That both beds had nubby, off-white bedspreads with fringe and little balls of stitching on them. She knew with a growing awareness that resembled dread, that Becca was not in the bed next to her. Her *notness* struck Laura in the center of the chest. The *old* smell accentuated her cousin's absence and the length of time that had really passed since Laura last saw her.

Behind the wood-paneled cabinets built into the eaves were old quilts, a collection of Nancy Drew books, and, if she dug deep enough back into the crawlspace, a dirty magazine she'd found in her dad's toolbox when she was ten and brought to Nonna's to share with Becca. She was embarrassed all over again by Becca's questions about the photos in the magazine, who were these women that they could look so bold posing like that, holding her fingers around their private places? Were penises really that big? The thought terrified them. In with that dirty magazine were secret love letters the girls had written each summer to various boys they had crushes on. She had even written one to Michael J. Fox, and Rebecca dared her to send it, but she didn't. Rebecca did send hers off to Adam Ant, including a poster-sized picture she drew of him. She never heard back. Laura wondered what Adam Ant was doing now, his heyday over, the Ants disbanded. He probably wasn't even cute anymore. He would have been lucky to have Becca, all grown up and gorgeous.

When Laura and Janelle came to visit, Becca would give Janelle her room, and she and Laura would bunk together. Janelle was happier that way – she hated Baltimore and was a total pill for each and every visit. She was Judy's girl. Laura ended each summer wishing she could leave Janelle and Judy and even her dad and live with Becca and Nonna forever.

But Becca was gone. The black hole in Laura's chest that had felt shaken or at least distracted in Bart's company churned around, rolled into a ball like a sleepy animal, and settled in.

She was so tired. Her limbs were leaden with the humidity, with the travel, with the back-in-time effect of the room, with the absence of Rebecca, with the humiliation of Dexter, with the awkwardness with Bart, and an underlying throb of an orphan who needed what she herself was lacking in childhood – was maybe still lacking now. Rather than being a place to dislodge all the darkness, Baltimore sank around her and trapped her body.

She buried her face in her mildewy pillow before she turned her head to the wall. She didn't really have anything to get up for. She might as well take advantage of this enforced vacation and sleep. Maybe Nonna would make something really nice for dinner. Something with a lot of noodles and cheese. But now she'd sleep, just a little more.

ADRIANA

Hollywood, California, 1940.

Rose had been out of work for several months now. The acting work wasn't coming so quickly, and with Adriana's income, she didn't seem to worry as much about it. She stayed home and worked on her scripts. The house was a mess every time Adriana got home, and dinner was no longer waiting for her. She supposed the honeymoon was over. Most evenings, Rose would be tap-tapping at her typewriter. Adriana knew that the stack of pages to the right of the typewriter was getting too thick for a screenplay. It was the width of a long book manuscript, and that worried her. She tried talking to Rose about the house and her lack of job prospects, but her love merely shrugged and kissed her. Sex had gone from the thrill of discovery to something with a purpose, an end. Rose used it to distract Adriana from something larger they weren't talking about. It was an unsettling shift in what before had been so free and fulfilling.

Things at work were picking up. The costumes for *The*

Lady Eve were a hit. Stanwyck insisted on Edith for her next movie, *Ball of Fire*. The black midriff beaded number Stanwyck's Eve wore had been the talk of the industry. Stanwyck seduced Henry Fonda aboard the ocean liner in a short-sleeved top and long flowing skirt. With its black beading and daring exposed midriff, the top had not only shocked and flummoxed Fonda's character Charles Pike but also numerous ladies from around the country who wrote in angry letters to Hollywood about indecency. Edith took this as a sign that America needed a little shaking up, and she wanted to take it a step further for Stanwyck's new role in *Ball of Fire* as nightclub singer and gangster moll, Sugarpuss O'Shea. Adriana got to work, sewing thousands of gold sequins into long strands, and then sewing three long strands together into ribbons which she affixed to the bodice in a delicate pattern sloping inward toward the seam in between Stanwyck's breasts. Then she sewed ribbons of these sequins onto the sheer sleeves and made a skirt entirely of the same-sized strips. It was painstaking work that resulted in aches and twinges at the end of the day. After three days of it, Adriana's shoulder froze up, and she couldn't turn her head for two days. She tried talking about her work with Rose, but Rose wasn't listening to her. She was listening to the noise in her head and the noise of the typewriter.

Then came that night that changed everything at work. When they watched the "Drum Boogie" dailies, Adriana's countless hours of sequin sewing paid off, and Stanwyck, with one hand on the shoulder, one murmur in her ear, the scent of cigarettes and cold cream, became Missy.

Adriana stepped out of the screening room into the cool night of a lot where most folks had gone home. The golden hour had passed, and the light hung suspended between day and night amidst the looming studio soundstages. The air was filled with the evening ocean breeze and the smell of sun-baked fennel and eucalyptus from the hills. She was full and heady with the hope and blush of new love. How could she not have seen it before now?

Missy was so considerate of her, shown her nothing but kindness, and Adriana had dismissed her as just another *actress*. But there was a mutual understanding there, and after hours of fittings and chatting, Adriana was comfortable enough with Missy to dare a hope, and that hope was electrifying. Missy was married, of course, to Robert Taylor; their love affair and consequent marriage had been spread across the movie magazines for years. But there had also been rumors about Stanwyck: that her maid, who always traveled with her, was provided for in contracts for press junkets. These rumors swelled Adriana's hope into desire. Such things were gossiped about hatefully in Hollywood. Like the fuss made over Cary Grant and his lover Randolph Scott, who were living Rose and Adriana's life, only in front of the press.

Rose. It was only when she got to her bicycle that Adriana remembered her. The unfounded elation over Missy and the fact that she had completely forgotten about Rose filled her with guilt. Rose had done so much for her, and now she was ready to throw it away for a crush on a movie star.

She would put Missy out of her mind. It was the only answer.

When she arrived home, she found the house dark. She unlocked the door, determined to surprise Rose with a night out on the town. It had been a long time since they'd gone out together, just the two of them. It was only nine, and there were plenty of clubs open. They could grab a meal and a drink at the Brown Derby. She needed to get more involved with what Rose was writing, maybe she could help her sort out the story. She'd been wrapped up in work, and the two had such a comfortable shorthand, that Adriana hadn't even thought to ask

Rose about her writing. She had been an altogether negligent girlfriend.

She opened the front door to darkness. She walked through the kitchen where the sink was still full of the dishes from that morning. The smell of sour milk and coffee grinds surprised her with a flash of anger. She went to the bedroom, but Rose wasn't there. She saw a small light shining in the office, and there was Rose, asleep on the daybed. A cigarette in her hand burned out long ago, and a pile of ash lay under where her arm draped down toward the floor.

Adriana sat down in the chair at Rose's desk and looked at her. Her hair was down and probably hadn't been brushed for a few days. She wore a silk red-and-blue striped blouse that had once been fancy but had been worn so often it had lost its sheen. She was beautiful as she slept, her lashes, without mascara, had a reddish tinge to them, as did her cheeks. Her lips were full and, without lipstick, softer, less confident and pronounced. Adriana looked at her love of over two years and was completely helpless. She didn't know how to do this. No one had brought her up on ideas of romance and love or long marriages. No one had talked to her about long-term relationships. Her father left her mother, her mother left them, her sister and her brothers left and, finally, she left the family that wasn't hers. No one told her that she would have to love a real, breathing, smoking, shitting, temperamental human being; someone who could be so loving and doting and then so withdrawn and inscrutable. Rose was the one to usher her into the film industry and gave her the strength and boldness to succeed, and now that Adriana was succeeding, Rose was ... was this failing? She didn't know how to help her, if Rose needed helping.

She turned to the pages next to the typewriter. Scripts always looked funny to her after books, all those lines running down the middle of the page. It was a conversation between Mary and James. The story on the top of the pile seemed to come in somewhere in the middle, and there weren't any page numbers. Adriana picked up a stack of pages from the top. Underneath, there was more conversation between James and Mary. She picked up about five pages more. There was no action, no scene description, just a dialogue, a long dialogue. She picked up ten more pages. The same. Ten more. The same. All the way through the stack of what must have been two hundred pages, James and Mary were having a conversation, two words at a time, sometimes one line or sentence. She looked for a part to grasp onto, some thicker chunk of dialogue that might reveal a plot. The only thing she noticed was that they said each other's names a lot. She couldn't read on.

She'd come right up against the truth that Rose couldn't write. Sadness flooded up from somewhere in her stomach and caught in her throat. Rose had been at this for so long. Adriana didn't know if she could bear her disappointment when whatever this script promised didn't happen for her.

Rose shifted in her sleep and made dry mouth noises. The sadness in Adriana passed her throat and started flooding her eyes. She left the room so Rose wouldn't wake.

She went to bed and cried. She hadn't cried herself to sleep since she was a child. It was strange but comforting. She was careful to be quiet. The windows were open, and she stared at the cartoon ghost shape of the dancing white curtain and drifted off to sleep.

She woke to a rattling sound and a low howling wind. She was coated in sweat, and Rose rolled over, putting her arm around her, hot and heavy. Adriana was trapped. She tried to move her blanket down gently, but it was no good. It was October, and this was the beginning of the Santa Anas, an autumn offshore wind that blew the remnants of the summer off the desert, through Los Angeles and out to sea.

Adriana never did well during the Santa Anas. They provoked a constant headache, burning eyes, and a soul-deep restlessness that would not settle until they had passed. She slid out of bed and went to the window to close it. That made it worse. The room must have heated up thirty degrees since she first came to bed. She looked at Rose, who was lying on her stomach on top of the blankets, her arm still drooped over where Adriana had lain. She had taken off her trousers, her remaining striped shirt, her white silky panties, and sprawled naked limbs made her look like some sort of murder victim.

Adriana went into the kitchen and opened the fridge to get a glass of milk. Rose hadn't been shopping. Of course. She ran a glass of water from the tap and drank it all. She refilled her glass, walked into the living room, and sat on their sofa. It was a handsome, sage green mohair with dark wood arms and feet. Rose had gotten it as a gift from a friend in the set department. It brought elegance to their terra cotta-tiled, sunken living room with curved arched ceilings and an enormous Moorish window. The tile was cool on Adriana's feet, but the mohair was the wrong substance to sit on when the wind already made her skin crackle with itch. She settled for the bentwood rocker in the corner. She rocked.

This was a good house. A better place than she had ever lived. She had someone who loved her more than she had any right to be loved. She had a job she was good at and where she was useful. It was good to be useful. Why did she feel like she needed desperately to get out? Why did she long for unknown adventures? For other places to live? For other women – okay one specific other woman – to love? How did one clamped hand on her shoulder and breath in her ear turn her so completely upside down?

She had never really made a commitment to Rose. Maybe she was just sort of her roommate. Maybe Rose took in other girls before Adriana, and her withdrawal meant it was time for her to move on. Maybe if Adriana hadn't stayed so long, Rose wouldn't be writing herself into a hole. Without Adriana's salary, maybe Rose would be out there getting work, not as a star necessarily, but as the best friend role. Even steady extra work paid the rent.

The wind bellowed again. They had an archway outside the house by the kitchen that caught even a mild wind and made it echo like a cave. The archway raged during the winds, exacerbating the mood of the house.

She could leave. She made enough money with Edith to find her own place, start over. In fact, without carrying Rose and the rent, she might be able to afford a few more luxuries here and there. In Bethlehem, with nothing but her own where-withal, she had ferreted away money for months and made that suit to make the journey across the entire country to get here. She had hidden her money under her mattress, under a loose board in the barn, never all in one place in case that prying diGiralomo girl should find it. She had skills, a job, she could do anything.

"Watcha thinking about?" Rose's voice startled her.

Rose stood, her hair down around her shoulders. She was wearing a white slip now and, leaning against the archway above the steps down into the living room, she looked like a star. Adriana wondered why, with all the things they could do with makeup and costume, they had never managed to capture the simple beauty of one's lover just after sleep. Too much makeup perhaps. But there stood Rose, who laughed gently.

"You've got your brows all knitted together, like ..." She

imitated Adriana's face. It made her laugh. Rose said, "Come to bed."

"It's too hot."

"You always get antsy when the winds blow."

Adriana stretched and writhed. "I itch. All of me, my muscles, my thoughts. *Everything* itches."

Rose walked down toward her, her bare feet padding on the cool tile floor. It was the loveliest sound Adriana had ever heard, the scuff of dry skin on the cool floor, the rustle of silk slip. Rose held out her hand and said, "Let's take a cold bath." Adriana took her hand, which was strangely cool in the heat. She followed her up the two stairs and down the hall to the bathroom.

She loved Rose. That was just about it. Whatever crushes may come, whatever winds might blow, she loved her.

As she sank to the edge of their tub in their pale, pink-tiled bathroom, Rose said, "I think I've hit a real turning point with the script." She plugged the bathtub and turned the tap on full.

A small round stone of cold fear manifested in Adriana's abdomen, but she used all her mental abilities to put it aside. "I love you, Rosie."

She knew she still meant it, even if it didn't sound as genuine as she'd hoped. She slid out of her slip and tested the water with her big toe.

She could hear an edge creep into Rose's voice as she said, "I love you too, hon."

LIZZIE

Laura kept not getting up, and after I did the dishes as loudly as I could, Nonna disappeared into the bathroom for way too long. It took Nonna forever to do anything. Getting across the kitchen. Going down the hall. She would go into the downstairs bathroom by her bedroom (it used to be some sort of office, but she moved her bedroom there after she broke her hip) and not come out for ages. After the forever it took her to shuffle her walker down the hall, I heard the door to the bathroom close. I flomped down on the sofa.

I picked up my sketchbook, which was on the side table, and picked up my pencil, but when I leafed through my drawings to get to a blank page, they all seemed stupid again. The motorcycle chase scene I drew was *totally* ripped off from *Akira*. My mutant little girls series seemed downright childish. Things had changed over the past month. Somehow, I had to draw to reflect that.

I thought about working on what was calling me from under the bed from upstairs, but I didn't want to go there again. Not with company in the house. I sat with my pen hovering over a blank page for about five minutes until I realized it was useless. I snooped again. The key to bringing Nonna back was somewhere in this house.

There were more old-timey photos on the bookshelf next to the fireplace. I reached up and grabbed down a snapshot tucked into a frame of another picture. It was a little blurrier than the one of Nonna and the movie star, but there she was with that woman from the other photo. They had their cheeks pressed together and were laughing for the camera. Having so much fun. The fact that someone so young and beautiful could get as old and bathroom-stuck as Nonna worried me.

They were amazing. The woman who wasn't Nonna was prettier in a glamorous sort of way, even though she wasn't wearing much makeup from what I could tell in the happy blur. There was a flush from down the hall and went to tuck the photo back in, when I saw the picture it had been hiding in the frame. There was the woman who wasn't Nonna in a really fancy, dark but sparkly dress, reclining on a chaise, one arm raised over her head, looking at the camera with her big, clear, light eyes (probably blue, but maybe green), made-up like a movie-star. She was so beautiful it stopped me. I put it back on the shelf before Nonna could make the shuffle down the hall. I guessed this friend of hers wasn't around anymore. You don't keep photos around when you have a real person visiting.

The girl at Video Planet looked up and smiled when she recognized me. "Hey, don't you have school or something?" I squinted at her name tag that read *Leticia*. She was really pretty. Her blue eyes were startling in her black-lashed eyelids, and her skin was almost white against her black hair. With those giant eyes and tiny nose and chin, she would make a perfect manga heroine. Could she be mixed like me? Had I found the one person in Baltimore like me? *Be cool.*

I said, "I just moved here. I start in the fall."

She blew a bubble and nodded her head, popping it. "S'cool." At first, I thought she was saying "school" but then I realized she meant it was *cool.* I didn't know why it gave me a charge, but it did. She said, "Whatzit today?" She had the ability to raise one eyebrow at a time and turn it into a question mark. I could totally draw this chick.

I put *Robin Hood* on the counter and fished into my pocket for the scrap of napkin I wrote the title on. I said, "Uh. *Bringing up Baby?*" I really did not want to watch a movie about babies, but Nonna said it was time for a comedy, and I liked *Robin Hood,* so I gave it the benefit of the doubt. I started over toward the Classics section now that I knew where it was. "I can find it though."

She said, "Suit yourself," And hopped up on the counter. Some slasher movie was on, there was screaming and cheesy music. She was watching it with a serious frown like she was studying something.

The movie was easy enough to find. It was black and white. No oozing gorgeous intense colors. Just Nonna's color-free existence. I tried not to be too jaded. It was another 102 minutes. Maybe after 102 minutes. Laura would join us, and I could figure out what her being there was about.

I smacked it on the counter with my five dollars. Leticia raised her finger *one minute,* taking her eyes off the screen. There was growling, high-pitched music, screaming, and something or other being eviscerated. I looked at the screen, feeling like I was getting away with something, like when I snuck a look in the wrong section of the graphic novel shelf at the library. But then something in my stomach shifted and I had a sudden need to look away.

I must have had a funny expression on my face because Leticia paused the movie. She said, "Are you okay?"

"Yeah. Fine. Fine." I was staring at the carpet, but something about the blood and the messy intestines stuck with me.

She looked at the movie box, concentrating, turning it over. "Cary Grant. I like that dude. Real suave." She looked at me doubtfully, "This your choice?"

"My grandmother. We're going to watch it with my cousin. She's in from out of town." Why did I have the need to tell her this? I sounded like a little kid.

Leticia said, "That's great. Cousins are the best. Have fun." She handed me my fifty cents change.

"Thanks."

I hung my shoulders and tried to act cool in the way I picked up the movie. I said, "Thanks, man." *Man.* Where did that come from?

She smiled. "Right, on, dude." She wasn't being malicious. Just gently teasing; that question mark eyebrow was working again.

I laughed and said, "Hang loose."

She nodded and flashed me a peace sign as I went out the door. "Groovy."

LAURA

Laura woke up again. It would have been really nice to stay in bed, but her bladder was yelling at her, and she was developing a low throb in her head that came from a lack of caffeine. She opened the door cautiously. Old movie banter echoed up from downstairs; screwball comedy from the sound of it. Long-days-in-Baltimore-with-no-idea-of-what-to-do-next-in-life in screwball comedies were non-existent. They may have someone look forlorn for about thirty seconds, but the screwball heroine always found her way out of these moments. If only Laura had a leopard. Or some roller skates.

She made her way quietly along the hall and went to pee, but by the time she got back to her room, she knew there was no way to go forward without getting some coffee and food. If she were a screwball heroine, she'd have a handsome butler to bring her a silver tea set with everything she needed. Toast, coffee. And the newspaper. That's why screwball heroines were so smart, they always read the morning paper.

She pulled the bedspread off her and wrapped it around like a protective coating. Somewhere in the course of the morning, the air conditioning had kicked in, so it was cool enough to do this. She walked downstairs and waved vaguely at the girl who looked up at her like an eager but anxious stray puppy.

She went into the kitchen and poured herself some coffee. The taste of it, burner-singed, made her cringe, but when she looked at the clock, she saw that it was eleven. She went to the fridge to get some milk. There was only non-dairy creamer. She would have to do some shopping at some point, but for now, she poured the hazelnut goop into the coffee. She walked through the dining room to the living room and slunk along the outside of the room, not ready for conversation quite yet. She sat on the edge of one of those horrible, uncomfortable wing-backed chairs by the fireplace. It was too narrow and not deep enough for any sort of comfort without a footstool, but if she sat on the sofa, she'd have to engage the girl.

She focused in on the dialogue of the movie and burst out, *"Bringing up Baby!"* before she remembered that she had been avoiding conversation.

Fortunately, Nonna shushed her. But the girl looked over and grinned that needy, expectant grin at her. She *needed* in a way that kicked Laura right in her metastasized black lump.

Laura deliberately turned her eyes to the television, sipped her burnt hazelnut sludge, and leaned back, trying to pretend she was comfortable where she was.

They were at the part where Katharine Hepburn was pretending that she was being mauled by a leopard to get Cary Grant to come over and save her. Cary said, "Susan! Oh Susan!" and he was off the phone and on his way. Laura wondered if maybe she had pulled a stunt like this, she wouldn't have lost Dexter. Or if she had worn more cunning hats. Or if she had a rich aunt from whom Dexter needed money.

The thing is, compared to the length of the relationship, the clever banter part had lasted about five minutes. Like if the relationship were ninety minutes, it had five minutes of romantic comedy before it turned into some sad movie from the seventies like *Lady Sings the Blues* – only around three and a half hours long. It could have benefited from a better editor. Or perhaps some outrageous violence in the middle. She imagined Dexter being blown away, cross-cut with the baptism scene from The Godfather. Moe Green, through the eye, Clemenza with the garrotte, Dexter. Dexter sitting at some big meeting with stars and a famous director. A man in a black coat and big hat bursts in, and pulls out a gun with a silencer on it ...

The chair wasn't going to do. Laura slunk across the floor and sat at the foot of the sofa, separated from the Stray by a coffee table. She sank back into the familiar world of the happy, funny little movie, a place she'd visited so many times she could name the next line and shot. She could pretend that the California on the screen was the Connecticut it was supposed to be, because it was in black and white, and there were David and Susan, chasing George the dog around, looking for the inter-costic clavicle, the dinosaur bone that started the hijinks. Cary Grant was so assured in his role as the bumbler. Katharine Hepburn purred, "David, you are so handsome without your glasses."

Laura pulled a pillow off the sofa and laid it on the floor. She curled around the corner of the coffee table so she could see. She was comfortable. Things might just be okay after all, as long as the movie didn't end.

LIZZIE

I didn't know what was up with Laura, but it was quite clear she was not going to be "fun." She came down for the movie looking all weirded out and didn't speak to either of us. All my waiting excitement over maybe having a new relative ... a new person ... sorta died. She wouldn't even sit with me. Which was just as well because she smelled funky. She curled up on the floor – maybe she had cramps or something.

Now that I looked at her, it was hard to believe she and Mom ever hung out. If she and mom *were* sister-cousins, that had stopped a long time ago because if they had been close any time in recent years, I would have met her before now.

We watched the movie, which was funny. It got noisy and crazy at the end but funnier. Every time Nonna laughed, she looked more real than she had the laugh before. I could see a shadow of the woman in the picture from the mantle. Black and white wasn't so bad when you got used to it, and the guy who played David was no Erroll Flynn, but he was nice and funny, and you could see these two nutjobs living together crazy ever after. They'd probably bicker all the time.

Mom and Dad bickered. They had this funny way of talking to each other like they were arguing, but both of them were kind of laughing, so they weren't *arguing* even though they were arguing.

Dad would say, "Because, of course, I'm going to find my sweater in my drawer, right where I left it because I only have two."

And Mom would say, "Yes, but one of those two IS the softest sweater in the house and extra toasty and nice smelling."

And Dad would say, "But some people had ample opportunity to buy a sweater that would be just as soft and toasty."

And Mom would say, "But why would I do that when I have a perfectly good sweater in the house?"

And I'm telling it all wrong. It didn't go like that. It was quick, and funny, and clever, and just an argument over a sweater, but it let me know how much they loved each other, and for some reason, the conversations in the movie reminded me of that. It was lunch by the time we were done, but Laura, still wrapped in that hot, hot bedspread thing, trailed it upstairs like some sad, defeated queen before we could ask her what she'd like to eat.

Nonna looked at me with a gleam, a twinkle, whatever they call that thing that shows an old lady's got something on her mind that will be fun for her and maybe not so much fun for you. Anyway, she said, "So, chef Elisabetta, what's on the menu for lunch?"

I didn't know why she put so much production into getting me to cook for her when she knew I was going to do it anyway.

But I remember seeing some kinda nutty bread in the fridge and some cheese. If I could rustle up some butter and mayonnaise, I could make a mean grilled cheese.

The bread was gross and heavy, and I was polite about it, but partway through chewing the grilled cheese sandwich, lost in thought and looking like an old lady again, Nonna looked right at me. Mouth still full, she said, "This is awful bread, where did you find this bread?" Like she was angry.

I sounded more snappish than I meant to, "It was in *your* fridge."

Her face still in a frown, she drank her water and then cracked a smile. "We need to go shopping tomorrow."

Going out! Where there were people! Maybe she'd go to the shops, see her friends. I said, "We could go this afternoon."

She shook her head, "We'll need Laura to drive, and I don't think she's up to it yet. I'll give her another day."

Going out. Maybe I could persuade her to come downtown first. To a park. *Somewhere.* Maybe once I got Nonna out of the house, she'd remember who she was.

"Should I make Laura a sandwich?" If I made her a sandwich, I could take it to her room, and maybe we could talk about *something.*

But Nonna said, "No, honey, she'll come down when she's hungry enough."

LAURA

Tomorrow she would get up, go online, and start looking for work. In Baltimore. Maybe she could get some work with John Waters or get a gig working on *Homicide*. There was filming in Baltimore. She came from LA, maybe she was a big fish in a small pond now. Maybe they'd be impressed by the title *Windblown*. Maybe things were homegrown and fun here. *Let's get together in that old barn and make a movie!* Or a TV show. She could do that.

Tomorrow, she would get her shit together. Get going. It was time to take charge of her life. She lay awake in the dark of the room, weaving pictures of what things would be like here in her new life. It took her about an hour to get over herself and get to sleep.

CHAPTER NINE

ADRIANA

While the bath soothed Adriana a bit that night, the Santa Anas blew ill that year. By the time she got back to bed, her skin was dry, and she was irritable again. Both agreed it was too hot to make love, and Rose fell asleep, her hand lying gently on Adriana's bare belly. That long, gorgeous hand and Rose's all too human presence became too much, and Adriana ended up on the daybed in the office.

She got up early the next morning and snuck out to avoid Rose. She chose her lightest linen trousers and a short sleeve white blouse and at six-thirty left the house to pedal into work. There was a breath of onshore flow, a reminder that the Los Angeles of yesterday was still out there, but the wind changed by the time she got to work. It was so burningly dry that the inside of her nose crackled, and she had broken a sweat. The sun hit her face with such severity that she could have been in a Western, in the middle of the desert, out of water. She waved to the security guard at the front gate and headed back to the shop. It would be cooler in there at least.

She loved those early moments in the studio when nothing

was bustling yet. The union workers were grabbing their coffee, waiting carefully until the clock struck seven before starting any work, so as not to disobey contracts. The commissary wouldn't see its businessmen, writers, and producers for a few hours. No actors were there, only working folk. She stopped in and grabbed an oatmeal and a coffee. The cooks and attendants knew her, so she could take her tray with her to the shop.

Edith usually got in at eight and would stay until late at night. She let Adriana go home earlier than her but would leave her tasks for the next morning. Adriana arrived to find a bolt of herringbone tweed, a pattern to cut for a suit, and two dresses to finish. She put her tray on a side table, took two bites of oatmeal and a swig of coffee, and got to work. Working with a purpose pushed everything else away: her irritation with Rose and with life in general, her brief flight of fancy over Missy.

Infatuation is all that was.

She pinned the pattern. For so long, she had kept her pins stowed in that lipstick case with Rose's heart – it hung from her neck and conveniently traveled with her across the fabric as she went. But somewhere around a month ago, she had left it at home, tucked safely among her underwear. She told herself the alternative was easier: a pincushion stuck to her wrist with elastic. It had nothing to do with Rose. It just wasn't the right use for the thing.

Tweed was complicated, as it needed to be cut on the bias, and the pattern had to flow. Edith had taught her to reverse the pattern with each panel, creating a larger herringbone effect on the garment. Adriana knew it wouldn't show in black and white, but detail was everything, and Edith would see it. She was down on her hands and knees, paper across the floor, cutting the pattern when the door blew open behind her with a slam against the outside of the building.

"Hey! I'm working here!" she hollered. She and the other

girls had a rough shorthand with each other; they worked like a large crazy family.

"I'm sorry, honey. The wind caught it." The soft voice shot through her with a familiarity that both electrified her and felt like home.

"Miss – Stanwyck ..." While she said Missy in her head, and that is all Edith called her, she knew it wasn't her place to call her by her nickname.

"Aw, please, honey. It should be Missy by now, don't you think?" She was wearing an adorable, tan linen calf-length A-line skirt with four buttons on the front. A short-sleeved white blouse made her look like she was ready for a day at work as a secretary, but the tennis shoes and colorful scarf around her hair gave her an off-kilter sensibility that only stars could afford.

She said, "Is Edith here?"

Adriana panicked and blood rushed in her ears. The star was here, the boss wasn't and somehow she'd mess it up.

"N-no. She's usually in around eight."

Missy said, "Right, I forgot how early it was." She threw herself in a chair near where Adriana was working and tucked her legs up underneath her. "I couldn't sleep last night. These damn winds." Adriana thrilled at their shared experience. She was in an awkward position on the floor, which now put her at Missy's feet, but there was work that needed finishing. She felt Missy watching her. She knew that if she looked directly into her face, she might just disclose something, so she went back to cutting her work. Her hands, usually so deft, were thick and clumsy. She cut slowly.

"How do you do that?" Missy's face had genuine awe in it.

Adriana said, "Oh, you do enough of these, and it's no trick."

"But you draw those patterns on the paper freehand? Just like that?"

Adriana wiggled the tape measure around her neck. "There is some measurement involved."

"Of course. Hey, honey, don't get up, and I mean that, you've got some ... magic going on there. But where do you keep the cigs?"

"Silver box on the worktable. Matches inside."

Adriana wanted to get up, bring her the cigarette, light it for her. She had a need for some motion of intimacy, but there wasn't room for it. She was a child forlorn when Missy walked away from her, five feet across the room to get a cigarette. She said a secret prayer, wishing her back to the chair, which was right next to her, and it seemed like her prayer worked because Missy returned to the chair after getting her cigarette.

She knew she couldn't rely on alterations to fix things. She had to get it right in the first place. The two pieces for the sides of the bodice were the easiest. The front and back were trickier. She had to allow enough extra fabric in the back for the zipper, enough in the front for the bust, and enough for adjustments. Actresses were always shrinking and growing by a scant half inch. If you fitted the dress too loosely at first, your work wouldn't look careful, and the dress wouldn't be well represented enough for the actress to feel taken care of. The dress could be nixed before it got to a second fitting. If you fitted it too tight, you risked shaming the actress for being fat.

Missy sat wordlessly for a while. Adriana thrilled at the comfortable silence and each inhalation of her cigarette. Such an intimate noise, the catch of the lips, the pull, the exhale. Missy smelled sensational but different from the night before. She didn't have any perfume on yet, just the soapy, clean smell of fresh-scrubbed self.

Missy said, "Edith told me that *Drum Boogie* dress was yours."

A blush rose under Adriana's hair, and she was grateful her face was to the floor. "Edith designed it. I just sewed it."

"It was a stunner, honey. All those sequins, it must've taken days."

"A few."

"I love the way it *moved*, you know? It gave that number a little extra *oomph*." From the rustle of clothing, she knew that Missy had just shaken her shoulders, like in the number. Adriana smiled but kept her face to the floor. She took the pencil from behind her ear and numbered the pieces she was working on so as not to lose track when they made their way to a pile. One piece in the wrong place, one fabric pattern running askew, and the whole jacket would be ruined.

Missy's voice got all soft and wondrous as she said, "Adriana." Then, softer still, "Adriana."

Adriana looked up, hoping the compliment about the dress would explain her blush.

Missy looked at her closely, something at work in her eyes. Adriana couldn't read her, and that made her uneasy. She smiled, and the smile was returned, but the mischief still played.

Adriana said, "Yeah?"

"That's better. I can see your face. You've got a good face there, Ade. Strong, but pretty, you know?"

No one had given her that nickname before. She was dubbed, blessed.

Missy continued, "Ever think of acting?"

Adriana shook her head and went back to her work. She made a point never to talk about her childish dreams when she arrived. Acting was a distant memory.

"No, of course. Why would you when you can sew like that?" She got off the chair, knelt down next to Adriana, and touched her chin gently, tilting it. "You're something else." Her face was serious now, and Adriana could see that she wore no makeup at all. She had freckles smattered across her nose, and Adriana could cry for her makeup-free eyes, so vulnerable and real. She felt as if she were going to be kissed, but she knew this couldn't be. She both wanted it to happen and was terrified that it would.

The door opened, the wind blew in, and Missy let go of Adriana's chin, rising to her feet without missing a beat. She shielded her eyes from the bright light from outside and hollered shakily, "Friend or foe?"

"It's blowing like Death itself out there!" Edith's sharp, nasal voice broke through the softness of the room. "Adriana, anybody else here?"

Adriana sat up and looked at her boss, who, despite the weather, had on a full suit, hat, and gloves. Not a hair out of place. "No. Just me. And ..." She wasn't about to say "Missy" in front of Edith, so she dropped off there.

Edith said, "Hi, Missy. I gotta grab some PAs or something to clear the fabric outta the car. Right back. You need me?"

Missy said, "No, I've been well taken care of, thanks, honey. I gotta get to makeup anyway."

She stepped over the pattern and the fabric, and Edith let the door slam abruptly as she went back out into the wind. The pieces of the pattern were pinned down, but as they rustled, Adriana instinctively reached out to stop them with her hands. She was overcome by a need to protect her patterns from the elements and whatever else was swirling around in that room.

Missy was opposite her, legs still as if she were planted there. Adriana, hands spread over the paper patterns, lifted them, and rose to her feet, uncertain of what to say or do. She faced Missy and smiled.

She was surprised to feel herself tearing up as she said, "Thank you." For the attention? For the compliment? It was the sleeplessness, the emotional rollercoaster, the wind. She was embarrassed, but it touched something in Missy. Was it concern, or something deeper?

"Don't mention it," Missy said, but her voice and eyes lent no original meaning to the words. She smiled, and the connection was definite. Unmistakable. She stepped out into the bright sunshine, the wind still for the moment. Adriana's heart was leaden and flighty at once.

LAURA

Laura woke up to knocking at her door. Thirsty again, hunger pulling at the bottom of her belly. But she couldn't get up. The sheet was as heavy as her head. The knock repeated.

"What?"

The needy voice of the girl said, "Can I come in?"

Laura said, "What time is it?"

"Almost eleven."

She couldn't move. She didn't want the Stray seeing her like this. She said, "I'll be right down!"

"Okay." She didn't hear Lizzie leave for a minute. Like she was thinking about opening the door, which sent Laura into a panic, like when Judy stood outside her door when she was a teenager. But soon the girl's feet padded off down the hall.

Laura didn't know how long after the knocking came again. She had fallen back asleep. "I said I'd be right down!"

But the doorknob turned, and a loud violent metallic thunk

smacked it open. She had a random fear that it was a police battering ram. Nonna stood there. She looked pretty natty in makeup and all, but she was breathing heavily. The stairs. Shit. Laura sat up straight in bed, shame pounding in her ears. Nonna didn't seem angry. She shuffled into the room with her walker and kicked the door shut behind her.

"Nonna, I'm sorry. I don't feel so great."

Nonna hadn't caught her breath but raised a hand to stop her. She swallowed. Took another deep breath. The more time she took, the sadder, more humiliated, and useless Laura felt.

"Are you okay?" she asked.

Nonna nodded. She swallowed one more time and said, "Ridiculous. One flight of stairs, and I'm gasping like a fish."

Laura was about to say something, but Nonna stopped her again. "Honey, I know you got shit going on, and I get it. Believe me, I get it. But we've got this kid here, and we need groceries, and I can't drive because of this fucking hip. So do me a favor. Take a shower, you stink. Drive me to the market, come home, eat something and I promise, I'll let you sleep another five days."

Laura had no idea what to say. She felt as if her pathetic existence in this room had been broadcast without her permission.

Nonna said, "Okay?"

"Okay."

Nonna turned her walker around, which involved about four moves and small hip swivels. She winced, and Laura saw for the first time that she must be in pain.

This was terrible. Laura said, "How will you get down the stairs?"

Nonna didn't turn around again. It would be too hard. She said, "I got a thing I do. It's fine." She stopped in the doorway and said, "Next week, though, you have to get a job. I have an interview lined up for you."

Laura went from pity to wonder to rage in one strange swoop. What kind of interview? What would Nonna know about jobs?

ADRIANA

Nothing sat well at home after that. As much as Adriana tried to go on as usual, everything Rose did irritated her. The way she swallowed, the way she smoked, the way she stopped taking care of the house, the way she wasn't getting a job. And every moment Adriana spent with Missy, on set, in the dressing room, was rife with the heady joy of possibility. They weren't left alone enough for the kind of intimacy they had in the work-room that morning, but there were looks and laughs, and Adriana was allowed in on every joke, every meeting. Adriana laughed too loud at dailies one time and got a stern look from Edith over the top of her glasses. She sobered instantly. She knew she was safe for the very taboo of same-sex attraction. No one would *imagine*. After all, Stanwyck was married. But Adriana knew that she had crossed a star/worker line over which Edith kept a jealous control.

The fun, fast-talking anxiousness and growing attraction in her gave way to the dread of going home every evening where she would inevitably find Rose asleep on the daybed or typing away at that damned script.

One Friday, Adriana arrived home to find the house dark. She stood in the hallway for a moment, fuming a tirade in her head, *You can't wait up for me if I work past five? It's only eight! You can't have dinner ready? You don't even seem happy to see me anymore. I'm the only income in the household now, you should show me a little respect.* The tirade got uglier and uglier in her head when she smelled something lovely coming from the kitchen.

She moved down the hall past the dining room, when she saw that it was lit with candles. She went back and saw Rose sitting there at the head of the dark wood dining table, wearing one of her most attractive dresses. It was simple, form-fitting and black with a shirt collar and short sleeves. It had red roses all over it. Rose's hair and makeup were done to perfection. She looked gorgeous, and Adriana felt instantly rotten for the speech she never delivered.

Rose got up from the table and moved toward her with a glass of wine. She took Adriana's satchel off her shoulder and moved her into the dining room, pulling back a chair.

Adriana said, "Honey, what ..."

Rose had a knowing smile on her face, a certainty she hadn't worn in some months. "Nothing. You've just been working so hard I figured I'd spoil you a little."

Adriana sat down in the chair at the head of the table while Rose disappeared into the kitchen. She came out holding two plates with wedges of iceberg lettuce and some creamy bleu cheese dressing on them. She put them at their places and sat down.

Adriana had only seen salad served this way at the Derby. She said, "This is fancy."

Rose smiled and gestured for her to start. Adriana did. Rose sipped her wine and said, "The thing is, Adriana, I've been in a rut."

ALTERATIONS

"No ..."

Rose put up her hand to stop her. "And I know it. And I'm sorry it's been a drag around here. I really thought I could do something with this screenplay. It was so close I could taste it, you know?"

Adriana knew it was time to listen. She pointed to her salad with her fork and made an approving face before taking another bite.

"But the joke was on me. We don't need men in our lives. We've been doing great, but apparently, it is the rare woman who gets hired for writing in this town."

Adriana thanked God for Rose not talking about her writing, for putting the blame on men. She took another bite.

"I didn't get that 'til I took the script to the third agent. He, at least, was frank with me. The others kept calling me 'honey' and 'baby' and didn't have any real advice, just said it wasn't for them ... the third guy said that unless I was Lillian Hellman or Anita Loos, I wasn't going to get hired, because I wore a skirt."

"Rose, that's awful," Adriana said.

"Yup."

"What did you do? I mean, aside from put together this meal ... and whatever that is I smell in the oven. It smells delicious, what is it?"

"Guinea fowl, marmalade glaze."

"Goodness!"

Rose waved her hand at her. "Charlie at the Derby did me a favor. He owed me one. All I had to do was heat it up. You've been cooking for me for so long, and I've been doing a half-baked job, so I thought I'd go all out tonight."

"What are we celebrating?"

"If you let me finish ..."

"Of course."

Rose went into a delivery she usually reserved for parties,

complete with gestures, exaggeration, and big faces. "After that, I went back to Larry who'd been taking care of my bookings, and I marched in all mad and said that I'd had it with being a day player and wearing maiden outfits and sitting in the background when I had *talent*, real talent. I musta yelled at the guy for like, five minutes. He was scared at first, then he got this look in his eye, and you know what?"

"What?"

"He took me over to RKO – he drove me in his car! Apparently, they were looking for an angry dame, and he thought I was it! So, guess what?"

She was so beautiful and excited and all alive again, guilt flushed Adriana over her morning with Missy, shame at ever having disloyal thoughts about Rose. Without thinking, she said, "Rose, I love you. I really love you. You've been so good to me, helped me, supported me, these three long years. I wouldn't be in Edith's studio if it weren't for you, wouldn't have a job, a place to do something I'm good at."

Rose's entire face dropped. "What, is this the big kiss-off?"

Tears welled up, and Adriana dropped her fork. "No. No, Rosie, I didn't mean that. I."

Rose was cautious, "You ... what?"

Adriana said, "I just never manage to tell you, and the moments pass, and it's always not the right time, so I had to say it now before I forgot."

Rose grinned and grabbed her hand. "Aw, honey, thanks. I love you, too. You know that."

Once she started crying, it didn't seem to stop. Her lack of belief in Rose's writing, her moodiness, her complaints about the housekeeping, all these unsavory feelings seemed to be traveling out of her in tears. She bowed her head and sobbed.

Rose got up, walked around the table, and put her arms

around Adriana. She gave her a squeeze and said, "You work too hard."

CHAPTER TEN

LAURA

Nonna got Laura out of bed early in the morning, rapping her walker on the door. "Get showered and dressed. You have an interview at ten thirty."

Laura didn't ask questions till she was downstairs after a brief bout of clothes trauma. She chose to wear one of her old suits. Chocolate brown linen. A pink and white pin-striped blouse underneath. Slick, but not too formal. She didn't know how much she had to walk, so she chose wedge-heeled laced shoes. Two inches. In case her prospective employer was short.

"Where are you sending me?" What possible connections could Nonna have in Baltimore?

Nonna said, "The aquarium."

"What?"

"The aquarium. They need a clerk or something. There will be light administrative duties."

"Nonna."

"There will be no arguments. You may feel free to look for a job on your day off, which is Monday when the aquarium is closed."

"Nonna, I was an *executive*."

"You worked for a producer who made *one movie*." What the hell did this old lady know about Hollywood? Nonna said, "You're going to work because I promised someone, and I keep my promises. Plus, we could use some money around here for groceries. Here are directions." Nonna handed her a printed piece of paper. Laura was surprised to see that Nonna had printed it out from a computer. Where did she keep a computer? "Use my car. I'm not going anywhere."

Laura took a deep breath and tried to grasp anything to hold onto. At least she'd get to drive the car – Nonna's mint-condition classic Nantucket blue 1967 Bel Air.

NONNA

If there's one thing Adriana's learned, it's that a step forward, even in the wrong direction, is a step. As long as she was stepping forward, Laura would figure the rest out. And it got at least one of them out of the damn house. When she heard the front door slam, Adriana settled herself in the BarcaLounger and waited for the kid to get back from the video store.

LAURA

The moment Laura stepped into the aquarium, she knew it was the wrong place for her. Memories of childhood humiliations on field trips came back, Judy's smushed peanut butter and jelly sandwiches on wheat bread while the other kids got burgers and fries at the aquarium restaurant. Not enough money to get anything of significance at the gift shop. Long stories about jellyfish and not enough time in the kelp bed.

The Baltimore Aquarium, known as the National Aquarium, was beautiful. Two huge buildings were stationed directly on the harbor as if the sea animals had swum up from beneath to fill the tanks. But an administrative assistant? She knew she wasn't qualified for much more in this place, but it seemed like an enormous step-down.

A chipper blonde girl with a geeky light blue polo shirt belted into khaki mom pants greeted her at the front desk. "Good morning, and welcome to the National Aquarium! What can I do for you today?"

Laura wanted to turn tail, but she was already there, and going home to Nonna without having done this was unacceptable. She knew she was overdressed. She coughed and said, "I'm here to see James Mackenzie." A look of annoyance crossed Blondie's eyes. Laura looked at her nametag and saw that she was Heather.

Heather said, "On what business?"

Laura stared at her for a long moment. She kind of liked watching her squirm. She must be James Mackenzie's girlfriend. Laura put her hand under the back of her hair and swept it outward. She said, "I had a scheduled appointment."

Relief washed over Heather, and she grinned. "Oh! The new administrative assistant! Go on back." She pointed to the door around the corner, and as Laura approached it, it buzzed. She opened it and stepped out of the blue wonder of the aquarium into a small fluorescent-lit beige hallway with white and beige checked linoleum tile. The smells went from carpet and wet stone to corporate: old coffee, bathroom cleaner, Xerox machines. She progressed uncertainly – the checkered floor and long hallway making her feel a bit like Alice – until a door next to her opened and Heather popped her head through. "Down the hall, two lefts, a right, and it's on your left."

Laura walked down what seemed a hallway so long that it was like one of those mini-mall bathroom halls that really take you around the block before you get to the restroom. She made one left, walked down another hallway that was too long, made another left and then a right, and the further in she got, the more she wanted to run home, and the more trapped she felt. She wished that she could go back to bed in her and Becca's room. A blanket and a long nap would beat the fact that these business shoes were not meant for walking, and she was sweating in her suit.

She slowed as she approached the door on the left of the last hallway, trying to slow her heart rate. She wiped her sweaty palms on her trousers. It was important to look cool. She didn't know why she was so nervous about interviewing for a job she didn't want. But as a rule, Laura hated new people, and the door promised a new person.

When she saw James in his light blue polo and pleated khaki pants, she got a sinking realization that she was probably looking at her future uniform.

James had a long face, craggy with what looked like a painful adolescence of acne now healed permanently into scars on his cheeks and chin. His eyes were narrow and sharply blue under heavy brows, and Laura thought he looked like a young Tommy Lee Jones. He wore an inscrutable expression and acknowledged her entrance with a raise of the eyebrows and a motion to the chair in front of him. No smile. His hair, in a longer cut, was still wet from his morning shower and combed tidily. Laura figured he was probably just a Heather in male form.

Laura sat and tried not to look awkward, as she realized her trousers were a bit tighter than they'd been when she last wore them. She tried not to look at her belly and rested her folder across it. Too much of Janelle's mom-cooking, road food, and no exercise. James sat back in his office chair, which angled him down into a casual leaning position. He put his hand to his chin and considered her for a long moment. She didn't know if she was supposed to talk first.

She said, "Hi."

James said, "So, tell me about yourself." He was so comfortable and in charge, it was annoying.

As Laura wasn't entirely sure of the position for which she was interviewing, answering this question became somewhat difficult. "Well, James, what do you want to know?"

"It's Jamey." No change in facial expression, just a correction. Or a scolding. Laura tried to fight the flush that rose to her cheeks. He said, "Just the basics, where you're from, what you've been up to, where you want to go."

The problem was that the basics were what Laura had lost her handle on. "I just moved out from LA, where I was a movie executive." Jamey stared, waiting for more.

She was embarrassed by the grandiosity of what she'd said and backpedaled, "Really more of a junior exec. Lunches, but a really small expense account." She laughed nervously. Her stepmother always said never laugh at your own jokes, but she had to fill the void somehow. The words "lunches" and "expense account" rang hollowly in this fluorescent-lit office. "I'm not sure what I'm going to do now that I've moved here. I moved to take care of my grandmother."

Jamey cracked a smile. This stymied Laura, who prattled on to fill the void, "But I'm a hard worker." She scrambled for her resume and handed it to him, "I know Windows, Mac, and Excel, can manage any office system and ..." she cleared her throat, "I'm so sorry, Nonna ... um. I never learned what this position is, exactly."

Jamey wheeled his chair to the side and motioned to the bank of file cabinets behind him. "Administrative assistant. Basically, I need someone to take over some of my duties down here so I can better tend to the management of the aquarium itself. I do a lot of processing and filing, and I've had interns help me out, but man, have you ever seen a college student file? They don't care where it goes or if you ever might want to find it again."

Laura asked, "How do you know Adriana?"

Jamey looked earnest. "She did my mom a big favor awhile back. Took care of her when my grammy died."

Laura's ears flushed with humiliation. This interview was a favor for her grandmother, and she was getting a job from a guy who said, "my grammy" in a business interview.

Jamey covered for her embarrassment by saying, "But by your resume, I see that you're self-motivated, that you can run things on your own. When can you start?"

She hadn't given it much thought. But she had no money, and a job seemed like something, and it was a lot cooler in this building than in her room at Nonna's. "Um, Monday? I mean, I guessed you're closed Mondays. Tuesday?"

"Good." This guy's facial expression was just not a change-able thing. She couldn't tell if he was happy she was coming to work, or if he had just mentally ticked off the interview from his list of things to do that day.

"Um. Thanks." Laura knew that thanking him for the job was the right thing to do, but she didn't feel the joy.

He said, "Check in with Heather at the front desk, and she'll give you a uniform."

She was right about the uniform. Jamey turned to his computer, and Laura left. As she walked the long corridors again, the weight of a job she didn't want, a direction she didn't want to go, and a life she hadn't actively chosen, closed in around her.

ADRIANA

Adriana had mixed feelings about taking Rose to the wrap party for *Ball of Fire*. She later wished she'd heeded them.

Rose was the reason she got this job, and she was friends with Dorothy, so she was a natural invite. Edith asked her to bring a guest, and when Adriana suggested her roommate, Edith said, "Of course, of course. She brought you to me."

When Adriana told Rose, she lit up like she'd been given an enormous gift; a mink stole, a diamond bracelet. When she hugged her, Adriana thought the invitation was sealed with such certainty that something would go wrong. She felt guilty for feeling that.

Missy would be there, with Robert Taylor, of course. Adriana was half thrilled to see Missy again, as she was now at a different studio working on another movie. She was half terrified that she would betray her feelings with a look or a glance, worried that this fragile web of desire would be ruined by the presence of the undeniability of spouses.

Wrap parties were not premieres, so the dress had to be casual. Adriana chose a tea dress she'd made for herself of burgundy crepe. With its sloped, triangular neckline, flowing skirt, and draping sleeves, the shape of the dress was garden party, but the color made it appropriate for evening. She pinned a costume brooch of rhinestones set in silver in a whirling circle where the neckline came to a point between her breasts.

Rose came out of the bathroom beautifully made up, her red hair ratted in the fashion of the moment, her makeup impeccable, her short sleeved black crepe curving in all the right places. Adriana was proud to know her and ashamed she had doubted bringing her along. Rose owned the room the way she did when Adriana first met her, ready to provide a sandwich, a pair of stockings, or a job to any girl who might need it. She twirled her finger at Rose who spun for her, beaming.

Adriana nodded, "You'll do."

Rose said, "In a pinch." She moved past Adriana to get her evening bag when Adriana grabbed her elbow and pulled her in for a kiss. Rose met her, but pulled apart quickly, laughing, "You'll mess up my makeup." She got her bag and went to the mirror by the front door, picking at her lipstick.

Adriana said, "Nothing could mess you up, you look gorgeous."

Rose winked, clicked her tongue twice, and said, "All right, sister. Let's swing!"

They arrived when the party was just getting started. Edith answered the door, and she looked like a different person. Instead of her usual severe suits and gloves, she wore an actual dress – black crepe seemed to be the going concern – and her chignon was placed higher than usual. She wore her tinted glasses and a killer diamond necklace. Adriana said, "Well, look at you!" before she caught herself.

But Edith smiled, relaxed in her home. A slender, mustached, kind-faced, balding older man appeared behind her and put his hand around her waist. He said, "Welcome to Casa Ladera. Come in, come in. Can I get you, ladies, a drink?"

Edith said, "This is my husband, Bill Ihnen. Bill, Adriana, and Rose. Adriana's my girl Friday."

Bill took her hand and shook it warmly, saying, "Pleased to meet you. Edith said you're a godsend."

Adriana was stunned to see Edith blush at the presence of her new husband. She knew Edith had gotten re-married the year before but had never met him. She was surprised by how approachable and friendly he seemed. Edith at home was a different woman, and Adriana liked her very much.

Adriana and Rose followed Bill to the bar, which was in the living room. The house was beautiful, a prime example of Hollywood doing Spain in the 1920s. No expense had been spared. It had hand-plastered walls studded with decorative tile and terra cotta floors. The room was lined with tall lead casements and multi-paned windows. They walked through an arched doorway, covered with an elaborate wrought-iron gate into the sunken living room, where the dark wood-raftered ceiling came to a peak from which hung a matching wrought-iron candelabra. It looked like the inside of a small church. She and Rose watched Bill mix gin fizzes as he talked.

"So, Rose, how do you know Edith?" Adriana was grateful he hadn't asked about their relationship specifically. So settled in their private lives, she had forgotten about the outside world and its attitudes. Now, moving in that world, she had exposed something fragile and precious to the air.

Always easy in conversation, Rose said, "I brought my roommate here to Edith when she first got to town. She had made this *incredible* suit ... by hand! Can you believe she was signing up to be an extra?" Adriana beamed at the compliment, relieved at Rose's ease with playing the correct role for the public.

Bill responded appropriately, "No."

Rose said, "Yes. Can you imagine that talent wasted?"

Bill handed them each a glass, cold and tall. Adriana sipped it, grateful for the alcohol and the coolness. Bill said, "Well, thank you, Rose. Edith's been under a lot of pressure lately. I'm glad that you can be there for her, Adriana." He said their names carefully, as if to memorize them. Adriana figured that he must play host frequently. "So glad to meet both of you. Company's on the patio, through that door. Follow the voices."

There was a quiet gentleman peering at a painting in the corner. He was slim, balding, but young, possibly in his early thirties. He had dark hair and a Mediterranean complexion. He looked how Adriana had imagined her brother Angelo but grown.

As they headed out to the backyard, Rose nudged Adriana as she sipped her drink. She raised her eyebrows and flashed a wicked but reassuring smile, and Adriana had to laugh. It was going to be okay.

There was a long table in the backyard, under a grape arbor. The evening had not yet fully settled, but candles hanging in lanterns around the arbor were already lit. The setting sun cast a spell on the garden, and its vine-colored walls made it look enchanted. Adriana was suddenly proud that she had been invited into this inner sanctum. Missy stood with a man at the back of the garden, her hair backlit by the setting sun.

Adriana thought of that moment in *Ball of Fire* where Sugarpuss O'Shea stood in the sunlight purposely to manipulate Potsy, who couldn't resist the lure of the light on her hair. The moment was funny in the movie but hard to see in black and white. Here, Missy's brown hair glowed red, a smile on her face. She wore slacks and a simple blouse. She saw Adriana, and her face lit up. She waved her over and Adriana's heart rose to her chest, thrilled and proud. She drifted toward Missy, trying not to look obvious, when she noticed the man standing next to her. It was the very handsome and very famous Robert Taylor. She knew she had no right to envy, but she was surprised to feel a protective and angry surge fill her chest. Only when she arrived at the couple did she remember that Rose was alongside her. Of course, she was.

Missy kissed her on the cheek and started talking quickly, excitedly. "Adriana, I'm so glad you came. We just saw a rough cut and boy howdy. That dress is going to make those old ladies' eyebrows rise. I expect *hundreds* of letters! Bob, this is Adriana, the miracle worker of the costume department, although don't say anything to Edith. In public, we know Edith did it all ... Adriana this is Bob," she lowered her eyes ever so briefly and blushed, "my husband. I've been telling him all about you. I'm so glad you could meet."

Bob reached out and shook Adriana's hand, smiling. "Nice to meet you." His hand was warm and strong. He had one arm around Missy's waist. He was genuine and immediate, and any hopes Adriana had of the press lying about their relationship dissipated. She forgot herself for a moment, but someone pinched her elbow. She looked over at Rose who was grinning like a teenage fan.

Adriana coughed. "Missy," she flushed, forgetting the usual formality, but pressed on, "Bob, this is my ... roommate, Rose." She hesitated too long before the word roommate. She knew that. She saw Missy flash her a look before she shook Rose's hand, "A pleasure to meet you."

Rose smiled and got demure, "Miss Stanwyck ... I guess it's Mrs. Taylor now. It's a pleasure to meet you."

"Oh, please, call me Missy. If Adriana can, you surely can."

Rose turned to shake Bob's hand, which he met warmly enough, but Adriana noticed his eyes were vacant, his mind on other things.

The group fell silent. Adriana looked at Missy as Bob roped his arm around her waist and squeezed her tighter. She saw a flicker of irritation cross Missy's face, as if this was not the place for that kind of intimacy, or maybe to keep him from laying claim to her at what was essentially her party.

Her eyes lit up as she thought of something, "Hey, Ade, have you met Coop yet?"

Coop. Gary Cooper. He never came to the dailies. He'd gotten too old and famous for that. She said, "Um, no."

Missy slipped out of Bob's arms and took Adriana's hand. She said to Bob, "Honey, forgive me."

Bob laughed. "I won't stop you. The man's an institution."

Missy pulled Adriana's hand through her arm and whisked her off, leaving Rose standing with Bob. Adriana didn't look back at Rose, but she knew she had committed a traitorous act. She and Missy were running away together.

Rose was with a star. She'd be fine.

Missy squeezed her hand as they ducked behind the arbor. "I'm so glad you're here. Sometimes Edith only invites the bigwigs. And you worked so hard."

Adriana stopped in her tracks, Missy with her. She turned, still smiling but saw Adriana's face. Concerned, she said, "Come on, I'm going to introduce you." Adriana had so much she wanted to say to her, none of it appropriate.

Missy looked concerned and said, "Aw, you're shy." She smiled.

Adriana was not at all shy about meeting the old man who was now only six feet away from her. She just wished. She wished. Missy's hand in hers felt so right and maybe ... She knew this was impossible. Missy squeezed her arm again, and Adriana flushed at the touch of her skin.

They passed the Quiet Gentleman from the living room. He was talking to Billy Wilder, who was laughing. The Quiet Gentleman looked up at her as she passed, and something lit up in his face.

Adriana hadn't seen that look on a man since she got to LA, and she knew she was in trouble. She ducked under the arbor with Missy.

It was a full half hour before Edith called from the dining room that dinner was ready. It was a buffet. Blushing with Missy's compliments in their conversation with Gary Cooper, Adriana found her way back to Rose, who was sitting alone on a bench, nursing what had to be – judging by the wobble in her head – her third or fourth drink. She looked up at Adriana, smiling, but her eyes flickered with hurt.

She was humming a song that Adriana recognized as *Be Careful, It's My Heart*. Her mood was dangerous.

Adriana said, "Honey, I'm so sorry. I got caught up."

Rose stared at her a moment before her gaze softened. "It's your party, hon. I'm fine. Bill makes a mean gin fizz." She waggled her glass at her.

Adriana said, "Come on. Let's get some food in our bellies." She reached out her hand and pulled Rose up from the bench. Rose put her arm around her waist and hugged her, too tightly, too long. Adriana gently pushed her off. "Rose. We need to eat. Come on."

Rose said, "That Bob Taylor's a pip! We talked about ranching. Did you know that he and *Missy* have a ranch together? A little slice of heaven out in the valley. I learned things about cows I never wanted to know."

Adriana took her arm firmly in her own and guided her toward the house. "You okay, Rosie?"

Rose laughed. "I'm fine, baby. Show me to the grub."

Rose was leaning on her so heavily as Adriana reached for plates, that she was worried she would fall into the food. No more drinks, some food, a quiet seat in the garden, and she would be fine. There was roast beef with potatoes, broccoli, and a clever salad made with beets and Roquefort dressing. She put extra potatoes on Rose's plate, hoping the starch would help. They retreated to the quiet corner of the garden to Rose's bench and ate together by the warm light of the lanterns.

Adriana tried to keep the conversation going, to soothe whatever had troubled Rose into three drinks on an empty stomach. She said, "They say that the movie should do pretty well. Gary Cooper apparently guarantees a sold-out audience."

Rose laughed, "And what of your Missy?"

"She's not mine, Rose. Please, this is work."

"I know, I know. I'm sorry. I'm just in a mood. The roast beef should set me right up."

She was having trouble cutting a piece, so Adriana reached over and cut a few bites for her. She peered over at the arbor, which had a mercifully full table. With Charles Brackett, Billy Wilder, Howard Hawks, Gary Cooper, and their wives as well as Edith and Bill, it made perfect sense for Adriana and Rose to be sitting where they were. Other secondary players were sitting in other parts of the yard, conversing quietly.

As she finished cutting Rose's meat, she looked up again, startled to see Edith's owlish glasses glinting under the arbor. The reflection of candlelight on her glasses made it hard to see at first, but Adriana realized that Edith was staring right at her. She sat up and away from Rose, uncertain of the reason for her sudden shame.

A pair of soft, brown, wool trousers appeared in front of Adriana. She followed them up to see a starched-white, beautifully crafted man's shirt, open at the collar. The Quiet

Gentleman approached. "Do you ladies mind if I join you?" He had a faint foreign accent that Adriana immediately recognized as Italian.

Adriana craned her neck, uncertain of how this would work, when the gentleman skidded a heavy wrought iron chair through the grass in front of them and took a seat. His eyes were kind, but Adriana felt that blind terror that the interest of a man always brought her. It never led anywhere good.

Rose said, "Sure! I know you from somewhere, don't I?" Clearly the food was not helping.

The gentleman took his plate in one hand and reached out his right hand to shake hers.

"Salvatore Morello. Electrician. I worked on *Robin Hood.*"

Rose shook his hand, and her eyes lit up in recognition. "Of course. Adriana, this guy is amazing. He can climb a scaffolding like a monkey, fix a light in the middle of the catwalk, and be down at the director's side to see its effect in a minute flat."

Feigning enthusiasm, Adriana said, "That's great. Were you on *Ball of Fire* Salvatore?"

Salvatore reached his right hand out to Adriana to shake it. "No. I'm a friend of the Ihnens, so they invited me along." Edith as an "Ihnen" sounded wrong. She'd always been Edith Head, signature and all. "And please, call me Sal." He held her hand for too long. She extracted it gently so as not to offend.

Rose burst out, "See? A *real* nickname. None of this Missy shit."

Adriana scolded, "Rose!"

A look of concern crossed Sal's face, and he looked over to the head table. No one was looking their way. He looked at Rose and then smiled at Adriana, saying, "They served dinner too late."

He was a gentleman. That, at least, was a relief.

As the meal went on, Rose sobered back into her sociable,

manageable self. Sal had worked on so many movies, and they shared stories of various characters they had met in their days in Hollywood. Sal was a generous conversationalist and got along well with Rose, but his glance kept sliding to Adriana, and he constantly shifted the conversation around to include her. If he and Rose were too deep in reverie, he would turn the discussion to the costumes on that particular film. This extra attention made Adriana queasy.

That night as they undressed for bed, Rose sighed a long, heavy sigh. Adriana said, "Rose?"

Rose said, "I do love you, honey. I'm so proud of how much you've done."

Adriana went to her and put her arms around her, holding her close. "Thanks to you, hon. Thanks to you." She knew she said this to remind herself. She was still angry.

Rose kissed her head just behind her ear. "That Sal was kinda sweet on you."

Adriana stiffened. This made Rose step back. "You're not going to go straightsville on me or something are you?" She was genuinely worried.

Adriana snorted. The idea was so preposterous that she started laughing. "Rose, honey, you don't have to worry about me and men. To quote Ms. Stein, 'There is no there, there.'"

Rose was relieved. She put her arms around Adriana's waist and drew her in firmly. "Good. I'm sorry I got a little drunk."

Adriana put her face in Rose's neck and her smell, mixed with processed liquor and face powder and perfume made her anger wane as desire filled its place. She said, "You recovered very well."

Rose said, "Did I?"

Adriana kissed her. She meant it to be a peck, but Rose felt so good, tasted so good and so ready. She kissed her further, realizing that this evening had cured her of Missy. She was married. Adriana was essentially married. She was so relieved to have the force of that extraneous attraction lifted. They could just be them again.

Still kissing Rose, she pushed her backward toward the bed with her hips. Rose said, "Hey there, lady, I have an early call in the morning!"

Adriana said, "You'll sleep better."

The next day at work, Adriana arrived to find a bunch of wildflowers in a small cut glass vase on her desk. Mysterious. Her heart surged from habit as she saw her name written on an envelope. Maybe Missy.

But no more Missy. Only Rose now.

She opened the note, which was written in a gentle, but masculine cursive, with large, looped Ls.

Sitting in the garden with you reminded me of home. These wildflowers did, too. Please have lunch with me. Sal.

She was being wooed. She didn't really have time for wooing. Was she supposed to get in touch with him and say no thanks? Write on the note and send it back? Was it appropriate to get a PA to take a note to him so she didn't have to see him? Adriana thought the best solution for the card was the trash bin. The flowers, she kept. Purple lemon lavender, rosemary, and tiny pink roses. They did look and smell like Italy. Long ago and far away. She set to work.

At noon, Edith sent her out to fetch some sandwiches for the girls. Ordinarily, one of the newer girls would run these errands. When Adriana reminded her of this, Edith just said, "You need some sunshine." And that was it.

Adriana rotated her arms as she left the building and

twisted the crick out of her neck. It did feel good to move her legs, as she'd been kneeling over a pattern for the better part of the morning. She picked up her walk to almost a run, just to feel the blood in her legs again. She skipped up the steps of the commissary and inside. She gave her order to Cookie, a friendly fellow in a paper hat, who always remembered the names of the regulars. Someone was staring at her. She looked over to her left and there, sitting at a table, was Sal, eating a bowl of soup. He smiled and waved at her, too eagerly. She would have to nip this one in the bud. She finished her order and strode over and leaned against the table.

She said, "Soup good?"

Sal lit up when he saw her. "Minestrone. Only not. You know, nothing's like Mama's."

Adriana said, "I get it, you're Italian. I'm Italian. Wouldn't it be lovely? Listen, Sal, you seem like a nice guy, but you're barking up the wrong tree." She knew she couldn't tell him why, that wasn't something people spoke of.

Sal rose to his feet and wiped his chin with his napkin. He was tall, and the way he leaned into her made her take a step back. He didn't speak for a moment, just looked at her, mischief in his eye. The moment went on too long.

Adriana said, "Did you hear the wrong tree part?"

Sal laughed. He said, "Will you have dinner with me tomorrow night?"

She said, "No." It seemed rude. She thought a moment and said, "I'm a working girl, Sal. I'm not looking for a husband or babies. I'm sure there are plenty of other Italian girls out there who would love to start a nice family with you. I'm not the one."

She thought at first that she was being harsh, but judging by the implacability of Sal's face, she hadn't been harsh enough.

He said, "I wasn't proposing marriage. Just dinner."

She heard Cookie call for her order and turned to go. She said, "Take care of yourself, Salvatore."

As she walked away, he called after her, "Chi la dora la vince." Adriana stopped for a moment, stunned. *He who perseveres wins at last.* This was going to be a fight.

When Adriana brought Edith the box of sandwiches, she looked up expectantly. Hijinks. Adriana said, "Did you sic that guy on me?"

Edith said, "Sal's a catch. Don't dismiss him so easily."

"He's not my type."

Adriana thought she saw a cloud cross Edith's face as she turned away, but she couldn't be sure. What was really going on only became apparent later. Years later, Adriana would wonder why she hadn't seen it coming and if she could have done anything to prevent it or change things.

LAURA

Laura's first day of work dragged. She had stacks of papers to file, some letters to write. Jamey left her a folder on his desk covered with stickies and things to do. She filed invoices for fish food, vet bills, invoices for the cafeteria, tickets, the gift shop, thank you letters from schoolchildren. "THANKS FOR TEACHING US ABOUT CRUCIFORMS!"

They were cute, but she didn't understand why they needed filing. She had data forms in files for fish intake, food intake, oxygen intake. Electricity bills to keep up weekly. Donation files. Jamey wasn't in the office when she arrived in the morning. At first, she liked the isolation, no one breathing down her neck, but then she found work in the windowless room endless and depressing.

As twelve-thirty crept up in painfully slow, five-minute increments, Laura decided to go to the cafeteria. She wasn't sure how long a lunch break she was supposed to take. Roadside Productions gave her two hours. But what could she do for two hours? The clock seemed to lose five minutes and then gain an extra five minutes, so by the time she looked up again, it was twelve-thirty-five. She rushed out of the room and down the long hallways. It was only when she burst through the door into the lobby, that she realized she wasn't really late for anything. No one had told her when lunch break was.

There were clusters of schoolchildren everywhere eating lunches out of paper bags. Some were sitting in groups at tables, others on the floor. She had to snatch an aquarium map from the front desk to find her way to the cafeteria. One of the cafeterias could be reached by going up a series of escalators or by going around a ramp in the Pier 3 Pavilion, which wrapped around the largest fish tank Laura had ever seen.

She chose the ramp, which circled up four or five stories and although she started out at a swift pace making her way up, she soon slowed. At least six different kinds of sharks were swimming in circles in the tank, which seemed vaster the further up she went. Some of the sharks had spots, some were gray. Why wouldn't they eat each other? She leaned in and looked up. The tank went up what looked like forever, at least as high as the building. She walked up another two circles and leaned in again, looking down. She startled as a shark skimmed the edge of the tank, swimming close enough to brush her cheek, had it not been for the glass. Their eyes held a blank, cold stare that carried a ferocity – an emotionless killing machine. Or perhaps she had seen *Jaws* too many times.

Someone tugged on her trousers. It was a six-year-old boy, looking anxious. His mother, nun haircut, wide fit into Bermuda shorts wore an expectant smile of pride as her son asked Laura, "Hey, lady. What kind of sharks are those?"

"I, I don't know." She saw the woman's face darken a little, disappointed that Laura was failing her son.

The woman said, "But you *work* here, don't you?" Laura was a bit alarmed by the level of the woman's anger, all that expectation turned into an energy that might turn on her. She was torn between wishing she knew more about sharks and wanting to shove the woman over the rail of the ramp.

She said, "In administration."

The woman said, "He asked a simple question. Maybe you should bone up on the basics."

One little push and this lady would make such a lovely crunch on the main floor three stories below.

A determinedly cheerful voice interrupted them, "Can I help you?"

Great, the boss. She cleared her throat and said with forced brightness, "Hi, Jamey. This boy here ... what's your name?"

"John."

Laura said, "John here was asking what kinds of sharks these are."

Jamey fixed that gaze – what was he thinking? – on Laura for a long, uncomfortable moment. It reminded Laura of Eisenstein's theory that she studied in film class. He said that you could take a shot of a man staring into space and turn it into an emotion by intercutting it with food, translation: hunger; beautiful woman, translation: lust; a child dying, translation: sorrow. Jamey could be looking at her judgmentally, disappointedly, noncommittally, or curiously. He stared another beat before turning to the boy.

"Well, John, these are sand tiger sharks, nurse sharks, and sandbar sharks. Do you think you can pick out which is which?" The mother-threat had passed, and Jamey clearly had things under control, so Laura continued up the ramp to the snack bar as quickly as she could.

Laura got into a rhythm in the afternoon. She tried to embrace the office as her own space. She turned on the radio to an alternative station; they played a few songs she liked. She got into a dancey groove. This would be okay. This was income. She'd save up. It was always easier to get a job when you had a job.

Next lunch break, she'd spend doing research on John Waters. He always made his movies in Baltimore with a Baltimore crew. If she could get on his Baltimore crew ... she'd be happy to be a P.A. She'd hang out with him and his hipster crowd, get to know the young artistic people of Baltimore. She'd be out of this aquarium for good. This was just income and a place to go.

This good vibe stuck around for what seemed like a long time, and then Laura looked at the clock. 2:00 p.m. Half an hour had passed.

This job was death.

When she stepped out of the aquarium to go home that night, her day-long air-conditioned fluorescent chill made the hot, moist air feel good, like a warm bath. She stood for a moment with her eyes closed before going to her car.

Someone brushed by her and said, "Good night." He smelled good – of soap and shaving cream. Laura opened her eyes to see the back of a guy wearing ripped jeans and a nice-fitting T-shirt. His brown hair was longish and shaggy, and the late afternoon sun caught some blonde highlights. It had been a while since simple man energy had made Laura's head turn. She watched him slyly as he approached a 1980-something Cabriolet and unlocked it. She looked away sharply and blushed ... it was Jamey.

She turned and walked to her own car as if she'd been headed that way all along.

CHAPTER ELEVEN

LIZZIE

Artists were commonly loners, so this summer was going to work in my favor. Laura left for work around eight, and Nonna disappeared into the bathroom. That meant I couldn't work on her for at least an hour. Not that I knew what to do. The trip to the grocery – although not to the markets like I'd hoped – was nice, but it hardly restored the Nonna I used to know. When I suggested going to a park, Nonna and Laura just looked at me incredulously. It was like ninety degrees out.

Video Planet didn't open until ten, so I went up to my room and fished around under my bed. I ran into something warm and fuzzy, and I squeezed him and kept reaching until I came up with my sketchbook.

If Calzone was under the bed already, the day was going to be miserably hot.

The picture, which had been haunting me/calling me for over two weeks now didn't look quite as impressive as I'd made it in my head. All the black watercolor I imagined in the photo when I was drawing it wasn't actually there yet. Just the windshield, the cityscape, the outline of the silhouettes of my parents, not yet colored in.

My heroine wouldn't be able to emerge until the worst had happened. Catwoman couldn't be Catwoman until she fell to her death. Bruce Wayne couldn't be Batman until he not only witnessed his parents' death but fell into a cave. What was my cave?

I got out my pen-and-ink set and started to fill in the lines. Once I had fully seen this panel, I could move onto the next. I had to decide whether or not to make the taxi-driver a character. Would he be a villain or just an unwitting idiot who turned the wrong way at the wrong time?

LAURA

Laura awoke to a clatter downstairs. Lizzie must be into something. She should go check. But the kid wasn't her responsibility, and maybe she wanted a glass of milk. Poor kid. Living with an old woman and a basket case of a 29-year-old. She hadn't been good enough to her. But teenagers were so hard to talk to.

It was Rebecca's kid. Maybe she'd bring her to the aquarium one day. She couldn't bring her on a workday obviously ... but on the weekend. She'd take her to the harbor. They could rent a paddleboat and talk about life. There was another clatter, and guilt overcame her leaden limbs and got her out of bed. She was in her underwear and a tank top, but they were just girls, and for God's sake, it was hot.

She slowed as she got to the bottom of the stairs, not wanting to startle Lizzie. She rounded the corner saying, "Lizzie? Is that you?"

Bart was sitting at the table with a full glass of milk and some Keebler cookies. He was wearing madras shorts and a worn T-shirt. The look on his face, the outfit, the cookies and milk made him look like a sneaky child – a strangely handsome and attractive sneaky child. It took Laura a moment to remember her own outfit. She raised her finger and said, "I'll be right back."

One bra and a pair of shorts later, she sat opposite Bart eating cookies. It was amazing how a little distance from LA made her forget entirely what was good for her to eat. Or maybe it was just depression. When she was on top of her game and living with Dexter, life had been a series of protein shakes, low fat, and low carbs. She had been gluten-free and sugar-free and exercised every day.

But right now, these cookies – the Keebler fudge ones with the waxy chocolate on the bottom with chocolate stripes on the top – were the best thing she'd ever eaten, complete with cold milk and the gorgeous face sitting across from her. Laura was embarrassed that despite fighting it, she was building a proper crush on Rebecca's husband's brother. Compounded by her man-energy moment with Jamey, it was downright mortifying.

Bart's sometimes arrogant face looked tired, helpless, and cute. He had something weighing on him. They had gotten past the niceties: he got in using a spare key Nonna had given him in case of emergencies. He suspected it was actually a little metal talisman of guilt. It worked. He had a week off work, so he drove down. Traffic was a bear through Philadelphia, an overturned big rig. He had driven over smashed tomatoes with the other cars. It smelled weird.

Laura said, "But why did you come?"

Bart looked at her, his former controlled look going wide and helpless. "Lizzie." He cleared his throat in a way that surprised Laura ... like he was going to cry.

She wondered if there was something about Lizzie she didn't know. Like some fatal disease. She felt awful. She'd been horribly selfish this past week, hadn't checked in with Lizzie at all. But the girl hadn't shown any signs of distress, other than the expected moping one would do given the circumstances. Laura really was a heartless turd.

She said, "What happened to Lizzie?"

Bart looked at her incredulously, and she remembered their trouble with communication. Her crush began to fade a little, which gave her more control over the conversation. Bart said, "Both of her parents died a month ago. *Violently.*"

Laura huffed, "I'm aware of that. Rebecca was my cousin. I thought you had some new information or something. Why'd you drive all the way down here?"

The anger faded in his eyes, and he looked for the words. She let him, getting up to refill her glass from the milk on the counter. Cold milk tasted like the only thing she should be consuming.

Bart let out a long sigh and breathed in. "George and I were very close."

"I know, I'm sorry." Sorry they were close? She needed to shut up.

Bart didn't seem to mind, "He always looked out for me, worried about me, lectured me. When Lizzie was born, I was at a ... transitional time in my life."

He wasn't perfect. Laura wished she had the luxury to say the same, that she could look back on whatever this time was with such confident hindsight.

Bart said, "George had me down to visit them a few weeks after she was born. It was amazing. They looked so ... *happy.* I mean there was Rebecca, all worn out and puffy, exhausted with this squirmy, helpless little thing. Newborns are gross. Have you ever met a newborn? They writhe and make the most horrible faces." Laura shrugged. She'd never been near one. She avoided Janelle's house for a year after Skyler and Tyler were born. She never understood all the fuss about babies.

He continued, "But the three of them were so *happy*. George was always kind of a didactic pain in the ass, but that weekend he was at his worst. There was some sort of like, newfound gravity to everything he said." Bart shifted in his chair and started pressing his fingers into the crumbs on the table to no apparent end. He said, "He was so fucking serious. He bugged the shit out of me. I mean, later he apologized – he said becoming a father for the first time makes you kinda weird. But there he was, going on about how THIS is what matters in life, and I'd better get my shit together."

Maybe everyone has a Janelle. Laura leaned forward on her elbow, something to let him know she got what he was saying. But he stopped talking. Was there more? Was it polite to ask?

She ventured, "My sister's kinda that way."

Bart went on like he hadn't heard her, "He made me hold the baby. Which I hated."

He dusted the crumbs from the table over the open pack of cookies, stretched his legs out, and sighed. "But one time during the visit, he made me hold Lizzie while she was asleep, her face all mushed up but calm. Her little lips were puckered from all that nursing. He had me sit in the rocking chair and take her in the crook of my arm. I could kinda see what he saw in her."

"And George said, 'This is your niece. I need you to promise me that you will *always* be there for her.' I didn't think much of it at the time ..." He trailed off. She really didn't want him to cry. She should hug him. Carrying this shit around.

She said, "He couldn't have known."

Bart sniffled. Cleared his throat again. "No, of course not. But it's my brother's kid up there, and I pretty much bailed."

"You can't be expected to adopt a teenage girl."

"No. But I should be expected *not* to bail. I have this week off. And ... Jesus. It's my fault anyway."

Laura went over to him, cautiously. She put her hand on his

arm, which he took in his. She said, "Shhhh." Nope. Still attracted. She lowered her arms around his shoulders pressing her face into the side of his neck. He smelled really, *really* good. He smelled like Bart, which right now, smelled better than Dexter.

He undid her arms, and she had a sinking feeling that he was prying her off him, but he got up out of the chair and took her in his arms. He kissed her.

Bad idea. Bad idea.

She kissed back. Their clinch and the awkward noises of kissing echoed in the empty kitchen. He pushed her up against the counter, and she felt a charge of animal attraction she hadn't felt since the early days with Dexter. She sat up on the counter, and he pressed into her, one hand gripped around her back as he pushed into her with his madras shorts, now hard, the other hand traveling up the front of her shirt and under her bra.

Definitely a bad idea.

As if he read her thoughts, he pulled his hand out of her shirt, pulled her into a hug and kissed her on the cheek. Then he leaned away, holding her hand.

She was suddenly bereft, the *all of her* that was actualizing everything they were headed toward was left reaching into the space between them. She was breathing heavily. She tried to calm her breathing and not let on how excited she was.

Bart made no effort in that department as he forced words out, "That would be a bad idea."

Laura said, "Of course."

They both said, "Lizzie."

Laura turned to go upstairs. Without turning around, she said, "There are blankets in the chest in the dining room. You won't need more than one tonight."

ADRIANA

Now that Rose was working again, home became home again. They started inviting company at the weekends, fellow day players and character actors, girls from the costume department. As the rains came for winter, the house was a warm center of good food and company.

Work had gotten chillier, though. Edith wasn't an outgoing, personal type, but she had withdrawn more from Adriana and kept their conversations strictly business, almost curt.

Ordinarily, she would share at least the news of the goings on about the lot, but Adriana got the sense she was being cast out of Edith's favors. Dorothy was called in for set visits, meetings with clients. Adriana was assigned only tasks of pattern-making or sewing.

They started on Missy's new movie, *The Great Man's Lady*, a William Wellman western. Bodices and skirts, familiar and painstaking territory. When Missy came in for fittings, she was friendly enough, but Adriana could see there was some strain involved. Whenever they had a small conversation, Missy would look over to see if Edith was paying attention.

Los Angeles entered its brooding, overcast season, occasioned by deluges of rain. Today it was warmer, and the skies were a constant, unshifting gray.

Adriana was startled to find a note on her desk when she arrived at 7:30 a.m. A PA had probably slipped it in.

She opened it quietly and read it, "Formosa Café, 12:30. Missy." Ordinarily, Adriana would be thrilled, but in light of the recent environment at work, it put her in a panic. The panic ran in an underlying current to a long morning of sewing boning into bodices.

Adriana longed for another modern romantic comedy. They were so much more fun to sew. She loved the art of designing a dress for flow and flattery rather than adhering to the stringent historical guidelines. The morning dragged more slowly than usual, the note and the whispering in the back of her mind running in slow circles. She knew she couldn't speculate about her meeting with Missy, but by the time it came to wrap things up for the morning, she was certain she'd been fired.

By the end of the morning, she finished the second fitting on a bodice and put it aside with a note that said *working* so that one of the finishers wouldn't take it off for its next step to be sewn into the dress. She put on her hat and raincoat, just in case, hopped on her bike, and headed out of the front gate, ringing her bell at Mort, the guard on duty. She loved this job. Edith wouldn't ask a star to fire her. She knew she was being ridiculous.

The clouds darkened as she biked up Gower and, as she turned left onto Santa Monica Boulevard, the rain started to beat down. When the rain clouds came off the ocean and hit land in Los Angeles, it didn't shower so much as flood. She pedaled faster, which seemed to make her wetter as she cruised through quick-forming puddles that splashed up under her trouser legs. Her tennis shoes were soaking. She glided under the awning of the Formosa, wheeled her bike to lean under the window, and went inside.

She checked her watch as she stepped through the door and felt like she was bringing the rainstorm inside. It was twelve-twenty-five. The maitre d' took her to her table, and she was surprised to find Missy already waiting.

She wore a tweed suit, and her hair was in a tight bun, which was unusual because she usually liked to wear it loose down her back. Adriana supposed it was about the rain, but it made Missy look like an older schoolmarm carrying bad news.

Adriana took off her slicker and slid into the booth opposite her but did not slide closer, leaving the wide table between them. She noted that they had the booth in the back and that no tables near them were seated.

Missy smiled at her, stirring her drink. She had a gin and tonic, an odd choice for the weather and the time of day. Adriana followed her cue and ordered one of the same.

Missy said, "Thanks for coming." There was a terrible shadow hanging around her, and Adriana's worry about being fired resurfaced.

Adriana said, "Thanks for having me?" She had no idea what to do. Apparently, Missy didn't either.

The waiter brought her drink and stood for a moment before saying, "Miss Queen, would you like to order?"

"Miss Queen" is what the crew and the people who waited on her at the commissary called Missy. Adriana always found it odd, but it was said with a kindly understanding rather than in a sycophantic way. Missy turned on the charm that Adriana had wanted and needed when she came in but focused it on the waiter. "Thank you, Gus. How's your wife doing?"

"Oh, she's much better, Miss Queen, thanks for asking. They sent her home, and we got her set up good and comfort-

ALTERATIONS

able. Thanks so much for the flowers you sent. They meant the world to her."

"I'm so glad to hear it. You send her my regards, will you?" She looked at the menu. "Let's see, I'll have the shrimp and vegetable stir fry. Easy on the snow peas. Ade?"

Adriana couldn't think about food. "I'll have the steak, rare, with a baked potato, thanks."

If she couldn't find the strength to eat, steak at least would keep until she got home that night.

Gus went off to handle their order, and Missy looked at her for too long, considering.

Adriana said, "Missy, what's going on? You're scaring me. Am I fired?"

Missy smiled, at least her mouth did, but her eyes failed to match. "No. No, honey. It's not that."

She took another sip of her drink. Adriana noticed the lipstick on her straw and realized she'd never seen Missy wear so much makeup mid-day before. Her hair had gray streaks in it. She'd come from the set, which explained the bun. To eat off-lot while shooting was highly unusual.

Adriana asked, "Then what is it?"

"It's Rose."

Was Rose being fired? Was there something about Rose she didn't know? Maybe a mysterious past, something she hadn't thought of? Had Rose been involved with Missy? Her panic must have made it to her face because Missy took her forearm and grasped it, saying, "It's going to be okay, honey. Have a drink. Breathe. Take a minute. I'm sorry, I'm just no good at the words for this." Missy drew herself up, never taking her hand off Adriana's arm. Adriana sucked down half her drink, trying to look as composed as she could.

Missy continued, "It's not Rose. It's Hollywood. I didn't mean to put this on Rose or on you. But Adriana, I know it's all free and easy here, and Hollywood seems liberal-minded, but the truth is?" She leaned in, "We may be able to order Chinese food and gin and tonics for lunch on a rainy day, but we're living in just another small town."

Oh. This really was about Rose. And this really was about Adriana. Her Garden of Eden just off Melrose was being invaded. The bliss had passed. Real life was setting in.

"And, honey, don't get me wrong. I understand you. More than you know." Here she leaned in close and held her eyes steadily, as if hoping to communicate what wasn't allowed to be said. Adriana was elated and crushed at the same time. She hadn't been wrong about their moments together, their exchanges.

Adriana had to say something but couldn't think of the right thing. She placed her hand over Missy's and squeezed. Missy's eyes darted over to the bar, where the waiter had his back to them, organizing their order. She sat back and extracted her hand.

Missy kept the intensity of gaze but from farther away and continued, softly, "We all have our passions when we're young, and that's all right. Sometimes you can keep things going, but it needs to stay on the sly. This town is many great and wonderful things, but on its underside, it's a mean gossip."

The food came to the table, and they both stopped talking. Adriana saw her steak, which smelled good, but she couldn't make her hands work and knew that once she got a bite, it would be hard to swallow. She raised her empty glass to the waiter, and he took it away to the bar. Alcohol would help.

Missy took her fork and started pushing her food around. She was obviously relieved for something to do. She said, "You're in your twenties now, you're building a career, and it's time to think about your future."

Did Missy think of this at the party? Was she a friend trying to help Adriana along or was something else involved? Adriana spoke the words slowly as they formed, "Did Edith set this lunch up?"

Missy took a moment and smiled. "It's not Edith's way, Ade. She spoke of her concerns to me, and I know how she can go *cold* on a girl. I just thought you could use some help about now."

"She's been pushing Sal on me."

"Sal?"

"Skinny Italian grip, quiet."

Missy ate a few bites of her food. Adriana thought she was doing it to buy time. She turned to Adriana, full of new resolve. "It wouldn't be a bad thing for you to think about getting married."

The rain interrupted with a sudden smatter on the awning outside the window above their booth. It wasn't loud enough for the betrayal Adriana was feeling. This needed thunder and lightning.

Marriage? She knew that people didn't accept women having relationships with each other, but was she really expected to marry someone she could never be attracted to? To share her life with someone she didn't care for? Because people expected it? She figured she would keep Rose quiet and be thought an old maid. An artistic old maid. Someday she would costume for a studio directly, and no one would question her singlehood, because she had chosen career.

Adriana said, "I don't understand." She did, but this information just didn't work for her. Living with a man meant ... well, sex. And sex with men had never held any appeal for her.

Missy said, "Honey, it's not so bad. I love Bob something awful."

Adriana didn't know how to phrase what was running through her head. What was she allowed to say? Not supposed to say? She decided to leave Missy out of it. "What's wrong with being a career girl? An old maid?"

"Once the rumors are started, honey, they die hard. Look at Cary and Randy. Cary got married, Randy went along for the honeymoon. He will never get past this."

Adriana said, "I'm not a movie star."

"It still matters. The studio needs to see you married. Settled. Like Edith."

"She was divorced!"

Missy said, "But Bill's known around town, and they're such lovebirds that it worked for them. People forgot."

Adriana loved her job. She loved Rose. She sawed at her steak, rather than talk, because she had nothing to say. The bright red blood pooled on the plate. This wasn't advice being given from a friend. There was something else at play here. She said, "And what if I just say, 'no thank you' and go on my way?"

The time it took for Missy to formulate an answer gave Adriana her answer. Adriana put down her knife and fork and said, "She'd really fire me?"

Missy said, "Edith has trouble – because of being so successful, because of being a woman. She and I can have dinner alone together, and the rumors start up again. 'Hen parties' they call it. That job was hard for Edith to get, and it's harder for her to keep. The boys' club at the studio doesn't want women running their departments."

Adriana had been under the impression that costumes was a department that women *should* run, but she realized that Edith had given her that impression. She said, "How did Edith get the job, then?"

"The opportunity arose, and Edith worked so hard it was too difficult for them to say no. They thought she wouldn't last, but she dug in, and she works like a machine. You've seen how hard she works, after hours, weekends."

Adriana had. But she thought Edith had a strong work ethic. She never thought of her job as being in jeopardy.

Missy said, "As successful as she seems, she's still fighting for that job every day." She took a sip of her drink. "And the kicker? She's half price."

"What?"

Missy's eyes darkened. She was angry now. She said, "Because she's a woman, they don't have to pay Edith as much. She's working all those hours, fighting tooth and nail because of her title. She does okay, don't get me wrong, but a man in her position makes twice as much as she does."

All of Adriana's arguments fell, empty, back to the bottom of her stomach. What had felt like an attack on her, was really a defense of Edith. Missy saw the state of women in film as something to be protected, fought for. Adriana had no ammunition against that.

They fell silent. Missy, relieved of her burden, started eating her food with a newfound interest. Adriana, used to her independence, having extracted herself from an untenable home, having built another with a woman she loved, felt like someone had laid a train track before her and was asking her to get on it. And that track made no sense.

The one thing in the world that had gained her this independence was her work. She was good at it. She was a woman bringing in a modest income, who spent her days in fine company creating things that would stay onscreen forever. She didn't have to depend on anyone else for food or shelter – she'd never again be stuck in a place that she hadn't deliberately put herself in.

She had a piece of this world of Hollywood, and if she wanted to stay in the game, if she wanted to be the next Irene or Edith Head, she was expected to grow up into the real world.

And that might mean leaving Rose behind, leaving their cozy little house. It wasn't fair.

Adriana didn't have to do anything right now. Nobody said she did. She'd go back to work, continue her day. Think about it later.

Missy must have talked to Edith, because that afternoon, she was her old self again, even more friendly than usual. Adriana was somehow complicit in an agreement to which she hadn't consented. She got back to work, grateful the freeze-out had stopped. She told herself that nothing drastic had to be decided right then.

That night she went home early and prepared a Caesar salad and a simple Southern Italian fish stew for Rose. She dug through her underwear drawer for the lipstick case with Rose's heart in it and put it on to remind her where it should be; next to her own. Rose got home at seven to find the candles lit and wine and crusty bread on the table. Adriana dressed up. If paradise was fading, Adriana was going to celebrate every remaining minute. She was ashamed for having squandered any of it.

CHAPTER TWELVE

LIZZIE

I had a dream that morning where Mom and I were sitting in the back of a taxicab at night. She was trying to tell me something. Something important. She was so worried – this was serious. I couldn't hear her or remember what she said. When I woke up, I was crying. I wondered if the pad of pictures I'd been drawing under the bed was really a good thing or if it was going to make me crazy.

I pulled it out to look at it. I couldn't get past the second panel with mom leaning her head on Dad's shoulder. I had to show the accident to get to the core of it, to advance the story, but instead, I started up a conversation between my dad and the cab driver. And it sucked. I tried one where they talked about the weather. I tried another where they talked about the play, which was something about angels. But it all came out stupid. I chucked it back under the bed and went downstairs.

When I got to the living room, I saw that Uncle Bart was on the sofa. He looked like a kid under Nonna's crocheted multi-colored blanket, one arm over his face. I coughed, trying to wake him up, but he didn't move. I walked up next to him. His mouth was open. He was snoring.

When he was sleeping, you could see he had really long, dark lashes like Dad. And you could see that he had a few freckles, like me. They were just over the bridge of his nose. He didn't look enough like Dad. He always looked like Uncle Bart. But his eyelashes and freckles brought a lump to my throat.

I gave one more cough, but he wasn't moving. I went into the kitchen where Nonna was already sitting at the table, reading her newspaper. I sat down opposite her with an extra metal scrape on the linoleum, but Nonna didn't look up from her paper.

I said, "Nonna, did you ever have a job?"

She gave me a sharp look over her glasses, and I could see the old lady face sorta disappear around it. Her eyes softened and crinkled, and she smiled, saying, "A few."

"Did you work in movies?" Duh. The photos. But I got the sense that with Nonna, it would be dangerous to presume. I had to tiptoe forward.

She looked into space, drawing up what I hoped would be a long story. A clue. She shook her head, sighed, and started clearing her space, putting her paper napkin into her bowl, shifting her chair out in the five-part ritual that would lead to her getting up. She said, "That was a long, long time ago, Elizabetta. Another lifetime."

"Good Morning!" Laura was there all showered and in full makeup and that really ugly aquarium uniform. She walked up behind me and put her arms around my shoulders, giving me a squeeze. She said, "You're a good girl, Lizzie." It sounded more like an assignment than a compliment.

I got so lost in her hair and was so surprised by the hug that I felt like crying, which pissed me off. I choked out a, "Morning."

She grabbed a banana off the counter, gave Nonna a kiss on the cheek and said, "I'm running late." Yesterday she didn't leave until eight-thirty, but today she was in a rush. She left by the kitchen door.

Only later, when Bart woke up asking where she was, did I realize that she probably didn't want him to see her in that dorky uniform.

Uncle Bart was going to be here for a week!

After he showered and came down in a new t-shirt, he said, "So, what're we gonna do today?"

He waited, like I'd come up with an answer. Grownups were supposed to decide what you did, not vice versa. It was bad enough I had to make decisions on meals and groceries. I hated the way my voice sounded when I said, "What do *you* want to do?"

Nonna watched me, like she was expecting me to behave a certain way or do a certain something.

Bart said, "Well, what's great about Baltimore?"

Which is why, three hours later, full of crab and soda, we were out in the hot, hot sun on the bay in an aquamarine, fiberglass paddleboat. We sat in blue plastic seats, paddling away. It was too hot to think, and I was dizzy. The water stank and had oil floating on top in purple-and-blue rainbows, ribboned by the wake of the boat.

I thought about how hard it was to draw a picture of water and the fact that the ease with which I could draw *this* water was wrong and gross. Every few paddles, we cut through floating trash: crumpled Styrofoam cups, bits of wrappers for various fast-foods, wrinkly paper. It was a tiny bit cooler on the water than in the parking lot, but out here, there was nowhere to hide from the sun. Even picturesque things, like the aquarium across the bay and the tall buildings didn't look nearly so pretty with the smell or the sounds of our pedaling and panting and the wet sucking of the paddles going in and out of the water. My pedal had a squeak.

Bart said, "I shouldn't have had that beer." We kept pedaling. "So ..." Uncle Bart blew a burp and then continued, "Do you know anything about your new school?"

"It's Catholic."

"Oh."

I remembered that he didn't know anything about that or what it meant. Truth was, I didn't either, except from stories my mom told me. I said, "Uniforms. Mean kids. Maybe nuns."

Uncle Bart said, "Do you need me to beat anyone up?"

I laughed and shoved his shoulder. It was solid and real. I missed my dad's hugs. "No." We pedaled more. "At least not yet."

"Cuz I will. I'll beat someone up if you need me to." He let out a huge belch and said, "Wow. Excuse me. Crab and hot weather."

After about twenty more minutes, it was pretty obvious that fun was not being had.

I said, "Uncle Bart. Uh. This seemed like a good idea and everything, but would it be okay if we took the boat back?"

He said, "Thank you. Stop pedaling for a minute." I did, and he managed to bring us around in a circle. The dock looked horribly far away, and turned around, the sun was in our eyes.

We pedaled quietly for a while, nothing but the drip and suck of the paddles, the squeak of my pedal and the occasional noise of a boat horn from across the water.

He said, "Where do you want to go after?"

I didn't answer. I'd let him figure this one out. I didn't want to be the one in charge for a little while. He said, "After we get something really cold to drink in a really cold air-conditioned Baskin Robbins or something."

That was better.

"Or maybe the aquarium," he said.

Maybe Laura could get us in for free.

NONNA

The house was blessedly empty for a moment. Adriana fixed herself some iced tea and eased her body with its sore, throbbing hip into her chair. She would sit and enjoy the quiet humming around her. Maybe nap. She was too old for all of this *need* that flowed into her house. She felt responsible for all these missteps happening, every single one: Bart, Laura, Lizzie. She wondered if perhaps she had brought this on herself.

But she was too adrift herself to manage *two* lost children. Just the mention of Hollywood had caused her entire being to shift with uneasiness. And that uneasiness shifted to pain at seeing Laura beaten down by life. Life would start making choices for her if she kept avoiding making them herself. Laura needed to get out of the house, even to a crummy job. A few weeks in that crummy job, and she'd look for something that suited her better.

If only Adriana wasn't so tired. If she wasn't so tired, she could make things nice for Lizzie. Do for her like she'd done for her mother, Rebecca. Beautiful Becca.

With the house empty, there was time for a little cry.

LAURA

Laura opened the door to Jamey's office and saw a large, old, dusty cardboard box sitting on the desk with a bright pink sticky on it. She knew it was for her. "Please file. Take your time. Play music." The last command seemed odd until she looked next to the box, where a stack of CDs sat. She started flipping through them.

Jamey's taste in music seemed to be less eclectic than erratic. He had the Stones with They Might be Giants, Kruder Dorfmeister, Nirvana, Miles Davis, The Talking Heads. She stopped looking; it felt a little too close and personal. She tuned around on the radio until she found a jazz station. Laura liked listening to music from the 30s and 40s. It took her into those romantic comedies, where everything was simple. Where she could be Stanwyck, and Cary Grant was out there, somewhere, ready to meet her. Only she needed a new fixation. Cary Grant reminded her too much of Dexter.

The box of papers was interminable. There were purchase orders, work orders, invoices dating back ten years. Random letters. Things that could have been left in the closet. But Billie

Holiday was singing "I Cried for You" with Benny Goodman's orchestra, and she had nowhere better to be.

The best part was, she didn't have to think. About Bart. About how he was an amazing kisser, and she was deeply attracted to him, but she wasn't totally sure she liked the guy. About how their dating would be too complicated. About what to say to him at dinner that night with Lizzie sitting between them, watching – and Nonna.

The yellow slip in her hand was hard to read, but she recognized the company from yesterday's filing. She went to find it.

Three hours later, she was inputting some records from three months ago into Jamey's computer. At least the work had changed. Dizzie Gillespie was heating things up at Massey Hall with Charlie Parker, Charles Mingus, Max Roach, and some other guy Laura couldn't remember the name of. The quintet was playing "Salt Peanuts." She had the music up loud and was in the filing zone. She didn't hear the door open.

Jamey hollered, "Salt Peanuts! Salt Peanuts!" at exactly the right time. Laura scrambled for the boom box to turn the music off.

She said, "I'm sorry. I'm sorry."

"No, no, I love this album. Did you ever hear Dizzy sing 'Salt Peanuts' with Jimmy Carter? Crazy."

She stood up, her legs cramped from sitting and kneeling by the filing cabinet, from her lack of sleep. She blushed, remembering why she hadn't slept much. After the clinch in the kitchen, Laura couldn't get to sleep for several hours. Three times she thought of going down to Bart, three times she talked herself out of it.

Jamey said, "Are you okay? You don't look so good."

She didn't know how to take that. In Hollywood, they say that just before they attack. She brushed off her trousers, which had accumulated bits of browned and crumpled paper. "Fine. Fine."

The song came to an end, a radio ad came on and Laura turned off the radio. There was an awkward pause. The fluorescent lighting buzzed. The absurdly tiny aquarium next to Jamie's desk bubbled. The goldfish gawped. Jamey seemed unperturbed by the silence. As he stared into space, expression-free, Laura found herself wondering if he smoked a lot of pot.

She ventured, "So ..."

He startled. "Right. No. Um. I came down here to give you a break. You haven't had an official tour yet, aside from our ergonomically designed back hallways ..."

She said, "Could we grab some lunch?"

He stood by the door and held it open, "The Rusty Scupper awaits."

Once outside his office, they went in a different direction and walked down a seemingly endless hallway, doglegging right or left. Jamey didn't say anything, and Laura was too tired to venture conversation. Any question that came to her head was already answered or seemed inane: *How long have you worked here? Do you have much contact with the sea animals?*

When they left the hallway, the echoing sounds of the aquarium surrounded them, packs of children, a screaming baby, the baritone voiceover warble from a movie about whales playing in one of the halls, and an overall background hum she couldn't place.

Jamey breathed deeply and smiled. "Aaah, freedom."

Laura said, "Great."

"I'm sorry. I was in that hole for seven years, so count yourself lucky you're only two days in. Follow me."

He started walking through the crowds, which seemed to part around him. Laura followed a few paces behind, finding her way littered with obstacles: a stroller, a very tall man in a

"Don't Mess with Texas" T-shirt, another surly mom, whom she gave wide berth. Jamey ducked into a darkened hallway filled with tanks. She lost him.

She scooted into the corridor, squinting in the dark. The only light came from the tanks, which lit up the faces of excited children, pixelated schoolteachers, and exhausted parents. She headed toward the light at the end of the hallway, when a hand grabbed her arm and pulled her backward, stopping her short. It was Jamey standing in front of a tank full of jellies.

He said, "Check it."

The jellies were large and beige with long ruffled pink skirts hanging below them. There was some feathery matter floating in the tank around them. Laura couldn't tell if the particles were made of jellyfish food or if they were bits of the jellies that had fallen off.

She looked for what she thought was a polite amount of time and said, "Cool." She looked at Jamey nervously, but he smiled. He looked almost handsome in this subtle lighting, his clear blue eyes reflecting the light of from the tank. Laura hadn't thought of aquarium light as flattering, but it was up there with candlelight.

She needed to eat something. Fast. She was getting dizzy.

Jamey said, "No, look closer." His finger touched the glass, and she leaned in and squinted.

The bits of material floating in the tank that were no bigger than a pinhead were moving in a familiar pattern. She retrained her eyes and saw baby jellies, swimming in tiny little pushing thrusts, an entire empire of primordial creatures in a space she'd imagined to be empty. A chill ran down her neck and up her arms. She said, "Wow. How many are there?"

"Thousands."

And just as quickly, he was off. She scrambled to keep up. They were standing in line at the cafeteria for a while before she noticed that the place wasn't called the Rusty Scupper at all. This guy had a sense of humor. She had to eat something.

She had the mess of Bart waiting for her back home, and there she was crushing on the aquarium dork who gave her a job because of her grandmother. She grabbed an orange juice from the case and cracked it open and took a slug.

Jamey said, "How are you liking Baltimore so far?"

"Sucks." She shouldn't have said that so quickly. "I'm sorry. I don't. Things are kind of." She stopped and regained herself. "I haven't gotten to see much of it yet, aside from Nonna's house."

Jamey laughed. He moved his tray up the line to the hot food section. He hollered, "How do, Jerome? What's good today?"

Jerome looked up. He was an older man in a paper hat. "Hey, there. Who's the new blood?"

"This is Laura. Laura, this is Jerome. Laura's saving me from my office."

"Bout time somebody did," said Jerome, "The barbecue's pretty good today. I'd stay away from the Mac n' cheese ... it's been out awhile. But Bobby was *inspired* when he mixed up his barbecue sauce last night, and I have to say ..." he leaned forward confidentially, "...it's pretty good."

Jamey plunked his tray up on top and said, "Hook me up."

"And for the lady?"

Laura put her tray up. "Load me up, too. I'm starving."

Jerome laughed and said, "I like a woman who eats."

An hour later, Laura was completely stuffed and wondering whether Jamey had just invited her on a date and what she thought about that. He sensed her confusion and said, "No biggie. It's just a couplea friends of mine who jam every Saturday at this bar. I could introduce you to some folks outside the octo-genarian set."

Not a date. Safe. But she really wanted to go home and curl up in a blanket. And could she bring Bart? She didn't want to bring Bart. They weren't really a thing, and he was going back to New York, and she was here. In Baltimore. She had a flash of Bart pressing her up against the counter, his whiskers scratching her chin, and his hand on her breast. She flushed.

Jamey said, "I'm sorry. I didn't. It's not a *date*. I mean it wouldn't look too cool for me to go hitting on you right after hiring you after all your grandmother's done for my family."

Laura had too many emotions going on to get a handle. Her stomach burbled, full of barbecue and French fries. Jamey looked embarrassed.

She stumbled, "No. No. Nonono. I didn't think. It wasn't. I know, you're just being extremely cool to me because I'm new here. It's the – The barbecue was great. It just isn't agreeing with me right now."

She and Bart had nothing in common. They had a partial make-out session. He was going back to New York. If she was going to have a life, she'd have to start working at it.

Jamey was still trying to soothe her nerves. "Not that I *wouldn't* ask you out. I just meant it wouldn't be *right* ..." He trailed off.

Despite the flutter in her throat and the feeling of a live animal shifting around uncomfortably in her stomach, she said, "I would love to come check out your friend's band. Thank you."

Jamey stopped looking at her and looked up over her shoul-der. He smiled at someone in that friendly, helpful way and said, "Can I help you?" Laura supposed he was always on duty, even at lunch.

"Hey Laura." Bart's voice sent a zing to her khaki trousers

and raised the hairs on her neck like a bad horror movie. She breathed in and got up. Bart looked sweaty and exhausted.

Lizzie was with him. She had a wolfish, hungry look, exacerbated by a purple something on her upper lip that brought out the fact that she was growing a tiny mustache. Was Laura going to have to teach her to wax, too? Annoyance, excitement, embarrassment. and sheer shock ran through her.

Laura said, "Hieee ... What are you guys doing here?"

Lizzie said, "We thought you could get us in for free ..."

Bart interjected, "I told Lizzie I could spot us a couplea tickets. We've just been enjoying the air conditioning and the sights. Thought we'd take a shake break."

He looked over at Jamey, who got up as well. Laura wanted everyone to go away.

She said, "Bart, Lizzie, this is Jamey, my boss. Jamey, this is Lizzie, my ... cousin or something. She's my cousin's daughter which makes her Adriana's ..."

Lizzie said, "Great granddaughter."

Laura said, "And this is Bart, he's my ..." *Dead cousin's brother-in-law?*

Lizzie offered, "He's my uncle."

Jamey shook both of their hands. "Nice to meet you both."

Bart said, "Didn't want to interrupt you." He looked to both Jamey and Laura. Laura realized he was trying to figure out their relationship. Was he interested in her for more than a quick scuffle in the kitchen? Attraction surged in her, and Bart said, "We just wanted to say hi."

Laura checked her watch. "Well ... hi. I gotta get back to work."

Jamey said, "Lizzie, did you get to see the baby otters yet?"

Her eyes lit up. "*Baby* otters? No way!"

He said, "Come with me." Lizzie was at his side in an instant.

Bart turned to Laura for a moment, his hands in his pockets. "Sorry. I didn't mean to interrupt."

Laura said, "It's fine. Fine."

He looked at her a long beat, a flicker of desire in his eyes, then doubt. For a moment, she thought he was going to kiss her and, even though it would have been enormously inappropriate, she wanted him to. She looked at Lizzie and Jamey who were at the far end of the cafeteria. She said, "You better catch up there, Uncle Bart. That dude is fast."

He stared at her a moment longer. No words. She started to feel uncomfortable, just as he turned and jogged after Lizzie and her boss.

Laura made her way to the ladies' room, which smelled pretty ripe from the post-lunch crowd. She went into a far stall, despite her fear of public restrooms, she pulled up the toilet seat and promptly threw up her entire lunch. She was grateful Jamey was male, no chance of his setting foot in there.

LIZZIE

It was the best day ever. At least since ... okay, it was the best day since I moved in with Nonna.

The baby otters were so cute they shook away the dark drawing under my bed, and Jamey also showed me the baby seals. Uncle Bart was just happy for air conditioning. He bought me a book about otters from the gift shop at the end of the day and picked up pizza and salad on the way back to Nonna's. I got the feeling that Uncle Bart made bank. Which would be a big argument for my going to live with him. I wondered if he could at least get Nonna cable. Or a new computer.

We got home after Laura. She had changed and looked tons prettier in a tank top and shorts than in that dorkwear from the aquarium. She was all bizarro when we got home. For a second there, I thought she had a thing for Uncle Bart when she first saw him and lit up – she could have had hearts in her eyes. But two seconds later, she was crabby and sniping at him.

They argued about four different things before they got to music.

She said, "Jazz is the center and the heart of American music. How can you not admit that?"

He said, "I never said it wasn't *important*. I just said I don't like it.

"That's like saying you don't like garlic."

"What?"

She said, "It's the base and the heart of all food, but you go ahead and eat your Bulgogi or whatnot."

"I'm *Japanese*."

"So, you don't like garlic?"

"*What* exactly is your problem?"

Laura said, "I don't have a problem. I was just making a point."

"Whatever." Bart popped open the pizza. I mixed up a dressing like my mom taught me, with vinegar, oil, a tiny bit of mustard, sugar, salt, and pepper. I put it on the salad and put the pouches of takeout dressing on the counter. Thousand Island. Ew. Nonna was strangely quiet. I was worried it was because I'd talked about Hollywood that morning. There had to be another way in.

When we sat down to eat, Nonna said, "Grace, please."

None of us knew what to do. I said, "What?"

She said, "Can you say Grace, Lizzie?"

I said, "Grace."

She looked angry for a minute but then smiled. Then she laughed, murmuring something in Italian. She said, "In the name of the Father and the Son and the Holy Spirit, Amen. Bless us, oh Lord, and these thy gifts, which we are about to receive, from thy bounty through Christ Our Lord, Amen." Laura and Nonna touched their forehead and their chest and their shoulders ... I forgot what it's called, but I'd seen it before in movies, at Easter at Nonna's, and then at the funeral. Uncle Bart only bowed his head, looking awkward and embarrassed.

Laura started serving up the pizza.

Nonna said, "We are going to have to give you a catch-up course in Catholic stuff, Lizzie, before I send you to school.

Laura said, "You're sending her to *Catholic* school?"

I think Nonna glared at her, but the back of her head was toward me, so I couldn't tell.

LAURA

.

Bart's an asshole. That's pretty much it.

Laura lay in bed that night unable to sleep, staring at the ceiling, fuming over dinner. She tried to put it from her mind, tried to think of jellyfish babies or filing, anything to settle her down, but sleep wasn't coming. He rubbed her the wrong way, and that drove her nuts.

At midnight, she crept out of her room and padded downstairs for a glass of milk. She sighed as she opened the fridge.

"Always in a huff." Bart's voice scared the crap out of her, and she dropped the milk, which started glugging out onto the floor.

She said, "Goddamn it." She recovered it, but there was still a good cup of milk seeping across the floor to that irrecoverable place under the fridge. A dishtowel dropped in front of the milk just as it got to the edge. Bart crouched down next to her. He smelled good. She hated that.

He said, "I'm sorry. I thought you knew I was here."

She didn't say anything but sopped up the milk and went to the sink for the sponge.

He said, "I couldn't sleep."

He was going back to New York. It was a flirtation, that was all. She was angry she was letting herself get so upset over a kiss and half a grope.

She sponged up the floor and tossed the sponge into the sink.

He said, "So, this Jamey guy, your boss ..."

"*Really?*"

He fell quiet.

She said, "Why did you kiss me?" It was a stupid question.

He said, "Cuz you're hot."

It was so instantaneous and stupid an answer that she flushed.

"Really?" She hadn't felt sexy in at least a full year, since Dexter made that comment about Roadside and her likelihood of getting a job.

Bart looked scruffy and adorable. He hadn't shaved yet and his brows knit together with concern, making him look like a perplexed child. But the bulging veins in his muscled forearm brought back the night before in a way that quashed her anger.

Which made her mad. She said, "So, what's it going to be? Are you going to keep coming around all the time?"

He said, "Of course, I'm going to keep coming around. Lizzie."

"I mean, can I feel free to get on with my life?"

Anger flashed. He said, "What, like I'm *stopping* you? Otter boy seemed pretty well ready to make a move."

Bart was jealous. That was cute.

She said, "What, so you want a relationship? After one kiss?" She regretted it the moment she said it. It diminished the power of what she had felt the night before.

The veins on Bart's forehead stood out. He blushed scarlet. And it couldn't unsay itself.

She said, "I didn't mean ..."

He stood up, and the chair scraped loudly against the linoleum. He walked over toward her with such intensity she worried he would slap her. He backed her up against the fridge and kissed her deep and long. Maybe she was more tired, maybe she'd thought about it the whole night before, maybe it was the way he was so *angry*, but she was weak in the knees. He pulled her into his arms. They kissed some more. Her hand crept up to his chest, another to his face, and they parted.

Very bad idea.

When they broke apart, she took him by the hand and led him upstairs to her room, closing the door gently.

They made love on the bed where she had her first sexual awakenings when, as a kid, she looked at dirty magazines with her cousin. Having sex with her dead cousin's brother-in-law was all wrong and strange. But she was pulling at his shorts, and he smelled so good, and when he kissed her sides and nibbled at her breasts with his hot breath through the shirt, all of that seemed not to matter. It had been a long time since she'd had basic, sober, amazing sex. Bart was somewhat embarrassed when he pulled a condom out of his wallet. She tried not to think about the kind of guy who has a condom at the ready. She was grateful for the protection and plunged herself into the desire at hand. Fortunately, these little beds didn't squeak.

They fell asleep in each other's arms after but woke quickly from the heat. Bart pried his arm off her, and it loosened with an audible rip. They both laughed. He kissed her again. He looked her over, worried. She knew the questions in his face: did this mean they were committed? Had he complicated things? She smoothed the worried wrinkles in his brow and kissed him.

She said, "Don't worry. I think we both needed that." His

entire body relaxed so quickly that Laura was resentful. She was forever letting men off the hook.

Bart sat upright and leaned against the wall, looking down at her, his finger tracing her shoulder absently for a few moments. She could see he was thinking on something, but the sensation of the tracings on her shoulder made her comfortable and drowsy.

Bart huffed, exasperated.

Laura said, "What?"

He said, "I'm sorry."

"Sorry you slept with me?"

"No."

This buoyed her a little. She smiled and said, "I'm sorry to be so complicated. I'm not in a good place right now."

He said, "Me neither."

"At least you have a job and your own place in a real city."

Bart looked up at her. She didn't say anything, knowing that he was making up his mind whether or not to divulge something. He stared across the room and said, "I miss my brother. I mean, not like we need to talk or like when someone goes away. But he was *there,* and now he's *not.* And I don't know what to do with the *not.* And I'm so *tired* all the time. And I can't seem to focus on anything. I go home from work, and there I am in my apartment ... don't get me wrong, I've got a nice place. I used to go out with my friends every night to some hip restaurant or to hear a band, but I just don't feel like it anymore. And the television isn't about much, and I don't so much read and even music sounds all wrong. And Matilda, I can't handle Matilda right now."

Laura stiffened, realizing, "Matilda's your girlfriend." She pulled the sheet up around her, the sweetness of the night turning into something else. She sat up opposite him, the sheet held to her chest like a towel. It was one thing to take this as a one-night stand. Another thing entirely to consider that there was a girlfriend in play.

"Was. Is. I haven't really called her in a while."

"Oh." Maybe it was over. Not like they were *on*, but the fact that it was over made things less awful.

He said, "I mean, I'm probably going to dump her."

His choice of words stung. Dexter had *dumped* her. He hadn't really broken up with her. He just slept with someone else. Guys were passive aggressive dumpers. Women broke up.

She said, "What do you do with all your time at home?"

He said, "Mostly, I sleep."

Laura laughed, nodding. "I did that for a while there."

Bart said, "And I think about George. I think about him more now that he's gone than I did when he was in the suburbs."

Laura said, "This is Becca's room. At least the room where we stayed when we were little."

Bart looked around, taking in the details, now lit orange from the streetlamp outside. He said, "I hadn't thought of that."

"It's weird."

He said, "I have this ..." he rubbed his face up and down as he came up with the word. She definitely had feelings for this face. "... thing. It's not a thing, but I've kind of turned it into a thing that I've been carrying around, and I don't know what to do with it."

Laura waited.

He said, "It was my fault, you know, the cab accident."

"What?"

He said, "I mean. It was their anniversary. Fifteen years."

This struck Laura. The last time she saw Rebecca in person was near her five-year anniversary when they caught lunch in New York when she was flying through. That made it ten years since she'd seen her.

"I got them tickets to *Perestroika*, you know, *Angels in America?*"

Laura said, "And?"

"They wouldn't have been in the city otherwise."

Oh. Laura thought for a moment. She could see how some guilt might be involved, how he might feel somehow responsible, but it wasn't like he cut the cab's brakes or was driving the other car.

A long moment passed.

Bart said, "I need to tell Lizzie."

"You do NOT need to tell Lizzie."

"She deserves to know."

Laura reached over and took Bart's hand in her own. "Don't tell Lizzie. It wasn't your fault. The accident. It sucks, and the timing was horrible, but whatever killed those two was bigger than some tickets to a Broadway show."

He didn't respond.

She said, "And Lizzie has enough shit to deal with. Don't lay this on her."

"I wasn't going to *lay* it on her."

Laura said, "Think about it. Who will it help if you tell?"

He looked at her. "It's horrible. I see Lizzie, and she's ..."

"She's so needy." Laura said that too fast. And it felt wrong somehow to be sitting here naked with Lizzie's Uncle talking about her.

Bart said, "She's really, really needy." He laughed. "Oh, God, I'm going to hell."

Relieved, Laura said, "You and me both. She's a raw nerve. Like me after my mom left. I feel so, so bad for her, but I don't know what to do with her."

Bart paused for a moment, then said, "The aquarium was a good thing."

"I can't take her there every day. I have to work."

Bart said, "I know it's good to spend time with her, but I'm not my brother, you know? I'm not giving her enough. She's always wanting, needing more. When she hugs me, I feel ..." he trailed off. He said, "Insufficient. And she's not George."

Laura snorted a laugh.

Bart said, "I mean. His *not* there is kind of stronger when she's around."

"She's definitely not Becca. Becca was *wicked*."

He said, "Poor kid."

There was a long pause. Bart said, "Now I'm depressed."

Laura said, "Cuz you weren't before?"

He leaned forward and kissed her on the forehead. He said, "Thanks."

She wasn't sure if he was thanking her for the sex or for the advice. She hoped it was the latter.

He said, "I'd better hit the hay."

Laura was still holding his hand. They looked at each other for an awkward moment, and Bart pulled his hand away, stood up, and put on his shorts.

He said, "I'm sorry."

She hoped he *didn't* mean about the sex.

She said, too forced, "Nothing to be sorry for. Goodnight."

He crept out, closing the door behind him. She heard him pad down the stairs, and she flumped down onto the bed. She was agitated but exhausted and drifted off into a sweaty sleep.

CHAPTER THIRTEEN

ADRIANA

It didn't happen all at once. Adriana didn't leave the Formosa that day resolved to go and live a married life. But the arrows in her life, one by one, started pointing that way.

She never told Rose about her conversation with Missy.

Rose's role in the movie went well, and once the movie opened, she was offered more and more supporting roles, the best friend, the sister, the aunt. She was home less often. Adriana didn't think much of it at first. Rose was happy and didn't seem to notice the subtle shift in Adriana's attitude toward their public role. They were both busy, so not going out for dinner was expected. Adriana became artful at declining public social opportunities, parties, dinners. Rose accused her of being a homebody and started going out with her friends on her own.

Despite Adriana's constant refusals, Sal did not let up the wooing. He left flowers, notes, baskets of food. Sometimes he would pick things up from an Italian deli and leave them on her worktable before she got to work in the morning. Flavors of the old country. He was sweet, really. And, if only to give the illusion that she'd listened to advice, she agreed to see him one day for lunch, for dinner the next. She let him take her to the Brown Derby. He was kind enough, and people around her affirmed her genuine affection for him. He made her laugh.

She saw Missy less often as she was loaned out to other studios. Moving between studios was a privilege Missy fought for. Usually when a studio had an actress, it owned her. But everybody wanted Stanwyck, and she had a gentle but unwavering will and managed to convince her superiors.

When Adriana did see Missy, she greeted her warmly. There was an understood friendship between them, but never again did they talk so intimately or frankly as at the Formosa. Adriana found that she was relieved by this new definition to their relationship; that if she didn't talk about Sal or Rose, she wouldn't have to admit that things were changing.

Adriana was invited to Edith's with Sal regularly. Edith and Bill had become the surrogate in-laws, quietly encouraging the relationship. One night, after too much wine, Adriana and Sal got into the car to drive home from Edith's house, and she let him kiss her. With no love or attraction in the kiss, she found it to be the sum of its parts, whiskers, wet, warm tongue, intrusive. It was not a kiss, so much as a not-kiss.

Adriana felt herself step outside and watch with curiosity. The black leather seats of the car, the bougainvillea, a fluorescent fuchsia in the dying light of evening. Sal's hand went to her waist and inched upward in an attempt to graze the side of her breast. This graceful, polite man had been reduced to the clumsy advances of a boy. How curious to have such intimacy without want or need. What strange animals, humans.

She let the kiss go long enough to encourage him but then pulled away. There was only so far you were allowed to let a man go before marriage. She thought what they did after might be problematic, but she might be able to cope. She got out of the car, and her heart sank as she realized that in reality, she was actually entertaining this absurd idea.

She went straight to the bathroom when she got in the house that evening and washed the kiss away. She saw that her chin was red from Sal's whiskers. Fortunately, Rose wasn't home yet. Rose was always shooting and home so little these days that she was completely unaware that Adriana had other social engagements. She had no idea about Sal. Edith. Missy. Adriana's new choice of lifestyle seemed more illicit than her life with Rose.

Summer came on, marine layer in the mornings, warm, dry afternoons, and long evenings. In celebration of a wrap of a particularly grueling movie, The Road to Morocco, or more specifically, to celebrate seeing Adriana regularly again, Sal planned a picnic in the Hollywood Hills. He said that Adriana needed air and dirt again, to become part of the earth or she'd turn to celluloid. She had to say she agreed. It felt downright wicked not working on a Wednesday, but Edith had mysteriously given her a day off. As a reward for her hard-working weekends, she said.

Sal packed the basket. She brought the wine and a blanket. Late afternoon, they hiked like mountain goats up a path in Bronson canyon. The higher up they got, the more Adriana heard her feet hitting the dry packed sand that passed for dirt in the hills and smelled the eucalyptus and fennel, the more she dreamed she was in Italy, a little girl, roaming the hills behind her grandmother's house. She laughed and went farther and faster. Sal panted to keep up. She reached the top first, exhilarated by the climb and the warm, dry air. She raised her hands up to the sky as a cool breeze blew the evening in from the West. It was not a bad life.

She spread the blanket and settled herself in before she saw Sal rounding the last corner of the trail, his breath laboring, his bald pate shining. She had to laugh. He saw her, and his face lit up in a broad smile. As he approached, she saw in his eyes that he was really and truly in love with her, and it saddened her.

She really liked Sal. She had developed a genuine friendship with him. They had a quick banter when they were together, and she laughed when he shook his head and tossed out Italian proverbs. They liked the same food. But never in her life, even with trying, would she be attracted to him nor could she truly love him.

He must have seen her smile fade, for his faded as well. "What's wrong, Adriana? Do you feel ill?" He sat down on the blanket next to her and took her elbow. She loved the way he said her name, like her brother used to. He would take care of her. That she knew.

"No. No. It must have been the hike."

Sal laughed and said, "Ha! I knew you were faking it. Sitting there cool as a cucumber while I ..." he clutched his chest and breathed heavily.

She laughed. He was a lovely man. She didn't want to hurt him.

He said, "Open the basket. I made a special treat for us."

She opened the basket and found a red and white checked cloth covering the food. On top of that cloth was a small velvet box.

Oh.

Her stomach flopped, and she saw white splotches. Sal's voice sounded distant and tinny as he said, "What's that? Someone gave us dessert first!"

He reached in and grabbed the box. Adriana steadied herself. What was she supposed to say? She knew what was coming, but if she said no right away, what would happen next?

Would Missy take her out again for a serious talk? Would Edith fire her? And Rose. How could she have done this to Rose? She led Sal on because it had been a safe place to be for a while, but now he was going to propose a long-term safe place. She loved her job. She loved Rose.

What would Rose say?

"Adriana, il mio amore, salete la mia moglie?"

Adriana blinked hard. If she breathed deeply, she wouldn't throw up. She had to say no, of course, but there was Sal, with his eyes all earnest, exuding his confidence in her appropriate reply. If she told him no. If she told him no ...

He said, "Have you forgotten your Italian?"

"Naturalmente, non."

"Non?" He teased, with a mock pout.

"Oh, Salvatore." She raised her hand to his cheek and looked at him a long moment. How one of Missy's speeches from her movies would have helped now. *Maybe not now, maybe not tomorrow, but* ... She fished around for words and said, "Honey. I need to think on this. It's so sudden." She would talk it over with Rose that night. She'd know how to handle it. She shouldn't have let things go so far.

He lowered the ring and closed the box, pocketing it. He said softly, "Capisco." *I understand.*

She kissed him on the cheek, put her arms around him, and hugged him for a long, comforting moment.

She looked into the basket and lifted the cloth, "So, what's for dinner?" She was surprised to find a half-bottle of champagne and two glasses, no food. She looked up at Sal, questioning.

He smiled, "We have dinner plans. Had. For after. Edith wants us to her house."

"Oh."

His face lightened again. "Come, let's go. You know she has

a wonderful cook, let's go and relax together, just the four of us. It will be a beautiful evening at Casa Ladera."

"We just got here." She objected for a moment but then knew. He had brought her up there for one reason. To propose, while Los Angeles lay at their feet bathed in June evening light. And she had ruined it.

She hopped to her feet and dusted off her skirt. "We're due." She held out her hand for him, and he smiled, taking hers. All the way down the hill, she didn't let it go.

Adriana hadn't thought about *why* they would have dinner at Edith's house on the same night Sal proposed, until the front door opened. Edith was standing in her entryway with a grin on her face and her arms wide open.

"There she is!" She hollered over her shoulder, "Bill, Bill, the lovebirds have arrived!"

Sal leaned in behind her and spoke into her hair, "I'm sorry. I ... I was hopeful."

Bill came up behind Edith, a cocktail mixer in his hand. "Congratulations!"

It would be okay. She would explain that she was thinking about it. Edith couldn't fault her for that. She'd make up a very good reason why the answer was no. It was customary for a girl to think these things over.

Edith hugged her, Bill hugged her, and soon the happy couple was whisked into the living room where Bill stopped at the bar and raised one questioning eyebrow as Edith continued on into the garden. Adriana's stomach churned as she heard a cocktail party's number of voices coming from the garden. She nodded vigorously at Bill who grinned and filled a glass with ice.

Sal said, "You have company?" His voice was so full of despair that Adriana clasped his hand.

Bill said, "*You* have company. Edith was so excited she put together a party for you." Bill poured some gin into the glass for Adriana's customary gin fizz. He put the bottle down.

Adriana said, "Straight, on the rocks would be great." Adriana saw the cloud of concern cross his face as he filled the glass, but she needed a stiff one to face whoever was in that garden.

She sucked down some gin and, anxious not to abandon Sal, put her arm tightly around his waist, and they headed out to see whoever was waiting. They were in this embarrassment together.

There was a flurry of friendly faces from the shop, and a cheer went up when they stepped outside. Missy walked up first, and Sal took Adriana's drink so she could welcome her.

She took both her hands and said softly, "Well, let's look at you, promised and all." She pulled Adriana in for a hug, whispering into her ear, "Awful, it's just awful." *The party? The proposal? The setup?* She was super intense, but fortunately, people were stepping forward to congratulate Sal. It also had to be awkward for him, as she hadn't accepted him.

It was when she broke the hug that she saw Rose lurking behind one of the vine-wrapped columns of the arbor, her face red – her eyes darting and angry. She started toward her when Missy grabbed her shoulders and pulled her in, holding her gaze, serious, worried.

She said, "I didn't know she was inviting Rose, or I wouldn't have let this happen. Edith's intractable about these things. Maybe take a minute before you ... just take a minute, okay?" The cautionary look on her face, the clutch of her hands on her shoulders and Adriana saw it all. This had only ever been about appearances. She pulled away from her and went to Rose.

She slowed and approached Rose who was sidling along the wall. Adriana had no idea what she could say to her, surrounded by people. When Rose saw her coming, she walked away along the outside garden wall, making her way back to the house. As Adriana got closer to her, Rose walked faster.

Adriana said, "Rose."

Rose turned around. Tears ran down her face. She grabbed Rose's elbow and, as Rose yanked it away, her eyes flashing. She opened her mouth to speak, but shook her head, wiping her tears as she looked back at the crowd under the arbor.

Rose said slowly, her voice shaking, "If you ever loved me, you'll let me go home. I'll talk to you at home. I cannot. I cannot possibly talk now. This is *beyond* imagining. Like some horrible dream or a trick."

"Rose, I didn't accept. I'm so sorry, I didn't accept, though. I won't marry him."

Rose looked at her, incredulous. Adriana could see volumes of words forming in her head and being cast aside. Rose spoke slowly. "Let. Me. Go."

When Adriana went back to the group, she wiped her burgeoning tears away, and tried to laugh. "She's angry I didn't tell her." At least that wasn't a lie. Everyone but Missy laughed.

Dorothy said, "Your own roommate didn't know! You sly dog."

The rest of the evening was a slow-motion nightmare of conversation, congratulations, and wedding plans that made this fake engagement harder to wiggle out of with every conversation. That one gin took the edge off, but Adriana was too shaky to drink more. She ate, nodded politely, and artfully turned every conversation toward the person who was talking to her.

She found that by asking a few questions, she learned about every marriage, courtship, and proposal in the group of friends, their family, and their distant relations. She devoted the rest of her energy toward making Sal feel better. A touch to the arm here, a kiss on the cheek there. They put on a fine performance of a couple, which, Adriana didn't realize at the time, was to be the first of many.

Adriana got home late that night, hoping Rose was asleep. She had nothing left to give. Sal was a gentleman and didn't press her for an answer. He merely turned off the car in the street in front of her house, got out to open her door, walked her to the front porch, and gave her a noncommittal and brief kiss goodnight.

She let herself in quietly, but as soon as she was in the front door, she saw the light on in the living room. Everything she had avoided, ignored, not spoken of for months was in front of her – and she somehow had to explain this puzzle of mistakes to the one person who truly knew her. The one person she'd probably lost.

Rose sat on their mohair sofa which rose like a throne around her. She was still in her party dress, an emerald-green satin number with a plunging neckline, bodiced center and flared skirt. She had probably been a knockout when she arrived at the party, but since then, she had cried off her makeup, and her hair was down around her shoulders. Now she looked worn, sad, and beautiful. She looked at Adriana steadily and fiercely. Adriana's heart quailed. Rose had likely been here for hours, thinking of everything she'd like to say, whereas she was unprepared.

Adriana sat in the smaller cane chair opposite her like an obedient child and Rose started in right away, "It's not humiliating enough being invited to what I thought was some sort of surprise party for a promotion or something only to find out that you're engaged to someone I thought you only met once at a party. But I was expected to stay and congratulate you." She stopped.

She sat up, leaned forward on her elbows, and softened her stance as she spoke slowly and carefully. "Everyone's so *happy* for you. Edith made a special point of telling me how very, *very* happy she is for you. She knows, doesn't she?"

Adriana nodded.

Rose thought for a moment and said, "She is a cruel and heartless monster. I'm sorry, but anyone who sets someone up like that ..." She smoothed her skirt and touched her hair, as if trying to feel the shape of it.

"Adriana. Honey. We've lived together three years now and while we've had our ups and downs, we do okay, don't we? I mean, don't we?"

The tears came to Adriana now. She only nodded and let them run down her face so as not to interrupt Rose. It was not her place to interrupt her.

"We joked. We used to joke – about guys who were attracted to me. I'd tell you about men who made passes at me. It was funny, right? Why didn't you tell me about this guy? I mean, why? You lied to me about him."

The tears were too heavy for Adriana to answer, and she didn't have a good answer. She couldn't tell Rose about Missy's talk with her. About her career. If she made this about her career, she would appear completely inhuman. This career that Rose made for her.

Rose continued, "Do you love him, Ade?" Her voice cracked, and Adriana realized that Rose's biggest fear was that she didn't love her anymore.

"No." Her voice came out like the weepy protest of a ten-year-old. "No. Rose, I love *you*. You know I love you. All this time. This life we have together."

Rose cleared her throat. She sat back and folded her arms and the sofa was a throne again. "We don't have this life together anymore, honey. Don't you see that? God, don't you *see* that?"

"Don't say that. Please don't say that."

"Wasn't that party pretty much evidence of *this* ..." she waved her arms around to gesture to their home, "being over?"

Adriana couldn't say anything because Rose was right. She had, through cowardice and failure to make decisions, backed her way out of what was once her life. Now she had this future that people crowded around her to congratulate her on. Now she had a future with someone she didn't love and a job she used to love.

She didn't think she'd be able to face Edith again.

Rose got to her feet.

Adriana said, "Don't go. Honey, I'll fix this. I'll do whatever I can. I can quit, you know. You can be the breadwinner. I'll cook for you. I'll open a restaurant. An Italian one, like we always talked about."

Rose laughed. The tears started coming again, and she shook her head. "Honey. I have to work in this town, too, you know." Adriana sniffed, breathing, but she could see the tears weren't going to stop. They were falling faster, a leaking pipe picking up flow.

Rose sighed, smiling, and walked over to Adriana, who was still sitting in the chair. She put a warm hand on her knee and crouched down to look her in the face. Adriana felt the electricity from her hand, familiar and fading, the air of wet warmth from Rose's face and the familiar smell of her face powder and soap. She smelled the Roseness of her. Rose said,

"This little slice of paradise has ended, hon. You made damn sure of that."

Adriana didn't say anything. Here was Rose, beautiful Rose, and everything she had broken.

Rose got to her feet. "I'm cooked, sweet. I'm off to bed. Your things are in the driveway. Call a taxi. I'm sure the YWCA has a room tonight, and maybe your movie star friend has a guest house you can borrow until the nuptials."

Adriana stood up to object, but Rose was off down the hall.

This couldn't be it. And there weren't going to be any nuptials. She hadn't accepted the proposal. And she couldn't leave; this was her home. And that was her love walking away.

"Rose," She called weakly and too late.

CHAPTER FOURTEEN

ADRIANA

In later years, Adriana found it difficult to remember the after. There was Rose and After Rose. The *After* era did have the YWCA's Hollywood Studio Club and, as Rose predicted, Missy's guest house. Adriana remembered that period only vaguely. During that time, she slept a lot. She worked only two more weeks for Edith before she got a job offer from RKO. Missy, on loan, had pulled a few strings, and she welcomed the chance to get away from the Edith portion of the recent unpleasantness. Edith gave her a hard time about leaving. After all, she had worked so hard to keep her there. But after the party at Casa Ladera, Adriana found it hard to fake the friendliness necessary to get through a day of business.

Sal and Adriana were married that spring in a small ceremony at the Taylors' ranch. Missy was her matron of honor. Adriana didn't attempt to contact her brothers. She told Sal she had no family left. In so many ways, it was true.

Their married life was companionable enough at first. Adriana didn't like sex with men, even this man whom she truly liked. After they got over the first time, which hurt, it was merely unpleasant. She thought she deserved this punishment for having abandoned Rose. For being a coward. She took each session of intercourse as one would twenty lashes or self-flagellation, like those monks she'd heard of in Italy.

But, as sex wasn't talked about at the time, she had no reason to assume that their marriage was anything less than average. She let him have at it once a week and that seemed to work. Their marriage settled into a comfortable routine. Work, cooking, and housekeeping. Adriana missed Rose, but this was the new life she had made for herself.

One summer night in their little Spanish bungalow in the Hollywood Hills, Adriana brought the gnocchi in lemon sauce to the table. Sal sat there, looking content and almost handsome in his cotton shirt. Adriana served him gnocchi and salad and sat down opposite him.

He smiled. He said, "Il mio amore, me fate molto felice."

He looked very happy indeed. He didn't make her *unhappy*, exactly. Rose's absence did that. But she couldn't return the emotion. She smiled and raised her glass of wine to him. For Sal, it was enough. She drank. It was bitter and awful.

She said, "Has the wine gone off?"

Sal took a sip. He said, "No, it's very good."

She took another sip. It tasted like rubbing alcohol with red wine dregs mixed in.

She didn't know that this meant she was pregnant. Two weeks later, when she couldn't keep her breakfast down, she realized what was going on.

Hollywood was amenable to a working woman who was married, but when Adriana started showing, she was surprised to find that she was expected to quit. She raised her objections to the head of the studio, William Gordon, who laughed, threw her a baby shower, and quickly hired a man in her place.

She found herself uncomfortably pregnant and unemployed. Adriana never watched another movie. At least not until she was very old.

Sal received an offer from a cousin in Maryland who ran an electrician's shop. He was guaranteed higher wages and part ownership in the company. Without Adriana's salary, Los Angeles was expensive, so the couple moved to Baltimore. Adriana saw that control of her life was a brief and charming period in her early twenties, a magnificent dream. In real life, she had all her choices made for her by men: leaving her job, moving away from Los Angeles, the house they would buy, the hospital where she would have her child, the women she would become friends with. Sal was charming and kind to Adriana; he was a devoted husband. But the lot of a woman in post-war America was strictly stipulated.

Overwhelmed by the uncontrollable forces in her life, Adriana gave birth to Anna Maria on the hottest May day on record in Baltimore, when the city was undergoing a biblical plague of seven-year cicadas. When she went into labor, Sal walked her down the front stairs of their brick townhouse, over hundreds and thousands of crunching, squirming bodies that crackled under her feet and left brown stains on her shoes and stockings.

The evidence of her grave crime against love consumed her. Labor hurt more than anything that Adriana had been exposed to before and went on for two days. The contractions felt like a vise had been placed over her entire body and clamped tight with blinding pain in every single nerve.

When Anna Maria was laid in her arms, Adriana knew that she couldn't love her. She was born of circumstance, not love. She was Sal's baby.

Adriana lay, depleted from labor, with this squirming,

squelching creature in her arms, and all she could think about were her last miserable moments with Rose. They played in her head in quick, humiliating succession: Rose at the corner of the arbor when she first saw her at Edith's party, Rose pulling away from her and leaving, Rose waiting for her at the house, Adriana's things in a heap in the driveway. Around and around, it engulfed her so that she could no longer see the world directly in front of her.

Sal came into her hospital room, beaming with joy. He put flowers on the side table and kissed Adriana on the head. He took the baby from her arms and rocked her in the crook of his own, murmuring, "Bellisima. Mi bambina bellisima."

Adriana couldn't understand how this man could call the little squirming piece of flesh and spittle *beautiful*. She had been looking at the baby for the past two hours and hadn't seen anything remotely beautiful about it.

He looked up at Adriana, concerned. He said, "Are you in pain, piccola madre?"

She thought being called "my love" by a man she didn't truly love was bad. But being called "little mother" was more than she could handle.

She started to cry. Sal's concern shifted to gentle, kindly, but belittling laughter. He spoke words of comfort not to Adriana but to the baby, "Anna Maria, you will have to be patient with your mama." He kissed the baby's forehead. "She has been through a lot. But you have the best, best mama in tutto il mondo."

When Adriana heard this, she knew with sinking certainty that her husband didn't know her at all.

Sal was alarmed by Adriana's despondency after the baby and had the neighbor women come by to check on her regularly.

After a few months of caring for the child, of getting used to her perplexing but regulated daily routine in Baltimore, Adriana managed to put Rose from her mind to the extent that she only came to her in her dreams only every so often.

In her dreams, Adriana was always so happy to see her: Rose was beautiful, across a room or in the yard, her red hair shining, flashing a smile, her lipstick perfectly lined. Adriana surged with love and relief and went to her. Rose turned, the smile still there until her eyes met Adriana's. Her face fell, and tears welled up, pooling beneath her blue irises, like they had that moment when she saw Rose in Edith's garden. Rose was always so disappointed in her. Adriana always awoke in tears.

But the life she was in went on, and Adriana recovered enough to muster cheer when necessary and tend to the child's basic needs. Parents in the late nineteen forties did not dote on their children every moment, so no one found it unusual, the lack of bond between child and mother. She had Sally four years later and was familiar enough with the process to produce smiles and false affection only one week after her birth.

Adriana soldiered on.

After five years of marriage, Sal, perhaps noticing the lack of devotion and love in his wife, began a flirtation with a bakery shop girl and brought home zeppoli, cannoli, and almond cookies in pastel shades of pink and green. He started singing Italian songs from his village, ones he had sung when he first married Adriana. She was grateful when she realized that he had taken a lover.

One wintry Saturday afternoon, Sal came in the back door, glowing, with his pink pastry box. The girls were at the library, where they seemed to spend much of their time when Sal wasn't home. He stomped his feet on the doormat to clear them of snow, and Adriana put a kettle on the stove for him. His cheeks and nose shone pink from the cold, and his ridiculous mailman cap, complete with hanging earflaps, made his gleeful look positively boyish. Adriana walked over and kissed him hard on the cheek. He pulled her in for a hug and held her a moment too long. She kissed him again and pulled away, saying, "I'm making some tea, do you want some?"

He didn't answer.

She said, "It'll go well with whatever's in that pink box, I'm sure."

He didn't answer, and when she turned around to see what was wrong, she saw that his gleeful expression had changed to one of sorrow. She didn't know if his tears were from the cold or something else, but Sal said, "Adriana, I am so sorry."

She knew what he was apologizing for. The bakery girl. But she didn't want to have that conversation. She threw her arms around him and kissed him on the cheek again.

She said, "Come in, take your coat off. Let me make you some tea."

He gave in and sat at the table, the weight of his affair hanging about him with such seriousness that Adriana laughed.

Sal said, "What's so funny?"

Adriana sat opposite him and clasped both his hands. She said, "Sal, you've been nothing but good to me."

The sadness in his face sank into despair. He opened his mouth to talk, but she shushed him.

Adriana couldn't think of what to say to assuage his guilt without mortifying him. She said, "I love you enough to want you to find happiness."

Sal's tears welled in his eyes again. Adriana said, "Any place you can find it. Do you understand? The cookies won't change the fact that we're married. And Sal. Without seeming callous, I want you to know – the cookies don't bother me in the least. In fact, I'm relieved."

His tears abated, and he considered her for a long moment.

He leaned forward, squeezed her hands, and looked into her eyes. "Truly?"

Adriana put her three fingers up in a joke they'd shared for years now, "Scout's honor."

He sucked in his breath and sat back. He sighed, shook his head and said, "Sei stupenda."

Adriana said, "No. No, I'm not."

That was the only conversation they had on the matter. Things lightened up around the house once this happened, as she was more comfortable falling back into their old comic banter.

LAURA

Bart bailed. Laura got up the next morning and found him gone. It pissed her off on so many levels. He had cut off the promise of a full week of entertaining Lizzie. The girl was all dismal and teenaged sulk at breakfast, pushing her food around. She wouldn't look up to say, "Good Morning." *Look at what he did to her. Selfish turd.* Lizzie was obviously crushed. Laura felt a slight burn of guilt as she realized she was no better than Bart, but it felt good to be angry with him.

She should call him and tell him off. But the truth was, she didn't want to tell him off. She wanted to chat. Talk. Get back to that place they were last night when he was so open about George. Where they were connected. Maybe she could learn a little more about contemporary music, have more to talk about. Going out with Jamey and his friends could make her more hip and in the know with Bart.

Stupid. Stupid. Stupid. Falling for a guy who didn't give a shit. Again. She choked down the remainder of her milk, said, "Bye," to Lizzie and Nonna and went off to work.

LIZZIE

Uncle Bart was GONE even though he said he would stay a week. People are always leaving. That meant I was left with Nonna who napped and Laura who was at work all the time. Nonna said *The Philadelphia Story* was one of Laura's favorites. I figured we could have a family night – like with Mom and Dad when we'd order in Chinese food and play board games. Or whatever. I liked that Nonna was here for me and that Laura lived with us, but there was zero, I mean *zero* family going on.

And the drawing wasn't happening. I got to the part where they were supposed to crash, and I couldn't do it. I couldn't make it happen. It would be like I was killing them. I tried a couple of times to draw something else, start a little comic about a girl who liked movies or something, but they came out stupid, so I stopped. Now any time I looked at any of my sketchbooks, they depressed me.

I got today's five dollars from Nonna, who told me to hurry, it was supposed to rain. Frankly, I couldn't wait to get back to one person in my life who I actually wanted to talk to. One person I had chosen for myself.

When I stepped outside, the sky was kind of yellow, and the air was hot and heavy. It was probably even hotter than yesterday, but the clouds gave relief from the sun, so it was less horrifyingly vampirey to step onto the sidewalk – no recoiling from the burning. Every smell was exaggerated in this air: the barfy dumpster outside the corner store, the garbage cans waiting for pickup. By the time I got to Video Planet, the sky had turned that dark, dark almost black-gray. I tried to take note of how things looked *different* in this light.

But I wasn't drawing anymore.

When I stepped into the ice-water cold air conditioning, I was relieved to see that Leticia was working. Not that I expected anyone else, but there was always that chance. Judging by the screams coming from the television, she was watching another horror movie. I said, "Does anyone else ever work here?"

She said, "Hey, squirt."

I said, "*Really?*" She may not have been in my age range, but this black-haired, jaded, horror movie-obsessed video store attendant might have been turning into some sort of friend.

She said, "Well, you never told me your name."

"Lizzie."

"Hey, Lizzie."

"Hey, Leti."

She gave me a look of mock anger and said, "Tisha. Leticia. Never Leti. I had this tía. Don't get me started."

I was embarrassed, but she didn't seem upset by it. I surged with a bit of hope at the word *tía*! She had another culture in her life. Someone who understood. I said, "So, does anyone else ever work here?"

"My boss is a manager, so he gets to sit in an office in the back. Taking inventory and jacking off. Oh, shit." She seemed embarrassed, slipping up in front of a kid.

I said, "I'm *thirteen*."

I don't know what that was supposed to prove, but I was glad I said it because she said, "I thought you were like ... eleven or something. I'm sorry." *Eleven?*

She paused the movie on the screen, and it got a jagged line through it from the tape being paused, and all I saw was blood and some sort of open mouth. I started thinking about a taxicab and what a crash bad enough to kill someone must have to look like. I would have to draw it. Maybe not yet, but soon. Or eventually.

Tisha said, "So, Lizzie, what'll it be?"

"*The Philadelphia Story.*"

She smiled. "Your abuela sure likes the classics."

I said, "She's so *old*." It came out in one breath of hopeless complaint, and I felt horrible the minute I said it.

Tisha laughed. She said, "Are you kidding? Old people *rock*."

I said, "I'm sorry, I didn't mean ..."

Tisha shook her head. It wasn't like she was scolding me. It was more like she wanted me to be clear she was dropping wisdom. "They have so many stories. Just get her to tell you stories about the old days. She'll get a ton more interesting, that's for sure."

She made me feel stupid and judgmental, but she also made me want to be pretty and clever and so certain of things like she was. I didn't have the energy to explain how Nonna wasn't always old. She wasn't old *before*. And how I didn't know how to get her back.

Tisha said, "Are these movies any good?"

"They're pretty good. They're funny. And I don't know, the black and white makes me feel less hot."

She laughed. Not in a condescending way, but like I was funny. She got the movie and rang me up, and I paid, but I definitely wasn't ready to go back to that house yet. It was becoming more and more obvious that place wasn't going to change, and my five-year sentence stretched out before me.

"What's wrong, Liz. You want to use the bathroom?"

How could I say the right thing to stay without being totally obvious and pathetic?

No clue.

She looked at me sideways a moment and said, "Hey, you know what? I need a little help sorting out the action section. You want to help?"

Yes!

One hour later we had put most of the action movies in order and had managed to talk about boys:

She said, "At the end of the day, boys are just big clumsy puppies. If you remember that, you'll stay out of trouble."

About living with more than one culture:

I said, "My mom met my dad's folks *once!* It didn't go well, no matter how nice she was. Maybe she was too nice. I don't know, they weren't the warmest people and Dad just stopped bringing us. They both died when I was little. I still have this kimono in my closet in plastic wrapping I have no idea what to do with."

She said, "Because I came out so white my cousins bust on me all the time, but they love me. We're really close."

My circumstances:

I said, "They died. A couplea months ago. That's why I'm living with my mom's gramma."

She said, "Wow, that sucks. Like, totally."

It was exactly the right thing to say, and we moved on. I did tell her about Nonna and how she wasn't always old. About Laura and how she was never home. Tisha asked about Uncle

Bart, but I told her he lived in New York. When she asked about Laura and looked worried, I *lied* for her. I said, "She works at the aquarium. Long hours. Feeding the seals." She nodded and went back to sorting. I don't know why I defended Laura. I suppose if I admitted my family was *that* bad, it might have been true.

I was getting giddy and super chatty. This was the first person I could really talk to in a long time. I was comfortable with Uncle Bart, but he wasn't much of a conversationalist. When I rambled on a little too much, I worried, but Tisha never made me feel like she was bored of me. Not like Laura. Tisha looked interested, worried, sometimes a little tolerant, but she *listened* to me. She had a look when I was telling her something serious, like about my parents. She lowered her head a little and stared at me directly, intensely. Her blue eyes were a dark blue, and instead of making me nervous, her stare told me I had her complete attention. Nonna gave me that look once in a great while, but I had to say something pretty momentous to earn it.

Every once in a while, she'd come up with another super-wise life observation that made me feel like an immature dope, but aside from that, talking with her was easy.

It turned out she went to the school Nonna picked for me. She said, "St. Casimir! Gawd!"

"What, is it awful?"

She looked at me – that look again – and I could see that a number of answers went through her head before she said, "No. I mean, don't get me wrong, I don't think middle school is good for *anyone*, but it's not so bad. Especially since Sister Ancillita died."

"Sister whoozit?"

"Sister everything-that's-wrong-with-the-Catholic-Church, but never mind."

I had a lot of other questions to ask, but I was staying too long. I could feel it. I said, "I gotta go. I need to ..." I stopped. I didn't know how to ask her.

She smiled. She really meant that smile. It wasn't put there because it was a polite thing to do. She jumped up and went behind the counter. Disappearing for a moment, she said, "Hang on, I got something."

After some rustling, she poked up from behind the counter and unfurled a movie poster for *Mars Attacks*. I hadn't seen the movie, but I liked the artwork. "You want this? I was gonna throw it out."

"Yes! Cool! *Really?*"

She smiled and rolled it up, "Really. And if any classics come in, I'll be sure to save them for you."

"No. I mean thanks, that's nice, but this is way cooler." At last, I had something to put over the depressing wallpaper on Mom's wall. "Thank you."

She said, "Will I see you tomorrow?" She meant it like she wanted to see me.

I nodded.

She smiled wider. "Good. I'm sure I can come up with some other work for you."

I knew she was just doing me a favor, but it was the nicest favor anyone had done me recently. Okay, maybe except looking at baby otters. She grabbed a video, a blue, modern one and put it on top of the pile. It was called *Hard Boiled* and had some Asian dudes with guns on the front.

I said, "What's this?"

She had a mischievous look in her eye. She said, "Just watch it and tell me what you think tomorrow."

It looked violent. Like adult manga violent. "Is it appropriate for my age?"

She laughed. She said, "Most definitely not." She leaned in

and whispered, "But it won't ruin your life or anything. It's good, clean violence."

Thunder rumbled. I took my contraband and bolted.

There wasn't any rain yet. It wasn't allowed – I had a cool new poster that still smelled thick with ink. I ran all the way home and hit the house just as the rain hit the sidewalks.

As I went through the door, there was a huge crack of thunder, and I screamed. Nonna looked up from her chair where she was reading a book. I realized I was breathing heavily and covered in sweat.

She said, "Did it getcha?"

"Nope."

"Come in. You're letting the cool out."

ADRIANA

Despite the newfound lightness in her marriage, Adriana had no new affection for her girls, whom she found to be whiny, self-absorbed little creatures. She tried to love them. She prayed to find love for them. But whenever she sat them down to try to have an easy conversation, whenever she set up an activity they could all do together, she realized they only made each other uncomfortable or irritable. She would end up being short with them. Anna Maria would storm off to her room, or Sally would collapse in a puddle of tears. Adriana stepped back and dealt with her guilt by viewing her parenting style as benign neglect.

She raised them as best she knew how. It was easier not to get too involved.

A few years later, Sal was on a friend's roof, working on their electrical main when he had a heart attack and fell. He was only 51 years old. Adriana was saddened by his death and made sure to let the neighborhood in. Anna Maria was fifteen, Sally eleven. They had a large funeral and invited everyone, including Sal's bakery mistress, Gina, whom Adriana kissed on both cheeks and said, "I know how much you meant to Sal, thank you." Gina was baffled for years after, particularly when her boyfriend's wronged wife started coming in for pastries and a chat every Friday afternoon. Local lore had it that Gina said her confession and swore she'd never have an affair with a married man again.

For a while after Sal's death, Adriana took in sewing for the neighbors. She did simple tailoring and adjustments, made a few dresses for the girls in the neighborhood. The neighbor ladies *oohed* and *aahed* over her work, and Anna Maria and Sally were stunned by her craftsmanship.

In a fit of memory and nostalgia, Adriana fetched her suit out of her closet, the one which she had made for her trip to LA. She showed the girls. Sally was stunned and open mouthed. She stroked the fine seams with the tips of her fingers. Anna Maria said, "I'm glad, Mama. Glad you found something you're good at."

She wasn't disingenuous, but her words stung Adriana in a way she couldn't understand. She would sew. It was something she was good at.

But every time Adriana found herself in a familiar position, bent over a pattern with pins in her mouth or doing a particular whipstitch along a seam, she broke into a cold sweat. A green pit opened in her stomach, and her chest tightened. She shook it off and took on more sewing because she had to support herself, now that Sal was gone.

For two months, she struggled through each assignment. When Anna Maria pleaded for a dress for a high school dance, Adriana took her measurements, drew a pattern, cut, and started sewing.

One Saturday, after Adriana had cut out the green satin pattern pieces for Anna Maria's dress, she pinned the bodice on the girl. Adriana had pushed for red, but Anna Maria insisted on green, a deep emerald. It was a color Rose loved. It brought out her blue eyes and went well with her red hair. It was the fabric Rose wore on that last night.

On Anna Maria, the color looked nice, but very much *not* Rose.

Anna Maria's off-the-shoulder dress was bodiced with an A-line skirt. Dresses on the fashion runways were getting shorter and tighter, but Baltimore was always a little behind the times.

Anna Maria crackled with excitement and energy. She was endlessly patient as Adriana pinned and re-pinned. Something about the texture of the fabric, the shape of the dress, and the act of pinning pieces of fabric onto a live model, made the green pit in Adriana's stomach flower and consume her.

She used her concentration on her work as an excuse for not talking. Anna Maria was talking to Adriana more than she had since she was five. She was going on in a way she used to with Sal. "We decided we weren't going to go with dates. We would go together as a group to the dance. I think it's better, don't you? And this'll be so beautiful, Mama. Thank you. I can't believe you're doing this all for *me*."

Adriana, pins in her mouth, said, "Mmmm."

"I got straight A's on my report card, Mama. Do you know what Betty's parents did when she got straight A's? They bought her a *charm* bracelet. Doesn't that seem a bit excessive? Buying a charm bracelet? Shouldn't she just be proud of herself?"

"Mmmm."

"I thought so."

There was something in Anna Maria's talking that was *pushing*, pushing for something Adriana wasn't sure if she could produce. Later in life she would replay the scene with deep regret as a missed opportunity. But at the time, she wondered what it was she was supposed to do. She had no doubt she was failing overall as a mother, but moments like this really cemented the fact. Was she meant to tell Anna Maria how proud she was of her? Sal always believed people should do well at what they do because that's what they did. And if she praised her at this late stage, it would sound completely out of place.

Sally said, "Straight A's! Way to go! I wish I could get straight A's."

Sally to the rescue. The girl could deal out praise and platitudes with equal measure, and it wasn't out of character.

Anna Maria wheeled around to look at her sister, skewing the bodice Adriana was straightening.

"Anna Maria!" Her voice came out more sharply than she meant it to. The green flood in her stomach had turned to pure ire. Anna Maria turned back around toward her, the joy replaced with fear. The fear then faded back to subdued. She had to mind her mama.

Adriana had ruined the mood, and she couldn't fix it. She simply didn't have the tools.

At noon on the Friday of the dance while the girls were at school, Adriana sat down to work on the dress and was drawing together the seams of the green satin bodice when her chest tightened and the pit opened again; but this time it could not be dismissed. Tears started dripping on the green fabric, but she didn't truly realize she was crying until she heard herself moan. She put the dress down. It took her two hours to stop crying. When she was done, she powdered her face, went out to Sears, bought Anna Maria a ready-made dress in a similar color, and laid it on her bed.

Anna Maria came to the kitchen where Adriana was stirring some soup on the stove. She held up the store-bought dress; there were tears in her eyes. She was angry.

"Mama, what is *this?*"

"It's a dress for your dance tonight." The emerald satin of the dress she was sewing had been irreparably stained by Adriana's tears. She threw it in the trash and emptied the morning's coffee grounds on it to ensure its demise.

"What happened to the dress you were making?"

I couldn't. I just couldn't do it. You wouldn't understand. I hope you never have to understand anything like it. But Adriana said, "Oh. I didn't have time to finish it."

"It was going so well, and you had all *day* today." It was a sharp tone she had not yet used with her mother.

Adriana marveled at the fire in Anna Maria's eyes. It wasn't the warm glow of Sal that she'd seen for years. There was genuine anger. Outrage. It was the first time she recognized a little of herself in her daughter. And it hurt. She had only been failing Sal's children. She hadn't thought of it as failing her own. Adriana said, "I'm sorry. I ran out of time." She didn't reprimand her daughter for talking back.

Anna Maria was crying. In a voice that would sound bratty to an outsider but spoke so much more to Adriana, she said, "It was *one thing*, Mama. One thing for *me.*"

She stormed off to her room, and Adriana's shoulders slumped.

She felt a little hand on her back, rubbing in small circles. She looked down at Sally's worried, skinny little face. Another person she had failed. Adriana turned from Sal's daughter, wiped her eyes, and stirred the soup. Sally quietly disappeared. She was always doing that.

Adriana went to work as a secretary in a local law office. The company was fine, and they were generous with her hours, letting her out in time to pick up the girls from school. She was happy to be useful again, and her skills in organization made her good at her job. She tried not to think about her time in Hollywood, a distant, pleasant dream. It wasn't relevant to her new reality. She tried to talk to Anna Maria a few times after the dress incident, but the girl had clearly given up on her mother. Adriana knew she deserved this surly treatment from her teen and went back to her original plan of benign neglect.

When she turned seventeen, Anna Maria raided Adriana's money jar and her jewelry box. She even took Adriana's celluloid lipstick case with Rose's heart in it before she ran away to New York City. To Adriana, the theft seemed appropriate. Anna Maria told her mother that she would never understand her. Adriana knew this was true, but she spent two years looking for her anyway. She gave up hope when a private detective and three hundred dollars failed to provide a lead. She knew she had botched any opportunity to be a good mother. The regret and the nagging absence of that lipstick case, which had become a talisman of that part of her life, reminded her of Rose, so she turned the private detective to a new task.

He found that Rose had steady acting jobs in the movies for ten years after Adriana left Hollywood. She then disappeared abruptly, with no forwarding address. All potential leads went cold. With no hope of finding Rose or Anna Maria, she was left with Sally and the years stretched out in front of her, long and unrelenting. Adriana realized she needed to find something to occupy herself.

She turned back to cooking. While Sally was in school, she started scouring used bookstores for Italian cookbooks. She looked through the books slowly, checking a few key recipes to be sure they'd gotten it right. When she had collected a good six or seven, she spent her afternoons looking around different markets in Baltimore to find the freshest ingredients.

This journey acquainted her with a city she had somehow missed in her early self-absorbed, self-pitying child-rearing life. She got to know the local greengrocer Mario and his family. She befriended the butcher Pete and his wife Cristina and brought them pastries from Gina's shop because they lived in the part of town that didn't have any Italian bakeries. She befriended the Portuguese fishmonger Maurizio and his family. Adriana cobbled together an unusual group of friends whom she routinely had over for coffee and Gina's almond cookies.

Every weekday afternoon while Sally worked on her seventh-grade homework, Adriana turned her attention to dinner, creating clever tarts out of tomatoes and leeks with lemon zest and oregano mixed into the crust. She worked new ingredients into gnocchi dough that sometimes worked (pumpkin) sometimes didn't (spinach – too watery). She became an expert bread maker and got very good at pastas: lasagnas, tortellini, ravioli, and orrachiette. She made osso-bucco, braised pork roast, meatballs.

Sally seemed to benefit from her mother's culinary adventures, turning from a scrawny, shifty-looking little girl into a stout and friendly loaf of a teen, well-liked by her classmates. Sally talked incessantly, often muttering to no apparent end, filling the room with noise and girlish thoughts and fluttery platitudes:

"Every dog has his day."

"Every cloud has a silver lining."

"There's no use crying over spilt milk."

Adriana thought that with her sister gone, Sally simply needed to fill the space.

Sally wanted to help, but she was always into things,

making a mess. Adriana shooed her away and got to work. She never did well with that newfangled "my daughter's helping" garbage some of the local mothers were into. It was a big fake, created solely for the ego-stroking of the child, and Adriana refused to participate in that lie.

One night when she finished cooking, she found Sally in the dining room, waiting at the dining table as she so often did, pretending to read a book. But this time, she was asleep, face mushed against an atlas open to the state of New York. Adriana looked at this pudding of a girl, drizzle of drool at the corner of her mouth, and wondered who had brought this creature into her life.

She pretended for a moment that Sally was Gina's child. She could feed her and send her home to her mama. That she, Adriana was a childless cook: a woman living alone in Baltimore, making meals for friends. This thought was tremendously appealing. She thought of Gina and Sally giggling together, doing the pretend cooking nonsense. And they fit.

And Anna Maria, whom Gina would dote on, buying her the right dresses and sharing high school gossip. Anna Maria would not have left Gina. She would not be lost in New York. She may even have been happy. And this squash-faced Sally would be a confident, blossoming girl. Someone who didn't mutter things all the time. Who didn't spew conversation and truisms to fill the space her mother couldn't.

But here was Sally. At this dining table. Where she slept because it was nine at night, and Adriana had not yet worked out timing and cooking, especially with a complicated dish like lasagna. She held out the china plate an inch above the table in front of Sally. It was heavy with a thick slice of lasagna dripping with cheese and sauce. She let it drop with a clatter that startled the child awake.

The moment the plate hit, she was ashamed by her cruelty.

Sally looked at her mother, her face scrunched in a frown of bleary confusion. She looked at the lasagna and smiled.

"Thanks, Mommy." She rubbed her eyes and picked up a fork, cutting into the soft layers with a moist noise, saying, "All good things come to those who wait."

Adriana couldn't stand to watch her eat. She gave her the smile she thought she needed and went back into the kitchen to wash up.

LIZZIE

That night Laura came home and didn't even say hello. She went right up to her room and slammed the door. Later, I heard the shower running. I was making dinner. Mom had this quick recipe where she'd take chicken, dump a jar of salsa on it and bake it. It was the kind of thing she'd "throw together" when she didn't have time to cook. But that made it easier to remember. I made salad and Spanish rice from a packet to go with. Nonna kept coming through the kitchen like she had business there but peeked over at what I was doing. The walker rattling over the aluminum strip in the entry to the kitchen made me jumpy and her hovering made me nervous.

I set the table for three, so nice. Nonna even showed me where the candles were, and she picked a camellia from out back to put in a glass. It looked so civilized I felt like crying.

Laura came down all dressed up, jeans, a swanky shirt, big hoop earrings, kinda heavy makeup that looked nice on her. For a minute I fooled myself into thinking she had dressed for dinner.

She looked at the table. She frowned, and I could see her

267

weigh a few things as she looked at her watch. She thought again and sat down at the table, looking like she was about to get a shot at the doctor.

She said in a forced tone, "Smells great, what's for dinner?"

I hated her. She let me know that I was something to tolerate – to get through – and it made all of the good feelings I was starting to have about the evening go down the toilet. I suppose that time I spent with Tisha had given me false confidence in grown-ups.

Nonna said, "Lizzie's cooked us a nice meal."

I said, "And I rented *The Philadelphia Story*."

Laura smiled, "I *love* that movie."

She'd stay. How could she not stay?

I said, "I've never seen it."

She looked me in the eyes for maybe the first time that week, maybe the first time since I met her, like I was a person who was actually in the room and said, "I can't *believe* you haven't seen it. Cary Grant *and* Jimmy Stewart in the same movie with Katharine Hepburn. Lucky girl, she gets wooed by both of them, and there's a funny girl in it who reminds me of you."

I nodded and smiled. Maybe she and I could be like Tisha and me. I said, "Really, how?"

Her eyes left, and with her brief ray of sun disappearing behind a cloud, I got a chill.

She said, "Oh, I don't know. She's funny is all." She looked somewhere across the room, maybe toward Los Angeles, and said, "I wish *I* could see that movie again for the first time."

I put some chicken on her plate with some rice.

Laura cut into it and started eating.

Nonna cleared her throat. "Laura."

"Sorry, Nonna." She crossed herself and said, "Thank you,

God, for food." She crossed herself again. She went back to eating before I had served Nonna or myself.

I always thought "wolfing down" was not really an appropriate expression for when people eat fast. "Inhale" is sorta better. But Laura *destroyed* the plate of food, cut it apart, moved it around, actually ate only about ten bites and left the rest. She wiped her mouth with her napkin – one of Nonna's linen napkins – and got a smear of red lipstick on it. She said, "That was *so* nice. Thank you, Lizzie. Good night, Nonna. Don't wait up." And she left. She *left*.

I didn't tell her she had a piece of rice on the chest of her blouse.

The door slammed, and I looked over at Nonna. She shook her head. She raised her water glass and said, "A toast to the chef."

I raised my glass back at her.

She said, "May you never become a self-absorbed twenty-something year old."

I worried, "Does it happen to everyone?" Does everyone become a raving self-centered asshole?

The wheezing laugh again. She almost choked on her water. "It happened to me. In a bad way ..."

She got that distant look. I was hoping a story would follow. Any story. But she said, "Elizabetta, if there is anyone who can avoid it, it would be you."

And maybe Tisha. But was she twenty yet? I didn't know. I wanted to ask her more, but there didn't seem a good way to put it. "So, Nonna, when you were self-absorbed ..." Even, "What happened?" seemed somehow inappropriate, so I said nothing.

We ate quietly for a while.

Nonna said, "Don't forget, her Mama left her, too."

I know Sally had divorced Uncle Bruce, but I never thought of it as leaving. But something about the way Nonna said "left her" kicked me in the chest. My parents left. They took the *big* trip. They weren't coming back.

I said, "Didn't Aunt Sally still see her?"

"She sent her postcards from her travels. She'd blow into town once in a while. But, no, Bruce raised Laura pretty much himself – with her stepmother, I suppose." I thought she was going to sink into a condemnation of raising children without manners, raising kids who would walk out on a meal cooked specially for them, on a movie rented specifically for them. But Nonna let out a long sigh and said, "Being a parent is very hard. Anyone can screw it up."

She stuck her finger into her mouth, picking at something in the back of it. I hated that every time I got to see Nonna as a person, the old lady in her would make itself known. She kept fishing, and I tried to remind her of herself.

I said, "You did it right. Mom said you were the best mom ever. Better than hers could have been."

Nonna took her finger out of her mouth let out a long, *long* sigh. She said, "Thank you, Lizzie. Thank you for saying that." She stopped for a moment and took a drink of water. I thought she had moved on, but she said, "One out of three ain't bad."

I know Mom's mom bailed on her, but I hadn't thought much about Mom's mom being Nonna's KID. And Sally was Nonna's kid. Weird. Maybe something really bad happened when they were little. I wanted to ask questions, but the moment seemed to have passed, and Nonna said, "What's for dessert?"

I had picked up some Klondike bars. I was excited to see the movie. And for Nonna to go to bed so I could watch Tisha's movie. *Maybe I can talk to Laura about it tomorrow.* It almost *seemed* like we were watching it together. Nonna and I cozied up in front of the television. I put the movie in and unwrapped my Klondike bar. I liked the movie immediately, black and white was starting to feel like home. Everyone was handsome and funny and smart and talked quickly with that Mom-and-Dad banter. It was a good night.

But then that obnoxious kid came on the screen. The one – she couldn't have been more than ten – who sang about the tattooed lady and wore a drooping diamond necklace. She was the one who reminded Laura of me. A black feeling settled in the pit of my stomach, and I wanted Mom and Dad so badly. I wanted back the two people in the world who really got me.

One good thing about living with a very old person is that they can't hear so well, and you can get away with crying in the same room with them. As long as you do it quietly.

NONNA/ADRIANA

This wouldn't stop. She had broken Sally who had broken Laura. And she didn't have the tools to keep dear, sweet Lizzie unruined. This would go on, and Mama would always be leaving her in the gravel turnout in Connecticut, to find her family elsewhere.

CHAPTER FIFTEEN

LAURA

Going out. Like, *out*. Without Nonna or Lizzie. Laura felt a little guilty when she left the house, but the exhilaration of being *out* overtook it.

She had rethought her outfit four times before she picked one, but driving the vintage car made her wish she had gone for some sort of leopard skin coat and bright pink lipstick. She needed to get some cat-eye glasses. Women had cat-eye glasses. Retro was in.

Instead, she wore jeans, a tank top, and a gauzy blue and black swirled long-sleeved shirt. Simple with a little flare. Big silver hoop earrings. She took some time with her hair and makeup for the first time in several months, plucking an alarming number of eyebrow hairs, and when she looked at herself in Nonna's scallop-edged antique mirror, she had to admit she looked pretty good.

She told Jamey she'd meet him at the club, which was harder and easier. It would be easier walking in with someone, but the idea of him picking her up at her grandmother's house was all wrong.

The Ottobar was a small, low-ceilinged space with every wall, door, and patch of ceiling painted black, like a shorter version of the Roxy. After being ensconced in a small group of people she'd circulated amongst for years in Hollywood, Laura was out of her element walking into a club where she knew absolutely no one. Right out of college, it would have been no problem. But now she wracked her brains for how to start a conversation while keeping it away from what she did for a living or where she lived.

Laura walked along the bar as if she knew where she was going and found herself at the back of the place a little too quickly. Maybe it was Lizzie and Bart, maybe it was living in LA for so long, but Laura was a little surprised that most of the people at the bar were white.

She scanned the wall of T-shirt-blue-jeaned men and women, who looked comfortable stood around, drinks in hand. She knew right away she was wearing too much makeup, and her shirt was totally wrong. She could hold a drink. That would be something to do.

She went up to the bar and squeezed between two men. They were facing away from her, each talking to a different group of people. The bartender passed her three times and didn't even look at her despite her attempts to flag him down. The man to her right jostled her, and the man to her left leaned back into her, making the space she had even smaller. She tucked in her elbows, so as not to elbow them. But they kept squishing in, and Laura was disappearing.

She felt a warm presence behind her, and a guy yelled, "Bobby!"

She turned around and realized she hadn't realized how tall Jamey was. Impressively tall. The men to either side of her parted instantly to make room. Laura instantly was both protected and visible.

The bartender walked up to her, and Jamey said, "Bobby, this is Laura. Laura, Bobby. Bobby, take care of my friend here, will you?"

Bobby flashed a smile that probably landed a lot of barmaids and said, "What can I get for you?"

Laura said, "Margarita, rocks, salt."

Bobby looked at her incredulously. He nodded, dubiously. "Okay ... um, let me see if we have any margarita mix." He started looking around the bar. He yelled to someone in the back.

"Hey, Jake, we got any Margarita Mix?"

A voice from somewhere Laura couldn't see said, "Yeah, it's down in the back behind the triple sec."

Bobby opened an old cabinet behind him and started digging through some bottles. Laura realized that ordering margaritas in LA was different from ordering them here. She said, "Never mind!" She had to holler because it was so loud, "What d'you got on tap?" By the relief on both men's faces, she knew she'd said the right thing.

Step one into Baltimore's young society: fail.

Jamey escorted her over to a table where his friends sat. One look at them told Laura that she wasn't interesting enough. She had walked into this bar secure in the knowledge that Jamey was a bit of a dork, and she was cool. Or once upon a time, she was cool. She was from LA. She had to be cooler than people in *Baltimore*. But Jamey's friends were clearly more artsy and self-possessed than she was.

Clad simply in black, which exacerbated the loudness of Laura's blue and black swirly gauze shirt, Jenny was long-haired and wore no makeup. She was gorgeous. She was a cellist. She worked days at a bookstore and got gigs here and there. Stewart was a painter, who commanded quiet respect from the table. Black-haired, bearded, and hefty, he chain-smoked and had scarlet and green paint in evidence up and down his arms with a solid concentration of green on one knee of his jeans. He winked at Laura, which made her blush with embarrassment and caused Jenny to shift her chair closer to Stewart, arm around him in ownership.

Jenny pointed out their two friends onstage with the band – the Ziggies – and filled Laura in on the details. Tall and slim, with a wispy blonde beard and shoulder-length blonde hair, Garth ran a used record and CD store. He stepped down between sets to exchange a few jokes and nod in a slouched, *it's all cool* sort of way. His girlfriend, Anu, a petite Indian woman with a pink-tipped black buzz cut, was fierce and quiet and could play a mean fiddle. Her fiddle brought a light, dancing undertone to some already dynamic tunes and was brighter and fiercer than her personality. She exuded sexual control and seemed an odd pairing with the slouching, amiable Garth.

The wild card was Petra. She dressed rock n' roll, but Laura could tell from her tidy, short hair and her conservative jewelry that she had a day job somewhere. Jenny told Laura that Petra was a physical therapist at an old folks' home. Petra made it clear from the start that she disliked Laura. It didn't take long for Laura to figure out that she was Jamey's significant Ex.

This group had known each other since college, and Laura was not only an outsider for not being local, she had a huge learning curve as far as the conversation went. They had a history of stories, inside jokes, and huge events that made their conversation swift, funny, and impossible to follow.

Any time a conversation opened up that Laura could participate in, Petra worked hard to make sure to close it with an inside joke or shared memory in which Laura could no way participate. She knew how to get by in the film industry, but in Baltimore, she was at a complete loss.

After a few feeble attempts at conversation and obvious

fails, Laura pushed her chair back from the table a little and pretended she was enjoying the band. What she was really doing was thinking about Bart. And last night. And wondering when she'd see him again.

And she thought of Lizzie. She should work harder with Lizzie. She'd been so angry about Bart's leaving that she was a total brat at dinner. It reminded her of when she'd behaved badly with Janelle – that feeling that pushed up during her teen years urging her to make her sister's life miserable. It came with a certain amount of shame. Lizzie didn't deserve that. Laura needed to try with her. Take care of her a little. Maybe if someone took an interest in Lizzie, she wouldn't end up out at a bar a few years down the road with a bunch of people cooler than her, completely lost about where exactly she belonged on the planet.

Every so often one of Jamey's group would ask her a question, and she'd put her hand to her ear and shake her head: *sorry I can't hear you.* When the Ziggies finished and a new band went up on stage, she complimented Garth and Anu, who actually smiled. Laura figured it was as good a time as any to leave. She gave Jenny a nice, long, warm handshake (she was the only one of them who had really tried), and, utterly sick of Petra, she gave Jamey a prolonged peck on the cheek before walking off. He smelled homey and nice, but kind of *not* Bart. Kind of *not a chance.*

ADRIANA

Adriana knew that her disappointment in Laura that evening was undeserved. She had certainly done worse at Laura's age than walking out on a dinner, ignoring the feelings of others. She had gone through most of that phase of her life ignoring the feelings of others. Rose. Sal. Her girls. The girls who she failed so completely that they had to go find out who they were elsewhere. In drugs. In traveling. Their own home offered no answers.

She readied herself for bed, leaving Lizzie to her own devices. She should shoo the child to bed, but what harm was there, really? She lay her creaking body down, sore hip up, turned out the light, but sleep wouldn't come.

Was it the age thing? Did being in your mid to late twenties make you so self-absorbed that you couldn't really think about your effect on other people? Was this a myopia that struck everyone? She laughed. That notion would absolve her of her sins and that was hardly fair. Laura would have to find her own path.

Laura's dressing up and going out to make new friends was

a good thing. That disappointment that surged at dinner was really more about herself than her granddaughter. And that disappointment was something Adriana couldn't change. She let that familiar black cloud of regret settle over her head as she drifted into an uneven sleep.

LIZZIE

When Nonna had gone to bed, I snuck back downstairs and put on *Hard Boiled*. It was all heavy music, smokey rooms, and liquor. Then there was this shootout at a tea house where people took their birds in cages to eat with them. I had never in my life seen so many people shot. It was horrible but kind of terrific at the same time. There was slow motion and dodging, and the framing reminded me so much of parts of *Akira*. In one slow motion sequence, this guy, the character's partner? was shot so many times, and there was blood all over his chest.

I got to thinking about taxicabs again.

The hero sought vengeance in a kitchen fogged with flour and spattered in blood, and when he finally took the bad guy down in a rain of gunfire and more blood, you saw his face, whitened like a ghost with flour and splattered with the red, red blood, and I turned it off.

I ejected the cassette. Why would Tisha want me to see that? I sat there in the dark for a long while trying to figure it out. I mean, on the one hand, it meant she thought I was grown-up enough to handle it. And I guessed that was cool. But on the other hand, *Men in Black* was about as violent as movies got for me.

I got this huge, *enormous* sadness from deep inside, but I didn't know what it was about. I took it upstairs, curled up in my bed, and cried.

I didn't want to be a grownup. I didn't want to be cool. I wanted to be somewhere where people understood me. I wanted to go *home.*

LAURA

It was one a.m. when Laura got back to Nonna's. She was exhausted, but too agitated to go straight to bed. She flumped on the sofa and turned on the television. She flipped around Nonna's meager ten or so available channels before she realized there was nothing on. She saw the video rental box under the television. She knew it was *The Philadelphia Story* and that would only remind her of Dexter. The one thing nice about her outing was it put her a very non-Dexter state.

There was another video box underneath. *Hard Boiled.* She'd heard of it but couldn't remember why. She popped it in. After the first extremely violent and artful shootout culminating in Chow Yun-Fat in a restaurant kitchen, flour-whitened face, blowing a bad guy away at close range, she remembered. John Woo.

Dexter hated John Woo; he didn't know why all the other guys in the business thought he was so amazing. Dexter was more of a Yimou Zhang groupie. "*Raise the Red Lantern* is a *real* movie. Brilliant, artistic, special. It brings something to the table. Woo does killer action, I'll give him that, but he's nothing to drool over." If Dexter hated this guy, that was good enough for Laura. She sat back, settling in.

Aside from some awkward acting, the movie was kind of terrific. The action was dynamic in a way she'd never seen before. Even more than in *Windblown*. In fact, *Windblown* had some very specific sequences that obviously were lifted from this movie. Fuck *Raise the Red Lantern*. Dexter was an idiot.

Chow Yun-Fat was very handsome and reminded her of someone. She didn't see it at first, all of the serious looks, the suits, and the way his head was shaped differently, but when he smiled, something about his expressions reminded her of Bart. By the time his character, baffled and overwhelmed, argued with his ex-girlfriend, Bart had somehow affixed himself onto Chow Yun-Fat or vice versa.

Laura found herself scooching to the floor for a closer look.

I mean look at this guy. Tough, cute, good with a gun, deeply brooding, and rescuing *babies* from the bad guys. In the hospital's nursery, Chow Yun-Fat was so endearingly bewildered by the dozens of babies in their little plastic cribs. Kind of like Bart and the cottura. Or Bart and Lizzie. Of course, he was bewildered. He'd never had a kid before. It made sense that Bart fled.

When the movie was finished, Laura went off to sleep yearning for Bart in a no more arguments kind of way. Too late to call him. She would call the next day.

Laura had some dreams about Bart that night. When she awoke, she was fuzzy on the details. There was something about babies and guns and funny conversations, but whatever the details, she woke up absolutely smitten. She would call him, but later in the morning. He was probably sleeping in.

She remembered her promise to herself to be better to

Lizzie. It had seemed like a good idea the night before, but when she heard Lizzie's door open and her *galumph-badumph* down the stairs, it seemed less feasible.

She pulled herself out of bed and threw on some clothes.

When she got to the kitchen, Lizzie was sitting over a bowl of morning cereal reading the morning comics. Nonna was nowhere in sight.

She said, "Good morning, Liz."

Lizzie looked up at her, her brows folded distrustfully, like, *You talking to me?*

This would take some work. Laura said, "Did you sleep well?"

Lizzie chewed and swallowed her cereal before saying, "Um. Okay, I guess. You?"

"Fine." Laura got herself a bowl from the cabinet and sat down opposite Lizzie. What did she talk about when she was a teenager? Sally was gone, and Janelle, Judy, and her dad were the only people around. She didn't talk. She watched movies and went on long walks. She slept. What was she interested in? Clothes? No. Boys? Yes, but she didn't know how to talk about that with Lizzie, and her teen self probably wouldn't have known where to start.

Too long was passing. The expectant look was gone, and Lizzie looked back at her comics.

Laura said, "Anything funny in the funnies this morning?"

Lizzie didn't look up. She said, "Not so much. What's up with *Gasoline Alley* anyway? It's never funny."

Laura didn't know what *Gasoline Alley* was. She said, "I used to love *Peanuts*."

Lizzie looked up at her. She nodded, trying to be nice, and said, "That's cool."

Okay, comics were out.

Laura said, "That movie you rented was awesome. I watched it last night."

Lizzie looked up from the paper again. Laura couldn't read the look on her face. Something upset. Something angry. Something hopeful. Lizzie said, "Uhhhhh. I didn't watch it."

"Oh."

Laura ate her cereal. What else? Books? What could she talk about that the kid would need? Lizzie looked down at the paper, but Laura could tell she wasn't reading. Just dying. Of awkwardness. It reminded her too much of herself. If it were teenage Laura sitting across from her, she would let her go. She always wanted to be alone anyway. Lizzie didn't *want* to be alone. She wanted her mother. And Laura couldn't give Lizzie her mother.

Laura wanted Lizzie's mother, too. She and Becca could sort this shit out. Becca would be excited she was interested in Bart – she might even try to play matchmaker. Or she'd warn her that he was a womanizer. And with Becca, Lizzie would be happy, and Laura wouldn't have to worry about her.

It took her a moment to realize that Lizzie was looking at her.

"Um. Laura?"

"Oh. Sorry. Thousand-mile stare. I'm famous for it in the mornings."

Lizzie said, "Okaaaay." And picked up her bowl, put it in the sink, and left before Laura could think of something suitable to say.

Laura waited two nail-biting hours until 10:30 to call Bart. It seemed late enough not to be desperate, early enough he might still be home. The moment she heard his voice, she knew she'd woken him.

He said, "Hello?"

She said, "Hi, Bart? It's Laura."

He said, "Is Lizzie okay?" He was worried.

She said, "What?" Because like, seriously, could he think of no other reason for her to be calling?

He said, "Lizzie."

"Lizzie's downstairs." She came off more snappish than she wanted.

He said, "Oh, well, what do you want?"

"Never mind." She hung up. *Fucker.* All the glow of her prior night's dream, of Chow Yun-Fat, of their night together when she actually felt a connection with him faded. He probably told his most intimate secrets to every girl he slept with. Sex, confessional, gone.

Laura yawned and stretched. It was one of those hot days where even though it was still cool in the house, the air felt heavy. Nothing else to do, she might as well go back to bed.

LIZZIE

The movie wouldn't leave me. The bloody man getting shot up. The blood on the hero's floury face. And the zig-zag on Tisha's paused movie at the video store with the open mouth and blood. After a totally *weird* breakfast with Laura, I got the sketchbook out again and started to draw. I drew without looking back or thinking. I drew what I had seen, in what? nightmare? In my imagination? It was what I had seen every day since Mrs. Dunford told me the words: *there was a terrible accident. A taxi. In the city. Your parents.*

The lines came out of my black pen, and they were in the right place. There were close-up panels of the fear on my parents' faces. There were panels of metal crashing, flashes.

SCRIIITCH! SCREAM. KRASH.

I drew until a grumble in my stomach was loud enough to startle me. I looked at the clock. It was noon. I looked at the pictures, the page. It was too awful, but I knew it was right, somehow. I had gotten it right.

CHAPTER SIXTEEN

ADRIANA

Adriana didn't exactly find happiness in her cooking, but she did find a certain peace and a sense of purpose. For Christmas Eve, she decided to create the complicated and elaborate Italian Seven Fishes Dinner. She invited the greengrocer, the butcher, and their families, and of course the fishmonger, as well as the baffled Gina who cried when Adriana issued an invitation on her usual Friday visit to the bakery. Gina was always so emotional. As Adriana got to know her better, she saw that Gina gave Sal everything she could not.

Adriana cooked for five days. She soaked the salt cod, prepared the sauces, baked the desserts, and soaked the olives in garlic and herbs. Fifteen people came to her house that Christmas Eve. They all talked, laughed, drank wine, and ate better than they had in years. Sally sat wide-eyed as they ate antipasti of olives and squid salad, secondi of linguini with clam sauce, followed by Baccala, the traditional dish of salt cod and tomatoes. After stuffed crab, fried scallops, codfish balls, and crab-stuffed mushrooms, a contented hush fell over the room. It was apparent that this was now a family tradition, but this was a family chosen by Adriana, not for her.

The second year she invited them, it seemed her friends not only expected the meal but looked forward to it. It satisfied a certain cavity in Adriana's soul to feed people again. Something about the basic murmur of a small crowd eating well and clinking glasses would bring Rose back to her for a moment, and she experienced an ineffable relief from worry, a fleeting contentment.

That spring she introduced a traditional Italian Easter feast as well.

Four years passed. Sally went to the College of Notre Dame of Maryland, a small all-girls school that didn't mind her lower grades or her general lack of ambition. Even though the school was in Baltimore, she came back only at holidays. It was soon clear that her attentions were wandering. Each time she returned, her clothing was more outlandish, her hair and her body looser and flowing. She seemed deeply interested in some hippie movement in San Francisco. Adriana clearly hadn't figured out how to be a parent. Her children were pretty much growing up on their own now, God willing Anna Maria was still alive.

On the fourth Easter celebration, just as Adriana brought out and presented the braided Easter bread to its usual "oohs and aahs," the doorbell rang. She deposited the bread to its place of honor at the head of the table and commanded, "Mangia!" before wiping her hands on her apron and heading to the door.

She thought it was a dark-haired druggie selling something, but on closer examination, the gaunt, unhealthy, acne-covered girl holding a baby in her arms was Anna Maria. She wore a scowl of defiance that made Adriana want to slap her. Relief, despair, worry, and guilt crowded her, and her voice shook when she said, "I'm so glad you've come. Please, join us." She stood back and pushed the door open wider to allow her in.

After a murmured introduction of her baby Rebecca, Anna Maria sat through dinner quietly, the baby on her lap. The baby looked to be about six or seven months old and was quite social despite being clearly malnourished. Her eyes were giant in her face atop a neck too skinny for her age. The company cooed over her, but Anna Maria's *stay away* scowl didn't leave her, so no one worked very hard to include her in the conversation. Adriana saw the diffidence with which her daughter held the baby, and guilt for Anna Maria's loveless childhood flooded her as if she were seeing it for the very first time. She had been so self-pitying and self-absorbed that she hadn't realized that she was raising a person; that she had some culpability in how this girl turned out. Even Sal's weekend ministrations of love and play hadn't saved this girl from Adriana's neglect.

Easter dinner went on as happily as usual with roast lamb and mint sauce, artichoke pie, salad, fruit, eggs, and chocolate. They toasted with Marsala, the baby squealed, and Sally sat silently communicating questions at her sister throughout the meal. Adriana knew that Anna Maria's return was tentative; a wild bird had alighted at their table. Too much attention and it would fly away.

When the spring evening shadows grew long, one by one, the guests stretched and excused themselves to go back to their lives. Gina stopped as Adriana said her goodbyes in the front hall. She kissed Adriana and clasped both her hands. Adriana didn't want her to cry again. She was already on edge. But Gina's eyes lit up, and she smiled, "Thank you. Thank you again, Adriana. You have no idea how much this means to me." She looked around as if someone would overhear and then said, "Next time, can I bring a fella?"

"Christmas isn't for eight months yet!" Adriana saw a

flicker of disappointment in Gina's eyes. She knew that her own jaded take on relationships had clouded the moment. She said, "But of course. If this is a special fella, we'd be delighted to have him. Would have been delighted today." Gina threw her arms around Adriana's neck and began to cry. Adriana pried her off, patted her hands, and sent her out the door. Gina's curves had changed shape as she approached middle age; Adriana knew that the man who fell in love with her now would stick. She closed the door. The girls were nowhere to be seen.

Adriana went upstairs to the room they shared under the eaves. She had bought the girls matching white bedspreads in the year before Anna Maria left, and the wallpaper was made of chic woven fabric. It was a very modern bedroom, and Adriana was proud when it finally came together. The girls were sitting, each on her own bed, talking to each other. The baby lay asleep on the bed next to Anna Maria, too close to the edge, but Adriana knew she didn't have a place to say anything. The girls were talking intently, and she hadn't thought yet of what to say to her runaway daughter, so she crept back downstairs to the kitchen and washed the dishes.

Anna Maria stayed with them for two months. Adriana helped with the baby.

One evening, she was bathing the baby in the kitchen sink. Anna Maria was out "with friends." Adriana never asked her where she was going, but due to Anna Maria's hours and lack of appetite, she knew drugs were involved.

Rebecca had dark hair like the rest of her family, and her eyes were a soft, warm brown. Her skin was not so dark as Anna Maria's, she was more snow-white rose-red than the tawny tan of Adriana's daughters. In her weeks at Adriana's house, she had put on enough weight to look healthy and well-fed.

Rebecca dropped a spoon that she was playing with into the water and let out a disappointed, "uh-oh" that made Adriana laugh. Rebecca looked up at her grandmother, brown eyes sparkling. She screwed up her face and blew a raspberry, causing Adriana to laugh harder. Rebecca laughed too, and Adriana knew that for the first time in almost twenty-five years, she had fallen in love.

Three months after she arrived, Anna Maria crept out in the dead of a muggy night, taking her bag of clothing with her and two hundred and three dollars from the false bottom of the flour tin. She left a note that simply said, "I can't." She left a longer note for Sally, but Adriana never learned its contents.

Oddly enough, the lipstick case Adriana had finally learned to stop missing reappeared on her chest of drawers. She opened it up, twisted her finger inside, and pulled out Rose's drawing of a heart, yellowed with age, the ink still as black as the day she drew it. She kissed the heart, put it back in its case, returning it to her underwear drawer. It was likely Anna Maria couldn't find a buyer for it. It would take a celluloid collector to bring it a decent price.

Rebecca didn't seem to notice her mother's absence, and Adriana knew in the small, warm, giggly bundle of baby, that she had been given a second chance. Two months later, Sally dropped out of college and went to Alaska to find herself, leaving Adriana with the first family that had made sense to her since Rose.

LAURA

Laura came home after work to find Lizzie bent over a notebook at the dining room table, drawing. She was so engrossed in her work and looked so much like her own person, with her own interests and worries, it jarred Laura. She didn't know where to start with this girl.

She slammed the door to announce her entrance, and Lizzie looked up, startled like she'd woken out of a dream. Lizzie said, "Hi."

"Hi," Laura said, "How was your day?"

That distrustful frown again. "Fine."

Laura dropped her purse, slipped off her shoes, and walked to the dining room. Lizzie seemed panicked by her approach and quickly closed her notebook.

Laura slid into the chair opposite her at the table, "Whatcha drawin'?"

"Just doodling."

"Aw, come on. Lemme see."

Lizzie acted like she'd asked to see her underwear. She said, "No."

Okay, talking about drawing was out. But damn it, she was going to talk about something with Lizzie. Do *something* in her life. Laura would succeed where Bart had failed.

Lizzie said, "How was the aquarium? Anything new with the seals?" She was speaking quickly as if she were covering for something.

What *was* in that notebook?

Laura said, "The seals were barky. The sharks are still circling."

Lizzie laughed.

An idea struck Laura, suddenly and urgently. "Hey. Let's go shopping."

Lizzie said, "Now?" She looked at her as if she'd asked her to pull off her nose and hand it to her.

"No. No. This weekend. For sure. You could do with some new clothes, and since I've got no rent, I've got a little money saved up."

She seemed uncertain. "I'll ask Nonna. Uncle Bart gave me some money when he left."

He paid her off.

Laura said, "Great. We'll go Saturday."

Lizzie smiled politely. She thought for a moment and said, "Oh, wait. I promised Tisha I'd help her at the store Saturday."

"Who's Tisha?"

Lizzie was flustered by the question. "Oh, just someone I met. At the video store."

"Tisha" was better than shopping with Laura? But Laura hadn't exactly been there for Lizzie. It wasn't surprising she'd find someone else.

Laura said, "Maybe Sunday then."

"Sure, maybe Sunday. But I don't really. Um. Need anything."

"Not anything?"

"Nope."

Nope. Laura wondered if she'd been this difficult as a teen. As a child when Sally visited her. Maybe she hadn't been charming enough, and Sally just gave up on her.

Despite Laura's invitation, Lizzie remained distant and difficult to talk to. Laura tried a few more times during the week to start conversation over dinner. She credited herself with *trying*. She was trying with Lizzie, not dumping cash on her and bailing. Trying was good.

Bart.

She couldn't stop thinking about him, but she tried to be practical. She told herself she was Bart's quick hookup, a one-night stand. It wasn't much more than that, and she had projected all sorts of things onto their conversations. She had deluded herself into thinking they had a connection. She was sympathizing with a guy who lost his brother. That was all. If only he wasn't so goddamned cute. That flash of a smile. That worry over the babies. Oh. That was Chow Yun-Fat. She was doing it again. Dexter had become her Cary Grant, and Bart wasn't even the *type* to rescue a hospital full of babies. He'd probably abandon the whole lot and let the place burn to the ground.

She went to work the next day hoping to avoid Jamey, still somewhat flummoxed by her awkwardness at the Ottobar. She ran into him out on the floor, and he gave her an affable smile and a steady stare that seemed somehow less warm than *before* their night out. She wasn't sure what she'd done wrong. Maybe his friends were a test, and she'd failed. It was all uneasy tension. Maybe he knew she was obsessing over Chow Yun-Fat on her grandmother's sofa in the middle of the night.

She waited until long past the lunch hour to sneak up to the

Rusty Scupper or whatever it was called, buy a hasty tuna sandwich, and sneak it back to the office.

What she needed was a year off men entirely. It was clear that she couldn't do anything right. She needed to focus on her career and learn how to be an amazing single lady. She needed no further emotional entanglements of any kind. The problem was that between Bart and Dexter and now Jamey, her self-worth was at about nil.

She filed for an extra half hour and started organizing some binders Jamey had wanted done (left with a sticky note of course). At five-thirty, she headed down the long hallway. She was nervous about running into Jamey as she walked out into the main aquarium and was relieved when she walked into the just-cooling subtropical air of the parking lot, which looked serviceable when full, but now, emptying, showed its cracks and weeds.

The heat from the sidewalk intensified as she stepped onto the asphalt. It was close to midsummer; the sun was still high, and an almost pleasant breeze blew off the harbor. She would never get used to the humidity. She would have to learn to breathe underwater and it was one long swim. It would be easier with no men. A flash of Bart tugged in her gut, and she almost welled up with tears for the want of him, for the knowledge that she never really had him. *Asshole* she assured herself. *He's just an asshole.*

Tomorrow she would set up some informational interviews. She could do that at least. Maybe someone would hire her as a production assistant. She'd have to suck it up and take a step down if she was going to start over in this insular teeny tiny film industry. Or she could try with television. It would be a learning curve, but it was her own fault she wasn't already working in it.

She fished for her keys, and she didn't see that she was

almost on him until she looked up. She breathed in suddenly and made a startled, "Aaah" noise. The breath and the humidity carried the smell of T-shirt, fresh shampoo, soap, and young *guy*.

Jamey was leaning against her car, wearing some dumb-ass aviator glasses from the eighties, a worn-to-death T-shirt for some long-forgotten band and jeans. He had a weird look on his face.

She said, "Jamey?"

He didn't say anything.

She said, "I finished the filing, and I've got the binders half done. I'll need some more work for tomorrow unless you've run out."

He said, "It's totally unethical, you know, to hire someone just so you can ..."

He trailed off and stepped in close.

Oh.

He didn't give her that lightning-dangerous palpitation that Bart gave her. But Laura knew her attraction to him was safe. She was the one in the driver's seat for this one. He was going to kiss her, and she was going to let him.

CHAPTER SEVENTEEN

LIZZIE

Laura was suddenly interested in *talking* to me. Which was kind of annoying after the past, like almost two months – well, one and a half – of *not* talking. And I didn't really want to go shopping with her. For one, she was hard to talk to. I could imagine shopping with Tisha. When I got around to shopping again. If I *had* to go.

Mom always did the clothes shopping with me. We had our thing. We *weren't* the mother/daughter combo with the dressing rooms, the lingering over lunch, the giggling, the shopping bags. That just wasn't us. We went in, got what we needed, made sure it fit, and then bolted. Our fun times weren't about shopping at all.

Sometimes we'd go for a hike or a bike ride. Other times, she'd take me into the city to a museum. Or, the best, we would park ourselves in Central Park or on the steps of the Metropolitan Museum and people watch.

Mom always made sure I had my notebook to draw in. We'd talk a little or laugh at situations going on all around us. Young people on dates. Bratty children. Old ladies dressed up all natty in hats and jackets. A lot of times we *wouldn't* talk. But that was comfortable. And kinda great. Mom would sit, chin in hands, watching, and I'd draw. We'd be *together.*

Even though Mom and I hated shopping, we hated it *together.* I couldn't imagine shopping with anyone else. Especially not Laura.

Nonna and I could hang out *not* talking comfortably. Which was nice. But sometimes I wanted to talk *more.* We had our conversations here and there, but I think she was so used to quiet, and lately, she seemed to have run out of material.

I wondered what happened to all Nonna's friends – those back in the day holiday people. The one time I tried to ask, she said, "Lizzie, you don't need to worry about your Nonna's troubles. We're fine. We're fine, aren't we?" She said it in a voice that made me think we weren't fine at all.

One determined afternoon, I looked all over the house for a little phone book, a rolodex. Maybe I could call these people. No luck. I thought about the public phone book, but it had been two years since we'd had a proper Easter, and I only remembered parts of names. *Mr. Lipsicki. Or Lisicki. Gina somebody. Maurice or Maurizio?*

Nonna was weird about the phone. She never answered it on Friday afternoons. Every Friday afternoon around three o'clock, it rang. She said a stream of things in Italian, and that was that.

One Friday afternoon at three, the doorbell rang. I got up to answer it, but Nonna motioned me to stop with her hand and put her fingers to her lips. "Shhhhh ..."

I couldn't see who was outside from the sofa, and Nonna made it very clear she didn't want me to move. The person knocked. Waited. Knocked again. Then whoever it was went away.

When I asked Nonna who she thought it was, she said,

"Just a pesty neighbor. Always wanting something." I wondered why that pesty neighbor always wanted something on Fridays at three o'clock. I would try to answer it next time. Even if she got mad.

Nonna slept in again one Thursday. There was no rousing her, even with a clattering of dishes, because her hearing aids were out. I hung out in front of the television and watched *The Today Show* with Calzone. He didn't want lap much these days because it was so hot, but he was good company and followed me room to room. Right now, he was upside down on the hearth. That meant it was going to be seriously hot.

Ever since Laura went to work, I was almost religious about *The Today Show* because Nonna had started sleeping in, and it looked like I was going to have to learn about the world through television. Laura and Nonna sure weren't sharing. And, while Tisha was good company, she mostly talked about horror movies and college. With Bart was gone, it was me and the house and the heat outside and the video store.

Near as I could make out from *The Today Show*, the world was about diets and recipes, new clothes and makeovers. It seemed that if you ate all of the recipes, you needed the diet, and after dieting, you needed the new clothes and the makeover. I'd watch this nonsense for an hour, tops, then I'd get a headache, and I'd have to turn off the television. TV education was work.

I didn't sleep well the night before. I couldn't shake what was in the sketchbook under my bed – I shoved it back there right after Laura almost caught me with it. Knowing that I had gotten it right at last ate at me. I pulled it out three times to look at it. It couldn't stay there, but I knew I couldn't tear it up. That last page. SCRIIITCH. SCREAM. KRASH. I tore it out and folded it into four. Then I folded it again. And again. As small as it would go.

I wedged it into my pocket. That wasn't going to do. I got mom's secret message holder down from the shelf and wedged it inside, twisting and shoving. The lid screwed on almost all the way. I hung it back on the shelf, but it sorta watched me. It couldn't stay in this room. I grabbed it and tiptoed downstairs, stopping at Nonna's door to listen.

I could put it behind the books on the bookshelf. But that didn't seem safe. What if Laura wanted to read something? How would I explain what she found? I couldn't put it in the fireplace because I remembered Nonna liked fires in the winter.

The blanket chest in the dining room.

Calzone twined around my legs as I opened the out of place dark wooden chest. It was meant for blankets. Mom had one like it in our old house, but usually those sort of things went in the bedroom. When I lifted the lid, the smell of cedar and mothballs rose. Calzone jumped into the box. Cats loved boxes. I pushed him out of the way and started digging. There were some nice blankets on top, and they got older as I went down. I lifted them out, trying to remember the order they were in there so I could put them back in the same way.

I reached in to grab the last one, and my knuckles hit something hard. A book. I pulled it out, and a rain of golden triangles and photos fell into the chest. I righted it and lifted it out flat. I had dropped five photos, which I caught quickly, but the gold triangles – those bracket things they used to hold photos with – were lost down in the blankets.

The album had thick, black paper pages. The pictures were of Hollywood. How awesome. Why was all this stuff hidden?

After watching so many old movies these past few weeks, I knew some of the faces. In all the photos I'd seen where she was wearing dresses and juggling kids – she'd always looked out of place. Kind of lost. But in these pictures, Nonna was dressed so hip – always in slacks and sneakers, short-sleeved, crisp blouses. She looked really beautiful and happy. Here, she was with a lady with glasses and bangs and a little tweed suit. Her head was back, and she was laughing, so young and toothy. She was confident, and I could almost hear Mom's laugh.

In the picture, they were standing over a sketch of some sort of dress. There was Barbara Stanwyck again. There was young Nonna with Katharine Hepburn. And with Fred Astaire.

There were photos of the woman from the pictures in the living room. Lots of pictures of them together, squinting in the sun. In a garden. In a kitchen. Laughing, smiling.

Must have been her roommate.

The pictures made me suddenly lonely for my friends.

The doorbell rang. It scared the crap out of me, and I dropped the album. Since Bart brought Laura to stay with them, the doorbell hadn't rung once, except for that Friday with the pesty neighbor. I put the album in the bottom of the chest, piled a few blankets on top of it, and then nestled the ivory case on the center of those blankets, its damning picture wedged inside. I shoved the remaining blankets in on top of that and closed it. It didn't close all the way, but the doorbell rang again. What was I supposed to do? Maybe they would go away. I listened for Nonna but heard no response.

Maybe it was a package. Maybe Uncle Bart thought to send some more of my parents' stuff.

I opened the inside front door, knowing the screen door would protect me long enough to call the police. I made sure I got the phone in my hand ... just in case. Although I hadn't heard of any mid-morning axe murderers in this part of Baltimore.

There was a dumpy, anxious-looking old lady at the front door. She was wearing one of those aprony housedress things that goes over a normal dress – the ones in bright colors with pockets at the front. I never knew what those things were for. It was a printed fabric made to look like patchwork and she had short sleeves on underneath. Her hair was dyed orangish. She squinted in. Maybe she was the pesty neighbor.

"Hello?"

She said, "Hello."

We stood for a minute and she said, "Is Adriana at home?" She had an Italian accent. She seemed familiar.

"Uh ... she's sleeping. Can I help you?"

She was out of breath. "Can ... Can I come in for a minute, honey? I hiked it all the way here from Eastern Avenue."

Not a neighbor. She didn't look like an axe murderer. I let her in.

When the screen swung outward, the hot wet air came in. Yesterday's rain hadn't cooled anything off at all. Another sucky summer day.

The lady sat on the sofa like it was hers, and I sat opposite her. She put a pink pastry box out in front of her. It was tied with white string.

I supposed I was the host. I didn't want to get Nonna up. Something told me she wouldn't want to see anyone with her teeth and hearing aids out and no makeup on. I said, "Can I get you something to drink?"

She smiled, looking at me. "Elisabetta, right? You're Adriana's great granddaughter."

"Yeah."

"My, but you've grown. Could you just get me a glass of water, hon? It's too hot to think about anything else."

When I came back with the water, she had the box open, and inside were those brightly colored pink and green Italian almond cookies, some with maraschino cherries and the sweet almondy smell that rose from the box transported me to better times. The Before Nonna always used to have them around.

Before. My face must have said *yum*, because Gina smiled and motioned to the box.

I took a pink one. Two bright pink kiss-shaped cookies with a wedge of raspberry jam in between. I took a bite. They were the real thing. The almondy kind that melt in your mouth. There were fakes of this, I'd eaten them, all powdered sugar and flour and no flavor. But these? The best ever.

She must have seen it on my face because she said, "You like these?"

I said, "I LOVE these."

She chuckled and sat back. She said, "Is your great grand-mother home or is she out?"

"She's sleeping. I said ..." I stopped myself. Musn't talk back.

"Is she okay?" She was genuinely worried.

I didn't know what she meant by okay. "Why do you keep asking?"

"Honey, your grandmother ... the great. She's stopped talking to all her friends."

"What?" I had thought maybe it was the other way around. I should have been doing something all this time here. All I'd been doing was trying to find a way to get her out, but I hadn't done the obvious thing: found her friends. I'd given up after not finding a phone book. Lame.

This lady would know where more of them were. We could have them over, get Nonna out of her rut.

"There're a handful of us. We come over every Easter and Christmas, but we'd always see her in between, out at the market. Then one day she stopped." I knew this, but I didn't really get how much Nonna was stuck until now. "I call every week – the same time we used to meet for coffee – Friday after-noons. But no answer. I came by once, but nothing."

"Oh. That was you." No pesty neighbor at all. I could have

let her in weeks ago. Here she was, but I felt suddenly protective of Nonna, like there was some answer I wasn't briefed on, and if I said the wrong thing, family security would be breached. This had to be done carefully.

I asked, "How long has it been since you saw her?"

"Four months. Easter Night."

Before Mom and Dad. So we don't have to talk about that. Thank God. Must have been the hip.

"Uh. She broke her hip."

Gina, at first gleeful to have heard the answer to the mystery said, "Aaaaaah," and leaned back on the sofa, nodding and sipping her water. Then a frown crossed her face. She said, "Why didn't she call me? I coulda helped. I could check in on her, bring her groceries. Why wouldn't she call me?" I felt like she was holding me responsible.

I said, "I don't know."

"She didn't think we'd take care of her? She shoulda called me."

She fell silent. I finished my cookie, and I wanted another one. They were the kind with chocolate kisses pressed into the top, and I knew those were good. Gina was upset, ruminating. I casually leaned in and took a pink cookie and began to eat it. She didn't notice.

The frowning stopped, and the lady put on her company face. "I'm so sorry, Elisabetta. Do you even remember me?"

I shook my head. My mouth was too full. It wasn't as good as the last one, and it was making me thirsty.

"I'm Mrs. Lipsicki. Gina."

I squinted sideways. I remembered Mr. Lipsicki. But recognizing her seemed really important, so I said, "Ohhhh ... yeaaahhhhh."

"The last time I saw you, you musta been. Five? Six?"

Then I remembered. "You had the boyfriend who sang."

She blushed and smiled, "He's my husband now. Mr. Lipsicki."

He was a skinny old man with wild Einstein hair, and he sang a song in a language I hadn't heard before. He said it was about a mountain goat. I remembered laughing. And Dad was laughing, too. Really hard. It was one of the times he came with us, and he'd had too much wine. He always turned bright red when he drank, which wasn't often. I leaned against him and his arm was on the chair behind me, a safe little tent. I was so happy that day.

I took another bite of cookie.

Mrs. Lipsicki smiled. She said, "How's your mama doing, honey? I haven't seen her in a while."

The cookie got stuck in my throat. I couldn't swallow it. I couldn't say anything, and it was hard to breathe. I held up my finger and went into the kitchen. I wanted to hurl into the sink, but that was going to be too embarrassing. I got down a glass, filled it with water, and drank one gulp. It almost came up. Two more gulps, and I was in the clear.

Aside from Tisha ... a girl I didn't know that well and who didn't know *them*, I hadn't had to *tell* anyone the news before. Other people did it for me. What was I supposed to say? *She's dead. He's dead too.*

And Nonna didn't even tell her friends. She just stopped calling them. It hit me that maybe Nonna was more upset about Mom dying than I knew. Like how Mom would be bummed if I died. I was stupid for not getting that before.

I pinched my finger with my fingernails so it would hurt so much I wouldn't have to think. I came back and sat down. Mrs. Lipsicki looked worried.

I looked down at the floor, still pinching, and it just kinda spilled out because there was no other way, "My mom and dad

died in a cab accident in the city. New York City. About ..." I
had to count. Had so long passed? "Six weeks ago."

The pictures I'd drawn ran through my head quickly.
Mom's head on Dad's shoulder. The taxi driver joking. The
taxi driver turning around to see them. The crash. *Scriiitch!*
The shatter of the windshield. The mouth open with blood, the
broken windshield just in front, like Tisha's paused movie.

I would not cry in front of this lady.

I tried to look at Mrs. Lipsicki more closely in order to stop
the images. Her face was soft and paunchy under the chin, but
she was definitely younger than Nonna. She looked worried.
Nonna was obviously important to her.

Wait. Nonna stopped talking to her friends, she was so
upset. Like they couldn't get her on the phone, and she
wouldn't answer her door. I didn't know why her being upset
made me feel better. But it did.

Mrs. Lipsicki said, "What? That's impossible. I just saw
Rebecca ..."

Was it a mistake? Maybe Mom had moved and was still
alive. Hope had a chance to lurch in my chest. She said, "Just
last year," and I realized that this was just a confused old lady
trying to find her place in the news. "She was so ..." Tears
welled up in her eyes and ran down her cheeks so fast I worried
she'd sprung a leak. I wished Nonna was there to take over. I
could go to my room and hide out with Calzone until Mrs.
Lipsicki left.

"Oh, Elisabetta. I'm so. So sorry. You poor kid." Her crying
turned into her own thing as she lowered her face in her hands and
sobbed. I gave her a minute, but I wanted to disappear. She looked
up and took a longer look around the room. "No wonder she hasn't
called. That poor thing." Her voice was wet and uncomfortable
and she wailed, exaggerated and desperate. "I need to see her."

Fortunately, that sounded so silly and loud it made me stop wanting to cry. I knew Nonna would not like anyone to see her without her teeth, hearing aid, or makeup, but she *definitely* wouldn't want to see this sopping wet mess of a woman.

"Mrs. Lipsicki?"

She sobbed, "Please. Call me Gina."

"Um, Gina? Nonna's okay. I'm here now. I'm sure she wants to get in touch, but it's been ... hard. We're getting by here. We just need." The word *need* hurt. I thought for a moment and said, "Time. We need some time."

She said, "I can help, you know. I can."

I said, "I know." And I believed she could. I just didn't know how.

ADRIANA

Adriana heard Gina's high-pitched voice in the living room and pulled her sheet over her head. She was having enough trouble getting up this morning.

It was going to happen sooner or later. Her friends wouldn't just disappear. For the past four months, she just ignored the phone and the front door. She screened calls on the answering machine. Gina's messages, always drowning in guilt, drove her crazy. "Hi, Adriana. It's your friend, Gina?" Like she wouldn't know. "I've been worried about you hon. We all have. You can't just shut us out. You need us."

They needed her to cook their holiday meals. She was always the one doing all the work. She knew she was selfish for thinking that way.

Gina spoke loudly to answering machines as if they'd just been invented. "Anything that's wrong, we can handle. If there's someone helping you, and you had a stroke or something, hello, Someone? Give me a call, we can help. We love our Adriana. We need to help her. Please call me at ..."

Gina called almost every day, and after a while the minute

she heard Gina's voice, she'd just delete the whole message without listening. The problem with people was ignoring them didn't make them go away. Ignoring them just made bad things happen around you. Unavoidable things.

Only five months before, Adriana had just been getting to a place of contentment in her life. Years before, when she was taking care of Rebecca she felt full of purpose. When Rebecca moved out, Adriana was spinning in space again with nothing to ground her.

She was depressed for a while, but her friends kept coming by. Pete and Cristina, Jerry and Anna, Gina, Maurizio. They would call ahead and drop by for tea and bring something nice. She realized that she had things pretty good. Friends who looked in on her. Daily walks to the markets. Her life was fine, and when Becca returned with Lizzie and George for holidays, it made everything okay. Becca, happy and successful in life proved to Adriana she wasn't a total failure. She'd done that one thing right.

That Easter, Becca said that she and George were going to spend Easter in New York City and have brunch with George's brother Bart. It was the third year they missed. But each time, Becca offered profuse apologies and sent a basket of fruit or a bouquet of flowers in her stead.

Adriana went about shopping for her usual crowd, which had grown some, as Jerry and Anna brought their kids, now in college, and Gina had Phil, whom she finally agreed to marry.

The familiarity of shopping for the meal was good, as was cooking it. The entire effort took a week, and when Adriana looked around the table at her friends, flush with wine and full of food, she was as happy as she got these days. Becca made sure to call and made her laugh on Easter day. Adriana thought *this isn't so bad.* It wasn't what she pictured, but her life was full of friends, and she was learning to enjoy it again.

She didn't get to the Sunday paper on Easter until after the company had gone. Easter Sunday night, she looked through the obits, which every so often would feature a friend or an old workmate. This particular Easter Sunday night, the obits inexplicably featured Rose.

It was that gorgeous glamour shot of her reclining on the sofa – only not. It was a different pose from the one Adriana had on her mantle – the one Adriana looked at on her blackest days. When she was only nostalgic, she'd look at the photo of them together young and happy, squinting in the sun. That was a picture of her youth. But the picture of Rose, reclined on the sofa, her eyes reflecting the studio lights, her gorgeous, full perfectly painted lips, the longing in her eyes – this was the picture that carried with it loss and regret and the career that didn't happen for Adriana, and worse yet, the career that didn't ever really happen for Rose. It carried the unfinished screenplay, the possible stardom, the support not given. It carried the Betrayal.

In the picture in the newspaper, her arm was down, not up over her head. Her lips were parted ever so slightly and her opposite eyebrow was raised. Rose caught at a time Adriana hadn't witnessed, Rose having another life without her. The photo hit her with a wave of panic, had she been in Baltimore all this time? Why was it in the local paper? The article read:

Rose Mallory was found dead in her Laurel Canyon home in Los Angeles on Saturday. The body's mummified state, enhanced by a space heater that had been left on, indicated that she may have been dead for almost a year. Neighbors say the reclusive Mallory did not often appear outside her home, but when her neighbor, Michael Gonzales, noticed her mailbox stuffed with envelopes, he called the police. She appeared to have died of natural causes. She was eighty-five years old.

Mallory was a bit player in the golden age of Hollywood and was best known for her role as the fiery sidekick in a string of B-movies for RKO in the late 1940s, including the Oscar-winning Heaven Knows. *Hollywood lost track of Mallory sometime in the 1950s, and she was rumored to have battled alcoholism. She resurfaced in the 1980s briefly with a guest spot on* The Love Boat. *There is no record of her having worked after that.*

Mallory had no living relatives.

All that time. And the detective couldn't find her. All that time, she was right there in the Hollywood Hills, alone. Probably a half-mile from their cottage on Melrose. So alone that she could die, and no one would find her for a year. Adriana was alone for so long, years they could have spent together. But the detective couldn't find her. And now she was in the local paper across the country from where she died, simply because of the unusual circumstances of her body's discovery.

Adriana sat for a long time. When old folks or friends passed, there was always someone to call. "So sad. She was still young. He still ..." But she didn't have anyone to call about Rose. She didn't know anything about Rose's life. Was her house nice? How did she pay for it? Did she work? Did she have a girlfriend who worked? Had she gotten married to a man, like Adriana?

Why did she ever marry Sal?

She left Rose. Sure, Rose kicked her out, but she should have fought for her. The regret rushed up in her and a desperation to reach Rose. Adriana always held onto hope that she was out there, somewhere. She had often fantasized about running into Rose on a street corner. Seeing her in a movie. Finding a phone number. That one reconnect, where they both recognized that Adriana had messed up, but they had enough years and experience between them to let it all go and just embrace.

She imagined Rose looking the same, maybe gray, but still healthy. That she had found some other career outside the industry. That she had anonymously been leading some sort of happy life. Walking in the hills. Maybe she had a dog. In Adriana's imaginings, Rose would be happy to see Adriana but had found someone else. Adriana imagined Rose's more understanding, open girlfriend, and she thought she would be jealous – but she deserved that. Entire lifetimes with Rose in it had played out in her head.

But there it was. No answers. No second chance. Rose died. Old and alone.

Adriana couldn't breathe. Here was her house, the house where she had lived a clumsily cobbled life with Sal. The house where she had unsuccessfully raised two children. Children raised in a lie did not thrive. She didn't love them enough. She didn't love Sal enough.

And she'd never loved Rose the way she deserved to be loved.

Adriana got up and threw open the front door, hoping some evening air would help. But it wasn't enough. She still couldn't breathe. She stepped outside onto the porch.

The evening was chilly and quiet, a lingering smell of flowers the only remaining sign of spring. The neighbors were inside, watching their televisions, their children safe in bed.

She heard the clicking of heels on the sidewalk a few houses down. She recognized that walk – that woman-about-town confident walk. She squinted down the street to see who it was. She knew it was wrong, but she recognized the long gait, the shoulders back, the head down, intent on its business. She recognized that jaunty little hat that cost her a whole five dollars when they could barely afford it.

Rose.

It can't be her, not really. She stood, rapt, worried she would scare away the apparition in front of her. Rose kept walking, never looking up.

Adriana called her name, but Rose walked on, the seams on her stockings straight as always.

Adriana stepped out after her and something CRACKED, and she fell down her front steps.

The ambulance man was so friendly and tried to keep things chipper. He made some corny jokes about her not running the marathon any time soon.

The hip surgery was painful, as was the recovery, but Sally came to take care of her. And Adriana just ... went inside for a while, to a safe place in her mind where she didn't have to think. She stared into space and tuned it all out: Sally's constant yammering about the universe doing things for a reason, concerned phone calls, doctor's advice.

When she slept, her dreams were all of their little cottage off Melrose. Cooking dinners. Making love. Sewing patterns. Edith. Missy. The dreams started out as joyful reunions. She came across Rose in her office, perched in her chair, cigarette burning, hand waving Adriana away so she could type out that next line. She and Rose were coiled around each other in the bathtub or in bed. She and Rose painted their dining room together. Adriana was dropped into a scene, and it was as real as being there.

But something always went awry. Sometimes Rose faded and disappeared, and Adriana was left with a hole inside her, a choking desperation. Other times, they would be so peaceful, so right together, and suddenly the knowledge of betrayal over-took Rose's face, and Adriana would tell her she was sorry. But all the dreams ended the same way: Rose fading away or walking off at her tight clip.

Rose leaving.

Adriana woke crying every morning for two months. The moment she opened her eyes, she saw, framed across from her bed, Sal's aerial photo of the Paramount lot taken in the 1940s, Edith's bungalow visible one soundstage away from the commissary. Her bedroom was now in Sal's "office," a room behind the laundry with enough space for a bed, a side table, and a walker.

The photo was a harsh reminder of her betrayal, of all the things that didn't happen. She didn't have the energy to move it and didn't feel she deserved the peace of having it gone. She got herself together as quickly as she could because if she didn't get out of her room by nine, Sally would come knocking on the door.

Sally drove her nuts, but Adriana figured she brought it on herself. Sally made up for Adriana's emotional absence by muscling through life in a noisy, self-affirming way. She talked at Adriana all day, but fortunately, she didn't seem to need much response. Her childhood muttering of platitudes had elaborated into monologues on the bits of philosophies she had acquired on her trip through the cafeteria of religions. Catholi-cism, Kabbala, Kickapoo, Buddhism, and Hinduism had all mixed up in her head to become some large, self-referential, bungled ideology. But it made sense to Sally, and that gave Adriana some comfort.

In the meantime, Sally graciously helped Adriana to the bathroom, cooked her meals, and cleaned up. She protested only a little when Adriana neglected to answer the phone or the door, but her philosophy included an acceptance of different "paths." Adriana didn't entirely understand it, but it kept Sally out of her business. After four weeks, when Adriana could handle the basics on her own, she sent Sally home.

Two weeks later, Sally was back. Becca had been killed.

Adriana supposed this was more punishment. That God would, of course, take away the one child she loved more than herself – the kid with whom she had finally gotten it right. She didn't deserve Becca and her family. George, Lizzie, and Becca glowed with the success of Becca's upbringing. Adriana didn't deserve to be proud of anything she'd done in her life. She had betrayed one person so miserably and had failed Sal and his daughters.

When Bart, George's shiftless brother dropped Lizzie off with her, Adriana knew she couldn't afford self-pity. It took her digging her way upwards through the heavy, gray blankets of sorrow and regret, closing her eyes to the photo of the Paramount lot, unseemly heaving through the sharp pain in her hip and muscles, and a walker that got her out of bed every morning.

But she did it. Sometimes later than she meant to.

She didn't know if she had the strength to take care of Lizzie or in any way be the parent that Lizzie so desperately needed, but it was becoming clear that Laura wasn't going to step up, nor was Bart. Adriana had another chance to screw up a human being for life.

Gina's sobs from the next room made it clear that Adriana had simply opted out of Baltimore, just like she did years ago when Edith foisted Sal upon her. She was hiding in her room avoiding things while real life consequences were going on outside the door. Hiding from the real world didn't help anything last time, and she lost her love. Real life was seeping in again in the form of one friend calling on her, so many others worried for her. And the collision of Lizzie and Gina, two people whose complications she was avoiding might create a whole new complication if she just lay here. It was time.

Rose didn't have a Gina to check on her. Rose was mummified before anyone thought to even look for her.

CHAPTER EIGHTEEN

LIZZIE

Over the summer, Uncle Bart called every Sunday. This went on for about a month and then, somewhere in the middle of July ...he stopped. I worried that it was because I didn't have anything interesting to report. Just what I'd cooked for dinner. That Nonna was napping. That Laura was out – she was always *out*. I guess after a while, he just didn't want to call anymore. I learned after the second time he called not to ask when he'd be coming down. I hadn't really learned to count on him. I mean, he *left* and all, and he didn't want me moving in with him. But I still missed him.

Laura started dating that Otter guy – Jamey – and he came by once and was *sooo* happy to see me and seemed friendly with Nonna, and we had a great time, but he didn't come back. I think it might have been because Laura didn't want him to, because Nonna kept asking Laura to bring him to Sunday dinner, but she didn't.

Nonna didn't have her friends over just yet. But she did talk to Gina on the telephone once a week – Friday afternoons at three. I only heard Nonna's half of the conversation, her patient tone, like she was dealing with a child. But the calls were good for her. She always seemed a bit more *there* when she hung up. She was definitely more *there* every day after Gina's visit. Like the visit, no matter how awkward, no matter Nonna didn't come out of her room, the visit opened some kind of door in Nonna and she could be present.

Tisha was extremely cool all summer. She let me hang out in the video store, and while Nonna showed me all the black and white movies, Tisha showed me some cool more recent movies like *Young Sherlock Holmes* and *The Pink Panther*. They weren't *that* recent, but they were in color.

And one day in late July, Tisha got *Akira* in. I'd read the manga a thousand times – Dad got it for my twelfth birthday – I didn't even know they'd made a movie. She told me it was an *anime*, which is what they called it when they made an animated manga or something.

We watched it on a rainy day when it was slow. Tisha made a big bag of popcorn, and I brought the soda from the corner store because the prices at Video Planet were ridiculous. She put it on the big television above the action movie section instead of the little TV by the counter. It was *beautiful*. Something about knowing the story, knowing those drawings, every frame from the manga, and how it came together in action clicked something bigger in my head. I had never been so excited about something before. The best part was that I knew that story backwards, forwards, inside out, and I could fill Tisha in on smaller story stuff the movie forgot to put in. She dug it as much as I did.

After that we started watching more violent real movies again. A lot of Hong Kong movies. Jackie Chan, John Woo. I watched *Hard Boiled* again and loved it. Getting those drawings out of my system helped. Tisha gave me awesome posters from the store, and my room was actually starting to look pretty cool.

And I was drawing again. My style was changing a little, and there was more violence in the comics I came up with. But it was all good – it felt right.

The rest of the summer wasn't so bad. Movies in the morning with Tisha while Nonna slept in, movies in the afternoon and evening with Nonna. We cooked and shopped. About the time Laura disappeared on us, Nonna got cleared to use a cane and drive. Once a week, we went to the supermarket. I asked Nonna about going to her regular markets, but she shook her head and grumbled. A suggestion of going to the park went over just as well.

In hindsight, I think maybe she was just depressed. I didn't get it then. After a while, she stopped doing her makeup for me. She didn't always get dressed every day. Sometimes she didn't get up 'til ten or eleven. I stopped trying to fix her and started getting used to the new Nonna. I loved her a lot. She just made me sad sometimes.

Sometimes Nonna was good to talk to about stuff. We talked a lot about the movies. About romantic comedies. About the characters and the dialogue and how funny things were. Sometimes I could make her laugh by saying a particular line to her. I begged her to tell stories about Hollywood. I never let on I'd seen her photo album, and I knew how to ask questions in the right way, but any mention of Hollywood would make her go quiet, and she'd make up some excuse she needed to lie down or something. I stopped asking after a while.

She enrolled me at St. Casimir's School, and it was really hard at first, being the only girl who looked like me and being the only girl who hadn't been in that school for eight or nine years already. Aside from one Peruvian kid, I was the only other kid who wasn't white in the whole place. But after a while, I kind of got used to it. Maybe all of that time over the summer made me not mind being alone. Now that I think about it, I was probably just depressed, too.

I made one good friend at school. Sometimes, that was enough. I still missed Mom and Dad something fierce. Certain things set me off – burnt toast, an old photo of Mom found pressed inside a book, Uncle Bart's voice. But overall, I got used to my new days.

I ate breakfast alone or sometimes with Laura, who didn't talk much. I was kinda grateful she stopped trying to have conversations. I walked to school. School itself wasn't much different from my old school, despite the scratchy uniforms and one nun who taught religion in a truly creepy way. My lunch was cheese and jam sandwiches – Nonna let me make my own lunches. One of the perks of being an orphan.

I walked home and did homework on Nonna's coffee table. I made dinner. I learned that sometimes with chicken all you needed was a variety of sauces to keep things interesting. Teriyaki, salsa, spaghetti sauce and cheese, Chinese black bean sauce. All served with rice or pasta, depending. Salad. We ate pretty well.

It didn't bother me at the time that Nonna didn't get up until late. That she didn't get dressed. I made my peace that she was an old lady. That was her place in things. She always showed up for supper, and that was nice. I learned not to expect too much from anyone anymore. Mom and Dad were like a far-off castle in my childhood, the happy part before orphanhood. Life was some sort of adventure I was on alone now. I grew comfortable with that.

I tried not to think about what would happen if Nonna kicked the bucket.

Laura checked in enough to remind us that she was mostly absent. There were a lot of nights she didn't come home. After the first two weeks, I stopped waiting up for her. She was such the *not*mom that I thought of her more as a curiosity in our life. Like the mailman. Only less dependable.

The heat broke somewhere around the end of September, and the cooling air brought fall. The leaves didn't change like they did at home in Pelham. They just got kind of yellow and brown and fell off.

Nonna made Laura take me shopping one weekend for new clothes. I had outgrown a lot of stuff over the summer, so it was necessary. Laura tried to be chatty, but we still weren't clicking. Some people were just like that. She waited at the counter while I tried things on. She was cagey when I asked her how much I should spend but bought me everything I put on the counter. It made me wonder if I shouldn't go overboard just to bug her, but I'd been raised to be a practical shopper. I got two sweaters, a pile of long sleeve shirts, and two pairs of jeans. One pair of corduroys and, on Laura's insistence, one dress. At least she took me to a store where I could get something halfway decent, a gray turtleneck sweater dress. Classy.

All the time we spent together felt like a chore. I have to say I did a pretty fair amount of teen sulking. After the shopping trip, I wasn't surprised when she didn't come home for a week.

My school was out the week of Thanksgiving. The whole week.

Nonna and I were watching *Meet John Doe,* which had a lot of slow parts. I said, "Nonna?"

"Mmm?"

"Can we? I mean. Like, DO Thanksgiving?" I was getting tired of chicken.

She didn't say anything for a while, but I could see by the way the television light stopped reflecting off her glasses that she was thinking. She oofed her BarcaLounger closed. She scooched around in her chair to face me. She said, "You know what, Lizzie?"

"What, Nonna?" It was a schtick we had. Our little bits of schtick were no substitute for real conversation, but they were comforting in their own way.

Nonna said, "I think it's about time we got the family together. Thanksgiving is a pretty good reason for it, don't you think?"

I blurted it out before I thought better of it, "Can you ask the neighborhood friends? The ones from the old days?" I was surprised that my need for the old Nonna was rearing its head again – that futile hope that she'd get out of her funk.

She didn't answer but turned back to the TV set.

Nonna was on the phone that night when I went to bed, and when I got up from bed in the middle of the night, she was still talking to someone. Maybe she was calling her old gang. Gina and all them. It gave me a little hope.

The next morning, Nonna was up when I was up. And she was dressed. She had some old grimy books out of the cabinet in a pile on the kitchen table. Her face was puckered into a frown as she looked through one binder filled with notebook paper and pencil scrawls. When I looked closely, I saw that they were recipes written in Italian.

"Are we having an Italian Thanksgiving?" I was worried. She talked about this fish dish or something, and I didn't want to be eating squid when everyone else in the world was having turkey.

That wheeze came again. She started laughing and muttering in Italian and shaking her head. She hadn't spoken in Italian for a long time. At least since Laura came. Since it came with laughing, I took it as a good sign, this time.

"No, no, honey. We'll have a turkey. And pie ... pumpkin

and apple. And my special cornbread dressing. And mushrooms. And green beans almondine. And sweet potato ..."

I said, "Gnocchi?" Mom always made sweet potato gnocchi at Thanksgiving. Her one Italian throwback. I didn't know it wasn't something served at the original Thanksgiving until about two years ago. I thought ynoki was a Wampanoag word.

Nonna said, "It's about time you learned how to make it." She held her finger on the page she was looking over, and she looked at me, long and hard. It had been a while since she did that.

"Lizzie."

Whenever a grownup addressed me by name, I knew it was going to be something heavy.

"Yes, Nonna?"

She wasn't making light this time. "Lizzie, I haven't been a good grandmother to you these months past."

Too heavy for me. I said, "Well, Nonna, that's because you're not my grandmother. You're my *great*-grandmother."

She smiled and laughed. I kept up, hoping she wouldn't get heavy again. "You're a great *great-grandmother*. I mean you're very good at being great. I mean. Who else would show me all those movies? And let me live in her house? And. And ..."

I started to run out of material, and I knew that wasn't good.

Nonna put her hand up to stop me. "It's no fair. No fair Rebecca and your dad left you. No fair you came to live with your one hundred-and-two-year-old grandmother."

"Wow, you're *that* old?"

She knew I was joking. She put her hand up again. "But I'm on a cane now. I'm feeling ..." she stopped for a moment, put her hands to her knees, and got up. She wheezed a little as she did so. "I'm feeling stronger now. It's time to teach you how to cook."

What was really good, aside from seeing Nonna have some purpose in her life, was having someone else in charge for once.

ADRIANA

In this dream, Adriana is stretched out on the horsehair sofa in the living room of their cottage off Melrose, wearing her silk-lined wool slacks and a blouse. She is reading a book. She can't make out what it is, but she knows that she loves it. Rose comes to the top of the stairs in the archway, looking at her – that look she used to thrive on – the one that let Adriana know she was understood, that she was desirable and merely being Adriana was enough. That look fills her with warmth from her toes, up her legs, over her body, culminating in a burst in her chest.

She puts her book down on the coffee table and stretches her arms in the air, luxuriously. She surveys her hands. Her arms are lean, tanned from the sun and so, so young. She runs her fingers down one arm and up another, loving the feel of her pliant skin, the strength in her needle-calloused fingers. She summons Rose to her.

Rose smiles, walks down the stairs and sits on the edge of the sofa next to Adriana, taking her face in her hands and kissing her, long and deep. Adriana can feel how supple her own skin is, how firm and young and compact her breasts are as Rose runs her hands down them, and her belly, soft but tight, no sagging or stretched out skin from pregnancies. She is in this moment, alive and young, and she dwells in her body, feeling every inch of it. But when Rose's hand gets to her hip, she feels a sharp pain. Rose sits up from kissing her and her brow furrows, "What's wrong, hon?"

Adriana's youthful body recedes, and her aged body returns to her, pulling her away from Rose who reaches for her frantically. Adriana says, "Rose!" but her voice is all cracked and weak and old and her arm is heavy and hard to lift, and she can feel the skin of her chin hitting where its soft aged folds rest against her breastbone.

Adriana woke up crying, looking at the Paramount lot. Her cane was draped on the end of the bed with her housecoat. And larger even than the loss of Rose in this dream, was the loss of the body she once had. The bicycling, running, dancing, leaping, lovemaking, free-standing body.

LAURA

Laura woke up with sun in her eyes, and she knew in two breaths that she was at Jamey's apartment. Again. He hadn't gotten it together to get curtains and, while there was a part of her that knew she could go out and *buy* him some curtains, she knew that would mean that she had agreed somehow to become the live-in girlfriend. It took her back to Dexter and his house that she bought and furnished. She decided that she could put up with Jamey's mattress-boxspring-floor combination as long as the sheets were clean, and he did his dishes.

The sex was nice. He knew what to do to make her feel good. He was a good listener and was deeply – perhaps too deeply – into her. In his eyes, the sun rose and set by her. He was a *really, really* good guy. He was nice and thoughtful to old ladies and children and knew everything about the animals and the tanks and spoke about them with such wonder and enthusiasm that kept money coming into the aquarium.

He made a steady living. He rubbed her back after a long day at work. He rubbed her feet just *because*. He cooked for her. He made a pretty good spaghetti Bolognese after she taught him how to sauté the garlic gently instead of singeing it. When he laughed really hard, his nose snorted, and he had a habit of putting his hands in the rim of his jeans when he was watching television. He liked movies okay, but preferred the really violent, contemporary ones. He watched basketball with Garth and Eric when they were into it but didn't mind missing a game. He murmured in his sleep some mornings, silly things about penguins, or he burst out exclamations such as "what are you talking about?" or, "I don't *think* so." That always made her laugh.

Laura had a deep, lasting affection for Jamey, but try as she might, she couldn't love him. Here she was in his bed again because greater than the dread of hearing him say, "I love you," one more time was the idea of his face when she told him that she didn't.

So far, she had gotten by on saying, "I don't think I'm ready to say that again, yet." Jamey was sympathetic to her terrible relationship with Dexter and liked to think of himself as her gallant rescuer.

It wasn't going to last.

That day when he kissed her in the parking lot, she was startled and flattered. They went out for pizza and drank some beer and wound up back at his place, and she forgot about making calls about the movie business and forgot about anything except that there she was, she had something to do after work, and for the first time in a long while, life seemed ... manageable.

And that was enough.

She tried calling Bart only twice more. Once, when he answered, she hung up. Another time, two months later, she called him on a night Jamey was out with his friends. They had a brief conversation in which he sounded happy to hear from her, then she went on too fast about something or other, and he got all irritated. "Why are you calling me?" Again with that dumbass question. She hung up.

She did like the attention Jamey gave her. She liked the playful notes he left on her desk in the mornings. She liked the look on Beth's face as she stood agape at the front desk when Laura walked to Jamey's car with him or on Petra's face when they showed up at another gig for the Ziggies. She liked not having to spend so much time at Nonna's house, trying so hard with Lizzie, missing Becca.

Laura did a lot of not thinking about things. She didn't think about the Baltimore movie industry – that thought only brought regret, resentment, and LA back. She had a job and a boyfriend, what more could a girl want?

She didn't think about Lizzie – this was easier the more nights she spent with Jamey. She didn't think about Becca, also aided by nights not spent in their childhood room. She didn't think about Dexter – definitely a positive change. She got really good at not thinking about Bart, although he crept into her dreams here and there, or into her daydreams at random, annoying moments.

LIZZIE

The last time I called Uncle Bart, it was a short conversation, and he had to go. He made me feel bad for calling, and then I was angry, I felt bad and mad at him for being that way, and I didn't feel like talking to him again. But after a while, I found myself wishing he would call and imagining what I would say when he did.

When Nonna told me to call him and ask him to Thanksgiving, I got all stressed out and full of butterflies like I was calling someone I had a crush on or something. I told myself not to be stupid.

I drew the phone once in my notebook – all black ink – and then hung the real phone up twice before I got the guts to dial his number.

I was relieved when I got an answering machine.

He called later that night, and I was glad Laura wasn't home because she's so weird about him anyway.

He said, "Hey, Lizzie, what's up? Everything okay?"

Cuz why should I be calling? *Argh!* "Yeah. Yeah, of course. Um. Nonna says you have to come for Thanksgiving."

He laughed, "*Have to,* huh?"

What, didn't he *want* to come?

I said, "I mean, *I* don't think you have to, I'm just telling you what she said. Did you have plans?"

"No. No. When does she want me?"

I said, "Wednesday or Thursday, whatever."

"How've you been, Liz?" There was a little guilt for not calling me in his voice. This was good. I'd take what I could get.

"Fine. Fine."

"How's school?"

"It's all right."

"Got any friends?"

I said, "So what time do you think you want to get here?"

He said, "I have to work Wednesday, so I'll come Thursday. What have you been up to?"

"The usual. School. Home. Nonna's been showing me a lot of movies. Old movies."

"Did you know that Nonna used to work in the movies?"

I didn't say anything because I wasn't sure if I was *supposed* to know. It made me feel like I needed to protect Nonna. From what I wasn't sure.

He said, "Lizzie?"

I said, "No. I mean. No kidding."

"Yeah, I was flipping around one night, and I got stuck on this old movie. There she was in the credits. Turns out she had this whole, like, career designing costumes – or being an assistant to a big-time designer. I looked it up."

"Wow." Designing costumes. Weird. My whole life I'd never seen anything Nonna sewed.

"Yeah, wow."

There was this looooooooong silence. His breathing got deeper. I didn't know why he was getting so heavy about

Nonna, when he said, "I miss your dad, Lizzie. I miss him something awful."

His saying that unscrewed something in me. Something I didn't know I'd been holding for a few months now. I said, "I miss him too." But it came out all husky because I started crying.

He said, "I used to talk to him about *everything*, you know?" I could tell he was crying, too.

I snurfed, but managed to get out, "Yeah? Like what?"

Uncle Bart said, "Stuff. You know. Life stuff. Girl stuff."

I laughed. "Eeew."

"No. I mean, *my* girl stuff. He loved your mom so much. She was the only girl he'd talk about. Unless it was you."

"Okay, then." It was okay I was crying. It was just sort of flowing, but I could still talk.

"I could ask him about *anything*, and he was always there with an answer. He had good advice on what *shoes* to buy. How to solve problems with friends. Problems at work. How to talk to my boss. *Anything*. Whenever I had a problem, I could call him."

I didn't say anything. I couldn't think of anything appropriate. I just wondered with my entire being where the hell Uncle Bart had been since Dad died.

"And do you know what I'd ask him? If I could call him today? Like right now?"

"No."

"I'd ask him how to talk to you."

"Um. Actually calling me on the phone would be a start." I couldn't help it, it came out.

He laughed, a "Ha!"

I said, "I'm sorry."

"*Touché.* I mean. You're right. I'm sorry, Liz."

"And coming for Thanksgiving. That would be good."

"Gotcha. And thank you for the invite."

"Of course. You're family." It was a foreign thing to say, but it felt more potentially real than if I'd said it before we both cried. "Okay. See you Thursday."

"Hey, Lizzie, before you go?"

I said, "Yeah?"

"I'm sorry I've been a total douche all this time."

"Um. Thanks?"

He laughed a short *heh*. "See you Thursday."

LAURA

Laura was toying with the idea of flying back to LA to spend Thanksgiving with Janelle. But Janelle had been hard to get on the phone, and whenever she talked to her, Laura hung up steamed. Janelle was the annoying, judgy, upper-middle-class white hausfrau again. That one moment of sisterly connection months ago – that moment Janelle had suggested she go to Baltimore – seemed never to have happened.

Janelle asked sharply, "Do you have a job?"

Laura said, "Yes."

Janelle said, "Well, where?"

Even answering the question was an admission of complete defeat. As Laura described her job to her sister, what she felt like she was really saying was, "I flunked life." But what she said was, "I'm working at the National Aquarium."

Janelle was hopeful, "Oh, with the animals?"

"No. No. I'm filing, organizing. Working for a junior manager there. Mostly paperwork."

There was a long, judgmental pause. Janelle said, "Well, I'm glad you've got a job. That's good. That's really good."

And Laura hated her sister from the bottom of her Chuck Taylors with the burning hatred that only a sibling can conjure. Janelle had essentially patted her on the head and given her up for lost. She got off the phone quickly, and Laura curled up in a ball on Becca's old bed, rolled up in her blanket, and groaned herself to sleep.

At least she wouldn't have to blow the money for the plane ticket.

The next morning, she made up her mind to embrace her new life and discard the old one. Again. She went to work singing under her breath, "I like filing, filing's cool. I like Jamey, he's so nice."

She rented *You Can't Take It With You* to take to Jamey's that night. She should have known it was a bad sign when she started renting a lot of black and white movies in a row; she rented like an alcoholic buys a bottle. She needed it, so she got it. She didn't think much about why. She didn't remember much about the movie except Jimmy Stewart being funny about a scream and Lionel Barrymore playing harmonica. She wouldn't rent anything with Cary Grant anymore.

Perhaps she was making an attempt to cast Jimmy Stewart as Jamey. Maybe that would help.

Jamey came home a little late that night. There was an evening tour of the aquarium for a special needs group, and he wanted to give it himself. He was a very generous guy, too. There was absolutely nothing wrong with Jamey.

Laura dug around in the cabinets and the fridge and came up with a simple dinner. Salmon patties, rice, and salad. She found some aging potatoes and carrots, cut off the rotten and rooted bits, and roasted them with olive oil and salt.

Jamey's face lit up when he got home and smelled dinner. He was always aglow after giving a tour – he really got into imparting the shit that he knew to interested people – and this made him cuter. And whenever he was very attractive, Laura was overtaken with an all-consuming guilt that this amazing guy deserved a truly amazing girlfriend who loved him more than she did.

He gave her a hug and a long kiss on the cheek and went off to the bedroom while she got dinner on the table. When he re-emerged, he was wearing old green cargo pants and his favorite Greenpeace sweatshirt. He wasn't muscular, but he had nice shoulders. They sat over their dinner sipping wine, and Laura thought, "This is really the ideal guy." That imaginary Dexter she'd fallen in love with, that black and white movie guy, he was a fake. Bart was a distant memory. Not the right guy. A passing phase. A one-night stand. Bart was an illusion.

Jamey toasted, "To the chef," and Laura imagined a thousand other dinners with him, with her in the role of chef. With Jamey rising to director of the aquarium, her sinking to the realm of wife, maybe mother. And a final nail in the coffin, Jamey said, "Your Nonna called me. We're spending Thanksgiving at her house."

Kachunk.

The Talking Heads song came to mind. *This is not my beautiful apartment. This is not my beautiful boyfriend.*

Laura poured herself a third glass of wine and drank quickly.

LIZZIE

They let us out of school for the whole of Thanksgiving week. Nonna and I went to the supermarket and had some serious fun. She seemed happy where she was for the first time in a while as we wandered through the aisles. She thumped on the squash, smelled the spinach, fretted over which turkey for waaaay too long, and ordered a half-pound of prosciutto from the deli counter. Her eye was sharp and critical. She muttered to herself in Italian. She sent the prosciutto back twice and scolded the man behind the counter, "Pete the butcher would never even display meat as bad as this."

To which the man responded, "Go see Pete the butcher then."

Nonna snapped, "He's *busy*."

I knew that Pete the butcher was one of Nonna's people. This made me worry about who was coming to Thanksgiving. I'd assumed she'd be letting Gina's gang back into the house. Something had been nagging at me for a while and Nonna, was in a good mood, so I figured it was as good a time as any to ask.

I said, "Can I invite my friend Tisha?"

338

She looked surprised. She said, "From school?"

"No, from the video store."

She eyed the deli clerk sharply and said, "Is she a good friend?"

The fact that Nonna didn't know the answer to this question really hurt. On the other hand, I'd never told her about Tisha. But she should have asked where I was all those mornings in the summer. I said, "She's the best. And she's twenty-two and has nowhere to go."

Nonna said, "Absolutely."

She made the deli clerk slice the entire slab of prosciutto in half to get the fresh part at the center.

She spent a long time over the potatoes, and I got a lecture about tenderness, graininess, and gnocchi. I listened attentively. I knew once upon a time Nonna had been good at *something*, but it was nice to hear her speak like an expert. From a place of wisdom. Like a great-grandmother with a lifetime of experience was supposed to.

Like the Nonna from before. Was she actually coming back?

We cooked all day. Put up the cranberry sauce – homemade of course – and the lemon curd for the tart. Nonna put the turkey in a brine of spices and salt and water and put it in a big stockpot in the fridge. It was only Tuesday.

On Wednesday I woke up before it was light out to the clanging of pots in the kitchen. I went downstairs, and Nonna had *everything* out. She grinned when I saw her and put her finger up *wait a minute*. She fished in her pockets, got her hearing aids out and after some high-pitched squeals, her ears were in.

She had the Kitchen Aid out on the counter. That thing weighed a ton, and I didn't know how she even moved it there. She had two pounds of butter out and an enormous earthenware jar which I'd tried to look in earlier in the summer, but the lid was wedged in tight, and I was worried I'd break it. It turned out to be flour, and it turned out Nonna used a curved partially melted plastic spatula to pry it open. Everyone's kitchen had those weird little things.

I got a lump in my throat for mom's junk-filled "all-purpose drawer" and our sticky wicker jam/honey/peanut butter tray that lived underneath it. I took some comfort in knowing that Mom had learned how to cook all that good stuff in this kitchen once upon a time.

Nonna handed me a one-cup measuring cup and said, "Two of these in the mixer."

I started scooping and scraped it level just like Mom taught me. Nonna started panting around the kitchen, getting various things from different shelves. She talked. "Your mama helped me when she was little. She was a very good helper. She knew where everything was, and after a while, she would get me something before I knew I needed it." She wheezed, laughing. I was glad she was moving around, even scuffing her feet along the floor, hitting her cane against the cabinets.

It was the first time since I got there that Nonna talked about Mom outside of being sad.

I asked, "When did you start to teach her how to cook?"

She stopped and leaned against the counter by the fridge and looked at me over her glasses. She got sad for a moment, but said, "She was about ... let me see. A tiny bit shorter than you."

"Well, that clears that up."

Nonna laughed. She walked to a lower cabinet and opened it up, fishing inside with her cane. It clanked against a pot and made two glass things clink together dangerously.

I asked, "So who's coming?"

She didn't answer. I knew she heard me because I was good

and loud. But she leaned over to reach into the cabinet. I could tell it hurt. She stood up. "I need you. Get down in there, will you?"

I crouched down and found a little-explored cabinet filled with bowls, leftover Tupperwares that didn't match, and various bits of metal I didn't recognize. Nonna said, "I need the pastry knife."

There were no knives that I could see. I looked up at Nonna, and she smiled. "Ah. It doesn't look a thing like a knife, I know. It's wire and curved, like a mezza luna, it has a wooden handle and looks a little like a boat."

I had no idea what a mezza whatta was but found something resembling what she described and handed it to her.

"Bene. Now, I need the ricer." I looked up at her again, blank. She laughed. "You have a lot to learn, honey. It looks like an enormous garlic press, only less shiny." I found something matching that. By the time we were done, the countertop was filled with cooking devices I hadn't seen before ... or at least all summer. A rolling pin, a pastry cloth, a flour sifter.

"What was Mom like when she was my age?" She had me chopping up butter into cubes and putting them in the mixer.

Nonna said, "Smart. Funny. Thoughtful. Quiet." She shuffled over to me and put her arms around me, hugging me tight. "She was a lot like you."

That hug was so good I wanted to cry. I didn't want to let her see I was going to cry in case she wouldn't hug me again.

She kissed me, and it hit my chin. I realized I had grown since the last time she kissed me.

We settled down in front of the television to watch a movie. The house smelled so good it gave me a sad/happy weepy feeling. Nonna had rented *Meet Me in St. Louis*. She said she'd save *It's a Wonderful Life* for Christmas. We had made some crust scraps baked with brown sugar and butter on top she called *crust grubbies,* and I had them on a plate on the table with some hot chocolate. The doorbell rang.

Nonna gave me that nose nudge of "You answer it," and when I did, there was a woman with strong, weird-smelling perfume who threw her arms around me and held me close and strong to her cold, damp wool coat. Her mohair scarf tickled my nose. I struggled and was terrified for a split second before I heard her jangly jewelry and realized it was Aunt Sally. Mom taught me the trick that if you hug a grownup back really hard, they tend to let go faster. I gave it a try. Sure enough, she released me.

Nonna yelled, "You're letting all the heat out!"

Sally said, "All right, Mama. All right."

I stepped back, Aunt Sally stepped inside, and the aluminum storm door squeaked closed.

Aunt Sally. Maybe Uncle Bart would come early. Sally dropped a duffel bag by the foot of the stairs and bustled over to Nonna to give her a kiss.

"Ma, the house smells like the old days. What you been cooking?"

"Oh, just a little something."

Sally chuckled and sank onto the sofa. Right in the middle so I couldn't really sit on it at all without being wedged right up next to her. I decided to sit cross-legged on the floor near the crust grubbies. I bit into one, and the slightly burnt brown sugar melted on my tongue. The crust was super flaky and tasty. Must've been the club soda.

Sally said, "What're we watching?"

Nonna said, *"Meet me in St. Louis."*

Sally said, "Another old movie? What's with the old movies, Ma? You're getting old with them!"

That made me mad. I mean, didn't she *get* Nonna? I said, "Nonna used to work in the movies you, know."

My tone was a little sharp because Aunt Sally did that back up and look surprised, *You talking smack to me, sister?* thing. She said, "Well, I know that. I mean I *know* that. But she quit a long time before I was born, honey." She turned to Nonna, "She got a mouth on her, Mama."

Nonna ignored Sally and looked at me for a long, surprised moment. I wasn't sure if she was surprised by my mouth or the fact that I knew about the movies. She turned and pressed play on the remote.

Sally said, "Where's my girl?"

I couldn't think for a moment who she meant by that, but then I remembered Laura. I knew logically that Sally was Laura's mother, but I couldn't connect the temperamental pretty sulker I'd spent the summer with and this blowsy perfumey lady.

Nonna said, "She'll be coming tomorrow."

"Where is she tonight? I thought she was living here."

"Be quiet, Sally. The movie's starting."

ADRIANA

The holidays made Adriana moody and mournful. Even in the best days of cooking a big meal for her friends, she missed Rose. And that year, because of Lizzie, she missed Rebecca, too.

She was already moody when she sat down to watch *Meet Me in St. Louis* with Lizzie and Sally. She wanted them to go away so she could enjoy some Technicolor and reverie.

Then Rose came onto the screen, startling her. She was cast as a pretty shopgirl. 1944. It was after they broke up. There she was in a very pretty brown-and-white striped shopgirl blouse that was pinned at the throat with a cameo and a carefully tailored blue apron and broad swinging skirt. Adriana had her issues with the period of the dress – the designer Irene was never as historically exacting as Edith – but Rose was gorgeous, her hair in a Technicolor red upsweep.

She delivered her one line flawlessly, her face so alive, extra-real. Adriana scrutinized her face for signs of sadness, but the scene was too brief and ended suddenly. She couldn't stop the tape without turning it into a thing.

By the time Lizzie and Sally went off to bed, Adriana had

moved from a general moodiness into a full-on wallow. She waited until the doors to the bathroom and two bedrooms had finished opening and closing, she pulled her tired, aching body out of her chair and went into the dining room. When she approached the chest, she noticed that it was slightly ajar. She opened it and saw that the blankets had been shifted. She flushed in shame, then in anger at her shame, then in remorse for the fact that she had relegated her old life – her one great love – to the bottom of a box of blankets.

She started pulling the blankets out one by one and reached in for the photo album when a clatter on the floor distracted her. She saw the white lipstick tube roll into the corner behind the radiator, and it was as if Rose had walked into the room.

"What? Are you ...?" Adriana looked around her at the dining room, as empty as when she left it. The thought was so absurd she laughed.

She had given the lipstick case to Rebecca for her wedding – something borrowed. With Rose's heart inside, it seemed appropriate, and at the time, Adriana had told herself that Rebecca was happy in love. It was time to move on. To pass the lost love of her life on to the unexpected love of her life. Rebecca had kissed her, pulled it over her neck, and let the case rest in the middle of the bodice of her ivory dress where it looked as if it had always belonged. She did not open it or show Becca the heart. Knowing it was there was enough.

How had it gotten here?

She put the faux leather album to the side and reached for the tube. The lid wasn't screwed on quite correctly. She gave it a turn, but it wouldn't give. She twisted it harder, and the top popped off. A curled paper folded too many times was wedged inside. She twisted it out, and it brought out Rose's heart with it. Rose's heart wrapped around the uncurling wad of paper.

Adriana unfolded it carefully. It was thick with black ink and unfolded to an impossible 8 ½ x 11 sheet of drawing paper.

It was a drawing someone had worked on very hard, shading and reshading every detail to the extent that the pen dented the page. She ran her fingers over the page, feeling its texture. It took a bit of computing to reconcile these startling images first with a reality she had visualized that terrible spring night, then with the shy, awkward, funny teenager she had taken into her home.

Thoughts of Rose fled as the knowledge of the life going on under her own roof was brought into stark relief.

SCRIIIITCH. SCREAM. KRASH.

CHAPTER NINETEEN

LIZZIE

I woke up the next morning excited. Kid excited. Then I felt guilty that I could feel this way without Mom and Dad here. Aside from watching *Akira*, which was different, it was probably the first time I'd been excited since. But I was here because of them. And Nonna was cooking a big meal for family, and Mom would have loved that. I closed my eyes and tried to imagine that Mom and Dad were here. At least their history was. I breathed deeply inhaling a sweet, rich smell floating upstairs.

I went downstairs, and the minute I got to the kitchen, Nonna, who was reading a cookbook at the table, handed me a potholder. Like she knew I was coming at that very moment. I pulled out a cookie sheet with four sweet potatoes on it, their skin brown with thick syrup bubbling up out of fork holes that had been punched in the top. I put them on top of the stove.

I had sweet potato skins for breakfast with milk and made sweet potato gnocchi with Nonna. It turned out the ricer did what Mom got by mushing the potatoes through a colander. I missed Mom's frustrated mushing and scraping and wondered why she never bought a ricer. Nonna gave me a huge hug. A meaningful it-lasts-a-minute-too-long hug. I made up my mind that instead of thinking about how Mom *wasn't* there, I would concentrate on how Mom *was* there. Nonna didn't let go, and I cried a little, but it was a good kind of crying.

LAURA

Laura woke up Thanksgiving morning with some cramping in her lower abdomen ... surely her period must be arriving. *Finally.* It was sometimes a little late, but she was going on five days, and it was about time. Relieved, she heaved herself off the mattress and went into the bathroom to check. She pressed a piece of toilet paper to herself and wiped it out. Nothing. She pressed it again, willing herself to bleed, and pulled it out – nothing. But cramping was good. Right?

She turned on the shower to a steamy hot, took off her pajamas, and got in. This apartment was freezing in the mornings.

The door opened. She heard the toilet lid clank up and prayed to herself as he took a leak that Jamey would leave the bathroom as quickly as he entered it. He didn't flush because flushing made the shower water scalding. He was always, always thinking of others. She clenched her eyes shut, but he opened the sliding glass door despite her psychic efforts to stop him.

"Good morning." He was always, always bright and sunshiny.

"Morning. Honey. Can I? I need to be alone this morning, I think."

He said, "Oh, Aunt Flo? I was wondering when she'd arrive. You're a few days late."

Anger rose in Laura at the double intrusion. This man had no business being up on her menstrual cycle. It served him right if she lied to him, "Yep. Just in time for a big day with family."

He slid the door shut to about six inches but kept talking at her. "Aww, it'll be fun. I love your Nonna. And we get to hang out with *Lizzie*." He spoke her name as if she were the most charming person on the planet. He had been bugging her to bring Lizzie into work. If she was a huge failure with Lizzie, how was she going to cope with a child of her own? A full-time child. A child of this guy whose very acne scars were getting on her nerves as he talked and talked and talked.

"Your Nonna's meals are legendary. Grammy used to go there all the time for Easter and Christmas – before she died. She talked about those meals for years. That's when your Nonna did my mom a solid, you know – when Grammy died. She managed her funeral." Both the fact that she didn't know this and the fact that Jamey was telling her rubbed Laura the wrong way.

She finished rinsing her hair and stood in the shower with the hot water turning the skin on her thighs pink. She aimed the water at her womb, hoping to somehow move things along. There was something about hot showers and blood flow from her fourth-grade hygiene class, but she couldn't remember how it worked. Laura needed to get out of the shower, but there was no way she was turning off the water before Jamey left.

"I'm going to the market. What kind of wine should I pick up?"

"I don't know, white, chardonnay, or something that goes with turkey. Now will you get out of here?"

He slid the glass door shut. "I see Aunt Flo brought her kids, the Crabbies, with her." He had mischief in his voice.

Some women might have found that charming. But it filled Laura's belly with a hot, liquid, loathing. The door closed, and she envisioned a future with this guy. Charming Dad, hammy jokes. A wedding in Baltimore. She would quit her shitty job to raise the kid, of course.

The kid would look like Jamey. It would get acne at age four and laugh at his dad's hammy jokes. It would grow up in this shitty little city and never need to leave, and she would grow old and live in a house like Nonna's with her Barca-Lounger and old movie rentals and would die alone.

She was being melodramatic – this made her somewhat hopeful that maybe her period *was* coming. She was prone to melodrama while in PMS. Or maybe pregnant women were melodramatic. Lord knows pregnancy made Janelle downright theatrical.

Laura shut off the water and swiped her towel down from atop the glass door. She wiped her face and breathed in deeply, inhaling towel, dryer, and soap smell. She wouldn't be able to find out until tomorrow anyway when she could sneak out to the store to get a pregnancy test.

Jesus, God, how could she even be thinking *pregnancy test?*

Dread overcame Laura as they pulled up to the curb in front of Nonna's house. She got out of the car with the bottle of wine. Jamey brought the flowers he'd gotten at the market that morning – some horrible autumn arrangement with fake leaves and mums and baby's breath, of all things.

They fought about his choice of flowers. He bit for a little while, but then put up his hands in surrender, "Okay, okay, I understand," implying that this was because of her period. Which she wasn't getting. His response sent her into a fuming silence that lasted until they parked the car.

Everything he did was grating on her nerves, from staying in the shower too long to the noises he made when he drank his coffee. He had gone from an agreeable boyfriend type who was so sweet to a blight on her existence. She did not want to spend the rest of her life with this guy. And worse than that, she was wasting his time: keeping him from some Petra-like woman who *should* be spending the rest of her life with this guy. Maybe this other woman was *right now* getting pregnant with someone *she* didn't want to be marrying, and it was all Laura's fault.

He came around the car as she waited at the bottom of the stairs and held out his elbow. She had to give it to Jamey, he knew when words weren't welcome. She reluctantly took his arm, and they scaled the stairs. They rang the doorbell, and he ran a nervous hand through his hair.

Laura was being a terrible brat, and he had to face her family. This guy couldn't help that she didn't love him. She squeezed his arm in solidarity as the door opened.

Sally stood there in all her Hippie glory. Anger, disappointment, fear, sadness, slight elation, and frustration ran through Laura's mind so fast that she couldn't fix on one. Then she found dread. She hadn't told Jamey much about her family history. Just that she grew up with her father and stepmother and that her mother had bailed on her.

To make matters worse, Sally opened the storm door, a glass of wine in her hand, and cooed like she was greeting a favorite kitty, "There's my girl! Where've you been?" This brought an angry monologue to Laura's mind.

My girl. You gave up your RIGHT to call me my girl when

you bolted on us. And you didn't have the decency to stay away, you kept coming by. And leaving again. What's a girl supposed to do with that while she's stuck with an alien family in Bumble-fuck, Alaska?

She didn't realize she was digging in her heels until she felt Jamey tug on her arm to pull her into the house.

The house smelled sweet, savory, spicy. Pumpkin, sweet potatoes, turkey. It smelled like the old days. Maybe the old Nonna was back.

Jamey took her jacket and his own and hung them on the newel post to the stairs. He looked to Laura a few times and held out his hand to Sally. "Hi. I'm Jamey."

With a clatter of bracelets, Sally took his hand and looked him up and down. "Ooh, Laura, I like this one. He's got a good energy about him."

Laura cleared her throat and said, "Jamey, this is Sally. Nonna's daughter."

Sally withdrew her hand from Jamey and looked at Laura, hurt. Laura squinted angrily at her, and Sally turned to go to the kitchen, saying, "I think I'm needed elsewhere."

Laura grabbed Jamey's hand and drew him over to the sofa. Sally was a crappy mom, and based on her stories about her older sister, Nonna wasn't very good at it for a while. There was no way she would subject another child to this family's bad streak. Rebecca was the only one who came out okay, and she ended up squashed in a taxicab on Central Park West.

She made up her mind then and there that if she *did* end up being pregnant, she'd get an abortion. This brought her a moment of relief. Then panic. Her heart sank to her bowels. She heard Sally's laugh from the kitchen and realized that her mother might be darkening her mood. Or maybe it was PMS. Hope surged once again.

Jamey said, "She's Nonna's daughter, does that make her your aunt?"

Without hesitating, Laura said, "Sort of."

She hoped this would suffice, but Jamey was going to keep at it.

Jamey said, "Sort of."

She cut him off. "Sweetie, don't try to figure out my family. All any of us have in common is that we're related to Nonna in one way or another. And here we are for Thanksgiving. And it smells good in here." She was starving. *Pregnant.* But during PMS, she could eat a buffet table. *PMS.*

There was galumphing down the stairs and Lizzie bounded into the room. Her boob buds were filling out to real breasts. Laura knew that she'd have to be the one to take her bra shopping soon. Who needed an extra kid when she already had one? Lizzie was wearing jeans and a nice green turtleneck sweater Laura hadn't bought her. It looked expensive. Bart. If Laura had a kid with Bart would it look like Lizzie? She blushed for entertaining the idea.

Lizzie's face lit up when she saw Jamey. She grinned and said, "Hiiiiiii." Her smile was Bart's. Her eyes were Rebecca's, only bigger. She leaned back shyly when she got close to the two and sat in a chair, knees together.

Jamey said, "Hey, Lizzie. How you been?"

"Good, Good." She nodded, and her hair moved with her. Laura realized that Lizzie had curled her hair with a curling iron. It was a mess and some of the curls flopped the wrong way, but it was kind of cute.

Jamey said, "They killing you over at St. Caz?"

"Nope. Only moderate levels of torture."

Jamey said, "Well, don't worry. Junior High is the ugliest phase of life, but it passes quickly."

Lizzie said, "Not quick enough for me."

She was growing up. She was holding a conversation. This teenager might someday become a grownup. Maybe Laura could try again with her. Maybe she'd outgrown the awkward wall Laura couldn't get through before. Maybe Laura had to try harder.

Sally sashayed into the room and floomphed in one of the uncomfortable armchairs. Laura couldn't deal with her right then and got up to go to the kitchen, but Sally grabbed her arm as she passed. "Laura."

Laura couldn't afford to lose it in front of Jamey; he'd want to do meaningful deep therapy of some kind with her after, and she didn't have the strength. Instead, she backed up and sat in the matching wing chair opposite Sally.

Laura shot her mother as convincing a *don't fuck with me* look as she could muster and said in a calming voice, "Hey, Sally. How've you been?"

"Fine, fine. I've moved to Santa Fe, you know."

The trick with Sally was to keep her talking about herself. Laura said, "You don't say." It came out more arch than she intended.

"Got a nice apartment. I'm working at a Native American gift shop."

Laura nodded. She noticed she didn't have a snotty comeback for this fact. She was a file clerk. She had the first thing resembling sympathy she'd had for her mother in a long time. She said, "They treating you well?"

Sally's brow furrowed, and she looked at Laura in one eye, then the other. "Yes, yes, they give me insurance, which is kind of unusual. That's sweet of you to ask. Very sweet." She took Laura's hand. "And how have you been?"

Laura said, "Good. Good." She really had nothing she could elaborate on that would make this exchange in any way okay.

Sally's hand tightened, which amplified all of Laura's feelings of being trapped. She said, "Honey, are you following your bliss?" She searched her daughter's face as if she could see the answer.

Sadness and anger churned in Laura. Her mother's pursuit of her own bliss took her away from Laura when she most needed her and left her with a shifting uneasiness in her life that made her unable to articulate her own bliss. *What is the bliss? What's working for you at the moment?* A true, deep, gripping passion that creates a path? Laura supposed her bliss was meant to be movies, but if it were, wouldn't she feel compelled to pursue it more deeply? Wouldn't she have been better at doing the pursuing while she was in Hollywood? Or was bliss making happiness with what was in front of you? Was contentment enough? She felt the seething in her chest go to her head and marveled, again, at how her mother could drive her from zero to crazy in one minute flat.

That was Sally. And Sally, in her completely clueless way, needed something from Laura that she couldn't provide.

Laura patted Sally's hand and answered the bliss question by saying, "Every day, Sally. Every day." With that, she got up and moved toward the kitchen, leaving Jamey with her mother. She was too tired to care what resulted from that encounter.

LIZZIE

The doorbell rang when I was tied up with Nonna in the kitchen. I was worried it was Tisha, so the moment I was free I ran to answer it, but when I got there, it was wide open, and it looked like Jamey and Uncle Bart were having some kind of a standoff. If I were drawing them, I would have added holsters, hats, and revolvers drawn and aimed. No joke. Their legs were planted in a widened stance and Uncle Bart stood right inside the front hall, door still open, breathing steadily and sizing Jamey up with a "what the hell are you doing here?" look.

Uncle Bart's face was pinched and pale from the cold. It did the same thing Dad's face did in cold weather, but mostly I was thinking how happy I was that he was here. It had been ... I counted. Five months.

Jamey turned and yelled, "Hey, Lizzie, your uncle's here!"

I saw Uncle Bart's face darken. Jamey turned, startled I was right behind him. I stepped between them and put my arms around Uncle Bart to hug him. I was taller, I noticed, so my arms went around his neck rather than under his arms. I held on really hard, and he smelled like family.

He said, "Hey, Lizzie." His voice choked.

I said, "Come, we've been *cooking*," and dragged him into the kitchen.

Nonna looked up, pleased to see him in a way that belied her years. "Bart! Traffic bad?"

He said, "No. Not too bad."

Laura looked up at him with a few thousand expressions on her face. Yep. She still had the hots for him. I hoped I'd be fighting off boyfriends when I grew to her age.

Crazy Aunt Sally came toward him with arms spread, chin tucked, wearing a deep sympathy pout. Uh-oh. Uncle Bart stepped sideways so the kitchen table was between them, but that didn't stop her. She came at his shoulder and put her arms around him. She rested her forehead on his temple, and I think he was trying to get away, but she wouldn't let him.

She said, "I am so, *so* sorry for your loss, honey. I didn't get a chance to tell you at the funeral because Ma wasn't feeling well, so I had to get her home. I lost my niece, and that's a tragedy, but losing a *brother*. I. I just have to tell you that I *get it*." She started to cry. "I lost a sister, you know. You never recover from that kind of grief."

Sally had tried to pull that number on me the night before, but I wasn't buying. Bart got away and looked up just in time to see Jamey curl his arms around Laura's shoulder and shove his nose into her neck. Jamey never did that kinda PDA in front of me before, so I figured he was kind of marking her. Laura stepped away from him with a sudden jerk that left him looking sheepish. She didn't want to play.

I looked back at Uncle Bart and saw a vein bulge out on his forehead.

This Thanksgiving had more going on than I thought.

LAURA

Why'd Bart have to look so frickin' cute? As if Laura didn't have enough on her mind, she had to look at his rakish hair, a bit shaggier than the last time she saw it, his worn leather jacket, his worn jeans, and the same t-shirt she had taken off his frame last summer. He had the most adorable crust of sleep in the corner of his eye that made her want to flick it out for him. Jamey was getting on her nerves already but giving her a full-on nuzzle stifled her. When she saw Bart at the other end of Lizzie's arm being led into the kitchen, it sent her reeling. She blushed. She felt like throwing up. *Pregnant*. She was furious. *PMS*. She wished Jamey would disappear, *PMS*.

When Jamey got Bart a beer, Laura took a moment to escape into the dining room for a breather.

The dining table was brightly set with her cottura. There was a mess of a centerpiece made of bits of bracken and such, probably courtesy of Lizzie. It was kind of beautiful, in an odd sort of way. The table was mysteriously set for twelve. Nonna had so many friends, but Laura hadn't thought of them as potential guests. She definitely hadn't thought of Sally as a potential guest. Jamey. Bart. It was all constricting in her chest and her abdomen felt heavy, full, and hot.

She hadn't had cramps like this before. *Pregnant.* Or maybe she was just paying extra attention today. *PMS.*

She sat down at the head of the table because the seat was closest to her.

Looking down at the row table settings, she thought of Dexter, so handsome, so together, sitting at the opposite end of their long, fancy cherry wood dining table in Beachwood set with the same china, killing her in increments. She thought of those fabulous dinner parties and that despite all her hard work, her presiding over company, it turned out that her position at the table was only temporary. *PMS.* And what if this baby – *Pregnant* – put her at the head of another table? Jamey's table? Charming Dad. Thanksgiving a year hence, they'd have their family around them. Including his straight-laced retiree parents who enjoyed golfing and luncheons.

And Lizzie. And Nonna. And Bart? She wouldn't be able to cook that much because she'd have the baby.

Stewing. *PMS.*

They hadn't heard anything from Bart in so many months. She thought of him as gone back to the world. He retreated into the same space of regret in her brain as Dexter and this one dumb but cute boyfriend from high school, Tommy, whom she couldn't quite manage to forget.

But here he was, and he was damned attractive. And screw him for leaving. What, he'd just abandon his niece and not even call? Any guy who would do that wasn't worth her time.

Guilt. She knew full well she'd been there for Lizzie about as much as Bart and she didn't have the excuse of distance. But Lizzie wasn't her niece. She was just her cousin. The more Laura thought about Jamey, Lizzie, and Bart, the more she filled with a heavy, deep self-loathing.

Jamey walked up behind her, put his beer on the table next to her, and started to rub her shoulders. He worked with purpose, as if he could fix her mood if he pressed the right buttons hard enough. It chafed her skin and made her want to squirm away. *PMS.*

She owed him some loyalty but couldn't muster it. She gently took his hands and patted them, as in *enough.* She got to her feet and took the bathroom as an excuse, but not before giving him a peck on the cheek. He smelled homey. Familiar. And done. She was sorry for him. He was going to be single again by the time he left to go home. She could at least be kind to him now.

LIZZIE

I went to answer the door, and there were Mr. and Mrs. Lipsicki. Mrs. Lipsicki was all made up and looked sweet in a dumpy older lady sort of way as she handed me a pink cardboard box (cookies!) and stepped into the house. Mr. Lipsicki seemed like a nice guy. He shook my hand for a minute too long and then patted it, shaking his head. It beat, "I'm so sorry for your loss," but it did kinda put a damper on things.

Then the Zimmittis came, Maurizio and his wife. Pete and his wife Cristina. And the Aguilars – the fish guy and his wife. The house was full of people laughing and chatting. Nonna got some scolding for not calling her friends for so long, and so did I, but they didn't mean it. They were just happy to be there.

Nonna let me boil the gnocchi, and she smiled with pride and nagged me about what to do every step of the way anyway. "No! wait til it's a rolling boil. A *rolling* boil. That's it. Cold water. Now. No, wait for it to come to a partial boil again. A *partial* boil." But when we got to the table and all of the food was laid out, Nonna had me bring in the gnocchi, which looked all orange and pretty in its creamy buttery sauce, poured out on an antique yellow platter that Nonna got out of the bottom of the china closet. Nonna announced, "And Lizzie made the pumpkin gnocchi." Everyone applauded. It was awful.

The doorbell rang again, and I took the opportunity to duck out. Tisha was there, cold and afraid with a bottle wrapped in a paper bag in her hand. She was relieved when she saw my face.

I gave her a big hug. We'd been doing that lately.

She said, "Am I late?"

"No! No. Come in." I took the bottle, which was weird because it was sort of the grownup thing to do. But I guessed I was Tisha's host.

I took her coat, tossed it on a chair, and led her into the dining room where there was some confusion over the seating arrangement. There was enough bustle going on for it not to be too crazy, but so much bustle I could tell Tisha was completely overwhelmed. I guess I would have been too.

Nonna had a firm idea of where everybody should be, and by the time she was done, it kinda made sense. I sat between Uncle Bart and Tisha, opposite Laura and Jamey. Laura kept giving Tisha the stink-eye, and it bugged the hell out of me. I introduced her around, and Jamey was really nice to her, but Laura and Bart were in some other world.

We were down the other end of the table from Nonna, who was surrounded by her oldsters. They talked in English and in Italian and laughed for so long I thought we were *never* going to eat. Laura looked at me questioningly, I shrugged and pointed to Nonna. She shrugged. Bart elbowed me. I didn't know why it was up to me. I guessed it was because I lived here the most. I elbowed Bart back, and he laughed. Tisha laughed. It was good to share a joke. Bart elbowing me, being in on something with Tisha and even Laura – it was nice.

I said, "Hey, Nonna? We gonna eat?"

The whole table burst out laughing, so I guessed it was okay.

Nonna held her hand out to me. I know she wanted me to say Grace. I'd been a trained Catholic for almost four months, so I started. "In the name of the Father, and of the Son, and of the Holy Spirit."

Everyone except Bart and Jamey crossed themselves and everyone except for Bart said, "Amen." I got a shiver hearing all the voices in unison like that. I ran through the regular grace, but it didn't seem enough for Thanksgiving, so, eyes closed, I kept going. It sorta just tumbled out. "And thank you, God, for everyone gathered here, friends and family, and for the really good food Nonna made and for friends and family at all. Please let us remember what a big deal that is."

There was a pause like they were waiting for more. I said, "Amen." Amens all around, and I looked up, embarrassed by how many people were looking at me. Tisha shoved me on the shoulder. I heard a sniff coming from somewhere. It was next to me. Uncle Bart coughed into his napkin and reached for the gravy. People never reached for the gravy first, so I could tell he was feeling emotional.

LAURA

Jesus H. Christ, I'm probably pregnant. This is my last Thanksgiving of freedom. Laura noticed that the idea of abortion had fled her. She tried to lure it back into her mind. *Get rid of it. No one will have to know.* But there was something about being twenty-nine and still single and pregnant that gave a girl pause. *Maybe pregnant, maybe.*

Sally sat, staring into her plate and eating methodically. She wasn't engaged in the conversation. She lowered her fork from her full mouth, stabbed another piece of gnocchi, and put it into her mouth with other food. Her eating was robotic; it looked self-punishing. For the first time, Laura saw in her wide face signs of the little girl she must have been in this house growing up. She didn't understand how Sally and Becca could turn out so differently, having essentially the same mother. If Sally had been more like Becca, Laura would be more like ... Lizzie? Lizzie, despite losing both parents, definitely looked more together than Laura was in seventh grade. More together than she was now. If Becca was Laura's mom, maybe she wouldn't be such a basket case.

But who was this chick Lizzie dragged home? She was really pretty and had no makeup or any sense of style. She wore her black hair in bangs and long pigtails, like a child, and her covetable skinny form made her ugly crew-neck blue sweater and jeans look like high fashion. She made Jamey laugh. What did she say?

Laura helped herself to a huge mound of stuffing and gnocchi. She took a little turkey to be polite but mostly as an excuse for gravy. *PMS.* Jamey looked at her with a tentative smile. She could see how unkind she'd been in the last hour reflected in his eyes. She reached under the table and squeezed his knee reassuringly.

Her hand startled as Bart said, "How's your job going?"

Jamey shifted to pull his knee away; he'd noticed the startle. She was cross with Bart now. She said, "Fine."

She hoped her tone would dissuade further questioning on the subject, but Bart was into it. "Did you ever make any of those movie contacts here?"

"No, why?"

"I was just asking. You were so gung-ho on the trip out here."

Was this guy for real?

Laura turned to Jamey and explained, "When my car broke down in Tennessee last summer, Bart came and picked me up."

Obviously upset that he hadn't known this earlier, Jamey said, "Well, that was nice of him."

Laura ignored him. She couldn't fix things with Jamey and, as she planned on dumping him later, there wasn't much point. She'd raise this baby alone. She turned to Bart and said, "I got ... distracted. I have to make a living, you know. Most places only offered day gigs or unpaid internships." This was a blatant lie. She hadn't made even one phone call.

Jamey said, "So, how's *your* job, going, Bart? Investment

banking, isn't it? Is it fun? You guys are so into the money up there. Do you have that Gordon Gekko thing going on? One of those great pads with the chrome and black leather furniture and big screen TV?"

Bart reddened.

Lizzie said, "I love Uncle Bart's apartment. It's so ... *clean*."

Bart reddened further. Laura was proud of Lizzie for standing up for her uncle, pleased that Jamey was making Bart uncomfortable, and hating herself for both these feelings. *PMS.*

Maybe it was really PMS and she could break up with Jamey, quit her job, start making phone calls on Monday. Time to follow *her* bliss after all.

Jamey said, "Not everyone does his or her passion for a living. Some of us like to work and live. Isn't that right, Bart?"

Laura forced herself not to smile. She never saw Jamey get worked up, but there he was, ready to get into a pissing contest with Bart. Over her. Her initial crush on him resurged a little, not enough to call off the breaking up, but a little.

Bart said, "I thought you loved your otters."

Jamey smiled like a man in love. He said, "I do, I do, man. I meant Laura. And you. Not a day goes by I don't think I'm making the planet a better place to live in."

And there went Laura's crush. Faded again.

Lizzie's pigtailed friend looked from one to the other of them as they spoke, trying to find a way in. Laura smiled a little that this motley group, Bart, Jamey, and Lizzie had a history. Miss Video Planet probably felt like Laura had that night at the Ottobar. She didn't belong there.

Bart stared at Jamey a long moment, and as if deciding he wasn't worth arguing with, turned to Laura. "They have movies in New York, too, you know. Tribeca Films and now Miramax is taking off there."

Is he propositioning me?

Jamey said, "Nothing wrong with Baltimore. Comfortable, cheap place to live. Plenty of movies here. John Waters." He paused too long and added, "*Homicide: Life on the Street.*"

They had to stop. Her stomach was heavy, her pelvis heavier. Why hadn't she called about getting work in the movies? She never even picked up the damn phone. Was she afraid they'd say no or that they wouldn't like her? Was she like Sally? Why had she sunk so easily into Jamey's life just the way she'd sunk into Dexter's? Why was Bart all of a sudden so interested in her film career?

She said, "I thought you said making movies was a waste of time."

Bart fumbled. "I. I don't think anything that you really *want* to do should be something you avoid, you know?"

Laura's ears burned and humiliation crept up her scalp. Bart wasn't allowed to be right. He was a clueless people-leaving jerk. He was not allowed to figure it out for her.

Lizzie piped up, "Nonna's given me a total film education this summer."

Finally, a change of subject. Laura started talking. Fast. "I don't know what it is, but we were never allowed to watch movies in the summers I lived here, and this summer it was like an indoor movie theater. Popcorn and everything. All the classics"

Lizzie looked at her in wonder and then glared. Okay, so Laura hadn't been here *all* summer, but at least Jamey had turned his attention to his plate, and Bart was looking at Lizzie like he really wanted to hear what she was going to say.

Tisha said, "Lizzie got me watching some of the old greats. I hadn't even ventured into black and white at work before, and I'm allowed to watch anything I want."

Bart smiled like he had a secret.

Laura said, "What?"

He said, "Nothing," in mock innocence and popped some turkey into his mouth. She hated this guy. Why was he so cute?

Laura tried to keep talking. She said, "Trisha. You work at the Video Planet, right?" She had not intended it to sound condescending, but most of her attention had been on Bart when she said it.

Lizzie got defensive, "*Tisha* just got into the NYU graduate program in film. She put herself through college and worked two jobs to do it."

Laura was obviously a monster asshole.

Tisha nodded self-consciously in agreement and turned her attention to her greens. She probably kept that figure on greens. Although the gnocchi and stuffing on her plate argued otherwise.

Skinny, too. How could this no-makeup crew neck be an artistic filmmaker type? That was supposed to be Laura's role in things. She had worked in Los Angeles, after all. Video clerks weren't even in her realm. Okay, except maybe Quentin Tarantino. And Kevin Smith. Didn't he work in a video store?

Bart said to Tisha, "No kidding? You found a place to live yet? When do you start? What are you specializing in?"

What, was she going to *move in with him* or something? Bart lit up in that way Laura had so rarely seen but had hoped for herself. Since when did Bart, the movie-hater, know about film school?

Tisha blushed, "I'm in the directing program. They liked a little movie I did with my friends at school this year."

Lizzie got all excited, "You should see it, Uncle Bart. It's a horror movie. Like tons of blood, and it's scary, but it's really, really funny."

Why couldn't it be a sad, slow movie about talking to a homeless guy on a park bench like the terrible student movies Laura had seen at screenings in LA? Not only was Tisha going to film school, she might actually succeed at something. This burned Laura.

The other end of the table was getting rowdier and louder. Gina said something in Italian, and Nonna roared with laughter. She must have had a bit of wine.

Laura ate more than was comfortable and was feeling nauseous. *Pregnant.* Pregnant and with no job prospects, she was in Baltimore while this pixie of a girl was moving to New York to live large and *make movies.* Any of those comfortable places Laura had created for herself in movies – herself as Stanwyck, Hepburn, Bette Davis – these faded. She might as well be a walk-on.

If she was pregnant, her life was officially over. She had to go to the bathroom to check again. But if she checked, her period wouldn't have started, and if she didn't check, maybe it would start. If she thought about it like a pregnancy, it would become one. Or if she thought about it like it was her period, maybe she would end up pregnant. This was nuts. She had a vision of a crater-faced, blue-eyed baby, sitting on Jamey's lap staring at her expectantly. Her stomach burbled, and she excused herself, leaving Tisha, Lizzie, and Bart to a discussion of the latest movies. Bart, who hated movies. Jamey was talking intently with Sally.

As she padded down the beige wall-to-wall carpeted hallway, Laura noticed that things smelled better than the last time she was there. Not just the food. The place was cleaner. Less decrepit. She passed Nonna's room as she got to the bathroom and opened the door to peek in.

It was a total pigsty. The bed was ruckled from the morning. There were piles of tissues and two glasses with lipstick marks on them next to the bed. There was at least a week's worth of clothing on the floor. The rest of the house may have smelled good, but this room stank. It reminded her of the sleeping porch at Janelle's when she was at her worst.

The idea of the old lady, the host of this enormous dinner and the only adult in Lizzie's life, being this depressed staggered her. There was too, too much going on in this house. With every fiber of her being, she longed for her teeny Beachwood apartment and Saturday mornings that demanded nothing of her. For life before Dexter, before Becca died. For life with opportunities she could go back and take advantage of.

Laura closed the door to the bathroom, slid down her jeans, and sat on the toilet. She found herself saying a prayer as she waited. She'd wait until after she peed. If she tried it now, there'd be no blood. Her heart beat faster. She pressed toilet paper to herself, and it came back bright red.

Period.

Thank God.

She felt like whooping in joy but resisted. She had a brief moment of remorse for the acne-covered baby and opened the cabinet under the sink to find her tampon stash. As she left the bathroom, she caught herself in the mirror grinning.

ADRIANA

When Laura came back to the table with a look of elation on her face, Adriana wondered if she was doing drugs. The girl was almost thirty, and she couldn't get her act together. Adriana had hoped that pushing her into a mediocre job at the aquarium would shake her out of whatever was eating her. Remind her to get on with her life. If she'd known that Laura would settle into the job and start dating her boss, she wouldn't have sent her on the interview. She should have allowed her another month or two of depression, and maybe she would have come out of it on her own.

As much as Adriana tried to do, all she ended up doing was screwing up more girls. Look at Sally, surrounded by people, a blank look on her face as she twisted her napkin. She looked as lost as she was at age ten.

Adriana knew she wasn't helping Lizzie either – her disturbed drawing of her parents' accident was solid evidence that Adriana's parenting was inadequate. She was able to muster some motherly love and cook with her once in a while, but those mornings when she couldn't get out of bed? And couldn't get out of the house? She was overwhelmed by the burden of ruining Lizzie, but she lacked the wherewithal to fix her.

All of these messy people, Sally, Laura, the missing Anna Maria, Lizzie, all of these were wrought from her mistakes. It wasn't that she would wish them away, but the weight of their lives pressed in on her.

When she saw Bart and Lizzie laughing over something, she knew she had made the right decision, but she needed to wait for the right moment to tell them.

Gina clinked her glass with her spoon for a toast. *Good lord, let this be a quick one.* She looked at her motley, blood-related family at the other end of the table and her cobbled-together neighborhood family.

Laura brought her own Sal: Jamey. A good guy. A gentleman. The kind of guy you marry even if you don't love him. Laura was so down when she arrived this morning that Adriana knew she had pretty much signed herself over to the nice guy. She'd have to have a talk with her.

Gina stood, clinking her glass, cleared her throat loudly, and said, "Ladies and gentlemen. I just wanted to say a few words."

Adriana saw by the way she wobbled when she stood up that there were going to be more than a few.

"We are all here today because of the beautiful blessings brought upon us by Adriana Morello."

There was a smattering of applause. Gina was an artist at saying exactly the wrong thing. Adriana closed her eyes and put her fingers together in a steeple on her lips, as if she was listening so she wouldn't have to look at Gina. She said a silent prayer for her to shut up or pass out.

"This beautiful woman, this amazing cook, and ... she's a beautiful, beautiful, forgiving woman." She stopped.

This was not going to get better. Tears entered Gina's voice, and she said, "This beautiful, forgiving woman, who took me in when I was in such need. Took me in even though I ..."

Adriana said, "Gina," sharply enough to keep her from continuing. Lizzie did not need to hear this crap. Sally either. And poor Phil.

Gina choked a sob. "I love you, Adriana. And when I think of you in here alone all those months, I ..."

Phil gently took hold of Gina's arm and pulled her back to her seat. He raised his glass and said, "To our gracious host and our two wonderful cooks." He made sure to raise his glass to both Adriana and Lizzie, who blushed.

Adriana leaned into Gina, who was flushed with embarrassment. She grabbed her hand and said, "Thank you, Gina. I love you, too."

The words that she had to churn up and force out on special occasions with her husband and her children came out so easily with Gina. She knew who Gina was and loved her for it. If only she had been able to *give* Sal a little more. If she had given Sally more. Anna Maria. Poor, lost, Anna Maria. Adriana's thoughts were following the downward spiral they had so many times in the past few months when she was interrupted.

From the other end of the table, Lizzie said, "Nonna worked in Hollywood for a while, didn't you Nonna?" Lizzie would let it go after a minute. She always did. But Adriana was irked that she brought it up in mixed company.

Bart said, "You are *so* busted, Mrs. Morello."

That didn't sound right. It wasn't like she ever denied it. She simply never talked about it.

Sally said, "Mama doesn't like to talk about the old days. It makes her ..."

Was she going to say, "sad?" Was Sally paying attention all those years?

Bart, that ingrate brother of George – George, who would have graciously steered the conversation back to a comfortable place for her – George, whose daughter sat, nearly grown and completely unguided at this mishmash of a table littered with Adriana's mistakes – Bart said, "I've been doing a little research, Mrs. Morello. You've got quite a few credits lined up. *The Lady Eve, Ball of Fire, Holiday Inn, Sullivan's Travels.*"

Her past was coming up in dark clouds around her in the room. Each of those names brought back a barrage of hope, love, remorse, and fear in equal increments.

Laura said to Bart, "So you're watching *movies* now?" It was said in simultaneous wonder and accusation.

Jamey said, "Tell us more about your past life, Mrs. Morello. It sounds amazing. Were you in Hollywood long?"

Bart squinted, "From what I can tell, it was three, four years?"

Adriana heard someone say, "Five." She was startled to realize that it was herself. Such regret was filling her heart, but the young end of the table was caught up in this new conversation. The oldster end of the table was looking at each other and murmuring. A whole life their friend had kept from them.

Lizzie said, "I've seen pictures of her then. Nonna was such a glamour puss. So full of work and life. And her friend. So many pictures with her friend." To Adriana's horror, Lizzie turned to her and said, "Your roommate, Nonna. What was her name?"

"Rose." She hadn't said Rose's name aloud in front of anyone in so many years that it opened a door and allowed tears to come out of her eyes. Unlike the times she cried for Rose in her room, she felt disconnected from the crying as if water were just running out of her face, completely beyond her control.

There were no sobs, just tears and tears. It was Laura who got out of her chair and came to her aid, Laura who put her arms around her shoulders and led her down the hallway to her room.

LAURA

Jesus. Nonna. All of that. I mean, who knew? Old ladies weren't just old ladies. Nonna had entire worlds in her past.

Laura got her to her room and went to get her some tea. It was sort of a strange, desperate thing to do, but it was the kind of thing Janelle would do – look after someone. So, tea it was. Laura poked her head into the dining room where people were talking in hushed tones. She said, "Look, she's fine. Just exhausted. You know, all this cooking? Don't let it go to waste. Get a move on with dessert."

She flicked on the electric kettle and got a cup and a teabag and prayed to escape the kitchen without ...

Jamey put his hand on Laura's shoulder and then encircled her with his arms. "Hey," he said, "Everything okay?" The caring and confidence in his voice, his confidence that they were still an item prompted her to pat his arms. Another *enough* gesture. She turned around to face him.

"Jamey? There's like, no good way to say this ..."

His face clouded immediately. His voice got thick, "Is it that Bart guy?"

"No. I mean." But really, it wasn't. It was kind of bigger than that Bart guy. "I'm at a. A place. Where ..." She turned back to the counter and said, "I'm gonna have to quit my job, too."

He leaned back and gave her that blue-eyed inscrutable stare – the first one he gave her on her interview. He had been so predictable lately that she was unmoored in a place where she wasn't sure what he was going to say.

She said, "I'm a wreck. You deserve so much better."

He said, "But you were the one I chose. I love *you*." He had never said it before. He stood there as if waiting for an answer.

She didn't say anything. There was nothing left to say. She felt him standing there, making up his mind what to do next.

Then he turned and walked out of the kitchen, grabbed his coat off the sofa, and closed the front door so gently that she had to look to make sure he'd gone.

He was supposed to make a big deal. Throw a fit. Give it some finality. But he had to leave it hanging with, "I love you." Which wasn't hanging, because she'd broken up with him, right?

The electric kettle clicked off, and she poured the water so quickly that she burned her hand. She threw the teabag in and went back to Nonna. But not before looking into the dining room. The home folks were smiling but more subdued. Lizzie, Bart, and Tisha were bent in toward each other – in cahoots. Laura wasn't in the mood to compete for the attention of anyone. She wasn't in the mood for much. But Nonna was waiting, and Jamey was gone. And for the latter, she felt lighter.

She bonked Nonna's door softly with her elbow twice and went in. Nonna was sitting up against the headboard of her bed, her legs stuck out in front of her. She was wearing a nicely-cut suit – sharp-looking for being off the rack. Her tweed skirt was scrunched up to reveal that she was wearing knee-highs in a color beige too dark for her pale skin. Her crying had ceased, and her face revealed nothing but wrinkles and distance in her brown eyes. Nonna had been through the wars. Of some sort.

Laura put the tea on her bedside table and climbed onto the foot of Nonna's bed. She realized that she had been handling her body with care all morning for fear of pregnancy. She stretched into a cross-legged position, felt the stretch of her muscles, enjoying a body that was fully hers. She waited for Nonna to say something.

Nonna said, "Oh, God, is everyone horrified?"

Laura shrugged and said, "I told them it was just an old lady getting tired thing. Making a giant meal and all."

Nonna laughed. She stared at Laura with surprise and intent, lowered her eyes, saying, "Thank you."

Laura cleared her throat and said, "You want to talk about it?" It came out forced. But there was Nonna in her room of depression, and clearly, she needed to talk.

And it did come out. And it wasn't what Laura expected. She had been thinking it would be something about missing her husband or Anna Maria or Becca. That something terrible had happened to Lizzie. That she had cancer. But what came out was this *story*. This incredibly complicated story about early Hollywood and love.

Laura said, "Wait, who's Missy?"

Nonna said, "Missy. Barbara Stanwyck."

Laura said, "You *knew* Barbara *Stanwyck*?"

Nonna said, "You're missing the point entirely."

Laura had always thought the picture in the living room of Nonna with Barbara Stanwyck was a Pose with a Star moment. Man, she was dumb.

Nonna continued her story. It was about intolerance and stupidity and time passing and children and a life a woman didn't want.

Laura's grandmother who had two children and a husband was *gay*. The love of her grandmother's life was someone – a woman – completely unknown to her entire family. How did she sit on that for fifty years? How did she stay married to a *man*? Laura said, "I don't get it. How could you marry him if ... I mean, forgive me, Nonna, but I'm assuming you weren't going to like the sex too much?"

Nonna looked at her a moment, and Laura knew she had stepped in it. But her story had been so intimate. A laugh started low in Nonna's throat and then took her shoulders, and then she threw her head back and laughed loudly. Thank God. Laura laughed with her.

Nonna stopped short, instantly serious. She said, "What are your intentions with Jamey, Laura?"

Total non sequitur. While she found it funny, talking about sex was apparently off the table.

She said, "Oh, I just dumped him." That sounded stark and terrible, so she backpedaled, "I mean, it wasn't going to work. I don't know. He's terrific. But he needs someone who loves him."

She looked to Nonna for a response, fearing she'd offended her. That she thought of Jamey only as her pet.

Nonna said, "Thank God. I was starting to worry about you. If there's one thing we can take away from this disaster area of my life, it should be that you should never settle for someone you don't love."

Nonna had this great love. The kind made in storybooks or movies. The kind that was supposed to last forever. And here she was in Baltimore with this collection of shopkeepers and straggling relatives, filled with so much regret that she burst out crying at simply saying her love's name.

Half an hour later, Nonna swung her legs off her bed and said, "Pity party over. Back to company."

"No. Wait. I. How can you?" But Laura didn't have any good way of saying what it was she needed. She needed not to go back to that room full of questions. She needed to process everything this little old lady told her – this little old lady who turned out to be an entire human being with a life. She was filled with remorse for having blown Nonna off all summer, having greedily eaten her cooking growing up – and never having thought of her as anything more than a minister for her own needs.

She needed to find a way to explain Jamey's absence without giving Bart the satisfaction of knowing about the breakup. She needed to think about what all of this meant for Lizzie. And what it meant to her mother – her mother who had grown up in a house leaden with regret.

But Nonna grabbed her cane, straightened her skirt, and opened the door to her room.

Laura sat for a moment, but with Nonna's absence, the room became a place she wasn't allowed to be.

LIZZIE

Nonna came back to the table. I didn't think the crying was only about cooking – she really loved cooking, and we'd planned it out. But we had gotten rid of Laura too, and that was good. Bart loosened up, and he and Tisha and I talked about New York.

Nonna looked okay. Less freaked out than she'd been at the beginning of the meal. Gina got mushy and grabbed her arm, but Nonna waved her off.

Laura straggled in after her, looking like someone had killed her dog. Even in her gloomy blanket-wrapped stage in the summer, I hadn't seen her so ... stricken.

I said, "Where's Jamey?"

The question startled her at first, but then she said, "He had to go."

Bart barked a laugh but cut it short.

I didn't know if she meant he had to leave the house or he had to go like some cheese that's gone off in the refrigerator. I figured it was the latter.

We moved on to pie. Nonna made a ricotta pie with a

cannoli filling. I had made a pumpkin pie from the can. It wasn't so good, and there was a crack across the top, and it got browner than it should have. But we had the lemon tart and Gina brought some really nice-looking pies: apple and pecan. And the cookies. Those cookies.

People were speaking normally again. I was glad Tisha started having a good time. Laura was still being weird with her, but Bart kept her entertained.

Company started leaving around eight. I was sleepy, and there was a lot to clean up. The oldsters left, and Tisha left with them. She gave me a big hug with a *squeeze* and said, "Thank you, Lizzie. See you tomorrow?" I nodded. We were going to do inventory. I didn't want to think about the fact that she was moving in January. We'd pretend things were normal for now. As much as any of these other people, she was family.

Laura and Sally and Nonna were in the kitchen, cleaning up. Sally said, "That was a really nice Thanksgiving, mom. Like the old days. Thanks."

She put her arms around Nonna's shoulders at the sink, hanging like an oversized albatross. Nonna turned around and hugged her back. Either Nonna was shrinking, or Sally's dad was enormously tall. I never saw Nonna hug Sally before, and again, it seemed strange that Sally was her kid. *Mom* was Nonna's kid. Not this lady.

Bart came out of the bathroom and said, "Well, I need to hit the road." Which was just like him.

Nonna said, "No. Help clean up." She didn't even look up from the sink where she was washing dishes. She was so short next to him that he looked like a kid who'd just been scolded.

He went deep red and went into the dining room where he started clearing dishes. I went to help him. I wanted a little more talking time. But he was rushed, anxious to go.

When the last dish had been put away, Nonna said,

"Everyone, dining room." She went in ahead of us, and we all just stood there for a minute. Nonna said, "Come. In. Here."

I was worried that this was about whatever she'd been crying about before. She motioned for us to sit at the table. The tablecloth was still on, looking like a child's bib covered with bits of cranberry sauce, stuffing, and pie. What had been so delicious and beautiful before looked gross. She had something big to tell us.

If it was about her dying of some sort of cancer, I was going to die myself. *I love Nonna, I don't want her to die.* And where would I go? This was my house. I was just getting to like my room with all its posters and was going to ask Tisha to help me paint it before she left for New York. School was okay. It wasn't great, but I knew what to expect. I kind of liked the church thing. And Nonna. I was just getting somewhere with her. We had a sort of ... family. Today felt like a family. And she couldn't leave me with Laura. Laura *hated* me.

Aunt Sally said, "What's going on, Ma, are you sick? Is there something you're not telling us?"

I was glad she said it because I didn't know if I was allowed to say it.

Nonna wrinkled up her face in a frown and waved her away, saying "No, no, no." Thank God. The wrinkles around Nonna's mouth always fascinated me. They shot out from around her lips like eyelashes, and sometimes I imagined her mouth was an eye.

She said in a haunted movie sort of voice, "You may wonder why I've gathered you here this evening."

I laughed. I was the only one. Nonna winked at me and, looking at the worried stares of Laura, Bart, and Aunt Sally Nonna said, "I'm putting the house on the market."

Oh. Just moving. We could move.

But Laura and Sally said, "What?" at the same time. Laura and her mother. It still didn't compute.

Nonna waved them to shut up and said, "It's become clear that I'm never really getting over this hip thing. The stairs are agony, and the three of you." I thought she meant the grownups, "Are going to have to step up."

"Step up?" Said Sally.

Nonna said, "As far as Lizzie is concerned."

Sally said, "Oh, Mama, I can't take on a child. I have a one-bedroom apartment, and while I have insurance, I can't provide any sort of life."

Laura shot her a glare. Aunt Sally left Laura on purpose. What would she do with me?

Nonna said, "Be quiet, Sally, and listen."

I couldn't go live with Aunt Sally out in a desert somewhere. I hardly knew the woman. I couldn't help it, I started to cry. Nonna was concerned but continued. "I can't take care of you properly, Lizzie. I love my great-granddaughter so much, but I'm a crusty, bitter old broad, and this is no home for a teenage girl."

I said, "I *hate* the desert!" It came out all whiny cry-y, and I didn't mean to sound ungrateful but was I going to have a Kickapoo name? Was I going to work in the gift shop with Aunt Sally?

Nonna reached and grabbed my hand. Her hand was icy cold and damp – the first indication I had that she was nervous about any of this. She squeezed it, reassuringly.

She looked at me and said, "I saw your drawing, Lizzie. Your beautiful drawing."

Which one? I'd been drawing bats around Halloween time and tried to make a stupid bat cartoon. But I saw the intensity in her eyes. I knew which drawing she meant. I slouched a little.

She squeezed my hand again and winked before turning to the other people at the table.

She said, "George, it seems, left her quite a bit of money. Bart, you're going to grow up for once in your life and take Lizzie to live with you."

Live with Uncle Bart in New York!

Why did he look so upset?

"There's enough money to put her in a good school and get her a proper art instructor. This girl has talent, and I won't have it squandered."

"Mrs. Morello, I have a *job*."

Nonna wouldn't let him talk. "You have a job, but you don't have a life. I know you two get along okay, and there are other working parents in the world. You'll figure it out. Lizzie will stay with me through Christmas and start the next semester in her new school."

New York! Art classes!

Laura looked like she had pulled a get-out-of-jail-free card.

Sally said, "But this is Pop's house."

Nonna said, "Sally, I'm a hundred and two."

"You're only eighty-two ..."

Nonna firmly plowed over her, "I need to move into a smaller place."

Sally said, "Where will you go?"

"Gina has a small apartment above her bake shop. There's an elevator, all the cannoli I can eat, and enough company to keep me from going completely nuts."

Bart said, "I don't know how to take care of a kid."

Nonna said, "She's not a kid, Bart, she's a person. And I think you know that. You two get along. You can't neglect her any more than I've done this summer."

I started to feel like no one knew I was sitting right there.

Laura said, "I can take a trip up once in a while."

Nonna said, "Laura, you're moving to New York." Laura's mouth fell open. Not exactly in horror but in a cartoon version of astonishment.

She said, "What?"

"You're in *Baltimore*, Laura. I thought the fact that you are nowhere would help you get your act together, but honestly, all you're doing here is burning time."

Laura turned red. She said, "There's a film industry here. John Waters. Television, *Homicide*."

Nonna wasn't having it. "And life is too short to burn time. You have something you want to do with your life and the opportunity to do it – no one can decide what you can and cannot do. You're allowed to love who you want to love. Pursue it all. Who cares if people say no? If you don't go after it, you'll never get anywhere. Life is your goddamned oyster. Eat it up."

Laura was angry at first, but her face changed, lightened, went soft.

Nonna turned to Aunt Sally who had started pushing crumbs around on the table with her too-long fingernail. Nonna's voice was softer when she said, "Sally."

"Mama?"

"Sally, can you stay for another month? I need your help to get things in order."

Aunt Sally said, "Sure. Sure, Ma."

"And honey, there are some things I need to talk over with you."

"Sure, Ma."

"Like why I was such a lousy mother."

Aunt Sally welled up with tears, "No. You were just fine. We all have our different paths."

Nonna took Sally's hand and held it. She said, "And how sorry I am."

Everyone had gone to bed, and I was lying on my bed with the lights on staring up at my *Akira* poster. Life seemed full of *possibility* for the first time in a while. New York! Uncle Bart! He didn't want me, but we'd do okay. I'd make sure of it. There was a knock on the door.

"Come in!"

The doorknob turned, and there was a thunk as Nonna opened it with her cane. She had the secret message tube dangling from a string.

I made motions to stand up, but she waved me back down. I scooched over, and she sat on the end of my bed, grabbing my ankle.

"Lizzie. Oh, my Lizzie."

No Italian today.

"I'm. Are you okay, Nonna? With the move and the ..." *the crying?* "... everything?"

She chuckled and grabbed my knee.

"What?"

She said, "I don't think you have to worry about that twenty-something self-absorbed stage of life. It just isn't in you."

I smiled. She stared at me too long and ran her hand over the side of my head, down to my chin. She said, "You're a perfect mix, you know. Of your mama and your dad."

I didn't feel like crying, but a lump came to my throat. She held up the tube and waved it at me. I wasn't ready to talk about the drawing. I liked that it brought me art lessons, but I wasn't ready to see it again or talk about it.

"Did your mama give you this?"

I felt like I was in trouble for a moment but then realized from the look on her face that I wasn't. I nodded.

She said, "I want to show you something."

She unscrewed it. My drawing was gone. I was relieved but

wondered where it was. She tucked her finger inside and twisted, pulling out the brownish paper I once thought was lining. She opened it up. There was an ink drawing of a heart on it. She smiled. Her eyes teared up but not in a totally losing it sort of way. She held it up to me, made sure I saw it, and folded it carefully, putting it back in the tube. She then pulled out a little slip of brand-new paper out of her pocket and rolled it up, tucking it in the tube before screwing it shut.

"Everything I ever loved is in this little tube. I am so, so happy that you have it." She lowered it over my head and kissed me on the forehead. She said, "Thank you, Lizzie."

"For what?"

She cleared her throat. She said, "For waking me." Before I had time to ask what she meant, she took her cane and shuffled toward the door.

"Good night, Nonna. And thank you."

She paused and turned around. She said, "For what?"

"For New York."

And she smiled. Instead of being tired or resigned, her smile shone pure. It was a happy smile.

I unscrewed the lid and took out the new piece of paper on which was drawn a heart and an address written inside in Nonna's hand. Another mystery. The tube seemed like the right place to put it.

LAURA

Sally snored from the bed next to her. Laura tried to think of her as an annoying auntie rather than as a crappy mother. Nonna said *she* had been a crappy mother. But she never left her daughter. She had lived with her daughter and cooked for her. Sally was the one to flee. And Anna Maria.

And who the hell was Nonna to tell Laura where to live? Could Bart raise Lizzie on his own? How was she going to afford New York? It was twice as expensive as living in LA.

A part of Laura was relieved to be freed from Baltimore – and the weight of that decision lay with someone else for a change. She wouldn't have to go back to the aquarium. Jamey could nurse his broken heart and find someone more worthy of him. He and this someone else could have crater-faced babies together and live in the suburbs. Her chance to be Artistic Girl was being given back to her. It was a new beginning. She was cagey with her freedom, irritated with Sally's snoring, and hungry in that strange Thanksgiving way where because you ate dinner at four, even though it was too much food, you were hungry again.

She opened the door and listened. Hearing nobody, she crept downstairs. She knew Bart was on the sofa, and a huge middle-of-the-night part of her wanted to go to him and wake him up. But her period and the fact that he was about to be a father dissuaded her. She crept downstairs where she saw the pies on the counter under plastic wrap.

She peeled back the edge of the pecan pie's wrap, just a little, and snuck a pecan–sugar-coated, sweet, with just a touch of salty. It was about the best thing she'd ever eaten. She snuck another. She needed milk, so she opened the fridge. When she closed it like a horror movie reveal, she saw Bart standing behind the door. She let out a small scream. He grabbed the milk as she dropped it and put it on the counter, saying, "We have to stop meeting like this."

She laughed and said, "Pie?"

"Yes." Bart went to the cabinet and got down two small plates. Laura poured two glasses of milk.

They sat at the kitchen table. But this time, Laura was in flannel pajamas, and Bart was wearing sweats with a worn "NYU" on the front of the shirt. They both had socks on. The house was cold. They ate in silence for a while. Laura was in no mood to break it.

Bart said, "Where *did* Jamey go?"

Laura smiled and stabbed at another bite of Lizzie's ugly pumpkin pie. It was tasty. "That wasn't going to last."

Bart smiled as well. She could tell he was pleased. Although he said, "And smiling about it. Aren't you the cool one?"

Maybe it was the lateness of the hour, the headiness of freedom, or just the fact that he looked adorable, but Laura said, "I kind of have a ... thing ... for you, you know."

He smiled broadly, a whole smile, so it couldn't have been a bad thing to say. His face sobered again. Then he smiled and said, "I hear you're moving to New York."

Laura coughed. "Apparently, that's been. Decided for me."

He said, "I'm glad."

Laura said, meaning it, all the way, "Me too."

CHAPTER TWENTY

LIZZIE

New York, 2012

Not that life wasn't weird before, but life got weird after that Thanksgiving. Then it changed into a new kind of normal. With some money from Dad and from Uncle Bart's job, which paid pretty well, we got a house in Brooklyn. I was enrolled in the public school there and went into Manhattan to visit Tisha when I could. School in Brooklyn was *so* much more normal, and nobody really cared about my Japanese last name or my hair. Everyone was part *something* in Brooklyn. People were much more into the things I was into also, like manga and movies. I had a few friends who actually liked *old* movies. I loved living with Uncle Bart. He was funny and mellow and paid enough attention to me that I didn't feel totally alone, but not so much attention to make it awkward. He worked a lot, but he hired Marta to hang out with me after school and in the summers. Marta, her family, and her eight grandkids probably had as much effect on how I see the world as Bart, my parents, and Nonna rolled together. Life was not terrible.

Yes, of course, Laura and Bart hooked up. She even lived with us for a brief patch, but it didn't last. She finally moved into Manhattan with a friend she made on her first movie job. She went on to be a pretty big-deal indie producer. At my high school graduation, she told me not to be afraid of rejection. That fear could paralyze a person. That if you wanted something, you had to go for it, and if you got rejected, at least you had tried. That seemed like a no-brainer to me, but for Laura, it was some sort of revelation. A few Christmases later, she apologized for being such a royal jerk during our time in Baltimore. It didn't make up for it, but it was something. Maybe it was because she was thirty something and she'd grown out of that twentysomething time Nonna spoke so harshly about.

Christmas was our last holiday in the old house. Most of the furniture was gone, but Bart got an itty-bitty tree, and Nonna cooked a great meal and invited all her cronies. Nonna was so much *happier*, lighter. We took neighborhood walks again. By the time we hit the road on New Year's Day, I knew she was going to be okay in her little apartment above Gina's bakery.

Bart, Laura, and I still went down to spend holidays with Nonna, who started hosting parties in Gina's house.

Aunt Sally went back to Santa Fe but she returned to Baltimore for the holidays, too. I didn't know what happened in her life, but after that Thanksgiving, but she seemed more together. Less anxious to please everyone. Less pushy.

Bart and I rented all of Nonna's movies one weekend. We made tons of popcorn and called her between each movie on speakerphone to ask her all kinds of questions. Barbara Stanwyck was her *friend*! She laughed more and actually told us stories about the old days. Bart told me about Rose, her girlfriend. Nonna finally told me all about her little house just off Melrose and Rose's orange tree.

Such a sad story. People were so stupid about some things back then.

Nonna died last spring. She was ninety-seven. It was peaceful – in her sleep. We never got that surround-the-deathbed moment, but when we went back for the funeral, it was so strange, all of us together again without her there. The Significant Others felt the charge in the room when we all assembled at a local Italian restaurant for a wake/celebration of Nonna's life.

Laura had an arty director boyfriend, and they were very cute together in their chunky glasses and leather coats. Bart got married the year I left for college at RISD in art. He and his long-time girlfriend, Andie, had gotten so sensitive about my feelings it was driving me crazy. I might have pushed them along a little.

Tisha, of course, did *great*. She started directing movies in Baltimore of all places and went the John Waters route – one movie every two, three years. Horror movies, of course. None really made it out of independent release, but she was happy. She was my saving grace in New York while she was at NYU, so I was bummed when she moved back home.

She came to Nonna's funeral with her girlfriend. Her girlfriend was very cool and worked in advertising in DC. We laughed that in all our years of friendship, Tisha had never brought up who she liked to date. When I asked her why, she said, "It didn't seem relevant."

Aunt Sally looked the same, only gray-haired, and despite the sorrow over Nonna, when she got going on the Nonna stories, I noticed that her laugh had gotten louder, more confident. She was easier to be around.

I came out okay. While I was at RISD, I did some storyboards for Tisha's movies and really enjoyed it. But I got into computer animation and, weirdly enough, after Nonna's funeral, I ended up moving out to LA. After hearing all Nonna's stories – which I drew out of her every holiday and during every Sunday phone call – LA felt like coming home.

My first stop after I'd gotten settled in was that address outlined by a heart Nonna had scrawled years before on the paper inside of the celluloid lipstick tube. I found out it was made out of celluloid a few years earlier when I had it appraised at a place that knows about those things. Celluloid seemed appropriate. It was made out of Nonna's movie years.

The house at the address on the note looked like it must have in the 1930s and 40s. A single-level stucco Spanish-style house with a Moorish front window and a terra cotta roof. There was nothing about it that was much different from the others around it.

I figured what the hell and let myself in the gate and knocked on the front door. No car in the drive, no one answering, I wandered down the driveway and around back, where a small postage stamp of a yard was lined with fruit trees surrounded by a garden wall. An orange tree was heavy with blossoms and tiny green fruits.

There was a little metal café table on the back patio outside what must have been the kitchen door. I breathed in. It smelled of dirt and orange blossom, and the sounds of noisy Melrose were somehow distant, cut off by the stucco walls.

I sat for a moment, and a sadness and happiness filled me up. I thought of Nonna and Rose, loving and living and hanging out with all the people who made those wonderful movies happen.

A child lived there now, as evidenced by a sun-bleached plastic slide and an abandoned tricycle.

There was a trowel sticking out of a terra-cotta pot on a low shelf behind the garage. Love was there again, and that was good. Life ended up being that patchwork Nonna talked about. A big mess of people and lives and events sewn together, but if you stood back, and made a few alterations, moving here, fighting there, working things out together, changing and adjusting until things were just right, it was beautiful.

I borrowed the trowel and dug a hole beneath the orange tree. I removed Rose's heart and Nonna's heart. I folded them together and buried them at the root of the tree. This couldn't possibly be the same tree, so many years later, but Rose and Adriana were reunited somehow, back where they had lived and breathed and loved.

Back when things were black and white and sunny.

ACKNOWLEDGMENTS

I was in Toni Ann Johnson's kitchen nook when she said, "Well, why aren't you writing about your love for movies?" We get so much support from our friends in unexpected ways, and I am so grateful for her for not only that moment but for later *seeing* my book where I could not, enabling me to get it into shape for market with her astute notes. She had an unwavering support of my characters. Any time I gave up on this book, Toni Ann was there nudging me about Adriana and Rose, assuring me they had a place out there in the world.

Thanks to the good folks at Running Wild for recognizing that. And to Aimee Hardy for helping me untangle sentences, sharpen verbs, and underline the larger themes of the book.

To Piper Selden, who suggested a short story concept that gave me Nonna and Lizzie.

Thanks to my dad, who ignored my protestations over watching black and white movies and immersed me in Astaire & Rogers, Barbara Stanwyck, Joan Crawford, Bette Davis, Cary Grant, Howard Hawkes, George Cukor, Preston Sturges and ... and ... and ... not a bad way to spend a childhood pre-VHS. I miss him every day, but our conversations will never leave me and I'm so grateful he got to read this book with a full mind. He really loved it.

Thanks to my ever-patient readers Diane Sherlock and Yuvi Zalkow, without whom I never would have found the end. And to my first ever and always reader, Kit Reed, who always says the best things. In this case, "This is great, now cut out everything that's not the book." A note I share with my students again and again. Her affirming checkmarks and exclamation points throughout (her way of writing okay! And this is good!) bolstered me as I untangled things.

I am so sad she didn't live to see this published, but I'm so grateful knowing she read it, deeply, twice.

Thanks to John Silbersack, who, when I embarrassedly and uncertainly, muttered the plot for this book that I had been throwing myself at for a couple of years let me know it was worth pursuing. Sometimes all we need is someone to believe in our stories. His patient and all-seeing notes helped make the book what it is.

Thanks to the books that helped me in my research. I owe a large debt to Paddy Calistro's *Edith Head: A Biography* and David Chierchutti's fabulous, *Edith Head: The Life and Times of Hollywood's Costume Designer*. Thanks for Mark Eliot's biography *Cary Grant*, Al Diorio's *Barbara Stanwyck: A Biography*. Both of these books got me going in the right direction. Cary Grant's heartbreaking relationship with Randolph Scott inspired Adriana and Rose as did my Great(great) Aunt Ruth and her partner Mary, who lived together when things like that weren't done, but saw it through to the end. This book is for anyone who chose (and choose!) love over society's strictures.

Thanks also to all the other fans of the golden age of Hollywood – you're my kind of geeks. From whoever had the brains to save menus from the 1942 Formosa Cafe, to those who post photos of early Hollywood, accessible to all, so that any street I chose gave me an accurate picture of the period.

Thanks to Wendy Ortiz, David Rocklin, Chiwan Choi, Jen Hitchcock, and Natashia Deon who all created spaces where this story could be heard. Somehow putting this story out there at Rhapsodomancy, at Roar Shack, at Book Show, at 90x90LA's

Dirty Laundry Lit gave it the faith it needed for me to keep rewriting and submitting.

Thanks to Women Who Submit who clapped and cheered each time I resubmitted this novel, to the ever supportive Antioch folk, teacher folk, 90x90LA folk, Poet folk, Horror folk, Library and small bookstore folk, to the living breathing Venn diagram that makes up Literary LA. I couldn't do it without you all.

And thanks especially to Ko, for being the forever guy, the never-even-a-doubt guy ...

Running Wild Press publishes stories that cross genres with great stories and writing. RIZE publishes great genre stories written by people of color and by authors who identify with other marginalized groups. Our team consists of:

Lisa Diane Kastner, Founder and Executive Editor
Cody Sisco, Acquisitions Editor, RIZE
Benjamin White, Acquisition Editor, Running Wild
Peter A. Wright, Acquisition Editor, Running Wild
Resa Alboher, Editor
Angela Andrews, Editor
Sandra Bush, Editor
Ashley Crantas, Editor
Rebecca Dimyan, Editor
Abigail Efird, Editor
Aimee Hardy, Editor
Henry L. Herz, Editor
Cecilia Kennedy, Editor
Barbara Lockwood, Editor
Scott Schultz, Editor

Evangeline Estropia, Product Manager
Kimberly Ligutan, Product Manager
Lara Macaione, Marketing Director
Joelle Mitchell, Licensing and Strategy Lead
Pulp Art Studios, Cover Design
Standout Books, Interior Design
Polgarus Studios, Interior Design

Learn more about us and our stories at www. runningwildpress.com

403

Loved this story and want more? Follow us at www.
runningwildpress.com, www.facebook.com/runningwildpress,
on Twitter @lisadkastner @RunWildBooks